THE
SUMMER
COUNTRY

THE
SUMMER
COUNTRY

A NOVEL

LAUREN
WILLIG

WILLIAM MORROW

An Imprint of HarperCollins*Publishers*

HarperCollins books may be purchased for educational, business,
or sales promotional use. For information, please email the
Special Markets Department at SPsales@harpercollins.com.

FIRST EDITION

Designed by Fritz Metsch

Library of Congress Cataloging-in-Publication Data
has been applied for.

ISBN 978-0-06-283902-2

19 20 21 22 23   LSC   10 9 8 7 6 5 4 3 2 1

To Oliver

The novelty of everything here, Plants, vegetables, seasons, slaves, Brutality of my species, the endeavours of our infant Society to open the Eyes of the people of Capacity & Feeling to amend many things that are amiss and the attention I give to model the government of my own Estates, so as to add to the happiness of my Slaves, without injury to myself, have so completely amused me, by finding constant occupation for me, that 5 years have passed over, in this eternal Summer Country, like only one.

—JOSHUA STEELE,
writing from Barbados to the London Society
for the Arts, 24 May 1785

THE
SUMMER
COUNTRY

CHAPTER ONE

Bridgetown, Barbados
February 1854

"EMILY!" ADAM SHOUTED.

Her cousin was standing by a barouche, a barouche so shiny and new that the black lacquer dazzled the eyes.

To be fair, Emily's eyes were dazzled already, sun-blind, rainbows dancing everywhere; she felt dizzy with wonder and delight.

When they anchored in Carlisle Bay just after noon, the island had seemed a fairyland drawn in pastels, houses bleached by the sunlight rising in tiers on the hills that circled the town, broad-leaved trees swaying on delicate trunks, the fronds casting their shadows over the blue waters, an illustration from a picture book, beautiful and remote.

But now they were here, unmistakably here, the brilliant sunshine like nothing Emily had ever seen, the heat baking through the heavy fabric of her dress and making the hair at the nape of her neck curl. The houses weren't pastels at all, but vibrant orange and yellow, blue and green and pink. The illusion of space had been just that, an illusion; people pressed close about, dressed in brightly colored kerchiefs, carrying baskets, chickens and donkeys getting underfoot, everyone talking, laughing, arguing, crying their wares.

Emily wanted to see it all, to peer into the baskets of fruit for which she had no name, to figure out whether the patterns on the handkerchiefs being shoved beneath her nose and waved about were seeds or beads or something else entirely.

But her cousin was waiting, his fair-skinned face flushed with heat and agitation. They were to dine at the house of her grandfather's oldest business associate, and Adam had worked himself into a pelter about it, chivvying them from ship to hotel and into evening dress, in a horror that they might be late.

"Emily!" Adam called again, jiggling from one foot to the other. His wife, Laura, was already in the barouche. "Are you coming?"

Emily made a face at him through the throng. Never mind that a new world pressed around them, strange and wonderful. A business contract was waiting. "I'm trying!"

The liveried coachman shouted, and the hawkers fell away, parting like the Red Sea. Emily gathered her skirts and made her way through the gap before it could close, glancing back over her shoulder as the crowd formed again, the hawkers descending on one of their fellow passengers from the *Renown*, who looked like she was destined to buy some fancywork whether she intended to or not.

"Do take your time, Emily." Adam shoved her up into the carriage with more vigor than finesse. "Is there anyone you'd like to stop and talk to before we go? A cold collation, perhaps?"

"Adam . . ." Laura moved aside to make room for Emily on the forward-facing seat. "Come, sit by me."

Emily squeezed her own modest skirts into the space beside Laura's flounces, as Adam tripped on the hem of her skirt and dropped, red-faced, into the seat opposite.

"It wouldn't do to be late. Not after Mr. Turner sent his own coach." Lowering his voice, Adam leaned forward. "They say he's the richest man in Barbados—the richest man in the West Indies. His fortune makes Grandfather seem like a pauper."

"Grandfather wouldn't like to hear you say that," pointed out Emily as the coach paused to let two women cross the road, large jugs balanced on their heads.

"No, he wouldn't, would he?" said Adam, and there was a catch in his voice that was audible even over the cries of the street vendors. "I keep thinking he's still there. That we'll go back and he'll be there in the house at Queen Street, barking orders to his clerks."

Emily felt an ache in her chest. She could picture it too, too well. Her autocratic, rough-mannered tyrant of a grandfather, who had loved her more than anyone in the world. He had been a self-made man, Jonathan Fenty, who had raised himself from poverty to riches through pure strength of will.

Well, will and an advantageous marriage. But mostly will.

No one, including their grandfather, had ever thought he might succumb to anything so mundane as death.

But he had, and there was a stylized angel in the churchyard to prove it, the carving raw and new, the chisel marks fresh on the stone, as the rain wept down, seeping into the newly turned earth. He was gone and they were here, in the land of their grandfather's birth, where the sun shone in February and strange birds sang. The heat and colors pressed around her, the women with their bright kerchiefs and the baskets balanced on top of their heads, the lilting voices and bright colors, a world away from the winter city they had left.

"Grandfather would be glad to see you carrying on," said Emily quietly. "It was what he wanted."

It shouldn't have stung to know that Fenty and Company would be Adam's. It was what she had always known. He was a boy, and a Fenty. Never mind that her grandfather had always said she was the most like him. That didn't extend to commerce. But he had left her a legacy of her own, one she had never expected.

"If he did, why didn't he bother to train me?" asked Adam.

"Perhaps because you didn't want to be trained? You were too busy stealing jam tarts."

"It was just the once," Adam protested. "You'll have Laura thinking she's married a ne'er-do-well. Laura?"

Laura shook her head as if to wake herself from a dream. She had always, thought Emily, had a talent for absenting herself. It had made the other girls at Miss Blackwell's Academy for Young Leaders declare her haughty and cold, although Emily knew it was quite otherwise: a combination of crippling shyness and an ability to escape into her own mind whenever something worried her.

"Is it the heat?" Adam asked, all concern.

"No. I'm quite all right." Laura's lace parasol cast dappled shadows across her face. "I was—I was admiring the flowers."

Emily rather suspected it had more to do with the topic; Grandfather hadn't approved of Laura and Laura couldn't bear criticism.

But she quickly said, "Flowers in February, can you imagine? Grandfather said it was always summer in Barbados."

"Yes, but he didn't like summer. He said it made the streets smell." Adam craned to look around as the barouche slowed. They came to a stop before a house fronted with yellow stucco, a gallery encircling the upper story. "Could this be the place?"

He sounded as if he hoped it weren't. The house and the galleries were freshly painted, the flowers carefully trimmed, but it looked nothing like the mansions of Bristol's burghers. A hen pecked at the dirt in the street. A small bird darted past, wings bright.

"It must be," said Emily. They were near enough to the wharves that Emily could hear the slap of the waves, the shouts and bustle of the dock hands. "Mr. Turner must like to live close to his investments."

"It isn't at all what I expected. I had thought it would look . . . different. Grander." Adam turned to Laura. "Is my cravat crooked?"

"Here," Laura said, and gave it a tweak, patting the edges into place where the starched folds had wilted in the heat.

Emily sat quietly back in her seat, feeling like an interloper. Of course she was delighted that her best friend and her favorite cousin had married; it was just that she didn't quite know how to behave with them now that they had a world she didn't share.

Adam displayed Laura's handiwork to Emily. "All right?"

"Nanny would be proud. . . . Thank you," she said to the coachman, who had held up a hand to help her down.

"You look very nice too," said Laura loyally.

Emily looked down at her own modest toilette. Her skirts were narrower than Laura's, her neckline higher, as befitted an unmarried woman on the verge of spinsterhood. "I'm tidy and respectable, at least."

Aunt Millicent would have been delighted to trick Emily out in her cousins' discarded dresses, to lace away her breath and trip her with flounces, never understanding, no matter how many times Emily told her, that she had no desire to play Cinderella with a borrowed slipper. She was comfortable in her poplins and twills, much happier to be busy and useful in her father's parish than she would ever have been sitting in Aunt Millicent's drawing room, pouring tea for the ladies on her aunt's myriad of charitable committees, most of which seemed to consist of vying to arrive with the newest hat or the most shocking on-dit.

Proceeding behind Adam and Laura down the walk, Emily felt out of place in her own skin, self-conscious in a way she had never been before, too aware of the hair escaping its net, the dress that had never been fashionable in England and was too heavy and hot for the West Indies. She had never thought of herself, in England, as a spinster. She was Miss Dawson, the vicar's daughter, always busy with soup or salves; Miss Dawson, Mr. Fenty's granddaughter, with the run of his house and warehouses; Miss Dawson, Miss Laura's practical friend.

Here, she was none of those, simply Mr. and Mrs. Fenty's companion, the spinster cousin in the outmoded gown.

They passed through a door hidden beneath the shade of a balcony. A maidservant stood aside to allow them to enter, leaving them blinking in the sudden gloom of the hall. It might have been England again, but for the fact that there were no doors to be seen; instead, arches separated a dining room and parlor from the hall. The impression was one of endless riches, the gleam of marble and wood, crystal and porcelain, spreading on as far as the eye could see.

A staircase rose before them, a smooth curve of mahogany. Emily heard a giggle and saw a whisper of white cambric, the bounce of a curl: two schoolgirls peering down through the banisters at the guests.

A man stepped through the arch on their right. He wore a well-cut suit, his face very dark against the starched white linen of his cravat. He must, thought Emily, be a superior sort of servant. "Mr. Fenty?"

"Ah. Yes," said Adam, and thrust his hat and gloves at the other man. "I believe your master is expecting us. If you would inform Mr. Turner—"

"My uncle," said the other man, enunciating very clearly, in a voice that spoke of Oxbridge and private tutors, "regrets that he was not here to receive you. He should be here presently."

"Your—" Adam stood frozen, his top hat vibrating in the air.

"If you will follow me?" said the other man curtly, and, without waiting for an answer, he strode back through the arch into the dining room.

Quietly, the maid took the hat and gloves from Adam's hand.

"Uncle?" murmured Laura.

"A charity child," whispered Adam. "It must be. It's been known to happen. A servant's child adopted into the family . . ."

Mr. Turner's nephew was waiting. Emily poked Adam in the arm. "Shall we?"

"Er, yes." Adam scrambled after their host, half dragging Laura with him, leaving Emily to follow along behind. "We must be—that is, we made very good time. The carriage—so well sprung. The road—so scenic. Your, er, uncle was very kind to send his own carriage."

"My uncle," said the other man flatly, "has several carriages."

"Naturally. That is . . . May I present to you my wife, Mrs. Fenty?" Adam said in desperation. He dug his elbow into Laura's ribs until she belatedly remembered to bow. "And this is my cousin Miss Dawson. Mr., er, Turner?"

"Braithwaite." Mr. Braithwaite bowed to Laura and to Emily, his movements as clipped as his speech. "My apologies. My aunt and uncle will be with you presently. If you would be seated?"

The settee was made of mahogany, upholstered in silk brocade that blended beautifully with the muted shades of the Aubusson rug. Bookshelves lined one side of the room, the leather bindings well-worn: natural history, history, poetry, religious works that Emily recognized from her father's shelves. Brilliant birds, stuffed and set on stands, peered down at them from above a curio cabinet. A pier glass above the mantelpiece reflected the landscapes on the wall, the rich drapes on the windows, the flushed and uncomfortable faces of the visitors.

Emily hastily took the indicated seat. Mr. Braithwaite stood by the mantel, his very presence quelling any conversation. He had, Emily noticed, a very thin mustache above his lip. It gave him a sardonic air. Or perhaps that was just his silence, pressing down on her, reducing the proportions of the room to the size of a nutshell. A very well-appointed nutshell, but a nutshell nonetheless.

Emily popped out of her seat, bustling across the room to a curio cabinet by the mantel. "Are those fossils? My father had one, but none so fine as these."

Mr. Braithwaite silently indicated the contents of the curio cabinet. In addition to the fossils, there was a fine collection of minerals, split to show their interiors, and shells far more beautiful than any Emily had seen when her aunt had dutifully taken them to bathe in the freezing waters of Weston-super-Mare.

Emily cleared her throat. "It is rather daunting, isn't it? It does make one feel very small to encounter a piece of rock that has been here since before the birth of our Savior."

"Does it?" Mr. Braithwaite's precise inflection made Emily very aware of her own West Country accent. It had never felt so thick as it did now.

"Well, very recent, at least," said Emily, resisting the urge to chivvy her cousin out of his seat. He could try to contribute to the conversation instead of sitting there gawking. "Were these collected on the island?"

"Yes."

Emily was spared making further attempts by the sound of foot-steps, as a man strode into the room. "Welcome, welcome."

Mr. Turner's deep voice resonated through the room, and for a moment, Emily felt her breath catch at the familiarity of it, the rhythm of his speech so like her grandfather's. It wasn't just the accent, the accent to which her grandfather had so stubbornly held all those years, throwing his island origins in the face of Bristol's elite; it was the air of command, the assurance that others would leap to obey, as Adam was leaping to his feet now, desperately trying to hide his chagrin as he looked anywhere but at Mr. Turner's face.

"I—it is an honor to meet you, sir, ma'am," Adam stammered. "May I—may I present my wife and my cousin Miss Dawson?"

Mrs. Turner murmured her own words of welcome, the rote greeting of the polished hostess. Her rose silk gown with its scalloped tiers of fabric, each edged in an intricate pattern of matching lace, was at least a season more recent than Laura's, so beautifully tailored it had to be from Paris. Her necklace, bracelet, and earrings were of rubies set with diamonds, elegant without being gaudy. Her black hair had been dressed in a series of rolls over her ears, elegantly arranged in a chignon at the back. She looked, in fact, like one of the ladies in the fashion plates Emily's cousins loved to study, but for one detail: the color of her skin.

Mr. Turner bowed to Laura and to Emily before turning again to Adam. "You needn't tell me who you are. Your face is your passport in these parts. You're the spit of your grandfather as a young man."

"You knew my grandfather?" blurted out Adam. "I mean—that is . . ."

Mr. Turner raised his brow. "That you hadn't thought your grandfather would do business with one of my complexion?"

Adam flushed. "No, certainly not. That is—"

"We'd never thought to meet anyone who knew him still," Emily jumped in, before Adam could embarrass himself further. "Grandfather was adamant about never leaving Bristol. He hated the sea. He always thought it was a great joke that he owned a fleet of ships on which he declined to sail." She was painfully aware that she was babbling. Mr. Braithwaite was watching her as though she were the dancing bear in a carnival, and a rather mangy one at that. "We had no idea he still had friends on Barbados. After so many years."

Mr. Turner regarded her with amused tolerance. "I was just a child when your grandfather left the island. But he was a memorable man."

"He was that," said Adam, a little too heartily. "How did you, er, come to meet?"

Mr. Turner smiled at Adam, and although his expression was perfectly pleasant, the room felt a little smaller. "I was the boy who held his horse. That was when I was a slave, of course."

Adam's mouth opened and closed. Laura sat like a marble statue, beautiful and still. Mr. Braithwaite's lips tightened, and he looked away.

"You weren't his slave, were you?" Emily blurted out. There were bits of his life in Barbados her grandfather had never shared; he had treated her father's passionate involvement in the British and Foreign Anti-Slavery Society with amused contempt—but he had never failed to make a large contribution. She had never been sure if it was out of a conviction he was reluctant to voice—her grandfather had scoffed at do-gooding at the same time that he had opened his purse and his kitchen to the indigent—or merely the desire to place her father more and more firmly in his debt.

Mr. Turner gave a bark of laughter. "Jonathan Fenty? He didn't own the clothes on his back, not in those days. No. My owner leased me to his employer."

"That," said Mrs. Turner, with a significant look at her husband, "is all in the past now."

Mr. Turner held out a hand to his wife. Mrs. Turner's hand looked pale against her husband's, the ruby of her ring very bright. "My wife's family have been free for some generations. I consider myself very fortunate that she lowered herself to marry me."

His tone invited them to share the joke.

The horror of it—the barbarism—that one person might lease
another, like—like a piece of farm equipment. Emily had read of it,
she had attended lectures and meetings, but to hear it spoken of so
frankly, by one who had, himself, been chattel . . . She should, Emily
knew, make the appropriate noises of distress, sympathy even, express
her delight that the institution was now ended, at least in this part of
the world. But there was something in Mr. Turner's countenance that
blunted sympathy, that made the words tangle on her tongue.

Donning a social smile, Mrs. Turner turned to Adam and Laura.
"Did you have a pleasant journey?"

"Yes, quite," said Adam, who had spent most of the voyage being ill
into a bucket.

"And your accommodations?" inquired Mrs. Turner, determined to
bring the conversation back to the mundane. Emily was reminded forcibly of Aunt Millicent. "Are they to your liking?"

"The inn is charming. It was very kind of you to arrange it for us,"
said Adam to the air somewhere beyond Mr. Turner's shoulder.

"My agent made the arrangements," said Mr. Turner. He nodded
casually to his nephew. "Has Nathaniel been looking after you?"

Adam glanced nervously at Mr. Braithwaite. "Mr. Braithwaite was
all that was kind."

"Dr. Braithwaite," corrected Mr. Turner pleasantly.

"I didn't—that is—no one said . . ." Adam looked as though he
wanted the Aubusson carpet to swallow him up. Laura stared at her
gloved hands.

"Educated in London and Edinburgh," said Mr. Turner, his eyes
meeting his nephew's across the room. There was an unmistakable similarity between the two men; before his hair had begun to gray and his
figure to broaden, Mr. Turner must, Emily thought, have been a handsome man. "We tried in vain to interest Nathaniel in commerce. He was
always mad after medicine."

"Best watch out, or you'll have Miss Dawson tagging along after
you," Adam said, a little too heartily. "Miss Dawson revels in the sick

and infirm, the sicker and more infirm the better, right, old thing? My cousin is happiest pouring nostrums down the throats of the unsuspecting. Don't stay still too long, or you may find yourself wreathed in bandages—whether you've broken anything or not."

"I have some training in the nursing arts," said Emily, frowning at Adam. To Dr. Braithwaite, she said, "I spent three mornings a week at the Bristol Royal Infirmary."

"You must see our hospital, then," said Mrs. Turner. "We are very proud of it."

"It was built by subscription," contributed Mr. Turner, something about the way he said it making Emily quite sure that a large part of the subscription had come from his pocket. "Just ten years ago now."

Dr. Braithwaite spoke from his place beside the mantel, his words slicing through the room. "It was built after emancipation. It was embarrassing for everyone to have former slaves dying in the streets of Bridgetown."

"That wasn't the only reason," said Mr. Turner.

"The poor are always with us, aren't they?" Adam put in quickly. He inclined his head to Dr. Braithwaite. "If the hospital is one of the sights of the town, we must see it, of course."

"If you have an interest in philanthropic endeavors, I can do no better than to direct you to my wife," said Mr. Turner blandly. Emily suspected he knew that Adam had about as much interest in philanthropy as Emily had in poultry farming. "She is the president of the Ladies' Branch Association for the Education of the Female Children of the Coloured Poor, secretary of the Bible Society, treasurer of the St. Mary's Friendly Society, a member of the committee for furnishing clothes to the poor and indigent, and—have I forgotten anything, my dear?"

"Only St. Paul's choir, the Library Association, and the lyceum committee," said Mrs. Turner patiently.

"Goodness," said Adam. "That's—very civic-minded of you."

"As you can see," said Dr. Braithwaite, "my aunt is largely responsible for the clothing, educating, and enlightening of the poor of Bridgetown."

"Well," said Mr. Turner, nodding at his nephew, "since you take care of their bodies, someone must have a care for their souls. And their linen."

There was an edge to their conversation that made Emily uneasy. Trying to break the tension, she said, "I should love to see the hospital and the charity school and the library, but first I should like to see Peverill House, if I might."

"Peverills?" Mr. Turner looked at her in surprise. It was an entirely different word on his tongue.

"Is that how you say it? I understand it is a plantation."

"It is indeed a plantation," said Mr. Turner slowly, "and was a very prosperous one at one point—or so I gather. Those days were well before my time. What do you want with Peverills?"

"It's not really so much what we want with it," Adam prevaricated. "Our grandfather—he appears to have owned it. We didn't any of us know anything of it until the will was read."

There was no reason, thought Emily, for Adam to look at her as though it were her fault.

"It was left to me," she explained to Mr. Turner, as though it were as simple as that, as though Aunt Millicent hadn't protested and Uncle Archibald stammered and the lawyer been forced to explain again and again that it was Emily's to do with as she liked, that there was nothing to prevent her inheriting it.

It was, Aunt Millicent had said, an absurd legacy for a young lady (this with a glance at her own three daughters, who had not received plantations, in Barbados or otherwise).

If it was indeed a sugar plantation, Uncle Archibald had said, looking deeply uncomfortable, it ought to be part of the holdings of Fenty and Company.

But it wasn't. This plantation—Peverills—had belonged to her grandfather and now it belonged to Emily.

Mr. Turner looked to Adam, who shrugged, looking mildly embarrassed. "It's true. The plantation belongs to my cousin."

"I see," said Mr. Turner, as though he didn't see at all. To Adam he said, "You mean to sell it, I assume."

"Naturally," said Adam.

"I mean to do nothing of the kind," said Emily. Both men looked at her as though she had run mad. "Surely, it would be unwise to arrive at any conclusion before I've seen it."

"You mustn't expect too much. Peverills isn't what it was."

"With the price of sugar what it is . . ." Adam ventured.

"The price of sugar has come down again—it won't command as much as it would have, say, ten years ago," Mr. Turner conceded, and Adam looked relieved, having feared to betray his own ignorance. "Mind you, a plantation's not a bad investment, provided one knows what he's getting into. I have two of my own. But Peverills . . . Had I known, I would have advised your grandfather against the purchase."

"Is there something wrong with the land?" Adam asked.

"Only neglect," said Mr. Turner. He looked at Emily, at her modest skirts, her white lace collar, her snub nose, her mid-brown hair looped in bunches over her ears, and Emily could feel herself bristling under his scrutiny. "But it will take time and care to put right again."

"And there's the ghost, of course," contributed Dr. Braithwaite from his post by the curio cabinet.

"Ghost?" said Emily.

"It's just a local story," said Mrs. Turner soothingly, with a reproachful look at her nephew. "People do make up stories about old houses. And Peverills is one of the oldest on the island."

"Perhaps," Mr. Turner interjected, "you might escort our guests, Nathaniel. You are the most familiar with that area."

Dr. Braithwaite lost his casual lounge. "I have obligations at the hospital."

"Not on Thursday," said Mr. Turner pleasantly. "You're often that way on a Thursday, aren't you?"

There was suddenly something in the air that made the hairs at the nape of Emily's neck prickle, a tension between the two men like the charged calm before a storm at sea.

"Is it so very near, then?" asked Emily. "It seemed rather far from Bridgetown on the map."

"Ours is a little island, Miss Dawson," said Mr. Turner genially. His eyes never left his nephew. "You mustn't judge it by England. Everything is more immediate than one would imagine."

It sounded as though he was speaking of more than distance. Emily bit her lip. "We shouldn't wish to trouble—"

"Nonsense," said Mr. Turner, still smiling, but there was something in that smile that made Emily see why prosperous Bristol merchants blanched at the sound of his name. "We would not wish to be behind-hand in our obligations to the Fenty family. Would we, Nathaniel?"

Beneath the mustache, Dr. Braithwaite's lips had compressed into a thin line. His eyes met his uncle's and he gave a terse nod. "As you wish. Miss Dawson, I shall be honored by the pleasure of your company on Thursday."

This, thought Emily, wasn't how she wanted to see her plantation, accompanied by an unwilling guide. But there was nothing to say but "Thank you, Dr. Braithwaite."

"Shall we go through to supper?" said Mrs. Turner.

CHAPTER TWO

Christ Church Parish, Barbados
February 1812

"I CAN'T REMEMBER when I've dined so well." Charles gripped the table with both hands, raising himself to his feet with difficulty. Mostly he had drunk well, his glass filled again and again by a silent servant who seemed to have no other purpose but to see him foxed. "Miss Beckles. Thank you for your hospitality."

Miss Beckles dropped a curtsy. He could see her only as a glimmer of pink silk and crepe, hovering headless in the gloom, her dark hair blending into the wood paneling of the dining parlor. Her voice was low and throaty, a soft burr. "Good night, Mr. Davenant. Uncle."

Charles should bow, he knew. But he was afraid he might overset himself if he tried. That would be one way to introduce himself to the neighboring gentry, tumbling flat on his face.

Too late. He blinked and Miss Beckles was gone, her maid following soft-footed behind her.

"Come, come." Miss Beckles's uncle linked arms with Charles, hauling him forward. "Now that the womenfolk are safely away, you'll share a drop of port with me?"

There had already been claret, claret and punch, made with limes and goodness knew what else. Charles felt as though the very walls were in motion, swaying like the cabin of a ship, and Charles swaying with them. Although the ship from England had never rocked like this, never with this sickening lurch at the pit of his stomach. Charles was a good sailor. He would have said he was a good drinker too, well able to hold his liquor, but the ports and clarets of Lincoln's Inn were as nothing to whatever had been in that punch.

What *had* been in that punch?

Charles blinked, hard. "You're very kind, Mr. Lyons, but—"

"Colonel Lyons," the other man corrected him, leading him through an arch from the dining room to the great room. Charles wasn't sure whether it was the drink that made the room stretch into infinity or the contrast with the cramped chambers he had left behind in London. "I've served in the militia these past fifteen years now. We'll have to find you a place now you're back. It's a good group of lads. Your brother, for one. He'll go far if he goes on the way he's started. Not but what it's hard for him being a second son, eh? But we all have our place. We'll have our port on the veranda, shall we?"

The colonel lifted a hand, like an enchanter in a tale, and shadows leaped to life, setting lights glimmering in the darkness.

Not shadows, people. People waiting to light lamps, pull over chairs, plump cushions. This wasn't a tale, it was Barbados, and the colonel was no Prospero, just a neighbor with exceptionally strong drink and a well-trained staff.

Charles clung to the shreds of sobriety. "I should be getting back."

There was something about the evening that sat ill with him, and it wasn't just the punch. The colonel was too friendly, too warm, like an uncle in a stage play; Miss Beckles too demure, a caricature of lady-like reserve. Miss Beckles had said little, but when she had spoken, tension crackled in the air, as though there were another conversation being had, one between uncle and niece, one Charles didn't understand. Maybe that was why he had drunk so deep, let Colonel Lyons press the claret on him again and again and again.

Miss Beckles had drunk only sparingly.

"Not just yet," said the colonel, and Charles found himself half dropping into a cushioned wicker chair, a crystal glass in his hand. "You'll not have me be chary in welcoming a visitor—not that you're a visitor, of course."

Wasn't he? He felt like one.

You've been gone too long. That's what his brother had thrown at him.

And it was true; Charles had forgotten more about Barbados than he remembered. He could remember now those early years in school in England, dreaming of Peverills, of the warm sun, the caves veiled with vines, the steady *plip* of the water through the dripstone. Over the years, Peverills had flattened into an illustration from a book, a botanist's rendering of something beautiful but remote. He might call it home, but his memories were increasingly attenuated, stories told again and again until they had lost their meaning.

And now . . . Charles felt as though he had slipped into a familiar pair of shoes only to find that they pinched. Everything felt strange, unfamiliar: the scents, the sounds, the accents. On the veranda, the smells of the island pressed in on him: frangipani, mango, lime blossom, rum, manure, and the ever-present cloy of the cane. He could feel it catching at the back of his throat. It didn't feel like home; it felt like the beginnings of an ague.

It wasn't Beckles. It wasn't the colonel. It was Charles; he was the odd one, wishing himself back in a London winter, back in his cramped quarters at Lincoln's Inn.

The colonel was still speaking. It took Charles an effort to focus on his voice. "How do you find Peverills?"

"Busy," he offered, for lack of anything better. *Busy* didn't begin to describe it. All his studies, his legal training had never prepared him for this, for the books and books of ledgers, the land, the people, the complicated patchwork of leases that rounded out the corners of their lands. "My father's affairs were—more complex than I had realized."

"Ah, your father. He had grand schemes, your father," said Colonel Lyons tolerantly. "A bit of a dreamer."

Charles stiffened. "My father, sir, is—was a gentleman and a scholar. His ideas were much praised in London."

Never mind that they had been left incomplete, left on Charles's head, unexplained, half-finished. Charles's head ached. Robert was right; he should have come home sooner, learned all this by his father's side. But there had never been any hurry. There would be time enough, that was what his father said in his letters.

Until there wasn't.

Colonel Lyons kicked back in his chair, stretching out his legs in their silk stockings and black evening pumps. "Oh, such things are all very well on paper, but—now, now, don't bristle so. I mean no offense. But if you need practical advice, Beckles is a short ride, as you see. My door is always open."

"Thank you," said Charles stiffly. It was a kindness, he knew. But something about the colonel set him on edge. "I wouldn't want to be a bother. I know you have obligations enough of your own."

"It's no bother, my boy. There isn't much about the land that I can't tell you. And my niece isn't such an exacting taskmaster as that." At Charles's involuntary look of surprise, Colonel Lyons added, "Didn't anyone tell you? It's my niece who owns all this. I manage it for her. Have done since her father died. I used to have a place of my own—on Jamaica—but when my sister's husband died, so young . . . well, family is family. I'm sure you understand."

What Charles didn't understand was why he was being told this at all, but he murmured what he hoped were appropriate noises of assent. "You've been here some time, then," he said.

"Since my niece was a mere babe in arms. It's been a burden, I'll tell you that, but I've done my best for her." The colonel smiled fondly, but there seemed to be too many teeth in it. He looked meaningfully at Charles. "The man who marries her will find him possessed of a rich dowry."

Charles coughed on his sip of port. "Oh?" he said weakly.

The colonel gave a rich chuckle. "We've had the fortune hunters at the door, sure enough. But they don't last long."

Charles stood, with an effort. The seat of the wicker chair felt deeper than it had been when he had sat down. "Your niece is fortunate to have you taking such care, sir. Now, if you will pardon me—" *I need to stick my head in a trough of very cold water*, he thought.

"No, no. You misunderstand me." The colonel stood too. He was a tall man, and spare. His hollow cheeks gave him an ascetic air. A misleading one. His glass had been refilled as frequently as Charles's, although he showed no effects other than a slight skew to his severe gray periwig, a coarsening of the skin around his nose. "Being new to the island, Mr. Davenant, you should know—my niece is not like other women."

"I am sure she is all that is accomplished and charming," Charles said politely. He tried to focus on the colonel, but there appeared to be two of him.

He was rescued by an unexpected source, a woman who came soft-footed onto the veranda from the great room. "Master John?"

The colonel went still for a moment, then turned. "Jenny. Can't you see I'm with a guest?"

The woman didn't flinch or falter. She wore, Charles saw, an apron over her gown, but it was of fine lawn, trimmed with lace. The candle she held obscured her face, leaving Charles with only a flickering impression of dark hair beneath a white cap. "Beg pardon, Master John. But Hamlet is in a bad way. He's asking for you."

"The cares of a plantation, Mr. Davenant. You'll know them soon enough. Hamlet is our head driver. There was a . . . mishap . . . in the mill this afternoon." To Jenny he said, "Tell Hamlet I'll be there presently."

Jenny didn't budge. Only the flame of her candle wavered. "I'm afraid it might not wait, Master John."

Her meaning was clear. The colonel bit down hard on whatever it was he was thinking of saying. "Right, then. Mr. Davenant, if you'll pardon me for just this little while—"

"No need," said Charles quickly. He was very aware of the

woman's—Jenny's—eyes on him from behind the candle. "I should be getting back to Peverills."

"Nonsense. At this hour? You'll stay the night, of course. There's no bother about bedchambers. As you can see, we have plenty of room." The colonel's avuncular smile reduced Charles to a stripling. "I'd be remiss if I let you make your way home alone on dark and unfamiliar roads. You won't have me explain to your brother how I let you break your neck."

Robert would probably thank him for it.

The thought sprang to his mind unbidden, and Charles was only grateful he had the wits left not to voice it.

The colonel took advantage of his silence to say, "Have another glass of port—or would you prefer punch? I won't be long. We can find you other entertainment if you like. The girls at Beckles are counted exceptionally pretty. Just look at our Jenny here."

The colonel's tone was so calm, so matter-of-fact, that it took Charles a moment to catch his meaning. He sounded as though he were offering the loan of a chess set, not the use of a human being.

"I—" Charles felt himself floundering, unsure what to do. Flight seemed the most sensible option. Quickly, he said, "If I must abuse your generosity, may I take advantage of the use of your coach and coachman? You're right, of course. It would be folly to risk my neck on strange roads."

Although he would if he had to. Every instinct screamed to get away while he could. Was he being tested? Was that it? Surely the colonel wouldn't really prostitute his niece's maid like that.

He'd heard the stories, of course. He'd spent his life contesting them, at Eton, at Oxford, at Lincoln's Inn. No, he'd said, again and again. The West Indies didn't decay men's morals. No, Creoles weren't creatures of uncontrollable lusts. The stories that were told—well, maybe it happened on some islands, on the French islands, the Spanish islands, but not on Barbados, not in Charles's family. Just because they owned slaves didn't make them monsters of depravity and decadence.

"If you're certain . . . ?" The colonel made a vague gesture toward

Jenny, who stood without moving, like Lot's wife turned to a pillar of salt. The torchlight flickered off her modest dress, hinting at the curves beneath, here then gone, all the more erotic for being hidden.

Charles could feel his cheeks slowly heat, as they hadn't since he was thirteen, being shown naughty etchings by candlelight with four others in Heatherington-Smythe's rooms at Eton. He shook his head in wordless negation.

The colonel shrugged, as one man to the vagaries of another. "Well, then. The carriage it is. Paris! Paris! Have Miss Mary Anne's carriage brought round."

"Master John." Jenny's voice was colorless, insistent. "Hamlet won't wait."

"Yes, yes." The colonel grasped Charles's hand, giving it a hard squeeze. "You see how it is, Mr. Davenant. I trust we shall see you at Beckles again soon."

"And you at Peverills." Charles would have said anything to be done with it. "Good night, Colonel."

Another hearty slap on the back and the colonel was gone, leaving Charles feeling like a moth who had flown into a lamp and found it too hot for his liking. His glass, he realized, was still in his hand. And it had somehow become empty. He set it down unsteadily on a table, listening for the sound of hoofbeats, wanting nothing more than his own bed. His bed in London, by choice.

He found himself missing it with a painful longing. His chambers had been cramped and narrow and always too cold, but they had been his, his alone. There had been a simplicity to them, no mosquito netting to tangle him about, no servants coming in and out without his bidding. He wanted to close his eyes and wake to the sound of the bustle from Kingsway, flower girls and costermongers and angry carters all disputing the right of way in strident London tones.

"Master Davenant?" The woman's voice took him by surprise. Charles had assumed she'd followed her master. The night had a strange, kaleidoscope feel to it, people sliding in and out of view.

"Yes?" He felt like a nervous virgin, drawing back as she approached. "It's—Jenny, is it?"

She didn't respond. He might be all embarrassment, but she was as calm as any judge confronted with a bumbling barrister. "My mistress has asked me to tell you that she will be riding tomorrow, a little before noon, by the path that runs along the boundary between Beckles and Peverills. She would be pleased to help you reacquaint yourself with the district."

Charles cleared his throat. "That's very kind of her, I'm sure, but—"

"I was not asked to bring a reply." That was all she said, but Charles felt thoroughly put in his place.

Below, the sound of carriage wheels clattering, the jingle of tack, heralded the approach of the promised carriage. It was an old-fashioned closed carriage, lacquered black, with lanterns on either side. To his relief, Charles saw someone had thought to bring his horse around and tether him to the back of the carriage. Not his horse, but one from the Peverills stable. He couldn't help but think of it all, still, as being his father's, on loan only.

Miss Beckles's maid dropped a small curtsy. "Safe journey, sir."

And she was gone, before he had time to tell her that he had no intention of riding with her mistress.

"WELL? WHAT DID he say?" Mary Anne turned from the window in a flurry of satin and crepe.

"Very little," said Jenny carefully. Her mistress was already quivering like a beast in a cage; there was no need to set her snapping.

Mary Anne traced a restless circle around the room, her flounces floating around her, her very hair crackling with tension. "You couldn't press him?"

"He seemed inclined to refuse. I preferred not to give him the opportunity." Below, Jenny could hear the sounds of the carriage rattling down the drive, down the long alley of tamarind trees, away from Beckles. Lucky man. "This way, he'll have the night to think better of his choice."

"Ye-es." Mary Anne stopped in front of her dressing table, dropping down heavily into her chair. "I can send him a note in the morning."

Jenny picked up the silk slippers her mistress had kicked off, setting them aside, out of the way. "You don't want to press so hard. You'll scare him off."

"If I don't, my uncle will first." Mary Anne began pulling at the pins in her hair, removing them with unnecessary force. "What did you think?"

Coming up behind her, Jenny firmly moved her mistress's hands away. "I think if you yank like that, Mistress Mary, you'll have a sore scalp."

Mary Anne scowled at Jenny in the oval mirror, her reflection uncertain in the candlelight. "You know what I meant. What did you think of him?"

Jenny could see Mr. Davenant as only a pale face in the darkness, features almost extinguished by the glare of the candle, fair hair cut short and unpowdered, as the younger men wore it. "He seemed pleasant enough."

"They all seem pleasant enough at first." Mary Anne gave her head an impatient shake as Jenny took the last of the pins out. Her hair, a thick chestnut, tumbled past her shoulders. "I don't need pleasant. I need desperate."

"Captain Harvey was desperate," pointed out Jenny, lifting the silver-backed brush.

Mary Anne made a face at her in the mirror. "Captain Harvey was too desperate. He would have run through my money within the month."

"Or," said Jenny, applying the brush to her mistress's hair, "he might have killed himself with drink. And you would be a widow and free."

Mary Anne gave a snort of laughter. "I couldn't count on his being so considerate. Just look at Uncle John."

Jenny's hand stilled. "Must I?"

The girls at Beckles are counted exceptionally pretty. Just look at our Jenny here.

Jenny's whole body burned with the humiliation of it. He'd been trying to put her in her place, she knew.

It wouldn't be the first time.

Don't you remember to whom you owe everything, girl?

But the colonel didn't own her. Not anymore. He'd given her as a gift to his niece when Jenny was little more than a baby herself, five to Mary Anne's two. He'd taken her from her mother and her people and brought her here, where she would have no one, no one but him. His tool. His puppet. But it hadn't worked the way he had planned.

Mary Anne's eyes met Jenny's in the mirror, her face bleached of color, her rounded features unusually stark. "I don't know how much longer I can stand it. There are times when I hope, when I pray, that he'll have one glass too many, that he'll take the wrong path on a dark night—that he'll offend the wrong man."

Jenny could only shake her head. The colonel was too canny for that. They both knew it. He treated the women of the field gang as his own harem, choosing his lovers as the whim took him. There were no jealous husbands to challenge him to a duel; for any man of the quarters to strike back would mean death.

As for the colonel, he played his hand cleverly, rewarding the women he favored with lighter work, their men with additional rations. It made Jenny sick to her stomach to think of it, but it worked, didn't it? He had half the plantation in his thrall, one way or another. As for the other planters, they thought him a reliable man, a good fellow. Just look how he had sacrificed his own interests to those of his widowed sister, who, being sickly herself, had produced no better heir for Beckles than a sallow and undergrown girl.

The colonel had done his work well.

They hadn't seen it happening, either of them. At first it had been visible only in the new reserve the neighbors had shown with Mary Anne. The curious, sidelong looks. The exaggerated concern her uncle had begun to display for her well-being. No one would say anything to Mary Anne, not directly. And no one would say anything to Jenny either. She wasn't part of the gossip in the washhouse. People watched their tongues around her. Mary Anne and Jenny had noticed only that childhood playmates had grown distant and potential suitors—the real suitors, the eligible suitors—had stayed away, leaving only the most desperate of fortune hunters to call.

It wasn't that Mary Anne was plain. She might not be the sort who made men stop and stare, but she was well enough, and a plantation as rich as Beckles was well known to transform plain girls into beauties.

But not when the mistress was rumored to be mad.

"We'd best hope for a bout of cholera," said Jenny, only half joking. "It will take too long for the pox to do him in."

"Uncle John has the luck of the devil. He'll never fall ill. The only way I'll ever be free of him is to marry." Mary Anne leaned her head back, her eyes half closing under the soothing pressure of the brush. "They say Peverills is in a bad way. He'll need money."

Jenny didn't need to ask who "he" was. There was only one "he" at the moment. Charles Davenant, newly come from England. From the moment she'd heard Davenant was returning, Mary Anne had begun weaving her schemes, with a cunning borne of desperation. And, per- haps, a bit of pique.

There had been a time when Robert Davenant had come calling, a time before the colonel had cultivated the younger Mr. Davenant, en- couraged him to join the militia, made him his drinking companion. Whether Robert Davenant had been paying court to her mistress or to her fortune, Jenny didn't know. But she did know that the cessation of his attentions had hurt Mary Anne more than she would ever say. To marry the older brother, to show the younger just what he had missed, would be a fine revenge. If Charles Davenant rose to the lure.

"He might borrow the money." Jenny kept up her gentle brushing. It was her role to play devil's advocate. So long as she knew when to stop. Mary Anne liked to be challenged only so far.

"Why borrow it when you can marry it? Our estates run side by side. He'd be a fool to look elsewhere."

"Men aren't best known for sense."

"He can be the biggest dolt in all Christendom so long as he gets me away from my uncle."

"He didn't seem a dolt." Jenny had been there, at supper, standing just outside the arch to the great room. Mary Anne liked to keep her close, for comfort. Davenant had been uncomfortable, yes, visibly so, but there was a measured tone to his voice, a thoughtful way about him, even deep in his cups.

But, as Mary Anne said, all men seemed pleasant enough. At first.

Mary Anne spoke into the silence. "I have to get to him before my uncle does."

Jenny set down the brush. "Push too hard and he'll think you really are mad."

"There are times when I wonder if I might be." Mary Anne sounded a decade older than her nineteen years. And well she might. The last five years, they had both lived like soldiers on campaign, constantly on guard against the next threat. The fact that it was Mary Anne's own house, her own land, only made it worse. She might be mistress, but her uncle was her guardian, and there was little she could do in her own defense, at least, not without confirming that she was as mad as her uncle implied.

And Jenny was only so safe as her mistress could keep her.

"You're not mad. Or if you're mad, then so are we all." Jenny divided Mary Anne's hair into three, weaving the heavy mass into one long plait. "Mr. Davenant seems a reasonable man. He didn't much like Master John, that much was clear."

That was putting it mildly. Jenny hadn't missed the way he had recoiled when Master John had offered Jenny to him.

A chill worked its way down Jenny's spine. What about next time? What if the next man didn't refuse? Her fingers turned cold at the thought; she could feel them prickling.

It was getting worse. Little reprisals, small cruelties. But they were mounting, day by day. And Jenny had no doubt that Master John had larger plans in hand.

"No, Mr. Davenant didn't seem taken in by Uncle John, did he?" Lost in her own reflections, Mary Anne didn't notice Jenny's abstraction. "We might be able to find our way free yet."

You, Jenny thought. *You might be able to find your way free.*

They'd been through so much together, she and Mary Anne, bound together closer than blood. She was, Jenny knew, privy to Mary Anne's every thought, every concern. But she was still her property. And she couldn't imagine that Mary Anne would give her up, not now, not while Mary Anne was still in this house, in her uncle's power.

Slaves disappeared all the time, losing themselves in Oistins, in Bridgetown, hiding with family members on other estates. But Jenny had no family to run to. Her people, whoever they were, were on Jamaica, lost to her before she was old enough to remember them. Her only family, such as it was, was in this house, in front of her.

Her cousin, who was also her mistress.

Her father. Who had just offered her to a strange man as if she were a Bridgetown doxy, for sale for a shilling.

But why should that surprise her? She'd always been a tool to her father, nothing more. The fact that she shared his blood was purely incidental. Except, of course, when he wanted something of her.

Mary Anne's braid was starting to unravel.

"One day at a time," said Jenny, and twisted a ribbon neatly around the tail of her mistress's braid. She smiled calmly into those gray eyes that were so much like her own. "You'll need your sleep if you're to charm Mr. Davenant in the morning."

CHAPTER THREE

Christ Church, Barbados
February 1854

THURSDAY MORNING FOUND Emily and her cousins on the road to Peverills.

Emily half expected Dr. Braithwaite to discover an emergency at the hospital, possibly involving plague. But the plague, if plague there was, stayed within bounds, and aside from an admonition that they must be on their way early if they wished to avoid the heat of the day, Dr. Braithwaite voiced no further objections.

The sun pounded down on Mr. Turner's barouche, reflecting off the road and the bright brass trappings of the carriage. After the gray of Bristol's cobbles, the white of the road looked as though someone had dunked it into carbolic and scrubbed. The world had been scoured clean: from the bright-painted pastel houses to the white road to the brilliant scarlet leaves on the trees. Emily had to blink and blink again, like someone who had emerged from the gloom of the sickroom. It made halos around her eyes and around the heads of Adam and Dr. Braithwaite, who sat in the rear-facing seats, their backs to the coachman. A picnic basket, stuffed to bursting by Mr. Turner's cook, rattled in tune to the rhythm of the horses' hooves.

"It is very bright, isn't it?" said Laura faintly. Her parasol was white lace, designed for the fugitive sunlight of Bristol summers. The starched fringes were already looking a bit wilted about the edges.

Emily furled her own sturdy green parasol and held it out, handle first. "Here. Take mine. It's larger."

"But what about you?"

"I have my bonnet," said Emily. One of Cousin Lily's, made over, the brim unfashionably deep. But like the outmoded pagoda sleeves on her dress, it was perfect for the weather. "You know I don't mind if I'm burnt brown."

"At least you don't freckle," put in Adam, who did. His hat was tipped down over his eyes. "Gran used to make me put lemon juice on my nose in summer. Much good it did me."

Dr. Braithwaite nodded toward a passing carriage. "Some women wear masks made of white gauze. The sight can be discomfiting for visitors. It makes them look like ghosts."

"Ah, ghosts." Adam sat up straighter in his seat. "You did promise us a ghost story, Dr. Braithwaite. Or must we wait until we stand at twilight by the ruins?" Turning to his wife, he said, "What was that poem you made me read? Something about waning moons and demon lovers." He pulled a face as he said it.

"Don't be such a Philistine," Emily scolded. She had always admired Laura's love for the written word, even if she didn't share it.

"Don't tell me you read it," retorted Adam.

"Well, no. But then, I never pretended to be poetical," said Emily apologetically. She turned to Dr. Braithwaite. "And as for ghosts . . . As a man of science, I shouldn't have thought you would give credence to ghost stories."

Dr. Braithwaite settled back against the squabs, provokingly aloof. "There are more things in heaven and earth, they say."

"Hamlet said, you mean," retorted Emily. "I hardly think he was a reliable source."

She surprised him into a grin. It made him look years younger, closer to her own age than she'd first imagined. "He did see ghosts."

"Wasn't he mad?"

"Only north by northwest." As if regretting his descent into whimsy,

Dr. Braithwaite said, "I haven't heard of any demon lovers at Peverills, but there are caverns. Some of them are quite deep. You won't want to go wandering about on your own. It's not just the caves. There are snakes, manchineel trees . . ."

"You make it sound like the Garden after the fall." Emily rather suspected Dr. Braithwaite of deliberately warning her off, retaliation for having to waste an afternoon of his time.

"If you eat any apples here, you'll be meeting your maker sooner than you intend," warned Dr. Braithwaite. "The Spanish call the fruit of the manchineel tree the apple of death."

"There's your Scripture for you, coz," said Adam lazily. "Like the apple in the Garden, which brought death to the world."

Dr. Braithwaite was not amused. "Only not quite so immediately. Or so painfully. Do not put anything in your mouth that wasn't first packed in that basket."

"I had thought the island was almost entirely under cultivation."

"It is," said Dr. Braithwaite bluntly. "That doesn't mean it isn't dangerous. This isn't Bristol, Miss Dawson."

Did he think Bristol was without dangers? Emily bit her tongue, settling back against the luxurious velvet squabs of the coach. He was right, though. She might know how to stitch an arm slashed by a knife, but she didn't know the first thing about snakebite.

The urban landscape of Bridgetown, so foreign in some ways, so familiar in others, was long behind them. The pastel houses by the side of the road had given way to an unbroken landscape of green fronds. The shoots swayed and whispered in the wind. It wasn't just the sound but the smell that surrounded them; Emily could feel it clinging to her skin, like the residue of a sweet. It tickled against the back of her throat.

The foliage surrounded them, the road the only sign of human habitation. Emily thought she could hear voices, just, and the thwack of something heavy, but the rustling of the leaves in the wind filled her ears, distorting all other sounds. She knew that one could cross the whole island in less time than it took to get from her aunt's house in

Bristol to their summer lodging in Weston-super-Mare, but the mathematics of the distance fell away against the impression of vastness, of endless cane, endless sky.

They were less than an hour from Bridgetown, but they might have been the only people in the world, Noah and his family in the ark, bobbing about with no set destination.

"It does go on and on, doesn't it?" said Emily, knowing she sounded ridiculous, but not sure how to put her feelings into words. She had grown up in a tiny house surrounded by tottering structures crammed with humanity, people pressing about on all sides. She wasn't quite sure how she felt about all this emptiness.

"This?" Adam wrinkled his nose at her. "This is no great distance. The last time I went to London . . ."

She didn't need to hear, again, about Adam's trip to London, which, apparently, had turned him into a cosmopolitan man of the world with one visit to Bond Street. Or at least to hear Adam tell it. "I meant the cane. There's just—so much of it."

Adam looked at her under the brim of his hat. "That is the point of a plantation, coz. Acres and acres of pure profit."

Yes, but how did people live in the midst of this? Emily couldn't say it, didn't want to admit to Adam that she might have any doubts about the course she had set. She would become accustomed to it, she was sure, just as her grandfather had become accustomed to Bristol.

"Just think, Emily," said Laura, making an effort to rouse herself. Beneath the flush of heat, she looked rather green from the motion of the carriage. "This might be your sugar."

"It's not," said Dr. Braithwaite. In the silence, Emily could hear a pattern of thwack and rustle, the far-off sounds of workers' voices, clearer now. "This is Beckles land. Your closest neighbors. They're the largest landowners in these parts—next to Peverills."

"Is Peverills that large, then?" asked Adam, looking significantly at Emily. "I can just see you, skirts kilted up, scythe in hand. . . ."

"You'll see nothing of the kind." The mockery was a bit rich coming from a man who had never ventured farther into the countryside than a picnic on the outskirts of town. She knew quite as much of agriculture as he, which, between the two of them, amounted to absolutely nothing. Emily turned to the doctor. "*Does* one use a scythe on cane?"

"No," said Dr. Braithwaite. "The usual implement is a cutlass—a form of machete. I wouldn't advise attempting it. Not unless you want to lose a leg."

"You know a great deal about it," said Adam, and Emily knew he was wondering, as she was, if Dr. Braithwaite knew it from experience, if he, like his uncle, had once been a slave.

"I've stitched up more gashes than I care to count. You can tell an experienced cane cutter by his scars," said Dr. Braithwaite shortly. "You wanted to know when we reached your land? Here it is."

"This?" Emily clutched at the seat as the barouche lurched over a rut in the road.

Cane stalks long dead lay brown and withered, surrounded by grasses high as Emily's shoulder, beige and brown in the heat. Vines climbed over the frame of an abandoned shack, like green fingers dragging the structure back down into the earth. An old wagon lay in pieces, one wheel fallen and cracked. The carriage lurched as they took a right-hand turn onto a narrower road, pitted and overgrown.

"This," said Dr. Braithwaite.

"Mr. Turner did say it was neglected," said Emily, trying not to show the jolt of disappointment she felt deep down in the pit of her stomach.

After all, what did she know of cane? Maybe this was what it looked like every season, before being cleared for harvesting. Wasn't being left fallow supposed to make the land more fertile?

"We might be the first people," she said with an attempt at cheerfulness. "I imagine this must be what the island looked like two hundred years ago, when colonists were first settling here."

"Except for the structures," said Dr. Braithwaite drily. He pointed to a stone cone that looked like something out of old Holland, but for the vines that twined it around and around. A snake slithered through the gash that had once been a door. "That's the Old Mill. The overseer's house is down that road. The bookkeeper's house is to the left."

"The stones seem sound," said Emily.

"It was built to withstand hurricane and riot."

The carriage lurched past a pair of stone gateposts thickly twined with dark green vines. An alley of broad-leaved trees spread out before them, and, at the end of it, loomed the house.

Chimney pots stabbed into the sky above high, arched gables. The casement windows had been made to stare out at the Sussex downs, not a Barbados cane field. It was a Jacobean manor house transplanted, all intricate brickwork and ornate finials. Only the wide, shaded portico set into the front of the house made any concession to the climate.

The leaves of the trees and the sun played tricks with Emily's eyes, making her think—no. It wasn't a trick. The walls stood jagged, blackened, empty windows opening onto nothingness. A pillar lurched crazily to the side, its mate toppled sideways in the long grass.

"I—" Emily found herself without words. It was majestic and horrible, a testament to the fleeting nature of man's vanities, and she knew she ought to be finding it all terribly interesting and improving, but all she could do was bite her lip and try not to let her distress show.

"This is as close as we can get," said Dr. Braithwaite brusquely, and Emily wasn't sure whether to be grateful to him for taking pity or annoyed with herself for needing it. "The central block is still standing. Although I wouldn't vouch for the roof."

Laura's hand slid into Emily's and squeezed. "It's very picturesque."

Picturesque wouldn't keep the rain off. "I suppose Grandfather must have bought it for the land," she said, trying to keep her voice level.

"He probably got it cheap," said Adam. "You know how he likes— liked—a bargain."

They all sat in the barouche, like castaways marooned in a rowboat, staring out at the ruin that was now Emily's.

"It must have been lovely once," said Laura. "Perhaps he remembered it as it was."

Lovely wasn't quite the word Emily would have used. Impressive. Grand. Ruined. "Is this recent?" she asked Dr. Braithwaite.

"It's been this way for as long as I can remember. When I was young, boys would dare each other to come up here after dark. Brave the duppies. Ghosts," Dr. Braithwaite translated. Bringing himself back to the present, he said briskly, "There was more than one ankle broken that way. Still is, I gather. I set one last week."

"There you are, Em," said Adam. "Shall we? There's the governor's reception tonight."

She wasn't ready to retreat to Bridgetown yet. "We've only just got here. And there's hours yet before we need to get dressed." She looked uncertainly at Dr. Braithwaite. "Could I . . . see it? Since we've come all this way?"

"There are snakes."

"I'm wearing boots. Stout ones." Looking down at Laura's dainty footwear, she said, "You'd best get started on the picnic. I won't be long."

Adam looked from Emily to Dr. Braithwaite. "I'll come with you."

And leave Laura alone? Laura, flushed with heat, was clearly in no condition to go adventuring. "No need," said Emily firmly. "We won't go far."

Adam looked like he might argue, then shrugged and leaned back. "As you will, coz. We'll be here, eating all the cakes."

"Don't blame me if you turn an ankle," said Dr. Braithwaite resignedly. Swinging down, he held out a hand to her. "Miss Dawson?"

"If I do," she said, "at least I have someone to set it."

She hopped down and landed heavily on what must have once been a fine sweep of gravel, but now was rutted from rains and neglect. The doctor hadn't, she realized, been joking about the danger to her joints. The ground ahead of them was full of bits of masonry and unexpected holes.

On the ground, rather than in the carriage, the full bulk of the house made itself felt, the blackened gables pushing high into the sky, the wings stretching on and on in either direction. It made Emily feel very small and insignificant; her grandfather's great house on Queen Street had been on a more human scale.

Emily craned her head, taking an involuntary step back. "It's rather large, isn't it? It dwarfs one, rather."

"It's meant to." Dr. Braithwaite steadied her with a hand on her elbow. "Careful now."

A flight of stairs led to an arched portico, missing pillars making it look like a jack-o'-lantern's grin. "Is that the entrance?"

"Yes, but I wouldn't advise entering."

Emily looked quizzically up at him. He was taller than she'd realized; she felt quite small beside him in her sensible, flat-heeled boots. "I thought you said the central block was still standing."

"Standing, yes," said Dr. Braithwaite. "But that doesn't mean it's sound. The floor is rotted out in parts; the stairs are treacherous. If you must go adventuring, I'll take you around the side."

"It's hardly idle curiosity. It is my house after all." Perhaps if one cleared away the debris . . . it might not be so bad as it looked.

"If you're looking for buried treasure, you'll be disappointed." Dr. Braithwaite led her sideways, not up the stairs but past them, down the length of the house. The ground-floor windows were all but obscured by a prickly hedge bristling with green fruit. "Anything of value is long gone."

They turned the corner, and the full scope of the destruction was laid bare. Large chunks of masonry had fallen at crazy angles, blackened beams resting on hollow foundations. Bits of intimate debris lay among the rubbish: a charred, cracked chamber pot. A child's doll, the limbs scorched, the face blackened.

Emily found herself leaning down toward the doll. "Snake," said Dr. Braithwaite tersely, and she jerked back.

"What happened here?" she asked.

Dr. Braithwaite navigated expertly around a blackened pile of rubble. "Fire."

"Well, yes, I gathered that." Perhaps it was the solidity of the central block that made the devastation so jarring. Walls still stood at various points, waist high, shoulder high, creating a crazy maze where once there must have been chambers and corridors. One staircase spiraled to nothingness. Another opened onto a fragment of what once might have been a gallery of sorts.

They paced the perimeter in silence, until Dr. Braithwaite said, "There was a rising here forty years ago. I don't imagine you've heard of it."

"I haven't. But I can imagine why." Emily stopped, looking up at him. "I belong to the Bristol and Clifton Ladies' Anti-Slavery Society. My father is a founding member of the British and Foreign Anti-Slavery Society. I heard Mr. Frederick Douglass speak when I was a girl."

Dr. Braithwaite raised a brow. "Then there's nothing I need tell you. I am sure you can imagine the whole of it." Before Emily could defend herself, he went on. "The revolt occurred for the usual reasons. It began in St. Philip and spread to Christ Church. Peverills was one of the plantations torched."

"Was the owner so cruel, then?" Even as she said it, she realized her own mistake, and quickly added, "Not that a man would need to be abused to break his chains. The very institution of slavery . . ."

"You can spare me the sermon, Miss Dawson. My uncle owned slaves when I was a boy."

"But—" Emily bit her tongue before she could commit another faux pas. But it was too late. A sardonic smile spread across Dr. Braithwaite's face.

"Like many of the worthy merchants of Bridgetown, my uncle was a proponent of emancipation only for his own relations, not for those who worked for him. Many of them signed a petition to the council, urging against emancipation—not that you'll find many who will admit to that now."

"But to enslave one's own people . . ."

"Is it more horrific than enslaving someone else's? Should my uncle be subject to sterner censure than the man who owned this estate? Or, for that matter, than those who traded in sugar, knowing whence it came?"

Dr. Braithwaite's curt tone left Emily floundering for an argument. Useless to tell him that their household had gone without sugar for a fortnight as part of her father's symbolic rejection of the slave system. It sounded as paltry as it was. Particularly when there was no denying that her grandfather's wealth, the wealth that had paid for her schooling, for the clothes on her back, for the plantation lying in blackened ruins in front of her, had been built on sugar. He hadn't grown it, but he had traded in it and made a fortune doing so.

Looking away, over the ruins of the plantation, she said, in a constrained voice, "It is strange the people who lived here didn't rebuild."

"Is it so strange?" Dr. Braithwaite didn't press the topic. Presumably, thought Emily, digging her toes into the rubble, because he knew that he had won. "Sugar planters were in a bad way forty years ago. They had better things to do than shore up houses that never made sense here anyway."

"Yes, but it seems strange not to have cleared away the rubble and done something with the bit that still stood. It seems a waste. And what of the fields? Why just leave it all? And don't," she added vehemently, "tell me it's all the fault of ghosts!"

Dr. Braithwaite was spared responding by a shout, underscored by the sound of hoofbeats.

"Ho, there!"

A man spurred his horse forward through what once must have been gardens, waving his hat in their general direction. The sun struck gold and bronze off his hair. He swung off his horse, striding forward toward them. His face was flushed with exertion and emotion.

"Apologies, madam, but this is private property. It's not safe. I'm afraid you and your guide—"

"I know it's private property," interrupted Emily, and thought she saw a spark of amusement in Dr. Braithwaite's dark eyes. "Dr. Braithwaite was merely—"

"Doctor? Braithwaite?" The man squinted at Dr. Braithwaite, holding up a hand to shield his eyes against the sun. "Nat! Is that you? I scarcely knew you in that getup. And that mustache."

"You look well too," retorted Dr. Braithwaite.

The other man choked on a laugh. "Is that your professional opinion?" With a dimple in his cheek and the color fading from his face, Emily could see that he was younger than she had originally supposed, close to Adam's age, or her own.

Bowing to the inevitable, Dr. Braithwaite said, "Miss Dawson, may I present to you Mr. George Davenant?"

Mr. Davenant bowed over Emily's hand. "Very pleased to make your acquaintance, Miss Dawson."

Emily looked from one man to the other, Mr. Davenant smiling, Dr. Braithwaite not. "I take it that you are acquainted?"

"We played together as boys," said Mr. Davenant easily, his cheeks creasing at the memory. "Some of the things we got up to—"

"Dares, for instance?" said Emily, watching the doctor's face.

Mr. Davenant grinned. "Among other things."

Dr. Braithwaite was not inclined to elaborate. "That was a long time ago."

"Before you went off to—Edinburgh, was it?" said Mr. Davenant.

"Among other places."

"I'd heard you'd returned." Mr. Davenant turned to Emily, so determinedly cheerful that Emily wondered if she'd imagined the note of reproach in his voice. "I hope you'll forgive me for my rudeness just now, Miss . . ."

"Dawson," provided Emily.

"Miss Dawson." Mr. Davenant smiled winningly at her. "We've had some trouble with trespassers. With the house sitting empty . . ."

"Trespassers?" said Emily, wondering, for a moment, if they'd got the wrong place. Perhaps this ruined shell was someone else's, and down the road they'd find the white painted villa of her imagining, humbler but more welcoming.

"You're the trespasser," said Dr. Braithwaite amiably. "Peverills belongs to Miss Dawson."

"Peverills—what?" Mr. Davenant looked as confused as Emily felt.

"My grandfather left it to me," explained Emily, who was beginning to feel as though she ought to have that embroidered on her forehead. What her grandfather had left her, it appeared, was a confusing mess.

A challenge, she corrected herself.

Mr. Davenant drove his fingers through his fair hair, making his hat skew at an odd angle. "Forgive me. I don't understand. We knew it had been purchased, of course, but . . . that was over twenty years ago."

"Twenty," echoed Emily.

Her grandfather had bought the plantation over twenty years ago and let it sit empty, fallow. Her grandfather, who squeezed a shilling until it squeaked in pain, who lectured the kitchen maids on waste and prided himself on driving only the canniest deals and hardest bargains.

And then he had left it to her, ruined fields, house, and all.

Mr. Davenant was still speaking. "No one's appeared or said a word since. So you can see why it comes as a bit of a surprise to me to find a claimant on the doorstep. And such a charming one," he added belatedly, with an attempt at a smile.

"Not a claimant," corrected Dr. Braithwaite. "An owner."

"Have you turned lawyer as well as doctor, Nat? But I do beg your pardon, Miss Dawson. I didn't mean to offend. It was a poor choice of word."

"An understandable one under the circumstances," said Emily, since Mr. Davenant's distress begged reassurance. She shook herself back to the present. "I haven't the slightest notion why my grandfather did what he did, but I can assure you, the papers are all in order."

"So it seems we are neighbors—of sorts." Mr. Davenant squeezed the brim of his hat between his hands, the gears of his mind visibly turning. "The house isn't habitable, of course. We might have told you if you'd asked. . . ."

"I did tell her," said Dr. Braithwaite drily.

Emily cast him a quelling look. "Is there anywhere on the property that *is* habitable?"

"The bookkeeper's house," said Mr. Davenant automatically, and then, quickly, "But you can't be thinking of living here! There aren't any of the amenities to which a lady might be accustomed."

He hadn't the faintest idea of what she was accustomed to. "Not all ladies require damask drapes and velvet cushions."

"You'll have a hard time finding help," interposed Dr. Braithwaite unhelpfully. "The house is accounted haunted."

"I'm not afraid of ghosts, Dr. Braithwaite. Or hard work."

"There's certainly plenty of that," said Mr. Davenant, smiling at her in a way that invited her to join in. "You should know you can call on Beckles for any help you might need."

"That's very kind of you," said Emily, taken aback. "You don't even know me."

"We're a small community and a close one," said Mr. Davenant. "You're the owner of Peverills now."

He was the first person who hadn't assumed she would be selling as rapidly as possible, and Emily was inordinately grateful to him for it. "Thank you. I may need more help than you know. I'm profoundly ignorant when it comes to agriculture."

Mr. Davenant pulled a wry face. "I should have liked to be more ignorant. It's my grandmother who loves the land. I've tried to love it, for her sake, but . . . What am I thinking? This is hardly a salubrious place for discussion." He looked earnestly at Emily. "Must you hurry back to town? I would invite you to take your potluck with us at Beckles. . . ."

"I should have liked to, but my cousins are waiting." Emily glanced back toward the carriage. "We have an engagement in Bridgetown this evening, a reception at the governor's house."

"You've plenty of time, yet. I hope I haven't offended with the lack of formal invitation. I know my grandmother will wish to make your acquaintance. And that of your party, of course."

"I advise you to accept Mr. Davenant's invitation," said the doctor, taking advantage of Emily's momentary silence. "Beckles is famed for its hospitality. You wouldn't want him to be behindhand in his attentions."

"Less so now than in my grandfather's day," he said with a self-deprecating dip of his head, "but we try as best we can to maintain the old standards. I can promise you a cool drink, at the least."

"You make it very hard to refuse," said Emily. "I must consult my cousins. . . ."

"Certainly. My grandmother will be delighted. As am I, of course." Mr. Davenant seemed so relieved that Emily didn't have the heart to tell him that she hadn't quite accepted. It appeared that, by omission, she had. "I cannot promise what you are accustomed to in England, Miss Dawson, but we shall be delighted to have you share our meager meal."

"By which he means," said the doctor, "that you may expect a banquet."

Chapter Four

Christ Church, Barbados
February 1812

"Do we always set out a banquet for breakfast, Robert?" Charles pulled out a chair, wishing that the legs wouldn't scrape so against the wood floor. The sound was like a pick being driven into his skull.

But it was the smells that were the worst: sliced cold beef, congealing on its plate; fresh ham, studded with cloves; peppers, swimming in brine; and, above it all, the pungent, unmistakable smell of pickled fish.

What in the devil had been in that punch last night?

Charles's little brother was already seated at the head of the table, booted feet propped up on the neighboring chair, a plate in front of him weighed down with beef, ham, fish, and something stewed that Charles couldn't name and didn't want to try.

"You need something in your stomach before you ride the fields." Robert speared a piece of rare beef. Charles tried not to wince as Robert let it dangle from his fork. "This isn't London."

"No," said Charles mildly. "It's warmer, for one."

Someone had placed a variety of beverages at the center of the table. Charles bypassed the decanter of Madeira and the bumper of hock negus and made straight for the porcelain coffeepot. It wasn't the silver coffeepot, the one they put out for company, but the one he remembered from his childhood, a conical thing of Chinese porcelain, with a dragon's head for a spout. If one squinted at it in just the right way, the chip on the dragon's mouth looked almost like a tooth.

Charles could picture his mother's hand on the curiously shaped handle. But nothing else. Just a pale hand in a sleeve edged with lace.

"All of this . . ." Charles poured himself a cup of coffee, black, without sugar. "It's a bit much for two bachelors, isn't it?"

Robert glanced sideways at him. "Preaching economy, brother?"

Robert's eyes were brown, like their mother's. Like the little boy, still in skirts, who used to follow Charles around on his expeditions, stumbling over his own chubby legs. It was hard now, to see that boy in Robert. He was tall as Charles, impeccably turned out in well-tailored riding togs.

It wasn't that Charles had expected to find the same adoring little brother he had left all those years ago, not really. Or maybe just a little. But he hadn't been prepared for the hostility his brother did little to hide.

Charles took a cautious sip of his coffee, waiting for it to burn up to his brain. "From what I've seen, economy does seem to be called for."

"Would you have us live like those poor beasts in St. Andrew, grubbing for a few roots?" Robert forked up something pungent and stewed. Charles looked away. "It all gets used, one way or another. The house servants would be up in arms if you stint at table. They think of the excess as theirs."

"They might prefer more on their own account, I should think." Bypassing the meats, Charles selected a plain roll and a sweetmeat of candied ginger. He took a careful bite of the latter, feeling the sugar turn to acid on his tongue, the bite of the gingerroot beneath.

"It's not *about* the food." When Charles looked at him blankly, Robert set down his fork with a clatter. "It's about their rights. The house servants have a right to the leavings at table. They eat it; they trade in it. It sets them above the others."

He said it as though it ought to make perfect sense. Charles wished he felt clearer headed; his night at Beckles had sucked him dry. "Wouldn't a full stomach be preferable to an empty honor?"

"Tell that to any courtier at Versailles."

"We saw what happened at Versailles," said Charles soberly. "And after."

Robert swung his feet down to the floor, looking full at his brother for the first time, and Charles was struck by the force of his resentment. "Do you want someone to put our heads on the block? Then go on and meddle with the way things are done. Never mind that you haven't been here. I'm sure you can tell us all about everything we've been doing wrong."

"Robert—"

Whatever Charles might have said to placate his brother was lost, interrupted by a servant bearing a note on a silver tray. It was written on cream paper, sealed with red wax. Inside were only three lines.

"From Beckles?"

Charles looked up sharply.

Robert shrugged, tilting back in his chair. "I recognized the seal."

There was something about his studied nonchalance that made Charles wish the note in his hand to perdition. Carefully, he said, "Miss Beckles has invited me to ride with her."

"That's quick work." The derision in Robert's voice could have stripped the painted paper from the wall. "Three days home and you've already secured an heiress. I wish you both very happy."

Charles tossed the note down on the table. "I haven't secured anyone."

Robert didn't deign to answer, only pulled the platter of ham closer, looking over the pieces with exaggerated care. "No meat for you, brother? Or haven't you the stomach for it?"

He hadn't the stomach for any of it.

Disjointed memories of the previous night chased themselves around Charles's brain. The veranda at Beckles, candle flames bobbing like will-o'-the-wisps. The colonel's barbed bonhomie.

Not but what it's hard for him being a second son, eh?

My niece is not like other women.

Mary Anne Beckles was an heiress; Robert a younger son. Was that what all this was about? Was Charles being cast as Count Paris to his brother's Romeo? From what he'd seen, Miss Beckles made an unlikely Juliet, quiet throughout dinner, but that might have been resentment only, resentment at being made to dine with the heir, the designated suitor.

Looked at in that light, the evening took on a distinctly different cast. The message sent by the maid—her uncle's doing, not hers? The offer of a woman for the night. Jenny. Charles could picture the maid, her apron ghostly white in the torchlight. All a test, like something out of a fairy story?

Charles decided he didn't care to know. He didn't want anything to do with any of it. He was here to take over management of the family plantation, not to engage in intrigues, romantic or otherwise. And if his brother had an interest in that direction, by God, he'd be damned if he ruined his chances.

Their parents' marriage had been a love match. Imprudent, some had said, an heiress marrying a dancing master, a younger son without prospects, albeit from a proud English family. But Charles could remember them still, sitting together of an evening, their heads close together, speaking in soft voices as Charles played on the floor with his toy soldiers.

"Did you have designs in that direction?" Charles asked neutrally. "Because if you do—"

"What, me? You can have the heiress and welcome to her." Robert pushed back his chair, sending pain exploding through Charles's skull. "I'm just a younger son, good for nothing but to be left at home."

"Would you like to go to England?" Charles demanded, trying to keep the irritation from his voice. He told himself he'd be patient with Robert, be understanding, be kind, but it was maddening to be made the villain for something that was none of his doing. "Is that what this is all about? I could arrange it, if you liked. Letters of introduction, lodging—"

"For what?" Robert's voice cracked, and Charles was reminded, jarringly, of how young his brother was still, never mind the breadth of his shoulders or the bold brass buttons of his coat. There were six years between them, but it felt more like ten. "So I can be told I'm a bumbling colonial? No thank you, Charles. I have no desire to go abroad to be sneered at."

"It isn't too late," said Charles, even though he knew it to be a lie. Or, if not a lie, then not entirely true. It had been bad enough for him at seven; it would be far worse for Robert at nearly twenty-one. "I have friends in England who would welcome you."

Not family. Their Davenant cousins, safe in the security of their Elizabethan estate in Essex, had nothing but mockery for their West Indian relations. Charles had spent several miserable holidays at Beauleigh Abbey those first few years in England. A dead rat in his bed, incongruously wrapped in cloth of gold, with a tag around his neck reading "nabob," had been the best of it. Charles had been only too delighted to abandon Beauleigh for the homes of his classmates, avoiding his relations whenever possible.

His head still aching, Charles said shortly, "If not England, then why not elsewhere? The Continent is hardly fit for travel, but you might visit America if you liked. Mother had cousins in Charleston."

"Trying to get rid of me, brother?"

"Hardly. I need your help even more than you know." Charles rubbed his aching temples. "If you wanted to go so badly, why did you never say?"

Robert rose from his chair, resting a hand against the polished mahogany of the sideboard. "Someone had to be here with Mother. She was entirely bedridden by the end, did you know? She liked to have me to read to her. Besides," he added abruptly, "there was no money. Father couldn't afford to keep two sons in school."

Charles stared down at his empty plate, lost for an answer. He'd thought himself so abstemious, so virtuous, all because he'd never wagered too high or developed a taste for expensive horses. But there had been a thousand expenses, all the same. All of it had seemed so reasonable at the time. Furnishings for his rooms at Oxford, new suits of clothes, just the standard perquisites of a gentleman. His father had never said him nay. And West Indian planters were all rich, everyone said. Charles's memories were of servants circling around him, silver shining from the sideboard, objets d'art from France and books from England.

Why had no one ever said?

Charles cleared his throat. "If I'd known how bad it was, Robert, I'd have come home years ago. Believe me. Father never said. I'd thought—"

That they were rich as everyone claimed. That everything at home was just as Charles had left it, eternally the same, gilded in sunshine and wonder.

Robert smiled, but it was a Medusa smile, beautiful and cold. "No, he wouldn't, would he? Could you see him admitting what a failure he'd been? Oh, no. Wouldn't want to tarnish that heroic image."

Charles shifted uncomfortably on his chair. "That's not entirely fair. The import duties—"

"And the prices, yes, I know! But we might have managed better. When we might have expanded our land, Father built model farms. *Model farms*. He had an idea he could turn the slaves into yeomen farmers."

Their father's ideas had been much praised in certain circles in London. "Was it such a terrible idea?"

Robert cast him a look. "Just look at the books."

"I mean to," said Charles calmly. "I have an appointment with the bookkeeper after breakfast. Fenty?"

Robert breathed in sharply through his nose. "Another one of Father's follies. Taking a Redleg from the charity school!"

That wasn't entirely fair. True, their father had taken a boy from the charity school, one of the poor whites who lived in the section of the island known as "Scotland" for its inhospitable terrain, but it wasn't pure charity. "Father said that the head of the St. Philip vestry told him that the man had the best mind for numbers he'd ever seen."

"He's a *Redleg*," repeated Robert, as though Charles were very slow. "Do you know that even the slaves give them alms? They're utterly shiftless."

"Perhaps that's because they've lacked the opportunity to be otherwise."

"You sound like Father." It was not meant as a compliment.

The two brothers stared at each other, the air between them thick with tension. Charles held his tongue, resisting the urge to snap back. Robert was just trying to provoke him, that was all. He felt slighted, and rightly. But that didn't mean Charles was going to tarnish their father's memory. Not when he agreed with him.

At long last, Robert said, as though he too were trying to curb his tongue, "Would you beggar us on a principle, Charles? The man was living in a cave. What does he know about the workings of a place such as this?"

"More than I, I imagine," said Charles quietly. They both knew it.

"But you're a *Peverill*. You belong here." The words came out gruffly. Charles could sense how much it cost Robert. He believed it, Robert. He believed the feudal myth, that they were somehow bound to the land, they in it and it in them.

But Charles didn't, and he wouldn't lie. "I could be a hundred Peverills and still as little use. Does blood count for more than experience? Lineage won't make our ledgers tally."

Robert made an impatient gesture. "Devil take it, Charles, there are customs, traditions—you can't reduce Peverills to numbers on a page!"

"I don't intend to—but you can't deny there's something to be said for numbers." Striving for a conciliatory tone, Charles said, "I'm seeing Fenty in an hour. If he's as incompetent as you claim, we'll find another bookkeeper. Would you like to come with me?"

For a long moment, Robert stared at him, as though trying to work something out. Then he gave his golden head an abrupt shake. "Some of us have work to do. I should have been in the east field an hour ago." Pointedly, he added, "An overseer is only as good as the estate manager."

He strode away, boots echoing on the planks of the floor. Charles was left sitting alone at the great dining room table, surrounded by a king's feast of uneaten food, one bread roll torn to crumbs—and a note secured with a red wax seal.

As Charles rose slowly from his seat, he realized, in his indignation about the bookkeeper, Robert had avoided any discussion of his intentions toward the heiress next door.

Vaguely, Charles thought it might solve two problems to send Robert to ride with Miss Beckles. But first, he had a bookkeeper to meet.

THE BOOKKEEPER'S HOUSE was only a short walk from the great house, but it might have been in another country.

Once Charles passed the lime hedge that marked the boundaries of the great house, the carefully cultivated oasis of mango, tamarind, and frangipani gave way to a more workmanlike world of sheds, outbuildings, and close-cut grass, the sounds of industry and the rustle of the cane louder than they had been before.

The overseer's house was closest, a white-walled building with a veranda that gave it claims to elegance. Some way past that sat the bookkeeper's house, a simple two-story block, roughly built of the local stone.

Although, Charles imagined, to a man raised in one of the tumbledown shacks in St. Andrew, this must seem like luxury indeed. He had, he realized, neglected to ask if the new bookkeeper had a family. Their last bookkeeper had. Two nearly grown girls, or at least they had seemed quite old to him then. He had no idea what had become of them, although he did know, from his father's letters, that the bookkeeper had succumbed to drink and been let go.

The sunlight was making Charles's head ache again. Or maybe it was this constant shifting between what was and what wasn't, nineteen years gone with only his father's letters in the between. Charles kept seeing the shadows of buildings and people that were no longer there, hearing the laughter of children long since grown.

The daughters, he vaguely remembered, used to feed him cake. There had been washing on a line behind the house.

Washing and daughters were gone now, as was the cake. Instead there was a man standing outside the bookkeeper's house, managing to give an impression of impatience even though he was standing utterly still.

"Mr. Davenant?" The bookkeeper doffed his hat, revealing hair once red, burnt by the sun into shades of orange and straw, roughly cut and clubbed back with a black ribbon. "I've the books ready for your inspection."

The man was of only medium height, but wiry, with an air of command that ill-fitted his station. Charles found himself following the man through the green-painted front door, feeling, obscurely, that he was being done a favor.

They passed through a sitting room, furnished in a Spartan fashion with leavings from the great house—chairs with upholstery faded by the sun, framed maps on the wall—and into a small office crowded with ledgers. Ledgers in various stages of decrepitude were stacked one atop the other on the shelves that lined one wall. Others, more recent, were piled on a table in the middle of the room.

"Sir," said Fenty. The syllable seemed to sit uncomfortably on his lips. He indicated the room's one chair, a straight-backed affair with a cane seat that looked more suited to penance than comfort.

Charles took it. "So," he said, wishing he had any idea of how to go on. "You have accounts for me?"

Not just accounts. His accounts had accounts. It was, Charles thought, a bit like the time a mechanically minded friend, after a few too many bottles of port, had decided it would be entertaining to take apart Charles's watch to show him how it worked. All of those tiny gears were fascinating, no doubt, but Charles remembered the disorienting sense of seeing something familiar reduced to incomprehensible components, and wanting, more than anything, for it just to be put back together again.

Seed, supplies, stock. They grew more than sugar. Charles had known that, he supposed, but here it was in black and white, so many acres of Guinea corn, of sweet potatoes, of yams. There were trees to be planted and felled, turned into wheels and barrels and wagons. Cows and pigs and horses. Sugar, in all its forms. Sugar planted, sugar sold, sugar turned to rum.

Then there was the human stock. Fenty was thorough, Charles had to grant him that. The slaves were divided into lists, male and female, subdivided by occupation. Sick nurses, midwives, cooks, water carriers, maidservants. Stockkeepers, drivers, coopers, carpenters, smiths, masons, boilers, basketmakers, field hands.

And next to each name: age, occupation. Value.

His father, raised in England, come to Barbados as a grown man, had had grand ideas of freeing their slaves. Not all at once, but gradually. *Like the ancient Saxons*, he liked to say, *moving from slavery to freedom. We'll start with villeins and turn them into good yeomen.*

The ledgers told another tale.

Betsy Rose, second gang, 100 pounds.

Sarcy Ann, second gang, 80 pounds.

Jubah, second gang, 75 pounds.

Thirty-four women and twenty men in the first gang, twenty women and seventeen men in the second gang. Page after page, on and on. The infirm gang. Infants.

The names and numbers, written in a cramped but tidy hand, danced in front of Charles's eyes. "So many souls in our care."

Fenty made a noise that was not quite a snort. "Fewer than you need."

Charles straightened; he hadn't realized how long he had been bending over the ledgers. His back ached with it. Sitting, he realized, also put him in the uncomfortable position of having to look up at his bookkeeper. "What would you recommend?"

"Lease," said the bookkeeper succinctly. "Beckles has people to spare. It's cheaper than buying, and faster than breeding."

In front of Charles was a page marked merely "Increase," next to another marked "Decrease." Five female infants and three male infants born, four men and three women deceased, with a resulting balance of seventy-five pounds.

There was an identical list for bulls and cattle.

He'd known they owned slaves, yes, but his father's letters had been full of elevated ideals, not these blunt valuations. His father had managed to make it sound more like a grand experiment than a trade in human souls, like an exercise in virtue, even. He'd corresponded with William Wilberforce, written enthusiastically in favor of abolition. Charles had dined out in reformist circles in London on the strength of his father's pen.

But this, these ledgers in front of him, was something else entirely. This was business, pure and simple.

Seventeen pounds, ten shillings for clothing for breeding women; forty-five pounds for nourishment. Rewards of six shillings, thruppence per woman for successfully bringing forth a child.

Charles closed the book with a snap. "Is that the last of them?"

"Almost." Fenty was holding another ledger in his arms, but he made no move to set it down on the table. "There are still the accounts for the house."

Charles straightened. "What is it?"

Fenty's calloused hands tightened on the book. Then he set it down with a decisive bang. "Someone is pilfering. Candles, linens, tea. Porter. Anything that won't be immediately missed."

"How long has this been going on?"

"Since before I arrived." Charles waited, saying nothing, and Fenty added, grudgingly, as though every word would be weighed against his account, "I tried to trace it, but the books before I got here—they were in a state. Entries missing, crossed out, books misplaced. I had to build the current accounts from scratch."

The way Fenty held himself reminded Charles of a pugilist, waiting for the other man to throw the next blow.

"You've done an admirable job of it," Charles said, and watched the man's wariness turn to surprise. Charles gestured toward the incriminating ledger. "May I take this with me?"

Fenty shrugged. "They're your books."

And that, thought Charles, was all the thanks he was going to get. Fenty wasn't going to win any awards for charm. But there was something obscurely reassuring about his very bluntness. Charles pushed back his chair, feeling the kinks in his bones as he stood. "Let me speak to my brother about this."

The bookkeeper turned away to put the other ledgers back on the shelf, his voice carefully expressionless. "I already spoke to Master Robert, sir."

"And?"

"He told me to mind my own damned business."

Of course he had. Charles swallowed a surge of annoyance, not at Fenty, but at Robert, Robert who couldn't bear the thought of a Redleg meddling in estate business.

Pride was one thing, but this was pure stubbornness. Charles remembered his father, long ago, telling him about his mother's family. *They're all proud as sin, the Peverills. They were cavaliers to the core and they'll never let you forget it.*

But he wasn't just a Peverill, whatever Robert might believe. They were Davenants too, and whatever Charles might think of his father's family, at least they weren't still mired in some forgotten dream of the seventeenth century, of feudal loyalties and great estates. This was the nineteenth century, for good or for ill, and changes would be made.

He couldn't criticize his brother, but he could say, "It's my business and you're meant to mind it. You've done as you should, Fenty."

Was that relief in the other man's face? He'd turned away before Charles could tell. "Thank you, sir."

The interview, somehow, had been terminated, and Charles wasn't the one to have ended it. "If you find any other, er, anomalies, don't hesitate to bring them to my attention."

"Yes, sir," said Mr. Fenty. "Shall I have the book brought to the great house for you, sir?"

"I believe I can manage it," said Charles, and was bending to pick up the ledger when they were interrupted by the sound of footsteps and a female voice calling.

"Mr. Davenant? I was told I might find you here." A woman appeared in the doorway, the train of her riding habit looped over one arm.

"Miss Beckles?" said Charles.

The voice he recognized, throaty and distinctive. Otherwise, he wouldn't have known her. Between the drink and the candlelight, he had seen her last night only as a blur of pink satin and crepe. In a red riding habit, she presented a different figure entirely. The blurred features of last night reserved themselves into a snub nose, a determined chin, and a well-set pair of gray eyes.

She was also, he realized, smaller than he remembered. In her bright habit, she looked like a little girl playing dress-up. But there was nothing girlish about the way she advanced into the room.

"It's best to ride early in the day," she said without preamble, as though Charles were responsible for keeping her waiting. Which, he supposed, in a way, he was. Did silence imply consent? He was sure his fellow students at Lincoln's Inn would have a grand time debating the point. Miss Beckles, on the other hand, looked as though she wouldn't brook any legal quibbles.

"I beg pardon," said Charles awkwardly. "I meant to send a message—"

"No matter," said Miss Beckles brightly, cutting him off before he could tender his regrets. And then, to Charles's surprise, she leaned over his arm to squint at the crabbed accounts lying open on the table. "Someone's been playing with your accounts. Those numbers are all wrong."

"Yes, I know," said Charles. "But how did you—?"

"Here and here. The numbers don't add up." She looked pointedly at Fenty's back. "No matter how good a manager one has, it's always best to review the accounts."

Her manager, Charles recalled, was her uncle. "Even among family?"

"Especially among family." There was something hard about her face, something that made her look years older. She put a hand on Charles's arm. "Shall we, Mr. Davenant? It's not kind to keep the horses waiting. Unless you'd rather I review your books for you."

"That," said Fenty flatly, "will not be necessary."

"I wouldn't trouble you, Miss Beckles," said Charles, looking down at that small, gloved hand on his arm and wondering just when the day had entirely escaped his control.

"It's no trouble at all," said Miss Beckles, and Charles had the sense that it was the most honest thing she had said. "I like numbers. And it's important to keep track of one's own books. People take advantage if you let them."

Fenty's back was displaying signs of indignation, like an offended cat. Charles hastily took Miss Beckles's arm, guiding her from the room. "If you could have the ledger sent on, Fenty, I would appreciate it. And thank you again for speaking to me of this matter."

"Sir," said Mr. Fenty. "Ma'am."

"You'd best watch that one," said Miss Beckles as they proceeded down the steps. "My father always said you could never trust a Redleg."

Goaded, Charles said, "And who would you trust?"

"My maid," said Miss Beckles, and there was a strangely defiant note in her voice. But before Charles could make too much of it, she affected a light laugh and said, "And there she is with the horses! I had yours brought round for you. It seemed simplest."

For whom? Charles wanted to ask, but couldn't. There were disadvantages to being a gentleman.

There were three horses inspecting the grass outside the bookkeeper's house, their reins held, not by a groom, but by a woman, clad in a severely cut riding habit. Her face was hidden by her hat, but there was something about her stance, a stillness, that touched a chord of memory.

Candlelight and white lawn; the colonel's hand on Charles's arm. *The girls at Beckles are counted exceptionally pretty.*

To hide his confusion, Charles turned to Miss Beckles. The feather on her hat brushed his nose. "You ride with your maid, not a groom?"

"Riding out with only a groom might lead to talk," said Miss Beckles, and there was a grim note to her voice that Charles didn't quite understand.

"It's not considered out of the ordinary in England," said Charles. They were closer now, and he felt unaccountably awkward at the idea of facing the maid again. Jenny. That odd interlude the night before felt like a fever dream. He might have imagined it. He must have imagined it.

"I would not wish to give any appearance of impropriety," said Miss Beckles. She smiled up at Charles a little too brightly. "And there can't be any impropriety with Jenny as my shadow, can there? She guards me as well as any groom."

"Guards?" It seemed a curious choice of word.

"Accompanies," amended Miss Beckles. "Would you prefer to ride first and then eat, or eat and then ride? Cook packed enough for a garrison."

"I—" Charles scrabbled to find a way to politely refuse but found himself at a loss as Jenny stepped forward, wordlessly handing him the reins of his horse. Her gloved hand brushed his, turning him tongue-tied with awkwardness.

"Let's eat first, then, shall we? There's a glade just between our properties that makes a splendid place for a picnic," said Miss Beckles, taking his silence for assent. "I'll show it to you."

CHAPTER FIVE

Christ Church, Barbados
February 1854

ADAM WAS ONLY too delighted to abandon their picnic for the promise of a proper meal.

"I do hope you will forgive the lack of formal invitation," said Mr. Davenant earnestly. He spoke to them all, but his eyes strayed to Laura. "We don't stand on ceremony here on our little island."

"You are very kind," said Laura.

"Not in the slightest. I could hardly leave you stranded here among these bare, ruined choirs."

Laura ducked her dark head. "I was thinking more *Time will rust the sharpest sword / Time will consume the strongest cord.*"

It wasn't time but fire that had consumed Peverills. Emily opened her mouth to say so, but Mr. Davenant got there first. "*Marmion?*"

"Marmi-what?" said Adam.

Laura shook her head. "It is Sir Walter Scott but not *Marmion*. Have you read *Harold the Dauntless?*"

"You have the advantage of me. Our library isn't as extensive, but I can, at least, claim to have committed those works we have to memory. Are you acquainted with *The Lay of the Last Minstrel?*"

Laura's cheeks pinked with pleasure. "*Breathes there the man, with soul so dead, / Who never to himself hath said, / This is my own, my native land!*"

"Your native land is Great George Street," muttered Adam, shoving his hands in his pockets.

Taking advantage of Laura's distraction, Emily took Adam by the arm. "If you will pardon us for a moment?"

"Do you intend to recite poetry at me?" said her cousin crossly, one eye on his wife. "Or do you mean to read me a lecture?"

"Neither. Did Grandfather ever say anything to Uncle Archie about . . . ?" Emily waved toward the smoke-blackened gables behind them. "About this place?"

"His own, his native land?" said Adam, but subsided as Emily fixed him with her best governess look. "You were there that day. Father was as surprised as the rest of us. If Grandfather were going to tell anyone, Em, it would have been you. You know that."

"But?" said Emily. Her cousin had always had all the subterfuge of a golden retriever.

Adam scuffed at the gravel with the toe of his boot. "Father did say that Grandfather worked as a bookkeeper on a plantation. Before he met Grandmother."

Emily looked up sharply. "Here?"

"It's the most likely answer, isn't it? It would be like him to take a fancy to own it."

"And let it sit empty?"

"Maybe. He was never exactly forthcoming about his life in Barbados, was he?"

"He was about some things," Emily said, in their grandfather's defense.

"Yes, the morality tales. Hoeing the ground in the hot sun, trying to grow enough Indian corn to keep body and soul together, a fourteen-mile walk in blazing heat to and from the market in Speightstown. . . . We all heard those stories. But the rest of it? Who knows. Maybe he . . ."

"What?" The tips of Adam's ears had turned red, a sure sign of guilt.

"Not fit for your ears, coz."

"You needn't go all prunes and prisms on me, Adam. I'm not"—

she'd almost said "Laura"—"one of your sisters. There's no need to spare my sensibilities."

The gap between her father's parish in St. Jude's and her cousin's grand house on Great George Street existed in more than just geography. There were times, at Miss Blackwell's, when Emily felt a world away from her classmates, divided by what she had seen and heard. Adam's sisters, she knew, understood it only as a matter of physical want; they made baskets and gathered up old clothes for Emily to deliver to "her" poor. Laura worried about their spirits; she put in impracticalities for them: sachets of fine linen and lavender, slim books of poetry, the items that she would want in times of duress.

But Adam, Emily thought, should know better. Or did he? He might have the run of the city, but he had never once visited her father's parish, never seen the children playing shoeless in the gutter, the women who knocked at the kitchen door late in the night, shawls covering their bruised eyes.

Adam cast a glance over his shoulder, made sure no one was listening. "All right, then. The governor had a notion that Grandfather did something dodgy, and that was why he ran when he did—and why he had enough money to set himself up after."

That, Emily was sure, was a distinctly abridged version. "Do you mean . . . he stole something?"

"Stole, reclaimed . . ." Adam made a helpless gesture. "A long time ago, Grandfather told me land was stolen from our family. He said the Fentys were lured to Barbados on the promise of land for work, that they had the work but never got the land."

"This land?"

Adam shrugged. "You know as much of it as I."

"So maybe that's what this was all about. He wanted the land. It would suit him, to even the score." Her grandfather was a firm believer in an eye for an eye. He wouldn't take only the eye, but the spectacles as well, as interest. But something didn't quite make sense. "Why leave it to me, then? I'm not a Fenty."

"Once you're sending plagues . . . Don't look at me like that! I didn't mean it. He always said you were the most like him of the lot of us. Maybe that's why." Before Emily could feel too pleased by that, Adam added, "And he did always feel that you'd got the short end of the stick, losing your mother and all. Remember when he used to bring out the bag of sweets?"

"One for you and two for me." The memory made Emily smile, despite herself. Her grandfather, with that crumpled paper bag he kept in his desk drawer. He'd lectured them all about frugality, but then he showered them with sweets. "I never liked peppermints."

"But you never told him, did you?"

"No. I gave them to you, instead." At Adam's suggestion, as she recalled. Emily narrowed her eyes at her cousin. "So, really, you had no cause to complain. You were hardly cheated."

His expression troubled, Adam reached out and squeezed her hand. "I didn't begrudge you the sweets, Emmy. And I don't begrudge you this. I just . . . I don't want to see you—"

"Toiling in the fields?"

Adam didn't return her amusement. "Caught up in some scheme of Grandfather's. You know how he was. He liked his surprises and his japes." Glancing over his shoulder at Dr. Braithwaite, he said darkly, "Look at him, sending us off to his old friend Turner without ever letting on that the man's a nigger. I'd wager he had a good laugh when he put that in the will."

Looking back, Emily saw Dr. Braithwaite watching them. She twitched her hand away from her cousin's. "That's not fair," she said flatly. "I don't believe Grandfather ever thought of that. He admired Mr. Turner for his business sense."

Adam shrugged. "Have it as you will. But you can't deny the old man liked to make everyone dance to his tune. He yanked us about like puppets."

He was, Emily suspected, thinking of their grandfather's opposition to his marriage with Laura, which had been fierce and vocal. "Only for the best," she protested. "He always meant it for the best, whatever it was."

Adam made a noise of frustration. "I just don't want to see you hurt. I know you loved him—I loved him too!—but he was no saint. My father always said there was more to Grandfather's past than we knew."

"Whatever it was," said Emily firmly, stepping away, "it was forty years ago. How can it touch me now?"

Adam looked as though he might say something else, then shrugged. "You've always taken your own counsel."

She'd offended him. Emily tried to make it right, just as she had, long ago, when they had played blindman's bluff and he'd had to be soothed when she won. "I appreciate your advice, Adam, truly, I do."

Adam knew her as well as she knew him. "You just won't take it."

"No," she said apologetically. As she watched, he turned again to look at Laura, who was speaking animatedly—animatedly for Laura—to Mr. Davenant. Emily touched his arm. "Would you take some from me?"

"That depends on what it is," said Adam, already moving away toward Laura and Mr. Davenant. "Ah, Mr. Davenant, shall we?"

Emily caught Dr. Braithwaite's eye and bit down hard on her lip. Maybe Adam was right. Maybe it wasn't any of her business. They were husband and wife now, after all. It didn't matter that she'd known Laura longer and better; it would be a point of pride to Adam not to take her advice, although he'd been glad enough for it during their courtship.

"My dear?" Adam held out his arm to Laura with aggressive courtesy. "If I might help you into the carriage?"

Laura looked slightly bewildered but accepted his help. "It was very fortunate that we came upon Mr. Davenant," she ventured, as Emily joined her on the seat.

"Oh yes, very fortunate," echoed Adam.

"Shall I ride alongside?" suggested Mr. Davenant tactfully, positioning himself by Emily's side of the carriage, well away from Adam and Laura. "Of course, Nathaniel knows the way."

"Oh?" Emily echoed, looking at Dr. Braithwaite. Hearing him referred to as Nathaniel was like seeing him in his shirtsleeves, an unimaginable invasion of his privacy.

Dr. Braithwaite's lips tightened at the casual use of his name, but he made no comment.

"Is it far?" inquired Emily, as the coach began to lurch again down the rutted drive.

"Not as the crow flies," said Mr. Davenant.

"Or by horseback?" suggested Emily. Mr. Davenant rode with the ease of a man who spent most of his time in the saddle.

Mr. Davenant dipped his head in acknowledgment. "My morning ride often takes me out this way."

"Trespassing?" said Dr. Braithwaite, and Mr. Davenant's fair face flushed.

"My grandmother likes me to keep an eye, make sure no one's making trouble. That was before we knew of Miss Dawson's arrival," he added, with a courteous bow in Emily's direction. "As to that, I've heard you've been making visits to Beckles. What are you doing poaching MacAndrews's patients, Nat?"

"Healing them," said Dr. Braithwaite. He propped one ankle against the opposite knee. "I'm surprised he noticed they were missing."

"Well, when the pest house is empty . . ."

"Pest house?" asked Emily.

"Our . . . infirmary, I guess you'd call it?" Mr. Davenant looked to Dr. Braithwaite for assistance, but the doctor didn't seem inclined to provide any. "Dr. MacAndrews comes once a week to visit the sick."

"And if they weren't sick before his visit . . ." murmured the doctor.

Mr. Davenant gave an airy wave of his crop. "MacAndrews does his best."

"The man's a sot," said Dr. Braithwaite bluntly. "The only thing he knows how to physic is his own thirst."

"I say, that's not fair. The man's been at Beckles longer than I have."

"So has beriberi," said Dr. Braithwaite. "That doesn't mean you want to encourage it to stay."

All around them, the wilted stalks had given way to tall green cane; the carriage wheels seemed very loud on the smooth surface of the road. "You might have asked before you started making house calls."

Dr. Braithwaite leaned back against the squabs. "Tugging my forelock and begging permission? The patients I'm treating are all freemen."

"Yes, in our employ." Blue eyes met brown. The blue eyes dropped first. Jokingly, Mr. Davenant said, "You might send us a reckoning, at least."

No answering smile touched Dr. Braithwaite's lips. "Oh no. This I do on my own account."

Mr. Davenant's horse sidled restlessly. "As you will. Your uncle is richer than Midas, isn't he? I don't imagine you miss the fee. If you look up ahead, Miss Dawson, you'll see Beckles."

"Where? Oh—I see now." There were no towering gables here, no Jacobean chimney pots. The house was wide and low, large parts of it all but obscured by enormous, flowering shrubs.

Mr. Davenant reined in his horse. "It isn't as grand as Peverills, but at least the roof still stands."

"It's lovely," said Emily. It was a meringue of a building, stucco gleaming white in the sunshine, capped by a red slate roof, which was, indeed, intact.

Mr. Davenant waited for the coachman to lower the stairs before holding out a hand to help her down. "But rather bland after Peverills?"

"I didn't say that." His grip was stronger than she would have expected; she had thought him more scholar than athlete. Emily gave her crumpled skirts a brisk shake as she stepped out onto the brick walk. Ahead of her, a flight of stairs led up to a broad veranda. "It's just . . . very different."

"Peverills is one of the oldest houses on the island. They don't tend to last, you know. Between hurricane and fire . . . Bridgetown's been rebuilt half a dozen times since I was born, at least."

"Hurricane?" said Laura as Mr. Davenant handed her out of the carriage.

"You needn't worry," Mr. Davenant hastened to reassure her. "Beckles was built to withstand hurricane. Our walls are two feet thick."

"Not to mention that it isn't the season for hurricane. You'll be back in England long before there's any danger." Dr. Braithwaite remained seated, making no move to follow them. To Mr. Davenant, he said, "Mrs. Davenant's carriage shall, I take it, be made available to return my uncle's guests to Bridgetown?"

Mr. Davenant nodded, seeming relieved. "Certainly. I'll see your guests safely back to Bridgetown."

Emily looked from one to the other. "You're not stopping?"

"I have obligations in town," said Dr. Braithwaite.

Those obligations hadn't prevented him from planning to share their picnic at Peverills, only from sitting at table at Beckles.

Emily frowned up at the figure in the carriage, reduced to a dark outline by the angle of the sun. "I hadn't realized—if it's inconvenient . . ."

Mr. Davenant offered her an arm. "Don't distress yourself, Miss Dawson. Our coachman should be delighted to convey you back to town. It isn't the least trouble."

It wasn't their return journey that was distressing her, and Dr. Braithwaite, at least, knew it. He looked at her as though daring her to voice her objections.

But how could she? No one had intimated that Dr. Braithwaite might be unwelcome. She would only embarrass herself and her cousins by pushing the point.

"Thank you," said Emily in a constrained voice. "And thank you, Dr. Braithwaite, for your escort today."

Dr. Braithwaite tipped his hat. "Miss Dawson. Mrs. Fenty. Mr. Fenty. Enjoy your luncheon." To Mr. Davenant, he merely inclined his head.

"Nathaniel—" said Mr. Davenant, but the carriage was already turning in the drive, bearing Dr. Braithwaite away.

"Stiff-necked, isn't he?" commented Adam lazily.

"I wouldn't say that. Shall we?" Mr. Davenant gestured toward the stairs. Something winked at them from the veranda, a sudden flash of bright light.

Emily blinked, seeing stars. "Do you know Dr. Braithwaite well?"

They ascended the stairs in silence, the air heady with the scent of flowers and sugar. After a moment, Mr. Davenant said, "Nathaniel used to work at Beckles."

Laura and Adam were several treads behind them, Adam deliberately keeping Laura to himself. Emily chose her words carefully. "Was that before the implementation of the Slavery Abolition Act?"

"Yes." Mr. Davenant's eyes met hers. They were, she noticed, a very pale, clear blue. "Nathaniel was the son of our cooper. We used to play hide-and-seek in the barrels—against strict instructions, I might add. But that was a very long time ago. I doubt either of us would fit in a barrel these days."

"No," said Emily. Impossible to imagine Dr. Braithwaite, in his impeccably tailored suit, squirming through the staves of a half-constructed barrel. A slave. "Were you of an age?"

Mr. Davenant paused on the veranda, giving Laura and Adam time to catch up. "Nathaniel is a few years older. I hadn't any brothers or sisters, you see. My mother . . . well, never mind that. Ah, here we are."

The front door opened and a maid emerged bearing a tray with four silver cups.

"Lemonade?" said Mr. Davenant proudly.

"But how—?" Laura looked up at him as he handed her a silver cup, sweating slightly in the heat.

Mr. Davenant pointed to a metal tube mounted to the railing of the veranda. "They'll have seen us coming some time since. I'll wager Sally has already laid extra places at table."

Emily took a cup, the metal cool beneath her fingers, incised with a coat of arms too faded to make out. "Is that a spyglass?"

"Yes," said Mr. Davenant, taking a grateful swig of his own drink. "It's an old planter trick, to welcome one's guests with the door open and a cold drink at the ready."

And see what one's slaves were doing, Emily didn't doubt. "May I?"

"Go right ahead," said Mr. Davenant.

The metal was warm to the touch but not hot; the hedges shaded the veranda from the sun. The road leaped out at her and, on it, Dr. Braithwaite in the barouche, making his way back to Bridgetown.

He had shifted to the forward-facing seat, his back to Beckles. Relieved to be done with them? No doubt.

They would not, Emily supposed, see him again, and she found the thought unsettling, although she wasn't sure why. The sense of a conversation unfinished, perhaps. Or the fear that she hadn't shown to good advantage—that all of them hadn't shown to good advantage—and she wanted to set it right.

The polished lacquer winked in the sunlight, disappearing behind the long stalks of cane.

"Don't keep it all to yourself," said Adam, and Emily obligingly moved aside. "Ahoy, mateys! I feel quite piratical."

"When I was a boy," said Mr. Davenant, taking Emily's empty cup from her and setting it back on the tray, "I thought my grandmother was omniscient. She knew whenever I was getting into something I shouldn't."

"Climbing into the cooper's barrels?" said Emily. "But I could see only the road."

"Oh, this is only one of many," said Mr. Davenant. "There are spyglasses all about the house. I'm sure I haven't found the half of them. My forebears liked to know what was going on about them. There wasn't anyone or anything on their land they couldn't see."

"How . . . enterprising," said Emily.

Mr. Davenant looked uncomfortable. "It's hard to explain how it was. One lived alone out here, surrounded by one's people. Not that one didn't trust one's people, but . . ."

The maid holding the tray stood impassive.

Mr. Davenant smiled at her. "Thank you, Polly. Will you tell Mrs.

Davenant that we have company?" To Emily, he added, "It's a formality, of course. She'll know already."

"How convenient," murmured Emily, but she couldn't help glancing back over her shoulder at the spyglass sitting so innocuously on its stand.

Was that how Mr. Davenant had seen them, all the way by the ruins? Could he see all the way to Peverills? It was disconcerting, knowing one was being watched.

"I think it's ingenious," said Adam. "I'll have ten of them put in at Great George Street, so that we can pretend not to be at home when my sisters call. Are you coming, Emily?"

"What? Yes," said Emily, and followed Mr. Davenant and her cousins through the front door of Beckles.

Chapter Six

Beckles
March 1812

"WHAT IS SHE doing riding out with Davenant?"

Jenny's father caught her behind the washhouse, her arms full of linens. That he'd lain in wait for her, she had no doubt. He'd have seen her from the glass he kept by his window and marked his time until she emerged. Jenny schooled herself to show no reaction. She wouldn't give him the satisfaction of knowing he'd startled her.

"Riding," said Jenny, and then, when her father's face darkened, she added, "If there were anything more, don't you think I'd have told you?"

"Would you?" The colonel gripped her chin in his hand, forcing her to stare up into the face that was so like hers. She'd gotten her looks from him, the long lines of her cheekbones, the deep-set gray eyes. Nobody dared comment upon it, yet everybody knew.

She wasn't the only one of her father's bastards at Beckles, but she was the only one he had honored with his attention.

Jenny forced herself to stand still, even though her heart was going like a blacksmith's hammer beneath the pile of linens. "I know which side my bread is buttered."

Her father released her, so abruptly that her head snapped back. "See that you do." There was no need to add an *or else*. He'd made the consequences clear enough. He might not own her anymore, not on paper, but what he wanted to do with her, he could. He had proved that well enough. But she wasn't going to think about that. Not now. "I don't want her seeing Davenant again."

"Stranger if she doesn't. Being neighbors and all." Jenny balanced her basket on her hip, trying to look as if the idea had just come to her. "They say familiarity breeds contempt."

Her father gave a short bark of a laugh. "Give her enough rope and she'll hang herself? There are times when you almost show sense."

"Sir." Jenny bowed her head, the picture of submission. As long as he couldn't see her eyes.

The colonel's booted foot tapped against the dirt path. She could see him working over the idea, turning it over in his mind.

"All right. Let her have her amusement. It will all be over soon enough." As if by chance, he added, "I've asked Dr. MacAndrews for dinner. These headaches my niece has been having . . . I don't like them. I don't like them at all."

"No, sir," said Jenny.

Her father didn't say anything else, just nodded abruptly and strode away, confident that his message had been received. Which it had. First the stick, then the carrot. That obscene pantomime with Davenant, followed, now, by this pretense of complicity. She could work with her father to destroy her mistress—or suffer the consequences.

It might, Jenny thought, making her way back to the house, have been more effective as a tactic if she'd had the least faith her father would stand by her. But she knew, knew from experience, knew from years of watching him, that as soon as her usefulness was done, so would she be. There would be no manumission, no tidy house in Bridgetown or advantageous marriage, the various plums he had dangled in front of her as his fancy took him. Instead, she was just as likely to be sold, an inconvenient reminder of an unfortunate interlude.

At least Mary Anne could be trusted to keep her promises—most of the time.

And that was just the crux of it, wasn't it? Mary Anne needed Jenny; she might even love her. But that didn't mean she was to be trusted. None of them were. And Jenny would do well to remember that.

Mary Anne had no such reserve. She came running down the steps to meet Jenny, in a welter of impatience.

"Well? Do you have my sprig muslin?" Lowering her voice, she added, "I saw you from the window. What did my uncle want with you?"

"The front breadth is spoiled." Jenny made a show of adjusting her burden. "He's asked Dr. MacAndrews to dine."

"*Doctor* MacAndrews." Mary Anne didn't bother to hide her contempt. Jenny cast her a warning look. The maid dusting the brasses, the boy sweeping the steps: any of them might be her father's spy. Any of them probably were. "What? He's no more been to the university in Edinburgh than I have. The only study he's done is of the bottom of a bottle."

Jenny kept her eyes down, her voice neutral. "The master wishes the doctor to alleviate the pain of your headaches."

"By removing my head?" Mary Anne muttered as they crossed the threshold into her rooms. The chambermaid didn't stop her sweeping, but her head moved slightly, listening. Mary Anne bared her teeth in a smile. "My uncle is all kindness, but he is mistaken. You can go now, Esther. Tell Cook there'll be one more at table."

Never mind that Cook already knew, probably had known long before her mistress. Mary Anne fought fiercely for the illusion that she had any say in the ordering of her own household.

The door had barely closed behind the maid before Mary Anne turned back to Jenny. "Is that his plan, do you think? To drug me into insensibility?"

Jenny busied herself laying out the linens, smoothing imaginary creases out of an impeccably pressed chemise. "He didn't say."

"You must have some idea." When Jenny didn't answer, Mary Anne turned on her heel, pacing her usual track from window to bed. "He means to put me in the madhouse, doesn't he?"

"He might do," said Jenny neutrally.

Or an accident, carefully staged. Poor girl, her mind was unbalanced. She never noticed that open window. . . .

"Might do," Mary Anne mocked. "What did he tell you?"

"Only what I've told you." Jenny held her mistress's gaze. "I'm not privy to his plans. Not anymore."

Mary Anne's eyes dropped first. She knew the reason for it as well as Jenny and the cost exacted for it.

She sat down among Jenny's carefully folded linens, never minding the mess she was making. "He's grown bolder."

Bolder wasn't exactly the word Jenny would have used. Her father was still playing a careful game, nothing that could redound discredit upon him. But he was enacting his moves with a grim determination that boded ill for Jenny's mistress. He was done playing a waiting game.

And Mary Anne . . . Mary Anne wasn't suited to subtlety.

"You might try to pay him off." Even as she said it, Jenny knew it was futile. Once, perhaps, it might have served. But not anymore. Her father would never settle for less than the whole. And Mary Anne would never willingly part with a penny of what was hers, even if she wrote her own death warrant in the process, and Jenny's with it.

Mary Anne shrugged the suggestion away. "And have him come back for more? No. But MacAndrews, now . . . How much do you think it would take to buy him?"

"I don't know," said Jenny honestly.

"Not much, I imagine." Mary Anne fingered the locket that hung from a ribbon around her neck. "The price of a bottle of brandy."

"You get what you pay for," Jenny cautioned.

"Meaning he'll be too foxed to remember he's been bought? In that case, we'll remind him." Mary Anne was already thumbing through the small box in which she kept her trinkets, the small ornaments her guardian had considered suitable to pass on to her. "My mother's pearl brooch. I never wear it."

"Would you offer it to MacAndrews?"

"No. You will."

Jenny's hands went cold. Her lips felt numb. "He'll think I stole it. If he goes to the master . . ."

Mary Anne looked as though she were about to argue, but something in Jenny's face made her reconsider. With a shrug, she said, "The filigree combs, then. They've never become me. I can gift them to you. I'll do it tonight, in front of my uncle."

Mary Anne looked dangerously pleased with herself at the notion.

"Don't tweak his tail too hard," Jenny warned. Those combs had been the colonel's birthday gift to his niece.

"Oh, hardly," said Mary Anne airily. "But I can't help it if he wastes his coin on bagatelles fit only for the servants. You can sell them—in Oistins. Or Bridgetown. Bridgetown would be best. You'll get a better price, I imagine. Don't worry. I'll give you a pass in case anyone questions you."

It was no use arguing with Mary Anne when she had the bit between her teeth; one could only hope that she might be distracted or forget. Once challenged, she would only dig in her heels. "What if someone follows me?"

"There's no harm to your selling something I've given you, is there? Whatever Uncle John suspects, he can't *know*." Having resolved the matter to her satisfaction, Mary Anne said, "Once I marry, he'll have no power over me. I can have him banned from the grounds if I like."

If her husband allowed it. But they would face that trouble when they came to it.

Against her better judgment, Jenny produced a folded piece of paper with a red seal from under her apron. "The Tremaines of Rosehall are giving a dance for Mr. Davenant."

Mary Anne frowned at the paper. "This is my uncle's seal."

"The master's reply. He regrets that you're indisposed."

There was a dangerous glitter in Mary Anne's eye. "Oh, am I? On the contrary, I am quite disposed to attend. Get me paper and ink. He'll never dare challenge my attendance once this is sent."

Unless he drugged her into insensibility first. Jenny watched as Mary Anne wrote her reply with such ferocity that the nib left a gash in the paper. "Go softly, Miss Mary."

"Softly won't serve." Mary Anne doused the paper in sand, setting up a shower of small grains as she shook the note in the air. "Here. See this delivered. No. Deliver it yourself. I won't take a chance on this."

"Yes, mistress."

Belatedly, Mary Anne glanced up at her, catching something in her voice or posture. "Will there be trouble for you? Will he know you took it?"

After a pause, Jenny shook her head. "Not this time."

Not if she went to him first, with the information that she'd delivered a sealed paper to Rosehall, professed ignorance when he raged, as he surely would, that she ought to have brought it to him first. He would be frustrated, yes, but he wouldn't punish her, not this time. He would see it as clumsiness, not treachery.

There were benefits to being underestimated.

"Good," said Mary Anne, dismissing the matter. "I'll wear the new jonquil silk. And my mother's diamonds. Let Mr. Davenant see just what he stands to gain."

Jenny paused, Mary Anne's letter in her hand. "Are you sure he wishes to be reminded?"

"What is that supposed to mean?"

Jenny bit her lip, weighing her words. "Mr. Davenant has . . . romantic tendencies." She could picture the two of them under the boughs of a tamarind tree, talking past each other, Mr. Davenant speaking of principles and Mary Anne of crops, Mr. Davenant of philosophy and Mary Anne of accounts; Mary Anne cited Lascelles's *Instructions for the Management of a Plantation in Barbadoes and for the Treatment of Negroes*, Mr. Davenant quoted a Frenchman named Rousseau. "He might not want to think himself a fortune hunter."

Mary Anne drew back her head and looked narrowly at Jenny. "You know him so well?"

"I listen. As you instructed me."

"He can be as romantic as he likes. That doesn't change the fact that the roof at Peverills needs repairing."

"You can't stand in the road and see the leak in somebody else's house," said Jenny softly. It was a proverb she'd heard in the quarters. Not in speech with her, of course. No one ever stopped and gossiped with her. It was all yes and no and averted eyes, as befitted her station as the voice of her mistress, the foreign by-blow of the master.

Mary Anne was not impressed. "You can when it's Peverills. They've lost half their leading. One hurricane and the house will come crashing down about them. I'll wear the diamonds."

"Yes, Miss Mary," said Jenny, and took the letter and her counsel away.

"Away so soon?" said Mrs. Tremaine, bustling over to Charles. Diamonds bounced in the deep V of her bosom. "If you find yourself in want of a partner . . ."

"Only of lemonade. The heat, after London . . ."

"It's very cool of an evening," said Mrs. Tremaine defensively, admitting no defect to her island. "Now, if you need a partner for the quadrille, my Becky—"

Charles wasn't sure which one of the Tremaine daughters Becky might be, but he was entirely sure he didn't want to dance the quadrille with any of them. The room was watching and waiting for him to choose a bride and sire an heir, preferably within the evening.

"I believe Colonel Lyons is looking for you," said Charles.

He took advantage of his hostess's distraction to escape, not toward refreshments, but onto the balcony, where he took several deep breaths of the warm evening air. The combination of hothouse flowers, candle smoke, and French scent was beginning to make his head ache.

But not the punch. Charles wasn't making that mistake again. He'd silently abandoned the many glasses pressed upon him, pretending to drink when necessary, trying not to choke on the fumes. From the smell of it, the punch was nine-tenths rum, with a hint of lemon and a generous scoop of sugar, fruits of the local bounty in their headiest form. Everyone expected him to toast and be toasted. He was the guest of honor. This party was, ostensibly, to welcome him home.

Nostos. That was the Greek word for it. Homecoming.

Had Odysseus felt thus when he sighted Ithaca after all those many years away? The pinch of expectation, like a suit of clothes tailored for another man, too heavy, too tight, choking him. This was his home, that place turned half myth by memory, and yet he had never felt more out of place or more alone.

It wasn't that people had been unwelcoming. Quite the contrary. He was overwhelmed with invitations and advice. He should join the militia, join the council, hire a new bookkeeper, try this or that with his crops. It seemed that every unmarried young lady in the district had been conscripted to play on the pianoforte or the harp for him; their mothers shared reminiscences of Charles's mother and demanded news of the latest fashions from London. Everyone wanted the pleasure of his company; he need never dine alone unless he so chose.

And yet. He was a novelty, an outsider. Charles didn't miss the way his neighbors' voices changed when they spoke to him, the rolling rhythms of the local accent clipped and strangled into something more like his own diction. Even Mary Anne Beckles, so forthright in her way, adopted what she fondly believed to be ladylike airs in his presence, never knowing that he preferred her as she was when she forgot herself, blunt and businesslike.

Everyone was kind, everyone had advice to give, but they weren't at ease with him as they were with Robert. Conversations stopped when Charles entered a room; fans were retrieved and cravats straightened.

The best thing he could do for everyone would be to depart, forthwith. Or would it? Robert might know more than he about practical management, but he would never further their father's schemes or keep his promises.

He had pledged his father. Not just his father but all the souls in his care, the men and women of Peverills. He couldn't shrug off that burden just because he found it didn't suit him to shoulder it.

But duty was poor company of an evening, and very lonely after the fellowship he had left behind in London.

"Master Charles?" A woman stood at the far end of the veranda, her white apron ghostlike in the darkness. She approached him warily, as one might a dangerous animal. "Are you ill?"

"No, not ill." Not in any way that might be physicked. Charles shook his head, feeling thoroughly sick of himself. He squinted at the figure in the shadows. "It's . . . Jenny, isn't it?"

"Yes, sir." She held herself very still, as if poised for flight.

Don't, Charles wanted to tell her. You have nothing to fear from me. But didn't she? He couldn't blame her for shying from him.

"Shouldn't you be enjoying the festivities?" said Charles, with false bonhomie. "My brother tells me the servants have their own dance."

Charles winced at himself. Servants. Not servants; slaves. It was too easy to fall into the local custom, mincing about with euphemisms, sidling past uncomfortable realities with half-truths.

"They do." The silence stretched between them. Charles could hear the scrape of the violin, the whine of the flute, the thumping tread of the dance, as she weighed her answer. "I wasn't invited."

"Whyever not?"

"I'm a foreigner."

"A foreigner?" Charles didn't quite manage to hide his confusion.

The maid was betrayed into something that might almost have been a smile, a barely perceptible movement of her closed lips. "Colonel Lyons brought me with him from Jamaica. That makes me a foreigner."

"Jamaica isn't so very far." Not to him, maybe, he realized. But to a woman who couldn't leave the parish, much less the island, it must seem as far as the moon. "How old were you?"

"A little more than five, or so I'm told." She shifted and the light from the windows fell across her face, highlighting the long bones of her cheeks, the shape of her face beneath her plain white cap.

Charles peered at her through the dim light, caught by an odd sense of familiarity, a resemblance he couldn't quite place. "Surely, by now . . ."

"I wasn't born here. It isn't something anyone forgets."

"Being born here doesn't seem to have done me much good," said Charles ruefully. "Do you miss Jamaica?"

"I don't remember it." But there was something about the way she glanced away from him, her eyes glinting silver in the light, that made him suspect she remembered more than she said. The maid dropped a curtsy, bowing her head. "Beg pardon, sir. My mistress will miss me. Do you have any message for her?"

Charles could feel his cheeks heat. What would anyone think to see him standing here, talking to his neighbor's maid? One of two things, neither of them to his credit.

"Only that I trust she will save me a dance," said Charles. In the ballroom, the set had finished. He could see Miss Beckles curtsy to his brother. And he could see his brother's eyes settle on him. "Will you tell her so for me?"

"Yes, sir," said the maid, and Charles was caught again by that tug of recognition. He had been standing on another balcony, another night. "I shall be glad to be of any honest service."

Another pair of pale eyes in a fine-boned face.

The girls at Beckles . . .

"Thank you . . . Jenny." But she was already gone, leaving Charles staring after her, fighting with the evidence of his own eyes.

"Trying to ingratiate yourself with the lady's maid?" Robert strolled over to join him, leaning an elbow on the rail.

Charles felt as though he'd bitten into something rancid. "That only works in the theater. And generally turns to farce. Are they cousins?"

"Who?"

"Miss Beckles and her maid," said Charles urgently. He didn't know why he was asking, when he was already sure of the answer. But if so . . . if so . . . it made what had already been gross, grotesque. "The colonel—is he the maid's father?"

Robert shrugged. "I shouldn't be surprised. He'd have to be a monk to refuse what's offered."

"What's *offered*?"

Robert folded his arms across his chest, looking narrowly at Charles. "What were you plotting with Miss Beckles's maid?"

"Not what you think," said Charles. Whatever the colonel might have offered. His own daughter. He had offered his own daughter. "We merely happened to be on the balcony at the same time."

"Are you planning to propose to Mar—Miss Beckles?"

"I'm not planning to propose to anybody! I've only just made the acquaintance of Miss Beckles."

Robert turned abruptly away from the rail. He wore his militia uniform and the gold braid winked in the light. "Have you heard what they say about her?"

"No, and I don't care to." The last thing Charles wanted to do was think about Beckles or its inhabitants. "Are we old women to gossip over our tatting?"

Robert wasn't deterred. "They say she has intemperate appetites. Why do you think she goes nowhere without that maid of hers? Her uncle doesn't trust her with a groom. . . ."

Charles cut him off. "Sour grapes, no doubt. She's not in the common way, certainly, but there's nothing the least intemperate about her." If anything, there was an innocence to her. No, not innocence. That wasn't the right word. A lack of coyness. Her attempts at flirtation were unstudied and awkward, alien to her forthright nature. "She lacks polish, but that's not surprising."

"I forget," said Robert. "We're all provincials to you. This must seem very flat to you after London."

"I dined out once a fortnight in London. This is an excess of gaiety in comparison." Robert made no effort to hide his disbelief. "I was a student, not a pink of the ton. Most of my evenings were spent with my Blackstone and a cold pork pie."

Or with his fellows, sprawled in someone's rooms, drinking cheap claret out of mismatched glasses. The circles in which he'd moved in London wouldn't have interested Robert, but Charles missed them, desperately. He missed the gray fog and coal smoke, the murky back-drop against which ideas blazed out with such clarity, words more real than objects.

Not like here, where the world of the flesh pressed around him, everything too hot, too earthy, too real.

"Has it ever occurred to you," said Charles shortly, "that Miss Beckles's uncle might have spread those rumors to ward off the fortune hunters?"

Robert's hand went to the hilt of his sword. "Like me?"

"Or me," said Charles. "You aren't burdened by expensive obligations."

"No, I'm not, am I? I haven't anything."

Charles cursed himself for imprudence. "I misspoke." He cast about for something, anything else to say. "Did you know someone's been stealing at Peverills?"

"Would you like me to turn out my pockets?"

"I wasn't accusing you." Charles felt suddenly deeply weary. It was no use. There was nothing he could say that Robert wouldn't interpret to his discredit. "Fenty said he showed you the books."

"What does a Redleg know about the running of a great estate?"

"Enough to add a column of numbers and find it wanting," said Charles. "You know the estate better than anyone. Is there anyone who would steal from us?"

"You might ask if there's anyone who wouldn't," said Robert savagely. "Including that Redleg of yours."

"He's taken nothing we haven't given him," said Charles. He'd worked closely with Fenty these past few weeks. Every shilling the man earned went back to his family in St. Andrew. For himself, Fenty lived a Spartan existence, his entire being focused on his work. Charles had invited him to avail himself of the table at the great house, but Fenty seemed to prefer to dine on whatever came to hand, gnawing a crust as he continued at his labors. His one indulgence was candles, burning late through the night. "I would vouch for his honesty."

"What do you know of him? He could be robbing you blind if he's as clever with numbers as that."

"He could," Charles admitted. The best way to blunt rage wasn't to fight it but to let it wear itself out. "But I don't believe he has. Not yet, at any rate. I can account for every candle he's taken, all burnt in our service."

Robert took a turn around the veranda, his boots clicking on the boards. "All right. If you must know. It's Old Doll. And I told her she might."

"You told her she might?" Old Doll had been the housekeeper at Peverills for as long as Charles could remember, her various relations filling the house as seamstresses, housemaids, nursemaids, the very upper echelon of service. She had her pick of the family's castoffs; she dined well on the leavings from table. Of all people, she would, Charles have thought, have had the least need to steal. "I don't understand."

Robert slouched away. "It's not as if I gambled away the family silver. Who's to miss a bit of tea and candles?"

"Hundreds of pounds of tea and candles," said Charles slowly.

Fenty had painstakingly reconstructed years of jumbled accounts, revealing a steady drain on the household. Old Doll must have made a pretty penny reselling the family's goods in Bridgetown. With Robert's connivance.

"You mean dollars." Robert glowered at him. It was, apparently, yet another betrayal on Charles's part that after all his years in England he thought in pounds rather than dollars; both might be used on the island, but the planters preferred their dollars. "Don't look at me like that! It's not like I was pocketing the money. I did it for the family. I did it to spare Mama."

He looked so young, his brother. So young and defiant and scared. In the place of the man in his militia uniform, Charles could see a little boy, still in skirts, holding a broken wooden soldier half behind his back.

Od's blood, but he wasn't prepared for this. Not any of it. Charles rubbed his aching temples with two fingers. "What did you do, Robin? If Doll has something over you . . ."

"Me?" Robert choked on a wild laugh, and Charles realized his brother was more than a little drunk. "That's rich. Not me. Father. Our sainted father. God rest his soul. Do you remember Nan? Doll's daughter Nan?"

"Nan? Of course." Doll's youngest daughter had been their nursemaid. Charles still remembered bringing her posies of wilted flowers; the wrench of being moved from the nursery to the schoolroom. She had, he knew, been made their mother's maid, her closest servant and confidante. "What has she to do with anything?"

"Father was tupping her." Robert glared at him, daring him to deny it. "We have—had—an arrangement, Doll and I. I turn a blind eye and she wouldn't shout the truth to the world. It seemed fair enough."

"No," Charles said. That was all. "No."

"What do you know? You weren't here." Robert's rage and frustration poured out like acid. "Mama was sick in bed and Father was rutting with her maid. I saw them. I saw them holding hands, making eyes at each other. . . ."

"Robin. *Robin*. I don't know what you saw, but it can't have been what you think. Father wouldn't." Not with their mother's own maid. Not at all. "He wouldn't do that to Mother, much less take advantage of a woman in his power. You know Father's views. . . ."

"Oh yes, fine words on a piece of paper!"

"What did Doll tell you?" He couldn't, he supposed, be surprised that Doll might take the chance to feather her own nest. With their mother so ill, a change of regime was sure to come sooner or later. And Robert, eager to protect their mother's feelings—he would have been an easy mark.

"You don't get it, do you?" Robert's hands clenched in fists at his sides. "It wouldn't have been so bad if he'd been an honest bastard. But Mama—it would have killed her if she'd known. I had to do what I could. I had to."

"Robert, I'm sure you thought you acted for the best. But whatever it was Doll told you—"

"He installed her in a house in Bridgetown. Nan. The minute Mama died." Robert shook off Charles's hand, catching at the veranda rail to steady himself. "They've a bastard there. A girl."

"I—" Charles's tongue tangled in his lips. "We have a sister?"

"No. Father has a by-blow. It's common enough. Why d'you think Father freed Nan and her child before Mother was cold in her grave? The brat was his. The fee damn near beggared us."

Charles felt on firmer ground. "He freed Nan and her child because he promised Mother he would. For her good service." The manumission fee had been steep, but it had been the right thing to do, a first step in the project of freeing all their people.

"Is that what he told you?" Robert gave a shout of laughter. "Trust Father to turn vice to virtue. He could roll in a pigsty and come out smelling of roses. At least in his own account."

"Robert." Charles's heart ached for his brother, left alone, coping with an ailing mother, a preoccupied father—oh yes, Charles had admired and loved their father, but Father was always busy, always away, wrapped up in his societies for improvement of this and that, his correspondence, his charities—left to stew in his own fears and suspicions. "I don't care about the tea and candles. It's past time Doll retired. We'll give her a nice little house of her own and forget about all of this. I'll tell Fenty it was all a misunderstanding."

"You don't believe me."

"I believe you believe it," said Charles tactfully. And little wonder. If the colonel was any example of what went on, it wasn't surprising that Robert should leap to the worst sort of conclusions. Perhaps he would benefit from some time away, some time in England. "I believe you meant it for the best. I'm sorry, Robert. I'm sorry I wasn't there. I'm sorry you were left to care for Mother alone."

"*Christ.*" Robert slammed a palm against the rail. "Do you really think I'm that green? I'll give you their direction. Take one look at the brat and then tell me who was mistaken."

"All right," said Charles. In the ballroom, people were beginning to turn and stare. He put a hand on his brother's shoulder, steering him back toward the ballroom. "Shall we have some lemonade?"

"I'm not foxed."

"Of course you're not," said Charles. Robert's cheeks were flushed and his eyes glassy. "But it is very warm."

Robert shook out from under his arm.

"Only for those unaccustomed to the heat. You'll see, Charles. Go to Bridgetown and bloody well see for yourself."

Chapter Seven

Christ Church, Barbados
February 1854

EMILY HAD NEVER seen a room quite so large as the front room at Beckles.

It stretched the length of the house in either direction, furniture perched at intervals along the walls, enough to stock a shop, and still the room seemed half-empty. A broad arch opened onto a second great room, this one fitted with a large mahogany table. Servants bustled about, laying out porcelain and silver. The spare elegance made her grandfather's drawing room seem stuffy and overwrought.

Emily wasn't used to feeling small, but she felt small, small and distinctly shabby, here in the center of this vast, elegant room.

"Goodness," she said. "Have you considered letting it out for assemblies?"

Mr. Davenant handed his hat and gloves to a waiting servant. "You're being kind. Beckles is modest compared to Peverills."

"As it was, you mean." The only household of which she'd had the managing had consisted of one cook/housekeeper and one scullery maid. Emily was accustomed to rolling up her sleeves and polishing whatever might need polish. At that, it might be for the best that Peverills was no longer standing; Emily would have been lost in it.

How many servants did it take to keep a house of this size running? Emily had already counted a dozen, at least.

"We make do," said Mr. Davenant. "Beckles isn't what it once was, or so my grandmother tells me. But we muddle along."

They muddled very nicely. There wasn't a speck of dust on the French porcelain arranged on top of the mahogany wainscoting or on the ornate gilded frames of the portraits that hung on either side of the arch.

"Is this your father?" Emily asked, indicating a man with fair hair who posed before an idealized landscape of cane fields, his arm resting on an improbably placed pillar.

Mr. Davenant joined Emily before the portrait. "My grandfather. I'm told I'm very like him."

"Are you?" Emily looked doubtfully at the picture.

The portrait failed utterly to capture anything of the subject beyond the fact that his hair was fair. Even that was debatable, given the muddy quality of the paint. He might have been in a uniform or a richly hued coat; his stock was a pale blur at his throat. Fields rolled up and down behind him, culminating in a house drawn alarmingly out of perspective. He had been painted with a horse standing behind him and a dog at his feet.

Mr. Davenant laughed. "It's a dreadful picture, isn't it?"

"The frame is very nice," said Emily. She peered at the gray-and-coral blur in the upper right corner. "Is that meant to be this house?"

Mr. Davenant hesitated for a moment. "No," he said. "It's your house."

"Peverills?" If one stood to one side and squinted, one could just make out the stylized outlines of the roof, so different from the long and low silhouette of the house in which they stood.

"It was painted before the fire, of course."

"The rising, you mean?" said Emily, remembering what Dr. Braithwaite had told her. The memory of her tactlessness made her squirm.

"Yes, that," said Mr. Davenant. "The portraits were a wedding gift from my grandmother to my grandfather. You'll see that she's standing in front of Beckles."

Emily obediently moved with him to the other side of the arch. The white of the house blended into the white gauze of the woman's Empire-waisted dress, making her look slightly hunchbacked. A woman stood behind her, her dark skin blending into the shadows, head lowered so that one couldn't quite see her face.

"Who is that with her?"

"Just a maid," said Mr. Davenant. "I'm not sure if she's a real person or just an idea the painter had, like the dog with my grandfather. My grandfather never kept dogs—not in the house—but the painter liked the idea of a dog."

Emily looked again at the woman in the background. For an imaginary person, she had a surprising amount of presence. Emily could feel the tension straight through the choppy paint, the sense of the woman watching and waiting. Waiting for what?

"My grandfather was a Peverill, you see." Mr. Davenant was still talking. He clasped his hands behind his back. "Well, really, he was a Davenant, but his mother had been a Peverill. When he married my grandmother . . . you might say there was a bit of Montague and Capulet in it. The properties had always marched side by side, but there was bad blood between the families dating back nearly to the very settling of the island."

"It sounds very romantic," said Laura, with genuine interest. The lemonade had done wonders for her. She had lost the sickly look and gained some color in her cheeks.

"It was," said Mr. Davenant gratefully. "The Peverills were Cavaliers; the Beckleses Roundheads. The Peverills supported the royal governor. The Beckleses championed Cromwell's man. There's a story that Sir Marmaduke Peverill personally trussed Praise God Beckles to prevent him sending word to Cromwell's fleet. Of course, the Beckleses were mad as fire and retaliated by lording it over the Peverills while Cromwell remained in power. And so it went."

"Until your grandparents?" Laura was clearly charmed by the story. "Did they meet much opposition?"

Mr. Davenant looked a bit sheepish. "By then the rivalry was more legend than fact. My grandmother's guardian made some objection, I gather, but it had to do more with finance than tradition."

"That's a pity," said Adam, who was roaming about the room with the air of a man who felt his time was being wasted. "I was hoping for a duel or an elopement at the least."

"There were those, or so I'm told, but in previous generations. There's a story—"

"Are you telling fairy stories, George?" A woman appeared at one of the arches, black taffeta rustling importantly as she stalked toward them. She was of medium height, a black lace cap on her gray-streaked brown hair. "Never mind my grandson. He spends too much time reading Sir Walter Scott and spinning pretty fancies for himself. Roundheads and Cavaliers, indeed!"

"But they were," protested Mr. Davenant, unoffended. "You told me so yourself."

"They were planters and Barbadians. All the rest is immaterial. We have a saying in these parts, 'Neither Carib nor Creole, but true Barbadian.' You, I take it, are not from these parts."

Mr. Davenant looked apologetically at his guests. "May I have the honor of making you known to my grandmother, Mrs. Davenant? Grandmama, may I present your new neighbor? Miss Dawson has recently come into possession of Peverills."

"Peverills?" Mrs. Davenant examined Emily with a concentrated interest reminiscent of Little Red Riding Hood and the wolf. "Welcome, indeed, then. Peverills has stood empty for so long, we had begun to despair of it."

"It seems my grandfather bought it some time ago." Some further explanation seemed to be required, so Emily added, "He came to England as a young man, but he always accounted himself a true Barbadian."

"He was well-respected in Bristol," Adam countered. He had never been comfortable with their West Indian origins, had winced away from their grandfather's stories, making himself as English as English could be. "He might have been an alderman if he had wanted to be."

Mrs. Davenant looked distinctly unimpressed. To Emily, she said, "And who might your grandfather be?"

"His name was Jonathan Fenty." Was. That *was* felt like a knife in her chest. She didn't quite believe it yet, that he was gone. "He left the island some years ago. I don't imagine—"

"Jonathan Fenty." Mrs. Davenant's face looked like a mask, frozen into place. She lifted a lace-edged handkerchief, coughing delicately into it. "I knew him. Not to speak to, of course. He was bookkeeper at Peverills. And a Redleg."

"A Redleg?" Laura looked inquisitively at Mr. Davenant.

Mr. Davenant's color rose. "It's a term for—for people who live in the area we call Scotland. They're mostly of Scots and Irish origin. When they worked in the field, their, er, extremities would burn in the sun. Hence the term."

"Dirt poor, the lot of them," Mrs. Davenant said, so viciously that Emily half expected to see welts rise on her skin from the venom. "I don't expect your grandfather ever spoke to you about where he came from."

"My grandfather," said Emily, "never made any pretense about his origins. He was proud to be a self-made man."

"I understood he married a wealthy widow."

"And made her wealthier by far." Emily didn't know what her grandfather had done to make Mrs. Davenant hate him so, but she refused to be intimidated. "My grandmother's inheritance was modest compared to what my grandfather achieved."

Not that her grandmother had ever gloried in wealth. She had been raised a Methodist, and, although she had come to the Church of England with her first marriage, the principles had remained. It had made Emily's grandmother an admirable, if not always a comfortable, figure.

But they had been well-suited, her grandparents. Emily remembered her grandfather's boyish glee at his wealth, and the way her
grandmother humored him—and continued to oversee the mending.
For that, her grandfather had been equally parsimonious about small
things. It was only in the large things that he tended to display, buying
jewels her grandmother would never wear and waistcoats so heavily
embroidered with gold and silver that they could light the way for passing ships.

Mrs. Davenant examined Emily so intently that Emily's nose began
to itch. "You loved him."

"He was my grandfather." Her grandfather and the one person she
could trust, always, to put her interests first. Emily swallowed hard
against a sudden rush of grief. "I would trade my inheritance in a moment to have him here with us again."

"Now here's a pattern of filial devotion for you." Mrs. Davenant
turned away with a rustle of starched linen and horsehair. Emily could
almost hear everyone begin to breathe again. "Not everyone feels quite
so warmly about their grandparents, eh, George?"

Mr. Davenant wrinkled his nose. "Grandmama . . ."

"Don't write me any poems." Mrs. Davenant stalked over to Adam,
peering at him through the lenses of her lorgnette. "I don't need to ask
whether you're a Fenty. You have the look of your grandfather."

"Sunburnt and penniless?" Adam tried to make a joke of it, but it
fell flat. "I can only endeavor to follow my grandfather's example in the
leadership of Fenty and Company."

"Fenty and Company." Mrs. Davenant rolled the words on her
tongue as though tasting something unpleasant. "How times have
changed. And is Peverills now the property of Fenty and Company?"

"No," said Emily. She felt as though a game were being played to
rules she didn't understand, with her family the butt of it. "Peverills is
mine and mine alone."

To her surprise, Mrs. Davenant lowered her lorgnette. "Hold to
that, Miss . . ."

"Dawson," supplied Mr. Davenant.

"Miss Dawson. There will be many who will try to tell you otherwise." Without waiting for an answer, she turned on her heel and stalked toward the dining room. "I imagine you expect to be fed?"

Laura looked imploringly at Mr. Davenant. "We don't wish to be any bother. . . ."

"It's no bother at all," said Mr. Davenant gallantly.

"George! You take in Miss Dawson. Mr. Fenty"— Mrs. Davenant eyed Adam with distaste—"your arm, if you please."

Mr. Davenant bowed to Emily. "If you would do me the honor?"

Emily began to think that Dr. Braithwaite had made the right choice in leaving; she would have been glad to decline. But they had no way back to Bridgetown but Mrs. Davenant's carriage, so she took his arm and said, "Thank you. We didn't mean to put you out."

"You haven't," said Mrs. Davenant, going unerringly to the head of the table. "The table is uneven. We're short a man."

They would have had an even number had Dr. Braithwaite stayed.

Mr. Davenant held out Emily's chair for her, a tall affair with spindly finials and a back made of cane. She sat gingerly, glancing around the table, uncomfortably aware of the contrast between those seated at the mahogany board and the servants positioned around the table.

Would Dr. Braithwaite have been invited to sit at this table, to share this board? Or would he have been snubbed, turned away?

"Pepper pot, Miss Dawson?" A footman was holding a tureen extended in front of her, a savory blend of meat and some sort of vegetable.

"Oh yes, please. Thank you," said Emily to the footman, who continued to look straight ahead. Of course he did. Aunt Millicent would never have countenanced any of her servants speaking to the guests. Emily ducked her head to her plate. "What is pepper pot?"

"I suppose you might call it . . . a stew? Do try some, Mr. Fenty," urged Mrs. Davenant. "It is one of our local delicacies."

"Delicious," gasped Adam as tears formed in the corners of his eyes.

"You might want to try it with bread," murmured Mr. Davenant to Emily, who nodded her thanks and took a large piece to sop the sauce. Laura, Emily noticed, had gingerly taken a bite.

"If you come again," Mrs. Davenant was saying to Adam, "we'll give you calipash and calipee."

"Turtle," explained Mr. Davenant, leaning sideways to Emily. "Well . . . part of the turtle. The squishy bit beneath the shell."

"Thank you, George," said Mrs. Davenant. "Did your grandfather explain nothing to you, Miss Dawson?"

Not about turtles, certainly. "We never had pepper pot. Or— calliope?" She looked inquisitively at Mr. Davenant.

"Calipash," he provided for her.

"And what did he tell you of Peverills?" Mrs. Davenant was looking at her with that disconcerting directness.

"Nothing at all." Emily surreptitiously gulped down half her glass of lemonade, trying not to pant too obviously. She would have suspected that the pepper pot had been served by way of trial by fire but for the fact that both Mr. and Mrs. Davenant were eating the dish with obvious relish.

"Did he tell you that Peverills belonged to the Davenants?" persisted Mrs. Davenant.

"Until we lost it," put in Mr. Davenant.

"You make it sound as though we misplaced it," retorted Mrs. Davenant. "It was mismanagement, pure and simple. The estate was run into the ground. The Davenants were decorative, I'll give them that, but they didn't have the slightest idea how to operate a plantation."

Mr. Davenant helped himself to more pepper pot from the dish held by a silent servant. "What about Grandfather?"

"What makes you think he was any better? He tried, I'll give him that. The damage had already been done. He meant well," she said grudgingly. To her grandson, she added, "You'll do better. I've had the training of you."

"With rigor," said Mr. Davenant.

Emily drained her lemonade and set her fork aside. "Might I trouble you for some of that training? I would be grateful for any advice."

Adam gave a little cough. "You don't want to bother Mrs. Davenant with all that. I'm sure her agent . . ."

Mrs. Davenant fixed him with a basilisk stare. "I am my own agent. Agent and estate manager and court of last resort. I gave up on hiring help. They were sots, most of them, more interested in the bottle than their work. Of course, there's George," she said, dismissing her grandson with a wave of a heavily incised silver fork. "But he's much to learn yet. You want to know anything about sugar, you ask me."

"I want to know everything about sugar," said Emily frankly. "I know about the use of it, but nothing about its cultivation."

"You'll have to if you want to keep Peverills," said Mrs. Davenant.

"You can't possibly—" Adam began, but Mrs. Davenant went on as though he hadn't spoken.

"You could hire someone to manage it for you, of course, but there's no guarantee he won't rob you blind. In fact, it's quite likely anyone you hire would. They'll have your measure in a minute: a woman. English. Absentee."

"And utterly ignorant," added Emily.

"Exactly," said Mrs. Davenant approvingly. "You might as well sign the estate over now."

"And," said Emily, "I imagine it would cost money to hire an agent—a good one. And I haven't any at present. Money, that is."

Adam winced. "Surely this isn't a proper subject for—"

"Land poor, are you?" Mrs. Davenant leaned both elbows on the table, her diamond earrings glittering in the light. "That's nothing of which to be ashamed—although I find it strange in Jonathan Fenty's granddaughter. I heard your grandfather was a warm man."

"My grandfather knew I could be trusted to make my own way."

Mrs. Davenant snorted. "I'd hardly call inheriting Peverills making your own way. You're an heiress, girl, whether you like it or not."

"The house . . ." put in Adam.

"Eh." Mrs. Davenant waved that aside. "A house is a house is a house. The land is rich, always has been. Those Peverills knew what they were doing when they staked their claim to those acres. It won't take much to put it right again. But it will take money. Money for equipment, money for hands. You haven't any jewels to sell, have you?"

Emily touched the plain oval locket at her throat, the other half of her legacy from her grandfather, worth less in coin but twice as valuable. "I could borrow the money, couldn't I? With the plantation as security."

"You could," said Mrs. Davenant. "If you want to lose it. You can't trust those moneylenders. Leeches, all of them. They'll suck the life out of you and then take your land once you've been bled dry. I've seen it happen before. I have a better suggestion for you. Sell me the southeast parcel. Use the money from that to cultivate the rest."

"Or you could just sell the whole thing," offered Adam, "and come back to Bristol."

To sit in Aunt Millicent's parlor and wind wool? Emily couldn't think of anything she would like less. To Mrs. Davenant, she said, carefully, "I wouldn't want to alienate any of the land until I had a better sense of the workings of the whole."

"Right now, the whole is rotting," said Mrs. Davenant. "And will continue to do so unless you expend some considerable funds. Would you consider leasing the parcel?"

"I would have to consult my agent in Bridgetown." That is, if she had an agent in Bridgetown. Mr. Turner, she knew, had served as her grandfather's agent in any matter of things, but that arrangement wouldn't necessarily extend to her. It would, however, give her an excuse to return to the Turner household. She wondered if Dr. Braithwaite would be in residence.

"Agents." Mrs. Davenant dismissed the breed with a tilt of her glass. She was drinking claret, not lemonade, although Emily noticed she only sipped sparingly. "In my day, such matters were dealt with between gentlemen."

"As we are?" said Emily, rather liking the notion. "There's just one problem. I don't know enough to even begin to discuss terms."

"Ah, well. It was worth an attempt," said Mrs. Davenant, unabashed. She raised her glass to Emily. "That's the first challenge. Admitting what you don't know. You would be surprised at how few can manage it." She looked pointedly at her grandson, who pulled a face in response.

Emily did her best to swallow her smile. "I am very sensible of my ignorance. But I'm a quick study."

"Speak to your agent. I'm sure we can come to an arrangement." Mrs. Davenant stood, abruptly signaling the end of the meal. "George, why don't you show Mr. and Mrs. Fenty our garden. There are views clear to the ocean if you stand in the right spot. Miss Dawson, you'll come with me."

Adam looked over his shoulder in surprise as his chair was magically pulled back for him. Saving face, he said importantly, "We do have an evening engagement in Bridgetown. At the governor's house."

"Those are always a sad crush. That Colebrooke sends a card to every stray who wanders off the wharves." Having rendered Adam speechless, Mrs. Davenant added magnanimously, "Don't worry. I'll get her back to you in plenty of time. Go along now."

"The gardens are lovely," said Mr. Davenant. Emily began to understand why he so frequently sounded as though he were apologizing. He was in the habit of it. Taking charge of Laura and Adam, he led them through yet another arch in the middle of the far wall. "Do you sketch, Mrs. Fenty?"

Mrs. Davenant took Emily by the arm, marching her in the other direction, back through the great room. "You have to be direct with men. They have no truck with subtleties. You don't favor your grandfather."

Emily was beginning to get used to her abrupt changes of topic. "I look very like my father."

Mrs. Davenant eyed her sideways, taking the measure of her features, the soft, mid-brown hair, the hazel eyes that were more brown than green. "Is he also from Barbados?"

"Yorkshire." It was strange how exotic it sounded here, in this large, light-filled room. The moors and mists of her father's childhood home might have been something out of a novel by Currer Bell. "But my father has served for some years as the minister of a parish in Bristol."

A very poor parish in Bristol. That had been by choice, not chance. Her father's convictions would suffer nothing more. Had not the Lord himself gone among the poor? Although sometimes Emily suspected it was less a matter of conviction and more that her father simply didn't notice such things. He would eat mutton as happily as beef.

Her grandfather had raged at his daughter throwing herself away on a penniless clergyman, a clergyman, no less, with no ambition for the higher orders, content to serve in the poorest section of the city. But her mother had never wavered. It was a story Emily had loved to hear as a child, how her mother had held fast in the face of all opposition.

"And what does the Reverend Mr. Dawson think of his daughter gadding halfway across the world?"

"He gave me his blessing." Never mind that her father's blessings were extended easily and broadly. And that he had, now, other interests. No, she wouldn't think about that. Not now. Not here. "He raised me to know my own mind."

Mrs. Davenant emitted a distinctly unladylike snort. "No one really expects a woman to know her own mind. You'll find that out soon enough if you try to take Peverills in hand. Every man jack of them in Bridgetown will pat you on the head and try to make your decisions for you."

They had stopped at the end of the great room, where a rectangular opening led into a small room containing several beautifully made bookshelves and a tall and narrow desk bristling with pigeonholes.

Emily looked at Mrs. Davenant, imposing and imperious in black taffeta. It was impossible to imagine her being patted on the head, at least not if the offending party wanted to keep his hand. "But you managed it."

"I married." Something about the way she said it forbade further comment. "What are you doing standing there? Come into my office. Oh yes, this is my office. I send George out to supervise the day-to-day running of the thing, but all the paperwork comes back to me."

Not just the paperwork. There was, Emily saw, a door that led to the veranda, a private entrance. And, next to it, a spyglass on a brass stand.

"It's good for him to ride the length of the land," Mrs. Davenant was saying. "I know every inch of my land; I know it in my bones. Do you ride, Miss Dawson?"

"Only shank's mare," said Emily.

Mrs. Davenant was not amused. "What, do you expect to be carried about on a palanquin?" she demanded, rooting about in a cabinet filled with leather-bound books. "If you don't ride, you'll have to learn. George can be of assistance in that, at least. He may have his head in the clouds, but he has an excellent seat."

Emily wasn't entirely sure she liked the way Mrs. Davenant was taking charge of her future. "I'm sure he has."

"You're too old to learn to ride well, but you can hack, at least." Mrs. Davenant thumped a book down on the desk, letting it fall open. "Ah, here we are. I thought you might like to see these."

Increase of horses, 1813. January 5. On the plantation: Charity, a bay; Hope, a chestnut.

Decrease of horses, 1813. June 3. Honor, a gray, sold.

The paper was yellowed, the ink faded, but the writing gave Emily a prickly feeling, like the faint sound of a familiar voice in a distant room. She had to stop from turning her head to see if her grandfather was there, behind her, standing by her shoulder to examine his work.

"This is my grandfather's hand."

"He kept the accounts for Peverills." Mrs. Davenant closed the book before Emily could take more than a quick glance at the neat columns of figures. "The world has changed considerably since Peverills was last a working concern, but this should give you some notion of the requirements of a plantation of this size."

The current accounts for Beckles might be of somewhat more use, Emily suspected, but she doubted that Mrs. Davenant would allow her to thumb through those.

And this had been her grandfather's. His life, his work. All those years of which he never spoke.

Emily touched the faded paper cover of the ledger. "Might I borrow this?"

Mrs. Davenant scooped it up again. "You may peruse it at your leisure—here at Beckles. You'll stay here," she said, as though it were already decided. "Your cousins too, if you wish."

"But—" A few hours ago, she hadn't known the Davenants existed; now she was being invited to join their household. Had she imagined the hostility when Mrs. Davenant had heard her grandfather's name? Or was that just her way? Either way, Emily wasn't sure she wanted to subject herself to Mrs. Davenant's rule. "We have obligations in Bridgetown."

"A nasty, festering place. No, you'll do better here." Mrs. Davenant raised her lorgnette, examining Emily as though she were a set of accounts that didn't quite add up. "We have, I think, a great deal to learn from one another. . . ."

Chapter Eight

Bridgetown, Barbados
April 1812

"GET YOUR CORN here! Corn!"

"Eggs! Fresh eggs!"

A chicken pecked at Charles's boot. "Pardon me," he said, and realized he was apologizing to poultry.

Broad Street was thronged with hawkers crying their wares. Charles had already refused guava, pickles, and aguacate pears, rum from a dipper, and lengths of fine lawn.

Charles's cravat clung limply to his neck. The jacket and waistcoat that had been quite comfortable in London were roasting him in his own sweat. He threaded his way through, past carts and donkeys, storefronts spilling out wares from foreign shores, wondering what on earth he was doing here and whether it might be wiser to turn back. But he had come this far. He had met with the plantation attorney that morning, and then, instead of sensibly returning to the horse he had stabled at an inn not far from St. Michael's, he had turned in the other direction entirely, down Broad Street toward the house where Robert claimed their father's mistress lived.

If his father had had a mistress. If there were such a house. Or even such a street.

They had never visited Bridgetown when he was a boy. Charles's tutors had lived at Peverills; his mother had shopped for ribbons in Oistins. Bridgetown was unfamiliar territory, merely a place to embark and disembark, a carriage ride through busy streets. The idea that their father might have a house here, another family here . . . It beggared belief.

His father had made periodic visits to Bridgetown, it was true. He had come to town to consult with the estate attorney, to meet with sugar factors, for meetings of the Barbados Society for the Encouragement of Arts, Manufactures, and Commerce, of which his father had been an enthusiastic and vocal member.

But he had never been gone long. Only a night here and a night there.

But that was before. Before Charles's mother had fallen ill, back when his parents still walked together in the garden of an afternoon, when his mother played the harp in the evenings and his father swore no angel could ever make a song so sweet. Nan had been there too, coming to collect Charles and Robert and shoo them back upstairs to the nursery, to scrub their faces and sing them songs.

They were all, Charles realized, frozen in his memory as they had been nearly two decades ago, before he had been sent away to school and never came home. Had his father not died, he would be in England still. There had always been an excuse to stay away. His father certainly hadn't chivvied him to come home; his mother's health had worsened so gradually, her illness had worn on so long, that there had never seemed any urgency. Or so his father said. Charles had assumed his father had acted selflessly, wanting to spare Charles, his time in England given as a gift.

But now he wondered.

A fool's errand, Charles told himself. That was what it was. Robert was getting his own back in the only way he knew how, taking his revenge on their father, for overlooking him, and on Charles, for having the gall to be born first.

The house to which Robert had sent him was past the customs

house, past the milk market, down Church Street and to the left. Like its neighbors, it was two stories high and built of brick. A gallery, painted green, jutted out from the second story, casting the door into shadow. The street drowsed in the midday heat, shutters closed. The thrum of Broad Street faded away. Behind doors and shutters, Charles could hear the muted sounds of voices calling, pots clattering, a pianoforte being played haltingly.

Charles should have liked to peer in a window, but the shutters blocked his view as surely as they did the sun.

Feeling like an idiot, he lowered the knocker.

The woman who opened the door stared at him as though she'd seen a ghost. "Master Charles?"

"Nan." Her hair was tied up in a kerchief, patterned in red and pink stripes. Her face was older, lines around the eyes and corners of her lips that hadn't been there in those long-gone days. It was strange, so very strange, to look down at her when once he had looked up. "My brother gave me your direction."

Nan stepped back, making a jerky gesture. "Would you like . . . Might I offer you a dish of tea?"

The hall behind her was modest but well-appointed. A pier glass reflected Charles's own strained face. And beneath it, a clock he recognized. It was of no great value. His mother had never cared for it. It was brass, and plain, but his father had had it with him on the ship from England and had prized it, as a relic of his wanderings.

Stealing, Fenty said.

Mistress, Robert claimed.

There were perfectly reasonable explanations. A gift, for long service. Something serviceable rather than valuable. "There's no need. I merely came to see that you were provided for."

Nan looked as though she were about to put a hand on his arm and then thought better of it, letting her hand fall to her side. "That's very kind of you, Master Charles. You always were kind. Even as a child."

The music had stopped. The ticking of the clock seemed very loud between them. Charles could hear it marking out the seconds in time with his heartbeats in the drowsy heat of the day. This was the woman who had soothed his childish nightmares and bound his scrapes; he had loved her second to his mother, and sometimes not even second.

But she wasn't that girl anymore. This woman was a matron, a prosperous matron, in striped muslin and a lace-edged fichu, and he was a man grown, not a little boy with a wilted bouquet in his hands.

"Well, then." There were so many questions he could ask, but he found, now that he was here, he wasn't entirely certain he wanted to know the answers.

"Mama?" A girl ventured into the hall, dressed in a white muslin frock tied with a blue sash.

"Is this your daughter?"

Nan hesitated slightly before answering. "Yes, Master Charles. Harriet, make your curtsy to Master Charles."

The girl obliged, looking curiously at him as she rose. Her dark hair had been plaited on either side of her face, tied top and bottom with bows that brought out the blue of her eyes. His eyes. His father's eyes.

It wasn't just the eyes. It was in the shape of her chin, the tilt of her head.

"How old is she?" Charles felt as though his tongue were glued to the top of his mouth.

Nan paused for a moment, then said carefully, "Just turned six."

Six. Six? His mother had predeceased his father by only four years. Yes, she had been sick for a time before that, a long time. But even so. There had been vows pledged, vows his father had claimed to hold sacred.

"Six and two months," said Harriet and, at a look from her mother, dropped another curtsy. "If you please, sir."

If oo plise.

Charles mustered a sickly smile. "Six! You are a great girl, aren't you?"

Gret gel. He was morbidly aware of the shape of his own vowels, so similar to hers, the linguistic quirk that gave them away. Not in all words, but some. His father's gift to them both.

Charles had no doubt that had she need to make reference to the color of his hair, it would be *yaller*, and the circle on her wrist a *goold brasslet*. His father, in all his years on the island, had never acquired the local accent. It was his mother who spoke with the lilt of the island; his father had retained the Whig drawl of his London years. And had, it seemed, imparted it to his children. To all his children.

If this was all his children.

The possibility hit Charles like a blow. If there was one, might there be others? Others scattered in little brick houses about Bridgetown? Working in his own fields? An infinity of betrayals made flesh, all speaking with the exaggerated accent popularized by a duchess an ocean away thirty years or more before.

How had they kept the truth from his mother? What stories had they told? It would have been easy enough, with his mother confined to her bed. The child could be explained as a result of a liaison with the old bookkeeper, with a neighboring overseer, a passing guest. Infants didn't look much like anyone in particular, not yet. "Master Charles? Are you certain you wouldn't like a dish of tea? Or a posset? You're looking peaky." Nan put a hand to his elbow, looking at him with such concern that for a moment Charles was six again and had tripped on the garden path.

"No," Charles said, stepping back so abruptly he nearly lost his footing. "I—I have an engagement. I mustn't stop."

"The master—he would have been proud to see you take his place. Whenever you sent a letter, he would keep it by him and read it again and again. He would read them aloud to me. . . ." Nan trailed off at the look on his face. Backing away, she put an arm protectively around her daughter. "It was kind of you to visit, Master Charles."

"Not at all. You were always good to me when I was a boy."

Had they been together even then? Nan couldn't have been more than sixteen at the time, his father thirty or more. No. He couldn't believe it. But then, he hadn't believed the rest of it either, and here the truth was in front of him, in blue bows and white muslin.

"I am glad to see you so well. And you," he said to the girl, and fled.

He could hear the girl's voice, raised in a question, and Nan shushing her, chivvying her back toward the pianoforte, as the door shut behind him.

His sister. He had a sister.

No, Robert had said. Our father has a by-blow.

Some men had untold numbers of half brothers and sisters, working their fields, pouring their drink, emptying their chamber pots. Charles thought of Mary Anne Beckles's maid, standing on the balcony holding her mistress's wrap, her cousin, her owner.

But not at Peverills. Not his father. He had decried the practice, had written about it, lectured about it.

Words, words, words, and no truth to them, all those letters, all those fine, fine letters.

How naive his father must have thought him when he wrote back! All grand ideals and philosophical abstracts. And all the while . . . The thought that he had shared Charles's letters, Charles's private letters, with his mistress made Charles so angry that the world around him seemed to blur and fade. He had stripped his soul naked in those letters.

When had it started? Was it after their mother had grown ill, when she had begun to take to her bed for long stretches in the morning, and then the afternoon, and then not leave her bed at all? His father's letters had been punctuated with his mother's movements, or lack thereof. A good day, when she had moved from bed to chaise longue. A bad day, when she could only lie against her pillows, with Robert to read to her.

And while Robert read . . .

Had he forced her? Had she seduced him? Each image was more monstrous than the last. Monstrous and impossible.

"You looking for a place to stay?" A woman in a low-cut dress positioned herself in front of him, leaning forward to make clear that she wore no fichu to veil her charms. "There's rooms at Nancy Clarke's."

A boy hurried over, elbowing the woman out of the way. "You'll find better at Betsy Austin's. Three dollars a night!"

Where in the deuce was he? Looking up, Charles saw a row of substantial houses. On a veranda, a pretty woman in a muslin gown and silk kerchief laughed with a soldier, toying with his tassels. From one of the windows, a woman waved to Charles.

Charles ducked, feeling his already flushed cheeks color.

"I'm not stopping. Forgive me." Charles veered around and away, picking an alley at random, hoping it would lead him back to Broad Street.

He found himself in the middle of a great market, ringed by stalls selling fruits and vegetables, flies buzzing over pools of blood beside the butcher's stall, women with baskets wrangling with vendors.

A constable wrestled a man into the stocks, to the great delight of the crowd, while hard by Charles's side a fight had broken out, with cries of false weight and other accusations lost in the general fray.

Charles dodged out of the way. He was, he realized, well and truly lost. He had no idea how he'd come from Nan's house to here, or even how long he might have been walking. He weaved through the crowd, feeling absurdly out of place, aware of the conversations stopping as he walked by, the suspicious looks, the people who ducked out of the way.

He thought he might know where he was. Robert had spoken of the market where slaves went to sell their masters' goods, blend into the crowd, and never return—or went to sell items filched from a master's house or garden. Did they think him a slave catcher? Charles felt decidedly conspicuous in his top boots and high-crowned hat. He tried to ask directions but couldn't seem to catch anyone's eye.

Until he saw the familiar line of a back at a jeweler's stall.

"Jenny? It is Jenny, isn't it?"

For a moment, Charles thought he had been mistaken, that it was someone else entirely. He had only ever seen Miss Beckles's maid dressed in a lawn apron and a white cap, while this woman wore a muslin dress, her hair tied up in a kerchief like half the other women at the market.

But then she turned, and it was unmistakably she. The kerchief seemed strange on her, like a costume. Charles thought vaguely that they were both in a play for which no one had bothered to teach them the lines.

"I've a commission for my mistress," she said quickly. She fumbled beneath her fichu, bringing out a folded piece of paper. "I have a pass."

"Of course you do. I never meant to imply otherwise." Charles tried to smile, but his lips didn't seem to want to work properly. "I—I seem to have lost my way."

Miss Beckles's maid looked at him with concern. "You've been too much in the sun."

"No. I . . . I've had a shock, that's all. My father— My father has a daughter. In Bridgetown." Black spots buzzed in front of his eyes, like flies. "My sister. I have a sister."

Miss Beckles's maid caught his arm, steadying him.

"You need something to drink." She smelled of flowers and linen left to dry in the sun. "Can you wait here?"

There was a murmur of voices, haggling, the clink of coins, the splash of a dipper. Charles's mouth felt fuzzy.

Jenny pressed a cup into his hand. "Drink this."

He did. The ginger beer burned its way down his throat, making him cough and gasp, but whether it was the shock of it or the liquid, Charles felt considerably better for it. He took another sip, more slowly, letting the ginger tingle on his tongue.

Charles looked down at Miss Beckles's maid. "Thank you. You must think me the rawest foreigner."

She looked away, giving him a good view of the lines of her profile, like a carving on a cameo. "You shouldn't stay outside when you aren't used to the sun."

Robert had said much the same thing, only he had been talking about other matters. "Was I so naive? My father always said we owed a sacred duty to the souls in our care, that only a beast would—"

He was raving as though he truly were sun mad. And maybe he

was mad, pouring all this out to a stranger, a slave. But to whom else could he speak? Robert? Miss Beckles? Jonathan Fenty? His world had shrunk, all his friends gone, an ocean away.

Charles slugged back the last of the ginger beer, fighting for normalcy. "Could you show me the way to St. Michael's?"

The last thing Jenny wanted was to shepherd Mr. Davenant to St. Michael's.

"It's not far," she said, hoping he would take her meaning and excuse himself, leaving her to fade back into the market, just for a time, just for a bit more, unremarked and unremarkable.

It was so tempting to imagine she might drift into the crowd, drift and keep drifting until she was well away, with money in her hand, enough to buy her a new name, a new life.

She might set herself up as a seamstress or a milliner, away, far away from Beckles and all the misery in that cursed house. She could sew a fine seam, none better. Mary Anne would feel betrayed, she might even genuinely miss her—at least, for a time. But Mary Anne would survive. She could look out for herself. And if she couldn't—hadn't Jenny paid her debt? Weren't they long since quits?

It would never serve.

She knew that. She'd known that even before Mr. Davenant had called her name, bringing her back, painfully, to herself. Barbados was a small island. Her father would find her. Even if he didn't, Jenny knew what became of a woman alone, especially a woman of her complexion. She'd seen the houses on Canary Street, which catered to the sailors just in port, the soldiers in the garrison, the planters come to town. Mulatto girls, that was their specialty. They were supposed, her father claimed, to have licentiousness bred in their blood, mongrels, purpose-made for a man's pleasure, borne of sin for the furtherance of sin. The closer to white, the higher the price, rented out as a temporary wife or just for the night.

She wouldn't be whored out. Or worse, caught. There was a cage where they kept runaway slaves, not five minutes' walk down Broad

Street. The smells emanating from it were so dreadful that the merchants of Broad Street had complained. Apparently, the stench of rotting flesh was bad for business. Jenny's stomach clenched. No. Her best chance, slim as it was, was with her mistress.

If her father didn't have his way first.

Jenny found herself recalled to the present by Master Charles. "Is it very out of your way? I don't want to inconvenience you."

He had to know she had no choice in the matter. "It's no bother, Master Charles. It's just down Broad Street. You'll know where you are soon enough."

"Did you finish your business?"

"What? Yes. It was only a small errand." She could feel the coins tied in a handkerchief burning a hole in her bodice, more money than she had ever had in her possession before. "Are you feeling better, Master Charles?"

"Yes, thank you. You would think I would be used to the heat by now." They walked in silence for a time. They garnered the occasional knowing glance; it was a common enough sight, a man with his mistress. Master Charles didn't seem to notice. He didn't notice anything. They were just shy of the Cage when he burst out, "My father set them up in a house. Here in Bridgetown."

"Is it the cost?" If Mary Anne was correct, the Davenants were in dreadful debt, a step away from losing everything.

"The cost?" Master Charles blinked at her as though she were speaking a different language. "The moral cost, perhaps. My father broke his vows. He betrayed my mother, he betrayed his conscience. . . . What price can one put on that?"

His voice cracked as he said it. Jenny looked at him curiously, torn between pity and disbelief. "Is it so different in England, then? Are all men noble and all women pure and virtuous?"

"No. To be sure. But— My father was different. I believed he was different. When I saw that Father freed Nan, I was proud of him. Proud."

"He freed her?"

"And her child. Their child."

Jenny felt a stab of raw envy. To be that child. The girl who would never have to live on a cousin's mercy, a father's whim. "There's many as wouldn't do as much."

"But he shouldn't have debauched her in the first place! He always claimed— It's no matter now what he claimed, is it? It was all a lie."

Jenny could hear the moans from the Cage. She turned her face away, toward Mr. Davenant. "People have their reasons. You don't know what happened between them."

"My mother was sick for many years. But does that excuse him? Breaking his vows, taking advantage of a woman in his household. Unless . . . Unless he loved her. Nan. I don't know if that makes it better or worse."

"Does it make a difference?" Jenny couldn't see that it much mattered one way or the other; it was what it was. But her companion seemed to care deeply.

He looked at her with clouded blue eyes, and Jenny knew he wasn't really seeing her, or anything else for that matter, too lost in the turmoil of his own thoughts. "She was Mother's maid. Mother relied on her utterly. Trusted her."

"She might not have had much choice in it." A room with a bed in it, mosquito netting around the sides. The light of a single candle casting grotesque shadows along the walls. A hand at the small of her back, shoving her forward. "Unless you think she tempted him to it."

"No! I didn't mean . . . I don't know what I meant. I want each of them to be at fault so the other won't be. I want them both blameless."

There was something strangely endearing about his naivete. Endearing and exasperating. "You're not talking about people, Master Charles. You're talking about saints."

"But shouldn't we aspire to better?" The sun touched his face, lighting it like a beacon. "My father always said that the institution of slavery is a disease that sickens owner and owned alike—but so much worse for the owner, who has choice in the matter. To own another person corrupts one. I knew that. I know that." He gestured helplessly in the direction of the wharves. "I look at those ships in the harbor and all I want to do is board any one of them bound back to England."

Jenny looked at the masts in the distance, the ships bobbing at anchor in the bay. Just a launch out to the ship, then . . . the promise of a new life, in England, where they said the very air made men free. She could have wept for the thought of it. "Why don't you, then? There's no one to stop you."

He looked wistfully out to sea, then shook his head, shoving his hands into his pockets. "I wish I might. But there are people who rely on me. My bookkeeper—my brother would have him out on his ear in a moment. If I might fall, what of Robert? He has no interest in my father's plans. He thinks it's all nonsense, that it's our right . . ." He glanced down at her, as though remembering, belatedly, to whom he was speaking. "Well."

It didn't take much imagination to guess what he might have said.

"And what do you think?" Jenny asked, even though she knew she shouldn't, that it was folly to engage in conversation.

She was meant to be seen and not heard. No, not even seen. Invisible in the background.

But there was something very disarming about Mr. Davenant. Perhaps it was that he spoke to her as though she were anyone else, as though she were Mary Anne and free.

Mr. Davenant paced forward, his eyes on the ground, working out his thoughts as he went. "Just because my father failed doesn't mean he was wrong. He was—he had a quicksilver temperament. He was charming and clever and mercurial. What it needs is someone willing to labor over the details. I've looked at the accounts for his model farm, and I think I see where he went wrong. If one divided the sugar fields into sections and granted each family an acre in copyhold . . ."

It was, thought Jenny, like looking through a glass: he made no effort to hide any of his thoughts or feelings.

What would it be to be free to be so guileless? It was both attractive and alarming. The world was full of opportunists. One might as well dangle meat in front of dogs.

And yet . . . there was something about the way he spoke, the way he stood taller as he voiced his plans, his hands moving in illustration, that made her almost believe she could see what he saw, a world made new and good.

". . . freehold. Not right away, but by and by." He came to a stop in the shadow of the tower of St. Michael's, looking at her almost bashfully. "Thank you."

Something about the way he was looking at her, the warmth in his eyes, made her look away. "I told you it wasn't far."

"Not just for leading the way—although I owe you thanks for that as well. Thank you for letting me talk like that."

As if she'd had a choice. "I didn't do anything."

He didn't allow himself to be deterred. "You gave me my father back. The better part of him, in any event." She had thought he would leave it at that, but he paused, looking at her as though trying to make out a puzzle. "Colonel Lyons—he's your father, isn't he?"

Jenny felt the air go out of her chest, as though she'd been struck. "So some say."

Mr. Davenant looked at her very seriously. "How do you bear it?"

For a moment, she suspected him of mocking her. But there was no guile in his face. He meant it, she realized, and something twisted in her chest, something bittersweet and painful.

"You bear what you have to bear." He looked at her, as though expecting something more. Jenny's nails bit into her palms. "Your father did a good thing when he freed his daughter. When you think of him, think of that."

She thought he might say something more, but instead he held out an arm. It took her a moment to realize he meant her to take it. "May I offer you a ride back to Beckles? I have my chariot."

As if she were a lady. "It's not a long walk."

"The sun is hot and the road is rough."

It was tempting, so tempting. It was a weary walk back, three hours on foot. But what if her father saw them? What then? She might be able to convince him that she was working in his interest, but one could never be sure with her father.

Reluctantly, Jenny shook her head. "It wouldn't be seemly."

Mr. Davenant dropped his arm as though struck. "I hadn't thought. . . . I ought, oughtn't I?"

He smiled at her, and it was a smile of such self-deprecating humor that Jenny began to think the greatest danger might not be her father; it might be Mr. Davenant himself.

"Godspeed, sir," she said, and escaped while she could. He might seem kind, but he was still trouble. They were all trouble.

Best to remember that a serpent was still a serpent. No matter how it held its bite, bite it would, sooner or later.

CHAPTER NINE

Bridgetown, Barbados
March 1854

A SERPENT COILED around a staff on Dr. Braithwaite's cravat pin. It was, Emily knew, the symbol of the Greek god of healing, but it looked remarkably unfriendly.

So, for that matter, did the doctor.

"I do hope I'm not disturbing," said Emily brightly.

Coming to the hospital had seemed a good idea back at Miss Lee's hotel, with Adam off engaged in unspecified business activities and Laura resting. But the reaction of the nurses and the staff when she appeared attended by only one of the maids from the inn had made her realize that the Barbados General Hospital might not be the Bristol Royal Infirmary. Truth be told, even the Bristol Royal Infirmary wasn't the Bristol Royal Infirmary. Emily had been permitted on the wards only at specific times on specific days, and never ever during the admission of outpatients, an exercise that was viewed as unseemly for a young lady.

"Oh no," said Dr. Braithwaite. "I only have fifty patients to see to."

"Never mind that, Braithwaite," called out one of his colleagues, who had been observing with unconcealed amusement. "I'll see to your breakdowns for you. Ma'am," he said to Emily.

"Thank you," said Emily. "I was told your hospital was one of the sights of the town, but I hadn't expected it to be quite so grand."

A pillared portico led into the hospital, set into a building graced with Georgian symmetry, marred only by the additional wings splitting off from one side.

"It was once a gentleman's residence," said Dr. Braithwaite, leading her inside with the air of a man making the best of a bad job. "When it was purchased for a hospital, extra wings were built. It was easier, I am told, than building new. Just through here, mind your step. You might want this," he added, digging out a handkerchief soaked in scent as they passed from the main block into one of the wards.

"No, no. I'm quite all . . . right." Emily breathed in deeply through her mouth, concentrating on not gagging. "Is that . . . waste?"

"Of the human variety." He didn't look at her, but Emily suspected she was being tested all the same. "We employ an earth system, but there is too much liquid in the soil to eliminate the stench."

On her mettle, Emily took another deep breath and said cheerfully, "Is that all? It's nothing to the Frome on a summer's day. In the winter, the cold blunts the smell, but as soon as there's a thaw, it becomes nearly unbearable for those who aren't accustomed to it."

"I would think that those who could afford it would leave town."

"Oh, they do," said Emily. She well remembered the hustle and bustle as Aunt Millicent packed up her household, transferring children, linens, and servants to a hired house in the country. "Did you think I . . . ? Oh, I stayed in town. My father would never leave his flock. He's a minister. He has a calling. Our Lord served the poor and so does he. As do I—as *did* I. Although I'm much better with bodies than souls. I clean sores and deliver beef tea. All the practical bits."

"I see," said Dr. Braithwaite, looking rather bemused. "A calling, is it?"

"I like to be useful. I'm not sure there's anything the least bit holy about it. But I am rather inured to stench. See? It's hardly noticeable now. You can put your handkerchief away," she added kindly.

"Oh." He looked at it as though he had forgotten he was holding it. "If you're quite certain?"

"Perhaps that poor man might like it instead?" One of the other doctors was breathing deeply into his handkerchief, looking distinctly green.

"He's just come from Edinburgh," said Dr. Braithwaite, stuffing the handkerchief back in his pocket. "It takes a bit for the new arrivals to grow accustomed."

Emily nodded understandingly. "There was a missionary visited us once who came with my father on his pastoral calls. He fainted and had to be carried back to the rectory. He was terribly apologetic, poor man. If you put a drop of oil of peppermint under your nose, it works wonders," she said to the Scottish doctor.

"Miss Dawson is visiting the hospital," explained Dr. Braithwaite. And then, after a moment, "You aren't what I expected of Jonathan Fenty's granddaughter."

"My aunt Millicent feels much the same way," said Emily, then caught herself and shook her head. "I shouldn't be unkind about Aunt Millicent. She means well. I'm a great trial to her. My mother always believed that it was more important to do good works in the world than be a lady of quality."

Her throat stuck. Even now, after all these years, she could hear her mother's voice, with that peculiar husky quality so her own, saying, "Sensibility? I trust I am more sensible of the suffering of others than my own."

She and Aunt Millicent had cordially despised each other, although Emily had always rather suspected that each enjoyed their loathing.

"I see," said Dr. Braithwaite. "Was it your mother who started you nursing?"

"My mother? Oh no, she was too busy fighting for emancipation, always writing letters and holding meetings."

"The Bristol and Clifton Ladies' Anti-Slavery Society, I take it?" said Dr. Braithwaite, and the irony in his voice was unmistakable.

Emily felt her cheeks color. "One does what one can. Even if it's only in a small way. My mother's great friend Mrs. More always said, 'Activity may lead to evil, but inactivity cannot lead to good.' One *must* try."

Dr. Braithwaite was unimpressed. "They also serve who only write letters?"

"If enough letters are written, people take notice."

"Do they? Or is it merely that circumstances change? Sugar grows less profitable; slavery becomes less attractive."

"That's very cynical. Surely moral sentiment has something to do with it."

"Do you also write letters, Miss Dawson?"

"I?" Emily felt herself floundering. It wasn't that she had expected plaudits, but people were usually impressed by her mother's principles, or at least pretended to be. "I would if—"

"If you thought it would do any good?"

Emily frowned at him. "If I had my mother's eloquence. As it is, I do what I can in a more practical way. We can't all be Marys; the world needs Marthas too." That was what her father had always said, placing a hand on her hair in thanks as she set a hot cup of tea in front of him or restored his lost glasses.

"Didn't the Lord say that Mary had chosen the better?"

Emily folded her arms across her chest. "In that case, oughtn't you to be a minister rather than a doctor?"

Instead of being put off by her rudeness, Dr. Braithwaite surprised her by smiling. "We're as bad as each other. I lived with a minister's family when I first came to England. I much prefer dealing with wounds one can lance and wrap."

"How old were you when you came to England?"

"Young." Dr. Braithwaite walked her at a fast clip down the ward. "I'm meant to be showing you the hospital, aren't I? We have seventy-five beds, all of which are presently filled. We interview patients every Monday at noon for indoor and outdoor relief. The majority are admitted for indoor relief."

Emily hurried to catch up. "I'm surprised. I should have thought it would have been the other way around."

"Many of the men here are suffering from little more than malnutrition and exhaustion."

"You sound as though you don't approve."

"They take room that could be devoted to the genuinely ill. This is a hospital, not a poorhouse."

"Poverty is an illness," said Emily seriously, walking with him down the ward. The majority of the patients were dark-complexioned, but there were a few fairer-skinned sufferers, their faces a sickly hue beneath the rash of old sunburns, red and yellow hair faded to straw by the sun. "I had thought the hospital was for the benefit of the formerly enslaved."

"It's for anyone who can't afford a doctor's fee."

"Redlegs, you mean. Like my grandfather."

Dr. Braithwaite looked at her sideways. "I doubt anyone would call him that now."

Mrs. Davenant had. Emily remembered Mr. Davenant's embarrassment. "I take it the term is not complimentary?"

"No," said Dr. Braithwaite.

When her grandfather had told her he was poor, she had imagined a familiar poverty, the slums of Bristol. It had never occurred to her that this poverty might be viewed as an ancestral stain, less a matter of wealth than of birth.

Dr. Braithwaite seemed disinclined to elaborate, so Emily took a breath and focused her mind on the matter at hand. "How many doctors are in residence?"

"Six. Five junior surgeons and one senior surgeon. I," he said, "am one of the junior staff."

He was also, as far as she could tell, the only one of color, but he hadn't commented on that. "Are you resident?"

"The hospital provides lodgings." He had not, Emily realized, answered the question. She wondered if he lived with his uncle and was ashamed of it. To be in luxury while seeing such poverty every day. Unlike his patients, Dr. Braithwaite had all his own teeth, and very nice ones they were. He gestured at the beds as they passed. "Scurvy, dysentery, exhaustion, malnutrition. As you can see, we treat a wide variety of complaints."

"What of infectious diseases?"

"Not permitted," said Dr. Braithwaite succinctly. "Only the curable sick are admitted."

Emily stopped short in a swish of petticoats, nearly tripping her companion. "But surely you can't mean that! Mightn't those patients be cured if they had proper care? To leave them to die—"

"Do you think I like it? Don't speak to me; speak to the Board of Governors. It was their determination." At the horrified expression on her face, he softened. "They're not entirely wrong. If we admitted one person with yellow fever, it would cut through the whole within days. Most of these people are already weak from disease and malnutrition. Admitting a fever case would be to sign their death warrants."

"But think of all the others exposed!" Her mother, the red flush on her chest, white fuzz on her tongue. Just feeling a bit tired, she had said. "If there were a ward devoted specially to infectious diseases—"

"Built with whose money?" Dr. Braithwaite asked bluntly. "The hospital operates at a deficit as it is. We've been forced to go hat in hand to the council for a grant of four thousand dollars a year."

"With a little economy . . ."

"I'm not paid for my work. None of the doctors are. What are we meant to skimp on? The patients' meals? Most of them come here primarily to be fed. They're poor and starving. On our implements? This may seem provincial to you, Miss Dawson, but I've performed at least a dozen major surgeries since I began at the hospital. I refuse to compromise the care of those in my charge."

"I wasn't suggesting that you should," said Emily.

"No, merely that we should be attempting a dozen other things besides." Dr. Braithwaite gestured down the row of beds. "You won't see many women here, or children. Half the children born in Barbados die before the age of ten. Their parents don't even bother to bring them to us; they know it's hopeless."

"But that's—" Emily clamped her lips shut at a look from Dr. Braithwaite.

"Can you tell me truly that it's better in Bristol?" Remembering the families her father had served, the children dying of cold, of hunger, of diseases a stronger constitution might have weathered, Emily could only remain silent. "We need a children's ward. We need a ward for infectious diseases. We need twice the number of beds merely for the curable sick. We haven't the funds or the staff. I'm at the hospital only three days a week. The rest of my time is devoted to private practice."

"And charity work?" she said, remembering the discussion at Beckles. "Perhaps your uncle . . ."

"Who do you think paid for this building?" Dr. Braithwaite pinched the bridge of his nose, wincing. "I beg your pardon. I had no call to bite your head off."

"You needn't apologize to me. It's very hard seeing people die when one feels that one might have done . . . something." Dipping a cloth into tepid water, mopping a brow, wishing she knew what to do, praying and praying until the words lost all meaning. She'd promised herself, after her mother died, that she would study, that she would learn, that next time she would outwit death. But all she'd learned was that even the most learned were powerless before the diseases that cut through Bristol's poorer quarters. She looked up at Dr. Braithwaite, her eyes meeting his. "With cuts and burns, one knows what to do. But with fevers . . ."

"Someday," said Dr. Braithwaite fervently. "Someday. We already have inoculations for smallpox. Snow and Budd are making great progress on the causes of cholera. . . ."

"Yes, I know," said Emily. "Dr. Budd speaks very eloquently on the topic."

The expression on Dr. Braithwaite's face made the whole visit, the smell and the sweat, entirely worthwhile. "You know Dr. Budd?"

"I had the privilege of working with him at the Royal Infirmary." Admittedly, working with him meant sponging patients' brows while Dr. Budd spoke to his colleagues, entirely unaware of her presence.

"His piece on the mode of propagation of cholera and its prevention . . . If he's correct, we have the chance of not curing the disease but eradicating it."

"Please, God." She had seen cholera. It had cut through Bristol five years before, while her father delivered sermons of hope to a church nearly empty of worshippers, those who dared to come the desperate and devout, everyone else too afraid of the tainted air.

She had thought her heart would break with the helplessness of it, spooning drops of soup into mouths that couldn't swallow, singing lullabies to children too ill to hear.

"God and the Board of Health," said Dr. Braithwaite. "We had two physicians come from England three years ago to set up a Board of Heath and take action, but . . . to call it a drop in the bucket would be to assume a bucket the size of the ocean. People are meant to throw waste in the sea, but half the time they simply fling it outside their door. And why should they bother to do otherwise? The well water here in Bridgetown is all tainted."

"All?" said Emily, thinking of Laura's lethargy, the fits of nausea that seemed to strike with no warning. "What of Miss Lee's hotel?"

Dr. Braithwaite blinked, and then sketched a dismissive gesture. "Oh, you needn't worry. The water you drink doesn't come from here. It's drawn from Beckles's spring."

"Beckles? As in the plantation?"

"It's a common enough name in these parts." Dr. Braithwaite shrugged. "It's peddled for half a cent a gallon. Few can afford to buy enough for drinking, much less washing, not unless you want to spend all your earnings on enough water for a sponge bath. We're ripe for an epidemic and every physician here knows it."

Emily could feel sweat pooling at the back of her neck. Her lips felt dry. "What can we do?"

"We?" He looked at her as though seeing her for the first time, then took a step back. "You needn't concern yourself. You'll be long back in Bristol by then."

"What makes you think I won't stay?" It felt as though a door had been slammed in her face.

"Your cousin said you sail back to England in June."

Trust Adam to say what pleased him in the assumption that time would make it true. "*He* sails back to England in June. I have a plantation to see to."

Dr. Braithwaite raised a brow. "Don't you mean you have a plantation to sell?"

He wasn't being sarcastic; he seemed genuinely baffled by the notion she would stay. Emily rounded on Dr. Braithwaite, venting all of her frustration in the direction of his cravat pin. "Why does everyone assume I mean to sell? Is it so inconceivable that a woman could run a plantation?"

"A woman, yes," said Dr. Braithwaite, and then ruined it by adding, "but one bred to it."

"I should think you of all people would realize that . . . that horticulture is hardly something that runs in the blood!"

"Agriculture," murmured Dr. Braithwaite.

"Agriculture, horticulture, anything can be learned with enough study." Emily flung up her hands in frustration. "You trained as a doctor. Why can't I train to grow sugar?"

Dr. Braithwaite went very still. "My training as a doctor was that unlikely, was it?"

"No! That's not what I meant at all." At least, she didn't think it had been.

"Isn't it? There were a number of my colleagues in Edinburgh who shared that view." Dr. Braithwaite smiled without humor. "Medical students aren't noted for their subtlety."

"Don't you think I heard the same at the infirmary? As if to be a woman were to be a simpleton!" Emily gave her skirts an agitated shake. "I can't change my sex any more than you can the color of your skin."

"Some women do," said Dr. Braithwaite. Emily detected a thaw.

"Yes," she said wrathfully, "in Shakespeare comedies, and very unconvincing it is too. Can you imagine me in breeches and a cravat, with a mustache drawn in charcoal on my lip?"

Dr. Braithwaite lost the battle with his lips. He grinned at her. "Now that you mention it, yes." Gravely, he added, "And I see your point."

There was something in the way he was looking at her that made the color rise to Emily's cheeks. "Well, then," she said, resolutely turning back to the matter at hand and away from the disquieting light in Dr. Braithwaite's eyes. "I only meant that one needn't be bred to something to master it. If that were so, shouldn't you be in business like your uncle? But you could be taught a new trade and so can I. Mrs. Davenant has invited me to stay at Beckles to learn the running of a plantation."

"Has she?" Dr. Braithwaite looked at her sharply. For a moment, he seemed about to say something. But then he shrugged and said only, "I'm sure you can learn a great deal from her."

"What do you mean?"

Dr. Braithwaite turned away, walking back the way they had come. "Precisely what I said. If you want to learn about the cultivation of sugar, there's little they can't tell you at Beckles."

And he would know. Emily bit down the urge to say that, asking instead, as she hurried along after him, "Is there anything I should know about Beckles? Or Peverills?"

Dr. Braithwaite glanced down at her. "You should ask George Davenant. I'm sure he would be more than delighted to tell you stories."

"Yes, fairy stories," said Emily impatiently, remembering Mrs. Davenant's term. "Cavaliers and Roundheads and elopements and romances."

Dr. Braithwaite stopped at the front door. A nurse regarded them with frank curiosity over her wash bucket before Dr. Braithwaite gestured her away.

"What more is there to know? Mrs. Davenant is a respected member of the parish. There have been Beckles at Beckleses since Barbados was Barbados. I'm just a humble surgeon. I wouldn't presume to comment on my betters." For a moment, they stared at each other, the terse words hovering in the air. In a very different voice, Dr. Braithwaite asked, "Do you mean to accept the invitation?"

She should go, she knew. There was no reason not to. She ought to be exceedingly grateful for the opportunity to see the workings of a plantation firsthand. It was pure foolishness to stall and dither, and all because there was something, something about Beckles that had made her feel unsettled. Vulnerable.

Nonsense, she told herself. If she meant to make a go of Peverills, she would have to learn to love the country. That was all it was, acculturation. With time, the sounds of the cane in the wind would become as familiar as the shouts and rattles of a city street. And it would certainly smell sweeter.

As for Mrs. Davenant—no, she must have imagined the rancor when her grandfather's name was mentioned. Mrs. Davenant had been nothing but kind after. Well, not kind, precisely, but helpful. Sometimes helpful was better than kind. It was an idiom Emily understood.

And it would do Laura good to get away, away from Bridgetown and its tainted water.

"Of course," she said lightly. "Why wouldn't I?"

CHAPTER TEN

Christ Church, Barbados
June 1812

"YOU MIGHT TRY to look as though you're enjoying yourself," muttered Robert. "Crop Over is a celebration. It's meant to be enjoyed."

"I am," lied Charles.

Outside, the sun glared, but inside, the louvres had been drawn shut and candlelight, expensive, wasteful candlelight glimmered off embroidered waistcoats and opal stickpins. Men dipped their glasses into vast bowls of rum punch, while women in long gloves held glasses of French champagne, regardless of the war with France. Here, in this room, one would never know that battles were being fought across Spain and Portugal, or that people were starving just outside their doors.

In front of them, the vast mahogany table was entirely hidden by platters of food. Never mind that drought had blighted the Guinea corn, that the people in the quarters had gone from subsistence rations to something that barely blunted the edge of hunger. The harvest festival at Beckles boasted jellied quince and haunches of ham, roasted fowl and French pie. Trifle rich with cream and sherry, candied sweetmeats, and platters overflowing with fruit.

"It seems such a waste," Charles burst out. "All of this when our people are hungry."

The ham was sweating on the table, slices beginning to curl. A stray grape lolled next to a platter, bruised edges turning brown.

"Not so loud," said Robert, fixing a fake smile and bowing to an acquaintance. "Do you want people to think we're up the River Tick?"

But they were. So far, they were drowning in it. Disaster had succeeded disaster. In May, dust had poured from the sky, turning the day to night. Cinders fell like the devil's own snowflakes, until the fields were black with ash, choking new shoots of plantain and Guinea corn. Drought followed, killing whatever survived.

Charles had sold his mother's jewels. He hadn't sold them himself; he had sent Fenty to do it, discreetly, so that their name might not be attached. He'd never asked how the man managed it, just taken the money and bought provisions, dear, so very dear, three times their price, but how could he haggle when his people were starving?

Charles had always thought himself a deist, but over the past few months, he had begun to feel as though he were being dogged by a vengeful Old Testament God, the sort who tossed prophets into the mouth of a whale and sent frogs pattering down like rain.

"They would only think the truth," said Charles. "We're in a bad way."

"For the love of God, don't let anyone hear you say so! Ah, Lascelles! How was your harvest?" Lowering his voice, Robert said viciously, "There's an easy solution. Hadn't you better go speak to the heiress?"

"You go," said Charles. "I'll join you presently."

Robert raised a brow. "You'd best make up your mind. Drink or pass, brother."

And then he was gone, pushing through the crowd, greeting and greeted, laughter and good fellowship following wherever he went. Miss Beckles stood with an older man and a dark-haired woman who wore her modest dress as though it belonged to her and her ruby-and-gold parure as though it didn't.

Miss Beckles's cheeks were flushed with heat. Her chestnut hair had been twisted into a knot at the back and teased into curls on either side of her face. She was, in short, in very good looks, with the sort of buxom prettiness that made one think of shepherdesses and milkmaids, earthy and inviting.

But Charles's eyes went past her.

There she was. Jenny. Standing quietly behind her mistress, garbed in a plain muslin dress and white lawn smock. The only hint of frivolity was a narrow band of lace, an indicator of her status and the festival day.

Standing so still, watching, waiting, always waiting.

It had become a passion of his to try to discover what she was thinking beneath that closed expression. Miss Beckles's every opinion emerged from her lips, but with Jenny it was a question of reading small signals, a tightening of the mouth, a lift of the brow. It was like learning to read a new language, finding pages and pages of text suddenly rich with meaning that might once have been blank. Every look spoke volumes; her carefully considered words sang like a choir by candlelight.

He called on Miss Beckles more often than he ought, but not, he had to admit, for the sake of Miss Beckles. It was her maid he came to see, although their communication was limited to a word and a look.

Oh, Lord. Was this what his father had felt for Nan? This pull like the moon to the sea, calling him like the tides, drawing him to her despite the knowledge that it was wrong, that there could be nothing between them. How could there when she was in no position to refuse?

That hadn't stopped his father.

But he wasn't his father. He wouldn't be.

Jenny's eyes met his across the room. Just a momentary glance, but he felt the hairs on his neck prickle, his cravat suddenly too tight, like a callow youth at his first assembly, sweating through his gloves at the embarrassment of making his bow to a young lady.

Miss Beckles spotted him over Robert's shoulder and her face lit.

Charles's heart sank at the eagerness in her face, the way she raised herself half onto her toes as she lifted a hand in greeting.

He bowed, but ignored the implied invitation, turning away instead so he wouldn't see the disappointment on her face. It was his own fault. He had raised expectations. He needed, he knew, to make a decision. Either marry Miss Beckles or cease his calls. Everyone was watching, he knew, waiting to see if he would come up to scratch. If he didn't, it would be embarrassing for Miss Beckles. No, worse than embarrassing, a confirmation of the rumors that Robert had taken pains to share, and that others only dared hint at.

But if he did marry her . . .

His entire being recoiled at the prospect. He wasn't being fair to her, he knew. There was nothing so repugnant about her. He even rather liked her, at times. But to like someone, at times—how could one make vows before God on the strength of so little?

Men had died and worms had eaten them, but not for love. So the poet said. But that same poet had decreed that to the marriage of minds there should be no impediment, and Charles knew, knew down to the depths of his soul, that their minds were of a very different mettle, that there were corners of Miss Beckles's mind that were anathema to him. She was an enigma to him, and one he had no desire to puzzle out. He could like her well enough, enjoy her blunt tongue, her forthright nature, so long as he didn't have to dwell too deeply on the opinions she expressed: her implacable contempt for Jonathan, based on nothing more than the circumstances of his birth; her acceptance—no, not just acceptance, her championing of a system that Charles found morally bankrupt at best and criminal at worst.

He wouldn't think of it now. This wasn't the place.

Jonathan was standing by the table, and Charles went to him instead, seizing on the excuse.

Charles had insisted he come, although Jonathan had balked at it, saying he wouldn't be welcome. Don't be absurd, Charles had told him.

But Jonathan had been right and he had been wrong. No one had done anything so obvious as snub him, but he hadn't been precisely welcomed either.

"Jonathan." They had progressed to first-name terms. Or, rather, Charles called Jonathan by his first name. Jonathan called him "sir." "How do you like the party?"

"They've a fine cook, to be sure." His plate was laden with food, but most of it was untouched. Gluttony, Charles had noticed, was not among Jonathan's weaknesses. The food was an excuse, a reason to stay by the table. He looked pointedly at Charles. "A man could get used to this."

Even his bookkeeper was asking his intentions. "Do you think I should marry her?"

Jonathan started to say something, then thought better of it. He shrugged. "Your books would balance."

That wasn't really an answer. Or perhaps it was, and Charles was just being naive. "Come with me. Let's make our bows." With Jonathan as shield, he might do the pretty without feeling as though he was making promises he didn't intend to keep. Miss Beckles would be too busy glowering at his bookkeeper to make eyes at Charles. "Who's that with them?"

"That's Mr. and Mrs. Boland." When Charles looked blank, Jonathan added, "The shipowner. Irish. He operates out of Cork and owns property in Antigua, but he's looking to start trading in Barbados sugar. Sir."

Charles didn't ask how Jonathan knew these things. He just did, the way he knew the best place to sell jewels on the quiet or arrange a loan. He was staggeringly competent in a way that made Charles, for all his learning, feel deeply inadequate.

"Shall we?" he said. "You can convince Mr. Boland of the superiority of Peverills sugar."

"What there is of it," murmured Jonathan.

"We'll do better next year," said Charles firmly.

Jonathan didn't say anything. He didn't need to. It was, thought

Charles, ironic that Miss Beckles and his bookkeeper disliked each other so much, when their opinions on how he ought to manage his land were so remarkably similar.

"Miss Beckles," he said, steeling himself against the hope in her eyes. "Thank you, as always, for your hospitality."

"Not at all," said Miss Beckles, her voice pitched higher than usual—with nerves, Charles thought, and cursed himself for causing it. "You know we regard you as family. Peverills and Beckleses have always been near relations."

"Yes, the sort that spar," said Robert, lazily popping a grape into his mouth. "Who was it again? Cain and Abel. Brother, may I make you known to Mr. and Mrs. Boland? They've come from Antigua to see the harvest."

"Ma'am. Sir. And may I make known to you our bookkeeper at Peverills, Mr. Fenty?" Charles made sure to accord Jonathan that "mister," which divided gentleman from servant. He could sense Jonathan's gratitude and Miss Beckles's disapproval. "He'll be able to tell you more than I about our harvest. His memory for numbers is nothing short of miraculous."

"If you ever find yourself seeking other employment . . ." said Mr. Boland with a grin. "I've no head for numbers myself, but I muddle along. I understand you've had a time of it this year?"

The transition was so smoothly done that Charles found himself nodding, and caught Jonathan's quick, sharp look of warning.

"I don't know what you've heard," said Miss Beckles quickly, "but we've never had a better harvest."

Mr. Boland's jowls wagged understandingly, but there was something in those shrewd blue eyes that belied his easygoing charm. "The dust didn't give you any trouble, then? It was something to be seen, I gather."

"It was," said Charles, with a rueful smile. He looked at Mrs. Boland, a decade younger than her husband, at least, but slight and quiet where her husband was expansive in both girth and character. "When

I woke and saw the darkness and the ash falling, I thought it was a judgment on us, like Pharaoh and the Israelites. First ash and then drought. Sometimes I wonder—I wonder if we aren't being punished for enslaving our fellow man. I expect frogs next or boils."

"Nonsense," said Robert, making little effort to disguise his displeasure.

"*'And the Lord said . . . I will send all my plagues upon thine heart, and upon thy servants, and upon thy people. . . .'*" Mrs. Boland spoke for the first time, the words rising up and down with a strong Welsh lilt. "'*For now I will stretch out my hand, that I may smite thee and thy people with pestilence, and thou shalt be cut off from the earth.*' Exodus, chapter nine," she added prosaically.

"Yes," said Charles hoarsely. Her words burned like a brand on his flesh. *Thou shalt be cut off from the earth.* "Yes, that's it exactly."

Mr. Boland chuckled, a husky, whisky-infused sound, reducing prophecy to so much chatter. "Yes, that's all grand, my dear, but these are hardly the people of Israel. You know what the Bible says about the sons of Ham. Servant of my servant, was it? So you've no need to trouble your conscience. Not until you see the frogs falling."

"Two plagues weren't enough to convince you?" said Charles drily.

Mr. Boland grinned at him. "Sure, and it took Pharaoh ten."

"In that case," said Robert, looking narrowly at Charles, "we've the slaying of the firstborn to look forward to. What do you think of that, brother mine?"

Charles could see Jenny standing behind Miss Beckles, listening, impassive. She might have been a piece of furniture for all the attention the others paid her. It was incredible to him still how many people moved among them daily, unnoted and unnoticed, the boys pulling the fans, the liveried servants removing empty glasses and refilling the great bowls of punch. So many to serve so few.

"I think that such retribution would be well deserved," said Charles quietly. "*Malo nodo malus quaerendus cuneus.*"

The wrinkles on Mr. Boland's forehead drew together. "Desperate diseases require desperate remedies, is it? I knew I remembered some Latin yet."

"Well, *I* think it's absurd," interjected Miss Beckles, who had time for neither plagues nor Latin. "It wasn't ash from heaven. It was ash from La Soufrière."

"And there you are," said Mr. Boland, his lips twitching with amusement. "You can't say fairer than that."

There was a great deal he could say, but it was, Charles saw, no use arguing. "Are you in Barbados long, Mr. Boland?"

"That depends on what I find." He yanked a handkerchief from his sleeve and pressed it to his mouth as a coughing fit overtook him, bending him double. Dabbing his lips, he said hoarsely, "I beg your pardon. We'll be here a month, at least. And if we find such hospitality, who's to say we'll ever want to go?"

"The doctors said to stay until the cough goes away," said his wife, frowning at him.

"Yes, yes. I'm meant to be here for my health," said Mr. Boland, stuffing the handkerchief into his waistcoat pocket. "But if all tables are set like this, it's gout I'll be after needing a cure for, not my chest!"

"You already have gout," said his wife pointedly.

"You see how she pecks at me? I'm not allowed the least pleasure."

"Only the pleasure of staying alive," said his wife sternly.

"We can do better than that," said Colonel Lyons, joining the group. "If you'll join us in the mill yard I can promise you a spectacle you won't soon forget. The Negroes have their party—and then we have ours. With ratafia and cakes for the ladies," he added with a bow to Mrs. Boland. "The ladies generally retire early. The harvest festival can become a bit . . . indelicate."

"Only to those raised on milk and water," retorted his niece. "I have the favors ready."

"Don't trouble yourself. I'll distribute them." Colonel Lyons placed a heavy hand on his niece's shoulder and squeezed.

Jenny took a half step forward, closer to her mistress, then stopped.

"Thank you, Uncle," said Miss Beckles in a strained voice. Charles could see the imprint of her uncle's signet in the bare flesh of her shoulder. "These are my people. It's my duty."

"And these are your guests. Besides, I wouldn't want you to overtax yourself. Not with your delicate constitution." As far as Charles could see, Miss Beckles was about as delicate as a mule. Colonel Lyons was smiling, smiling, his voice raised so that the room could hear. "Let me take on the burden for you. That's what I'm here for, after all."

"I am most grateful for your service." Miss Beckles's chin went up, and Charles saw Jenny tense, the look of alarm in her eyes, as the heiress said, very clearly, "I am sure you will miss Beckles when you return to your own home."

Colonel Lyons was smiling again, but beneath it was something raw and ugly. "After all these years, I feel Beckles is my home. If you'd do me the honor, Mrs. Boland? Allow me to escort you."

Balked of a response, Miss Beckles took the arm Mr. Boland offered her, falling into step behind her uncle and Mrs. Boland, staring at her uncle's back with such undisguised hatred that Charles could feel the heat of it like a sunburn.

Jenny fell into place behind her, gently touching her arm. "Don't forget your sunshade, Miss Mary Anne. You don't want to be too much in the sun."

Miss Beckles glared at her maid. Jenny met her gaze calmly.

"All right," said Miss Beckles grumpily, taking the proffered parasol. "I'll stay out of the sun."

Charles couldn't help but suspect they weren't talking about the weather.

"Well?" said Robert. "Are you going to dawdle there all day?"

Charles gave up and joined the procession through the garden, past the hedge, and down into the mill yard, the gray stone tower improbably decked with ribbons and branches of flowering shrubs for the occasion.

Colonel Lyons had arranged for a curtained gallery a little way back from the yard for the ladies, with small cakes and pitchers of ratafia and chairs lest they feel faint from heat.

The gentlemen congregated farther down, closer to the mill and the press of bodies as everyone came from the quarters to celebrate the end of the harvest, all dressed in their best, with flowers tucked into the folds of kerchiefs and the brims of hats, or braided into the little girls' hair.

"I'll stay with the ladies," Mr. Boland declared when Colonel Lyons invited him to join the party. "Sure, and where shall I find such loveliness otherwise? And such cakes!"

Jonathan stayed behind with him. Charles would have liked to do the same, but he knew how his choice would be interpreted, by Miss Beckles and others. So, reluctantly, he found himself part of the circle around Colonel Lyons, who had tapped a barrel of rum and was handing around cups of the raw beverage.

"Made here at Beckles," he said proudly. "You won't find finer."

The liquor burned down Charles's throat, making him cough. "Too strong for you, Mr. Davenant?"

"I think I prefer mine in punch," said Charles, setting his glass down on the top of the barrel.

"With sugar and lemon like the ladies?" The colonel laughed. "You'll have more, won't you, Robert, my lad?"

"Of course," said Robert, and knocked back the dram with a defiant look at his brother, who didn't know whether to shake him or march him home.

Not that he could do anything of the kind. It was too late, for one. And for another, Robert wouldn't be the first who tried to prove his manhood by drinking too deep. Charles had done the same his first year at Oxford and been fortunate to discover rather quickly that it wasn't worth the aching head in the morning. And, too, he had found other friends, better friends, who cared more for ideas than for who could piss the farthest.

Charles found himself missing them, and those days, with a painful yearning. All dispersed now. Carruthers, returned to Northumberland to set the family estates in order; Farleigh, a newly ordained clergyman; St. Aubyn, who had the sharpest mind of their generation, gone to the Peninsula as a soldier to please his father, trading his books for a sword.

And Charles, here in Barbados, confronted with everything he had so long denied.

A cry went up as the first of the carts was sighted, rumbling from the fields toward the mill yard.

The cart was led by a young woman garbed in white, a single red flower burning in the white folds of her kerchief, holding the long skirt of her gown carefully in one hand, the reins in the other.

"Last year's was prettier," commented Robert, regarding her critically through a lorgnette provided by the colonel.

"They're all the same in the dark," replied Colonel Lyons equably. He clapped Charles on the shoulder. "Eh, my boy?"

"Eh," said Charles.

He was spared further conversation by the appearance of the carts, gaily decorated with strips of cloth and bright branches of oleander and hibiscus. The rattle of the wheels and the cries of spectators drowned out any reply Colonel Lyons might have made.

Charles seized the opportunity to drift away, distancing himself from the cluster of young bucks around the colonel. They were, he noticed, all considerably younger than their host. The colonel's entourage consisted of boys like Robert, young bloods still keen to prove themselves men. The older men, the respectable married men, had formed their own cluster, farther away, beneath the canopy with the women.

The carts circled the mill, one, two, three times. Children ran along behind the carts, cheering and waving handkerchiefs or switches made from cane. Women in bright kerchiefs and men in knotted cloth hats with long streamers rode astride the loads of cane, waving to the spectators, who roared in response, hooting and shouting. There was a great deal of banter between the riders of the carts and the crowd in the mill yard; these were, Charles gathered, the best and strongest of the cane cutters, given this one moment of fame for all their labor.

But even their festival attire couldn't hide the scars on arms and legs from billhooks that had slipped while cutting the cane, the raised flesh that came of being seared with drops of boiling sugar, men with arms lost to the crush of the cane press, women with stripes on their backs from the lash of the whip.

Robert accounted himself a lenient master because he denied the drivers the use of the thonged whip. Only a small cat was used, he had told Charles, of five strands, and no more than three lashes applied for any offense. If a driver exceeded his authority, and overapplied the lash, he would be punished. Accidents did happen, of course, it was unavoidable, and toiling in the cane took its toll, but he made sure the members of the first and second gang were given two dressed meals a day, and salt fish and molasses besides, to keep their strength up, and there was no needless violence at Peverills, only what was required to keep the workers in line. Really, did Charles think he was so careless of their stock?

Robert was nodding and smiling now as the carts rolled forward, waving to the workers on the wagons, joking with his friends about the stamina of the women of the first gang, struggling all day to fell the long, long cane.

Colonel Lyons stepped forward as the carts rumbled to a stop, saying a word in turn to each of the riders, handing each a bright coin—he made sure, Charles saw, to display them, the copper winking in the light—a kerchief for the women, and a necktie for the men.

In defiance of her uncle, Miss Beckles came forward, following the colonel, making sure to add her own words of congratulations.

An elderly man stepped forward and began a speech of thanks, looking uneasily from Miss Beckles to the colonel as though unsure to whom he was meant to be speaking.

"Thank you all," said the colonel, stepping in front of his niece and pitching his voice to carry, "for your good work this harvest. Come and

enjoy the fruits of your labor! There's rum aplenty for every man—
and woman too! And I've a gift of sugar for you all."

Miss Beckles's lips pressed together at that "I." "We have a gift of
sugar for you all," she corrected, but Colonel Lyons didn't heed her.

He raised his glass, calling out, "Strike the fiddle, pour the rum, and
let's say farewell to hard times and hello to plenty!"

Like Prospero conjuring spirits, fiddles and drums began to play as
if by magic. Cups circulated around the crowd. Two men dragged from
the last cart an effigy of a man dressed in a rusty black top hat and frock
coat.

Bending, Colonel Lyons murmured something to his niece, who
looked at him from under her brows, but complied, trudging back to
the tent where the women had gathered, directing them toward the
house, away from the music and revelry.

"Who's a flame for me?" demanded Colonel Lyons, and the girl in
white, blushing, was nudged forward, a flaming brand in her hand.

Colonel Lyons caught her around the waist, giving her a squeeze
as he lifted the torch in the air. A cheer went up from the crowd as he
touched it to the effigy, which blazed up with alacrity, making the people nearest jump back in delighted horror.

"That's Mr. Harding," said a quiet voice beside him, and Charles
looked to see Jenny standing there, not quite next to him, a little behind, as though she too just happened to be viewing the scene. "The
one they're burning."

"Mr. Harding?" Charles tried to keep his voice level, as though he
weren't as unsettled by her presence as his eyes were by the flames and
his head by the rum. Everything seemed to dance and leap around him,
heat prickling his skin.

"You didn't have Mr. Harding at Peverills?"

"I don't remember," Charles confessed, although now that she mentioned it, he thought he remembered seeing something burning. But did
he truly remember it, or did he only imagine he did?

He couldn't be sure. Their own Crop Over had been a muted affair in comparison; he had distributed a ration of sugar to each man and woman on the estate as tradition dictated, and then retreated to allow them to enjoy their own celebrations, without the inhibition of his presence. Or, at least, that was what he had told himself. In truth, it was cowardice, an inability to be among the people whose labor clothed and fed him, knowing how much he owed them and how far he was still from expiating that debt. His brother would think him mad, he knew.

Charles shook his head to clear it. "Who's Mr. Harding?"

"Hard times," said Jenny, and then paused for a moment before saying, so quietly he could hardly hear her, "Might I speak with you? Not here."

"Of course." Charles tried to ignore the way his palms turned sweaty, the mingled anticipation and fear. It was nothing to do with him, he was sure, at least not like that. Jenny's eyes were on her father, watching him as one might a snake. "It would be my pleasure. I'm in your debt and would be happy to repay in any way I can."

Jenny looked at him sideways. "Any way?"

"Within honor." He looked at her closely, feeling a strong urge to go out and battle dragons on her behalf. Or at least Colonel Lyons. "Is it as bad as that?"

Jenny pressed her lips together and looked away. Speaking rapidly, she said, "Do you know where the Old Mill is?"

"The ruin? When?" The ladies had already retreated to the house, and Colonel Lyons, having disposed of Mr. Harding, was beginning to look about.

Jenny was already beginning to slip away, into the crowd. "When Mr. Harding is ash."

"It's done," said Charles, but she wasn't there to hear. Colonel Lyons was looking at him, so Charles made a show of locking his hands behind his back and strolling around the mill yard, examining the tubs of blackstrap and molasses, the tables laden with bowls of rice and peas, cassava pone, and salt fish.

"Was that one of the maids with you?" Colonel Lyons strode over to him, his entourage stumbling behind.

Charles schooled himself to indifference. "Yes, I believe so. She wanted to know if I needed more rum."

"If you have to ask," said Colonel Lyons, with a glint to his eye, "why then, the answer is yes."

Behind him, Charles could hear Robert's drunken laugh. Charles looked up to see his brother with three other men, one of them fondling the breast of the girl who'd led the carts.

Colonel Lyons looked at Charles as though daring him to say something.

"What I really need," said Charles, biting back the sharp words that rose to his lips, "is the nearest convenience."

"You can piss anywhere you like. They do." At the look on Charles's face he chuckled. "If you must save your modesty, there's a chamber pot behind a screen next to the arbor."

"Thank you," said Charles, and then, because he couldn't help himself, "That girl . . ."

"What? Do you want her? She's taken, but I imagine I can find you another to your liking."

Charles's stomach turned; he bit back a comment about pimps and panderers, saying instead, "No. No, thank you. If you'll excuse me . . ."

Charles escaped to the chamber pot, grateful for the screen that protected him from the colonel's watching eyes. Let them mock him for being unable to hold his liquor. It was better than the alternatives. He waited a few moments before slipping carefully away in the other direction, away from the mill, toward Peverills and the Old Mill that once, a very, very long time ago, the two estates had shared, over a century ago when sugar cultivation was in its infancy. The mill was on Beckles land, a bone of contention that had continued long after the mill itself was out of use.

The sun flared out, the sky lighting orange and purple. In the short dusk, Charles covered the last few yards to the Old Mill, blinking at the darkness inside. It was cool in the mill, the air heavy with the scent of wet earth, the sharp sap of the vines that circled through the old stones, and, incongruously, the crispness of sun-dried linen.

"Jenny?" he said softly. The act of saying her name felt like an indiscretion, as though he were taking a liberty.

"Here." Her voice came from a corner of the wide, conical room. She must have taken off her white smock; her dark dress blended with the shadows, rendering her all but invisible. "Did anyone see you come?"

"The colonel, you mean?" Her silence was answer enough. "No. Was it he—has he done anything to cause you discomfort?"

He felt like an idiot as he said it. Of course he had.

Jenny didn't respond, not directly. Instead, she said, in a strange, abstracted voice, "Did you mean what you said before? About God's retribution?"

"Yes. And no. I don't mean to say that I didn't mean it. What I mean is, I've never believed that the Lord visits vengeance as they have it in the Old Testament." In the darkness, Charles's voice sounded unnaturally loud. He tried again, scrounging for sense. "But it was He who made Nature's laws. When we broke those laws, we set the world out of joint, and nothing will be as it should until we put it right again. If we assume that in the state of nature all men were born equal and that no man can, in logic, contract away his own freedom, then slavery, by its very nature, is an illegitimate institution and an offense to the laws of Nature. That's the theory, in any event."

The silence pushed against him like a living thing. Charles began to wish he'd said yes and left it at that.

"I . . . Perhaps our Methodist friends are right and we're courting brimstone. I'm beginning to see the appeal of that. Theory is all very well, but there are injustices that call for action. Human or divine."

Charles's ears strained, attuned to the drip of moisture down the stone, the rustling of leaves outside, and then, finally, the sound of Jenny's voice. "I wouldn't share those views if I were you, Master Charles. You won't make any friends that way."

"I had gathered that," said Charles, letting out a deep breath he hadn't realized he'd been holding. "But you—you wanted to speak to me about something. If there is any way in my power to be of service . . ."

"Yes. There is." She took a step closer and then another, near enough that he could hear the gentle sway of her skirt and make out, in the gloom, the tension of the hands clenched into fists at her sides. "I need you to marry my mistress."

CHAPTER ELEVEN

Christ Church, Barbados
March 1854

"ARE YOU SURE this is quite necessary?" Emily looped the skirt of her borrowed habit over her arm and looked at the beast that awaited her in the stable yard.

Horses, she decided, looked a great deal larger when detached from a carriage. Also less friendly.

The creature whiffled in her general direction. Emily took a step back, tripping over the hem of her habit.

"Steady there," said George Davenant, who seemed, for once, a great deal more confident than she. "She's only trying to make your acquaintance. Hold out your hand to her."

"Should I offer her my calling card?" The horse nosed at her fingers, leaving a patch of slime on her kid gloves.

"You can, but she would most likely prefer a carrot," replied Mr. Davenant mildly.

Emily had strenuously resisted being taught to ride, but Mrs. Davenant had insisted that riding lessons were the very first priority, and there was nothing at all she could do until Emily could sit the back of a horse without being tossed about like a sack of meal.

To Emily's protests that she could very well read a ledger from a desk chair, Mrs. Davenant turned a deaf ear; one had to know the land to tend it, and to know it, one had to ride it.

Adam's comments about sedan chairs and bearers were not well received by either lady.

Emily had hoped her lack of a habit might provide a suitable delay, but no sooner had she mentioned it than one appeared, as if by magic, across the foot of her bed, rather disconcertingly tailored to her proportions.

"Well, yes," Mr. Davenant had said awkwardly, when quizzed. "The maid will have taken one of your dresses to measure for size and the seamstresses will have done the rest."

And would the cobblers hammer out boots for her too? Emily was afraid to ask lest it happen. She hadn't quite fully appreciated just how self-sufficient a world Beckles was, every possible need provided within its grounds. When Aunt Millicent wanted a dress made, she had to beg her modiste for the privilege of spending large sums of money. At Beckles, new clothes were run up overnight by elves.

Not elves. Former slaves, Emily reminded herself. Although they were free now, that level of service was still rather disconcerting and she found it innately suspect.

Not to mention that it had ruined her best excuse for avoiding riding lessons.

Mrs. Davenant had caught her at breakfast, bundled her into her habit, and chivvied her out the door, allowing her grandson barely time for a cup of coffee and a hard roll before he too was ruthlessly propelled in the direction of the stables, pursued by directives.

Emily rather suspected that if she looked back at the house she would see the glint of light on a lens, Mrs. Davenant watching to make sure her instructions were being obeyed.

"All right," said Emily resignedly, retrieving her hand and surreptitiously shaking off the slobber. "We've made friends. Now what?"

"Now you mount."

Emily regarded the saddle, a million miles up on the horse's back. It was a fearsome thing, studded with two large protrusions. "Have you a winch?"

"No, but we do have a mounting block," said Mr. Davenant, holding out a hand. "I'm afraid I don't know much about riding, er, sidesaddle, but I'll do my best."

"Is it your grandmother's saddle?" Emily asked, stalling for time. Even from the mounting block, the horse's back seemed very high and the saddle very uncomfortable. She wasn't sure how one was meant to sit with those hillocks sticking out.

"Grandmama? Heavens, no. She's very particular about her saddle. No. This was my mother's. It hasn't been used for some time. Not since I was a boy. Shall I help you up?"

"You may," said Emily, resisting the urge to quiz him further. He rarely mentioned his mother. "But I'm not at all sure where I'm meant to go once I get up there."

A flush rose in Mr. Davenant's fair cheeks. "I believe you place your, er, nether limb between those two pommels."

"My leg, do you mean?" Emily laughed at the expression on his face. "Don't worry. I'm not missish. I have it on the best authority that most creatures are in possession of legs, myself included. So I place my right leg between those two bumps?"

"Pommels," said Mr. Davenant, looking rather bemused. "May I?"

Emily would have liked to say no, particularly as she was conscious that there seemed to be rather a large number of people gathered around the stable yard, ostensibly performing tasks, but really waiting for her to make a fool of herself.

Better to get it over with quickly, she decided, and said, "Yes."

Remembering what Mr. Davenant had said about the pommels, she vigorously flung her leg up into what she thought was the right spot. It wasn't. She kicked out with her other leg to try to push herself up and found herself suddenly flung back, her right leg stuck at an odd angle between the pommels, her skirt trailing behind her, and her hands grasping for any purchase at all as the world raced away in a bizarre view of sky and tree branches and the very top of the windmill, all swirling together.

"Wait! Don't—hold on!" There was a great deal of commotion in the stable yard involving many people shouting and running, most of which Emily missed because she was too busy trying to pull herself upright and thinking distinctly unkind thoughts about horses and people who made other people ride them.

"Are you all right?" Mr. Davenant demanded breathlessly, peering up at her from what seemed like an odd angle until Emily realized it was she who was at the odd angle.

"Yes, quite." Never mind that her back felt as though she'd just been paid a personal visit by the Inquisition.

Emily clawed at her hat only to realize it had fallen off. Someone very helpfully handed it to her. Emily regarded it with disfavor—it was somewhat the worse for its adventure and looked as though it had been trodden on, most likely because it had been.

Emily jammed the hat back on her head, securing it with the one remaining pin. She didn't like to think of the whereabouts of the others. "I'm so sorry. I didn't mean to make it run like that."

"Her," said Mr. Davenant. "You didn't mean to make her run like that. She's a mare."

"Oh." Emily had been regarding her mount rather as an extension of a carriage, the bit that made it go. She hadn't really thought of it— her—as a creature with a personality and, most likely, opinions. The thought was distinctly unsettling. She preferred not to sit on anything sentient.

"Shall we try again? Maybe try not to, er, kick this time." Just to make sure, Mr. Davenant summoned two grooms, both of whom stood at the horse's head as Emily maneuvered her nether limbs into the approved position, wincing at what she was quite sure would be a truly spectacular set of bruises in locations that would make Mr. Davenant blush.

Emily looked down. And down. "The ground looks very hard."

"My grandmother would say, '*Try not to fall on it, then.*'" Mr. Davenant's imitation was so perfect that Emily was surprised into a grin and had to clutch at the horse's mane to keep from unseating herself.

"I don't think I could fall if I wanted to," complained Emily, shifting uncomfortably. Her right leg was very firmly pinned between the pommels, her left foot wedged in a stirrup that appeared to have been made for someone who took a smaller size of boot.

"That's good, then, isn't it?" said Mr. Davenant. "Shall we get started?"

Emily didn't miss his glance over his shoulder, back at the house. He'd had little breakfast and was wasting the better part of his morning when he doubtless had other obligations to see to. Mrs. Davenant had told her that she didn't trust hired overseers; she preferred to rely on her grandson and the head drivers. So Emily nodded and let Mr. Davenant lead her twice around the stable yard at a pace best suited to funerals and the conveyance of gouty dowagers.

The mare went docilely enough. Emily suspected her of biding her time.

Once they had safely completed a third circuit without the mare bolting, Emily felt secure enough to say, "I'm terribly sorry to be keeping you from your obligations."

"Don't be," said Mr. Davenant, with one of his disarmingly sweet smiles. "My grandmother is only too glad of the opportunity to seize the reins for a day. Er, don't seize the reins."

"Oh, I'm so very sorry." To the horse, she added, "I do beg your pardon."

The horse snorted at her. It sounded remarkably like Mrs. Davenant.

Mr. Davenant laughed, looking far more relaxed than Emily had seen him since they arrived. "You needn't apologize—to me or Petunia. You want her to know that you're in control."

"But I'm not," protested Emily, and was rewarded with another fleeting smile. "Couldn't I learn to drive instead? I think I should be rather good at driving."

Adam was always claiming he could drive to an inch, which, translated, meant he spent a great deal of time getting new wheels and axels fitted to his curricles.

"May I?" At Emily's nod, Mr. Davenant removed his jacket. Stripped to his shirtsleeves and waistcoat, he looked very at home in the stable yard. As they made another circuit, he gave thought to her question. "You could learn to drive, but it wouldn't serve the same purpose. It depends on what you intend. If you wish to engage yourself in the business of the plantation, then a mount is a necessity. If you mean to hire someone to manage for you, then a carriage will serve to carry you to town."

"Do you mean Bridgetown?" Emily asked, suppressing the sudden yearning to find a carriage, any carriage, and have herself conveyed back to the city forthwith.

It wasn't that they were unkind at Beckles. On the contrary, she had been offered every luxury. And she could hardly complain of quiet or loneliness when Beckles was a village unto itself, with dozens of servants in the house and hundreds in the fields. The night was busy with the sounds of dogs barking and babies crying and men shouting and the ever-present rustle of the cane. But the sounds weren't the sounds she was used to.

Most of all, she disliked the sensation of being marooned. All her life, she had been able to go anywhere she needed with a pair of stout shoes and a sturdy umbrella. Now, those stout shoes would take her only so far as the end of the drive, like a medieval ship skirting the edges of the map, with the unknown beyond. Peverills might be as far as the moon, for all that she was able to reach it. She was entirely reliant on the pleasure of others for her transportation, something that made her feel distinctly twitchy.

"Are you ready for a trot?" Mr. Davenant did something to the lead rope and the horse began to jiggle Emily up and down in a most uncomfortable way. "My grandmother prefers to do her marketing in Oistins, but I'm always glad of an excuse to come to Bridgetown.

Beckles is very well, but . . . I'm not making a very good job of con-vincing you to stay, am I?"

"I suppose it's all a matter of familiarity breeding contempt," said Emily, clinging to the horse's mane in what she doubted was approved style as she tried to relieve the pressure on her maltreated nether limbs. "I've always lived in town. Our vegetables come to us already shaken free of dirt and our meat nicely butchered and wrapped in a brown paper package. It seems rather exciting to be so close to creation."

"We are that," said Mr. Davenant ruefully. "If you wish to see pigs slaughtered, you've come to the right place. We grow all our own pro-visions. My grandmother is adamant about that. We're as self-sufficient as Robinson Crusoe on his island. There were some rather bad famines in the past between harvests—the hungry time, they call it—so my grandmother likes to make sure we always have enough and then some."

"Your grandmother seems a remarkable woman," said Emily, rather grimly.

"She is," said Mr. Davenant, his tone mirroring hers. His face light-ening, he added, "She took to you too. Says you remind her of someone."

"Most likely my grandfather," said Emily, frowning at the horse's ears and wondering just how one stopped one of these things.

"I don't think so," said Mr. Davenant thoughtfully. "She seemed to mean it kindly and—well. Did you say something?"

"No," said Emily through clenched teeth. "That's just the sound of my teeth coming loose."

The days took on a pattern. After breakfast, she and Mr. Davenant would retire to the stable yard, and if Emily had to spend some time afterward in a darkened room with ice wrapped in linen applied to ten-der parts of her anatomy, only her maid Katy knew it. By the end of the week, Mr. Davenant pronounced her ready to leave the stable yard and escorted her, still holding the lead rein, as far as the end of the drive.

Mrs. Davenant eluded her requests for instruction, telling her there would be time enough when she had seen the elements of the plantation, and Emily admitted, grudgingly, that there might be some sense in it as

Mr. Davenant, on their morning rides, took her day by day to the fields, to the mill, to the boiling house, demonstrating the uses of each.

Emily half suspected Mrs. Davenant of designing the tour to discourage her; she hadn't realized until Mr. Davenant took her about just how much there was to learn, how many steps from the holing of the cane to its triumphal transmutation into sugar, molasses, and rum. But Mr. Davenant brushed aside her doubts, insisting that if he could manage, anyone could.

"I have no head for business," he confessed, "or for management. I'm like a parrot that's been taught to squawk in tune."

"But with lovely plumage, at least?" teased Emily, who was beginning to enjoy shocking her host. It was so absurdly easy.

A groom accompanied them for propriety's sake (and, Emily privately suspected, to administer aid should she come to grief), but Adam and Laura remained behind. Laura spent long hours sipping weak tea in a quiet corner of the veranda, chasing the shade as the sun shifted. Mr. Davenant would often join her there, reading to her or speaking softly together of poetry and art, until Mrs. Davenant would invariably come to roust him out and send him about his business.

Adam, meanwhile, was conveyed almost daily back to town by Mrs. Davenant's own carriage, where he engaged in unspecified business dealings that Emily suspected had a great deal to do with the icehouse and less with the exchange.

Emily's schedule was determined for her, without discussion or opportunity for dissent. In the mornings, she rode with Mr. Davenant. In the afternoons, Emily sat by Mrs. Davenant as she entertained callers, ensconced like a queen in a cane-backed chair in the great room. Tremaines, Alleynes, Piles, Collymores, Burkes, Walkes, Thorpes, and dozens of others whose names Emily forgot but who all seemed to be related to one another, all longtime landowners, and, as Mrs. Davenant would have it, true Barbadians.

Which, of course, had the effect of reminding Emily that she was not.

Emily noticed that Adam was seldom invited to these gatherings.

The owner of Peverills was welcome where Jonathan Fenty's grandson was not.

Or, rather, the owner of Peverills was tolerated, pending further inspection.

Day bled into day and week into week. March gave way to April. Easter Sunday saw Emily sitting in the Beckles pew, crammed between Adam and Mr. Davenant. And still there was no discussion of departure. When Emily protested that they were overstaying their welcome, she was fed bromides about Creole hospitality. No one seemed inclined to hurry; Peverills might sit fallow a hundred years at this rate, while she rode a little farther each day and took tea with yet another cousin of a cousin of a cousin. She chafed at it, but found it strangely difficult to break free.

It was the first of May, over two months into their stay, before Mr. Davenant pronounced Emily capable of riding across the field as far as a tumbledown structure referred to as the Old Mill.

"Laura would adore this," said Emily, looking ruefully at the ivy-twined stones, the gaping arch where a door might once have stood.

Laura was rather a good rider—her father had had aspirations toward retiring to a country estate and setting up as squire one day—but Laura had been so subdued, so oppressed by the heat, that Emily doubted she would ride that far.

When they returned to the house, she would have to check on Laura and make sure she wasn't sickening for something.

"Bare, ruined choirs where late the sweet birds sang," said Mr. Davenant, swinging down and helping her dismount, a process that Emily accomplished about as gracefully as a bear dancing a quadrille.

"Don't you mean bare, ruined millstones?"

"That's not nearly as euphonious," protested Mr. Davenant.

"Can we go inside?"

"There's nothing to see," said Mr. Davenant quickly. "It was emptied long ago. It hasn't been in use since the very end of the seventeenth century, if that."

"It doesn't look empty," said Emily, peering into the darkness. "Someone left a blanket in there."

"It has a reputation for being, well, um, something of a trysting place." Mr. Davenant was red clear up to the tips of his ears. Hastily turning her in the other direction, he said, "You can see your land from here. This mill is on the dividing line between the properties. It served both long, long ago."

He pointed in a direction Emily thought might be north. Or possibly east. "Before the Peverills and Beckleses fell out?"

Mr. Davenant grinned. "I'm not sure there was ever a time when the families weren't on the outs, but they put their differences aside long enough to make some money out of it. We might make much of our gentlemanly birth, but the men who came to Barbados were adventurers at heart, Peverills and Beckleses both."

"Does that make you an adventurer too, then?" asked Emily doubtfully.

"My grandmother would say the old blood wears thin." Mr. Davenant dropped down on the rug the groom had set out and began rooting in the picnic basket. "Would you prefer cold chicken or ham?"

"Chicken, please." Over the scrub and the strange, skinny trees with their shock of broad leaves at the top, Emily could see the ruined towers of Peverills. "You must think me the worst sort of interloper."

"Shall we say the best sort of interloper?" Mr. Davenant hesitated a moment, busying himself with pouring lemonade, before asking, "Have you decided what you mean to do with Peverills?"

"Will I sell it, you mean?"

"Well—yes." Mr. Davenant handed her a glass of lemonade, miraculously cool. The bottle had been nestled in shaved ice, a luxury that Mr. Davenant appeared to take for granted. "Forgive my clumsiness. It's not my place to know."

"If it's anyone's place, it's yours," said Emily frankly. "I don't know yet. I should like to make a go of it, if I could."

Mr. Davenant toyed with his lemonade. "I should warn you—my

grandmother will be after you to sell. I'm surprised she hasn't already. She's never been reconciled to Peverills having been sold. It's been her dream to see the two properties reunited."

"Do you feel the same way, Mr. Davenant?"

"Me?" Mr. Davenant choked on his drink. "Not in the slightest. Reckoning my life in barrels of sugar, constantly worrying about the weather and the harvest and this blight and that bug. I'd just as happily chuck it all aside."

"Why don't you?"

"I'm the only one my grandmother has left. I can't leave her. She may seem strong—she *is* strong—but she . . . she isn't an island unto herself, however much she may pretend to be. She needs me more than she admits. I'm sorry. I shouldn't have said—"

"My grandfather was the same way. He would thunder at us and complain, but he was always happiest with his whole family about him." Losing her mother and then her grandmother had diminished him; he had seemed, somehow, a little smaller with each death. Emily quickly mustered a smile. "It's all the same with these domestic tyrants, isn't it? He would scold us and tell us we were useless—and then give us sweets."

She wondered if the plantation was only a larger and less digestible sort of sweet, the gift her grandfather would have offered her mother if she had lived.

But no. It seemed more likely that her grandfather had bought it planning to make something of it, and, finding it too large a task to manage from afar, and reluctant to admit having made a miscalculation, had simply let it sit, bequeathing it to her on the assumption she would take charge, as he had trained her to do.

"You must miss him terribly," said Mr. Davenant.

"I do," said Emily simply. "Very much."

"But you do have other family in Bristol?" Mr. Davenant asked diffidently. "I don't mean to pry. I simply wondered if you wouldn't be homesick for your own people if you stay on in Barbados."

Emily shook her head. "I don't imagine so. I don't have a home in

Bristol anymore. That's not entirely true. My aunt and uncle would be happy to offer me a home. But my own home—" She bit her lip. There was no point blundering about. She might as well get right to the heart of it. "My father remarried last year."

Mr. Davenant leaned back on one arm, looking up at her face beneath the brim of her bonnet. "You don't sound pleased."

Emily shrugged. "My father is very happy."

"Do you dislike his wife so very much?"

"Nooo. . . . Not dislike her, precisely." One didn't dislike Hester. One weathered her, like a gale. A gale scented with carbolic and puffed with improving aphorisms. "We don't fit well in the same place."

Emily didn't need improving, thank you very much. She had been running her father's household since she was ten, ministering to his motley flock, carrying baskets to the deserving poor, forcibly scrubbing the undeserving poor, and making sure her father's spectacles were always in reach.

Hester had provided him with a little cord on which to hang the spectacles. She had rearranged the furniture in the drawing room, removed Emily's mother's pianoforte ("Sentiment is all very well, but it does look rather *worn*, doesn't it?"), and taken on the preparation and delivery of charitable baskets. It was her right. Emily knew that. But it didn't make it any easier to be displaced.

Did her father even notice? Sometimes she wondered, and there was a sting in that too.

"Did she make you scrub the scullery and sleep in the ashes?" asked Mr. Davenant sympathetically.

"I don't mind a bit of scrubbing." It was the lack of purpose that rankled. "No, far worse. She wanted to marry me to the curate."

Mr. Davenant squinted up at her, shading his eyes against the sun. "And what about the curate?"

"I'm not sure he was permitted to have any say in the matter. I half expected to return home one day to find the parlor decked with orange flowers and Mr. Curtis trussed to the altar."

"With an apple in his mouth?" Mr. Davenant pushed himself back up to a sitting position, his smile fading. "My grandmother arranged my father's marriage. It was a disaster. They were both terribly young, and . . . Well, I shouldn't complain, should I? I wouldn't be here but for it. And we did round out the northwest corner of our lands."

There was an uncharacteristic bitterness to his tone.

"I'm so sorry," said Emily. "Have your parents been gone long?"

"As long as I can remember. My father ran off to Paris when I was still in swaddling clothes."

"Oh. I had assumed . . . Never mind."

"That he was dead? No. Merely absentee. My mother as well. She went on an extended visit to relations in the Carolinas and never came back."

"Oh," said Emily, entirely at a loss. Nothing short of death would have induced her own mother to leave her, and while Emily might have railed at death, she had never doubted her mother's love. "Was she—have you—does she visit?"

"Sometimes. Infrequently. They said she went away for her health, but I think it was more that she couldn't bear life at Beckles. She's very happy in Charleston, I understand."

Emily plucked at a thread on her skirt. "Did you ever think of going with her?"

"I'm heir to Beckles and the last of my line. I couldn't do that to Grandmama. She's lost so much already." Mr. Davenant looked at the sky and jumped to his feet with an exclamation of distress. "It's later than I'd realized. We should get back. If you don't mind, that is."

"Not at all," said Emily, taking his hand. The sun still shone, but the day felt darker than it had been before.

They rode back in silence broken only by comments about the weather. There was a new constraint about his manner as Mr. Davenant helped Emily down from her mount in the stable yard. And who could blame him? Emily suspected her pity showed on her face, and she hated herself for it.

"Miss Dawson," he said as he handed her down.

"Hadn't you better call me Emily?" Emily blurted out, in an attempt to make amends. "It seems silly to stand on formality."

"Emily," he said, looking down at her hand in his as though surprised to see it there. He released it and stepped back. "Then you must call me George. I've overstayed my time. I'd best see to my work, or my grandmother will have my head."

Emily watched him go with a frown, feeling that she'd thoroughly put her foot in it. She hadn't asked him to confide in her. Well, perhaps she had, just a little. But she had never imagined that there might be such unhappiness beneath Mr. Davenant's easy air.

It made her feel a little sick to think of the baby he had been, being left behind. No wonder he wouldn't leave his grandmother. She was the only one who had stood by him, even if standing by him did seem to mean nudging and guiding him.

Emily looped up the skirt of her habit as she climbed the steps to the bedroom floor. She would go in and tell Laura about the Old Mill, she decided. It might be just the thing to get Laura moving again. Not today, of course. But tomorrow, in the cool of the morning, perhaps she might persuade Laura to ride out with her. Mr. Davenant—George— could do without her for one day; they could both use some time apart after today. She felt silly for complaining about Hester when George had real sorrows with which to contend.

Before Emily could knock, Laura's door opened, and Adam came out, stopping short at the sight of her. He closed the door behind him, but not before Emily heard the sound of retching.

"You reek of the stables," he commented.

"And so would you if you had been riding. Is Laura ill again?"

Emily made to go past him, but Adam stopped her. "Just a touch of heat. Don't fuss at her, Emily. She wants to be let alone."

"She's been ill since we arrived. Don't tell me it's just the heat." Emily glanced back at the door. "If you won't let me look at her, perhaps a doctor ought to be called."

Adam made a face at her. "MacAndrews?"

"That's not funny," said Emily sharply. MacAndrews came to supper once a week, on Wednesdays, and it didn't take a doctor to diagnose his shaking hands and yellowed skin. "I wouldn't trust a cat to his care. I thought Mr. Turner might make a recommendation."

"His nephew, for one?" said Adam, as though it were a great joke.

"Why not? He's better trained than most doctors here."

"Don't be ridiculous." Taking her by the arm, Adam turned Emily and marched her away from Laura's door. "There's nothing wrong with Laura that a bit of rest and some tea won't cure."

"Yes, but—" Emily twisted back, but Adam held fast.

"Hadn't you better look to your own affairs?" he demanded. Seeing a passing servant carrying linens, he lowered his voice, tilting his head toward hers. "The old dragon had me to tea today while you were off gallivanting with young Davenant."

Emily suppressed the urge to point out that Mr. Davenant was at least as old as Adam and possibly a year or two more besides. "Yes? That's hardly surprising under the circumstances."

Adam stopped at the landing, raising his brows at her in an infuriating way. "But don't you want to know why?" Without waiting for Emily to answer, he said, with some relish, "She quizzed me about your mother. Where was she born, when was she born, what was she like, who did she favor. . . . It was, I would have you know, a most pointed inquisition."

"She knew Grandfather." Even if she hadn't liked him. "I'm not surprised she wants to know about his children."

"Not his children. Child. She couldn't have been less interested in Father. What do you imagine that means?"

"That she was making conversation with a guest and thought it a topic of mutual interest?"

"And all of those morning rides with young Davenant?"

"Do stop calling him that. I expect she thinks I'll get discouraged if I see how much work it all is and sell Peverills to her cheap."

Just as those endless teas were a campaign to show her how little she belonged, how little she understood their traditions and family ties.

It was a lowering thought. Emily rather liked Mrs. Davenant, because of—not despite—her toughness, and she thought Mrs. Davenant felt the same. But she should know, after all those years with her grandfather, how little weight liking held when there was money at issue.

Adam folded his arms across his chest, leaning back against an old mahogany chest. "Why do that when she can get it for free?"

Emily wasn't sure she liked where this was going. "What are you on about, Adam?"

"Surely you can't be that naive."

"Apparently I am," said Emily in frustration. "Do stop speaking in riddles."

"It's as plain as the nose on your face. Inspecting the family tree . . . trotting you out in front of all the local worthies . . . tête-à-têtes on horseback . . ."

Emily had an unpleasant sense that she knew where this was tending. "Oh no—" she began, but Adam was faster.

"Oh yes," he said triumphantly, as pleased with himself as if he'd marched her down the aisle himself. "She means you to marry her grandson, of course."

CHAPTER TWELVE

Christ Church, Barbados
June 1812

"MARRY YOUR MISTRESS," Mr. Davenant repeated.

"It would be a very good match," Jenny said, and winced at how strident her voice sounded. Honey, not vinegar. But she was desperate and it was very hard to be honeyed when the devil rode at her heels.

"As the world accounts such things," said Mr. Davenant quietly, and Jenny knew she was losing him.

No, she had lost him before she had come, she had seen it, that moment when he saw her mistress, checked, and turned away. Her father had seen it too, and there had been no mistaking the triumph on his face.

Through the dust and the drought, her father had bided his time, but now, now that harvest was in, the blow would fall soon, she was sure. She wasn't sure what her father had planned for her, but whatever it was, she knew it wouldn't be pleasant. At best, she would be sold. At worst . . .

"Please," Jenny said, the word scraped from the back of her throat, raw and hoarse. "Please, before you say anything, there is something you should know. It touches on my mistress. And the colonel."

"The stories he tells about her?" Mr. Davenant was quick, she would grant him that. "I don't believe them, if that's what you're concerned about."

"That is only the smallest part of it."

The loamy atmosphere of the Old Mill pressed hard around her. She looked up at Mr. Davenant, a charcoal sketch of a man in the gloaming, threatening in the abstract. One word from him and she would find herself flogged. Or worse. But she clutched to her the memory of that afternoon, the way he had spoken out against the breaking of Nature's laws. This wasn't a man to throw her over to the courts, to see her stripped and flogged.

She hoped.

Over the months, she had searched relentlessly for a crack in his facade, a sign that his civility was a ploy. But there had been nothing, nothing to show he was other than he seemed. Jenny, expecting hypocrisy, had been first skeptical, and then baffled, and, finally, reluctantly intrigued. She had never met anyone like that before, a man who wore his heart on his sleeve as Mr. Davenant did.

What would marriage to Mary Anne do to him?

She couldn't allow herself to think of that. Pity was the privilege of the powerful; she could afford none.

Jenny took a step toward Mr. Davenant, her palms sweaty against the fabric of her skirt. "I—I know I have no right to ask you for anything, but may I ask that what I tell you remain in confidence? It is more than my life is worth should any of it be known."

Mr. Davenant straightened, looking very solemn. "On my honor."

Honor. A word men used among themselves, but never to her. "You say that now. When you hear—you may think otherwise."

"Whatever you say to me here stays between us. No other will hear. You have my word."

Words, only words, Jenny knew, but they rang out like the trumpets of an avenging army, and she found herself, strangely, reassured. Reassured and unsure.

"I hardly know where to begin," she confessed.

"At the beginning," suggested Mr. Davenant.

And so Jenny did.

"When I was five years old, Miss Mary Anne's father died." Jenny took a deep breath, striving to keep her narrative simple. "The colonel sold his holdings in Jamaica and came here, to Beckles, to manage the plantation for his sister. I believe—I believe the colonel's properties were heavily mortgaged. The luck had run against him."

"He plays deep, I understand."

"You know?"

"One hears. It isn't considered a demerit in a gentleman, any more than drinking deep."

"But you don't."

"No. I don't. Whether that makes me virtuous or merely dull, I can't tell you. But I've never had much sympathy for rakehells. It's shameful that we call manly in the wealthy what we would account beastly in the poor." He checked himself. "But you didn't summon me to hear a homily. So the colonel sought to recoup his fortunes at his sister's expense?"

Jenny nodded. "Yes, but nothing so clumsy. My fath—the colonel made a pet of Miss Mary Anne. He lavished her with gifts. He bought her gold bracelets and French dolls and—and me."

He had dressed Jenny to match the doll, in cambric and lawn, with a gold necklace like a chain about her neck, her hair scraped back and hidden beneath a lace-edged cap.

This is your maid Jenny. I brought her from Jamaica especially for you. She's yours now. I've deeded her to you.

You can do with her what you like.

She could remember the day the letter came from Barbados; how her father had come for her in the quarters, telling her that she was his best girl, his very favorite girl, and she was to accompany him on a grand adventure, and if she was very good, there would be a new dress in it for her. A new dress and gold locket.

It wasn't until they were leaving Jamaica that the reality of it had hit her, that they were leaving her mother behind and her little brother. Couldn't they come too? she'd begged her father.

And for what? He'd sold them, her father told her, indifferent.

When she'd asked where, he'd told her to mind her manners or he'd do the same to her, sell her somewhere they'd throw her into a black pit of a mine to grub for gold. Or would she prefer the fields? he'd inquired with mock civility. He could set her to hoeing sugar, out in the fields until her skin burned black and her back was bent and she looked an old crone at eighteen. There'd be no fine dresses for her, oh no, and no gold lockets either. She was nothing—except insomuch as he chose to distinguish her with his regard, and she should be bloody grateful he had.

She had cried that night into the sleeve of her new dress, bought so dear, too dear, feeling, somehow, obscurely guilty, as though she were responsible for the loss of her mother and half brother.

The locket had been taken from her upon arrival, gifted to Mary Anne. Jenny's neck had been nothing more than the case for the carrying, a method of display, like a dog with a message in its mouth. More fool she, to have been tempted and believed, if only for a moment, that such things might be for her.

She still dreamed of her mother sometimes, of the feeling of arms around her, a hand stroking her forehead, a soft voice singing her a lullaby. She dreamed of her, and woke with tears on her cheeks, longing for something she barely remembered she'd had.

"Jenny?" said Mr. Davenant.

"Dust in my throat," said Jenny huskily, grateful for the darkness. "I was to stay beside Miss Mary Anne in all things, to brush her hair and listen to her confidences and do her lessons. But what I didn't realize was that my father—the colonel—had other tasks in mind."

Mr. Davenant leaned forward intently. "Does he acknowledge himself your father?"

"Yes. When he wants something of me, he reminds me of the blood that binds us. Other times . . ." She wouldn't think of that now. Only the story she had to tell. "Miss Mary Anne adored her uncle. She was his darling. But the year she turned twelve, accidents began happening. Little things at first. The horse she was riding bolted. There was glass in her stew. A kitchen maid confessed to having dropped the glass and was sold as punishment."

Mr. Davenant lifted his head, looking at her sharply. "You said 'at first.' What happened after?"

"The colonel began to be away a great deal, for business. At least, that was what he said. Whenever he was away, something would happen. Not every time, but often enough. There was a spider in her bed. Sarah Bess got bitten changing the linen."

"What happened to her?"

"She died." Jenny's throat tightened at the memory. Sarah Bess's arm had swollen and festered, and nothing they had done, no poultice they put on it, did any good. She had died shivering and crying out, so hideously swollen that not even her closest family could bear to be near her. "The colonel—he joked that Miss Mary Anne must have a guardian angel looking after her."

Mr. Davenant shifted, leaning back, away from her. She couldn't see his face for the shadows, couldn't tell whether he believed her or not. "I see."

"We didn't see, not then. We didn't even see when the colonel started asking after her health. Miss Mary Anne had headaches, from the time she was a girl. They came on during the rains. He made it sound like—oh, like there was something wrong with her mind. But you know that already."

"Yes."

"It's not true, any of it," Jenny said fiercely. "If she's become hard, it's since then, because she's had to be. Miss Mary Anne, she never got on with the other ladies, but all the boys used to call—Will Alleyne and Johnny Clarke and—"

"My brother," finished Mr. Davenant for her.

"Yes," said Jenny gratefully. "He more than any. They climbed trees together and threw rocks and scrambled down in the gully. . . ."

"Yes, I remember it." Mr. Davenant seemed very distant, worlds away. "I was a child here too, once."

"He stole a kiss once." Slightly more than a kiss. Jenny twisted her hands together. Mary Anne had laughed and told her not to fuss. "There was nothing in it, they were only children together, but—well. But they, all of them, started staying away. We know why now, but we didn't then." All those afternoons, looking out the window for carriages that never came. Calling at other houses to a frosty, formal reception. "But that wasn't enough. It wasn't enough to discredit her. A man might be desperate enough to marry a madwoman for her fortune."

"Like me?" said Mr. Davenant wryly.

"No!" said Jenny, and was surprised by her own vehemence. "A fortune hunter. There are enough of them who come to the island. If they can't make a fortune, they won't scruple to marry it. He couldn't risk that, not when he'd come so far."

"What did he do?"

"My father"—oh, he had been her father then, had insisted on it— "came to me. He told me I was his good girl and if I did what he said, he'd see me set for life. He had—he had made a paste from the manchineel. The death apple. I was to put it in her morning chocolate. To hide the taste."

Oh, he had been clever, so clever. The chocolate was bitter, mixed with quantities of sugar to take away the bite. Mary Anne drank her chocolate every morning, from her very own porcelain chocolate pot, that had been her mother's before her. No one else used it. Only Mary Anne.

"And you told him no?" Mr. Davenant asked carefully.

"I told him yes." Jenny looked him straight in the eye, daring him to judge her. "And then I went to my mistress and told her all. She didn't believe me at first. She didn't want to believe me. She loved him, you see."

Mr. Davenant shook his head. "And who could believe that such things could happen now? It's positively Gothic. Horace Walpole, Ann Radcliffe . . ."

"My mistress doesn't read novels."

"But you do. Or how would you know the names? But never mind. You convinced her, I take it?"

"Do you think I'm making it up out of a book?" Jenny felt a creeping horror that all of this might have been for naught, the risk, the pain.

"No!" He started forward and then checked himself, yanking off his hat and plunging a hand through his hair. "I wish I did. It's . . . horrific. Unthinkable. How old were you?"

"Fifteen." It had hurt all the more because she had loved her father too. She had known that he wasn't perfect, that he used people, that he was careless in his affections, but when that careless affection had fallen on her it had felt like a holiday, like Crop Over, fiddles playing and feasting for all.

Mr. Davenant stared at the hat he held in his hands. "When I was fifteen I was at Eton, with nothing more worrisome than construing Horace. Not decisions of life and death. . . . What did you do with the chocolate?"

"We broke the chocolate pot." Jenny pressed her eyes shut, remembering the sound as it shattered, the viscous liquid seeping across the floor.

"You were very brave."

"Or foolish." His sympathy unnerved her. Jenny dug her fingernails into her palm. "We pretended it had fallen. But my father knew. He knew."

They had planned it so carefully, timing it to look like an accident, making sure a maid was there to witness it, Mary Anne shrilly berating Jenny for clumsiness, Jenny weeping and protesting that it was Mary Anne's arm that had knocked her hand, that she would never . . . They had made a great show, and all for naught.

Mr. Davenant made a movement, his eyes seeking hers in the darkness. "Did he hurt you?"

"That's not important." A lie. He'd chosen his revenge with diabolical accuracy, making her see just how vulnerable she could be, how little her mistress could protect her. Jenny mustered a shrug. "After that—he knew we knew. He had to be careful. But he also knew we couldn't say."

"Why didn't you go to someone? The constable? The council? Surely, with your mistress's lineage . . ."

"Against my father's word? The colonel is a member of the militia, a good fellow." She couldn't stop the bitterness that dripped from her words. "Miss Mary Anne would have been sent straight to the madhouse. *Poor thing, her mind is disordered.* And I— Who would believe a woman and a slave?"

"I do." Mr. Davenant seized her hands, pressing them in his. His hat fell to the floor, rolling to one side. "I believe you. Who else knows?"

"Only you." Jenny looked up at him uncertainly, her hands still in his. She didn't want to offend him by pulling away, she told herself, but it was more than that. How long had it been since anyone had touched her in anything other than anger? He had removed his gloves and his skin was warm against hers, his touch soft, gentle. It made her want to lean toward him, to rest against him. Which was madness, of course. Jenny pulled back. "Miss Mary Anne and I—we've carried this alone."

Mr. Davenant looked earnestly into her face. "You're not alone anymore. We'll see justice done. I swear it."

It wasn't justice she wanted, only safety. Jenny rubbed her hands against her sides as if she could make the print of his touch go away and, with it, the craving for more. "Then you'll do it? You'll marry her?"

"I— There must be another way."

"But you called on her," Jenny protested. "You called again and again."

"It was wrong, I know. I called, but not to see her. I came to see you." Mr. Davenant took a step back, away from her, speaking rapidly. "If there were any way I could, in honor, say yes, I would. But I cannot. Bad enough to be thought a fortune hunter. Worse to be like my father and be always looking over my wife's shoulder at—at her maid."

Jenny's fingers were ice-cold; her cheeks burning hot. She felt frozen in place, unable to move or look away. "There are some who would think that a boon."

"Do you truly think that of me?" Their eyes met and Jenny could feel the force of his longing like a physical thing. Or maybe it wasn't his longing but hers, a desire that took her by surprise, as strong as the craving for water after drought. To be cared for. To be loved.

"Would you have married her—otherwise?" Jenny asked hoarsely.

"If I had, I would have done both of us a disservice."

The silence resounded between them. Jenny could practically feel the warmth of him through the well-tailored layers of wool and linen he wore, not the master of a plantation, not her mistress's suitor, but a man, laying his heart bare to her.

Mr. Davenant cleared his throat, locking his hands behind his back. "My brother has feelings for her, I think. I'm not sure he knew he did until I returned home, but he's been like a dog in a manger these past few months. If he were to come up to scratch . . ."

"She cared for him once. Before."

"There's a play, *Much Ado About Nothing*. The hero and heroine refuse to admit their feelings for each other, so their friends make a plot. Each is told that the other is sick with love."

"I know," said Jenny, and then realized how rude she sounded. "I attended my mistress's lessons with her."

Mr. Davenant looked at her in a way that made her feel warm through. "And profited more from them, I'll wager."

"My mistress was always more at home with numbers than words." Jenny wasn't quite sure why she felt the need to defend her. "She can add a line of numbers faster than any man in the parish."

Mr. Davenant nodded. "If I were to speak to Robert, and you to Miss Beckles . . . I could tell him that she refused me on his account."

Jenny turned the notion over in her mind, testing it. "And I could tell her that you refused her on account of your brother's feelings."

"It even has the benefit of being true!" Mr. Davenant beamed at her, his golden hair rumpled across his brow, looking to her for approval.

Jenny frowned at him. "But the colonel—Master Robert—"

"Is in his pocket? I know. But I think Robert will want Beckles more. And Miss Mary Anne, of course," Mr. Davenant hastily corrected himself.

Jenny rather thought he had the right of it the first time, that Master Robert would want Beckles first and Mary Anne second. But, then, Mary Anne felt the same way about Peverills. She was not a romantic. Not like Mr. Davenant.

"It will do Robert good to come first in something," said Mr. Davenant seriously. "He minds not having Peverills. If he marries Miss Beckles . . . it will give him something to do. I doubt the colonel will have much hold over him once he has a purpose of his own."

"It might serve," Jenny said cautiously.

"It will serve," said Mr. Davenant, as though saying it could make it so. "They seem to me to be well suited. I think they might make each other very happy. So you see, we won't just be averting a tragedy, we'll be doing both of them a good turn."

There was something about the eagerness in his face that made her chest twist. "Do you always believe the best?"

"I try to." He grimaced. "There's a ridiculous character in a Voltaire satire, a Dr. Pangloss, who's always insisting that all's for the best in the best of all possible worlds, no matter what horrors befall him. I like to think I'm not so naive as that, but I do believe that one can create the good by working toward it. God gave us reason so that we might raise ourselves above our baser natures. There is no ill we cannot cure if we set our minds and our wills to it."

"No ill?"

"Well, the man-made ones. I'm not sure what we can do about tempests and plagues, but I can promise that I will do all in my power to help you."

Jenny twisted her hands in her skirt to keep from reaching for him. "To help Miss Mary Anne, you mean."

Mr. Davenant winced. "Er, yes. That is—I'm sorry."

"For what?" In the distance, Jenny could hear the sound of music. Crop Over was being celebrated with drums and dance and song in all its joyful glory, but in here the sounds were muffled, softened. She felt miles away from everything and everyone, in this dark, safe place, forgotten by the world.

"For putting you in an awkward position. Of course I'll do all I can to help your mistress. I only—I only wanted you to know why I felt that it would be wrong of me to marry her. I wouldn't want you to feel in any way constrained, or put upon, or—"

Outside, far away, people were drinking rum and blackstrap; they were dancing to the sound of the drum and the fiddle. Men and women were kissing and coupling, not because they were constrained to do so, but because the rum and music coursed through and around them, and what did they have but the pleasure of the hour?

Jenny had never had that. Between the house and the quarters, belonging to neither place, her father's weapon, Mary Anne's tool. She had never kissed a man from desire. Her skin had tingled at a touch, yes, but with loathing, not lust.

Defiantly, Jenny stepped forward and put a hand on Mr. Davenant's shoulder and pressed her lips to his, stopping his mouth with a kiss.

He was tall, even without his high hat; she had to stand on her toes to kiss him. She could feel his quick, indrawn breath, the way his muscles tensed beneath her palm. But he didn't grab at her, didn't reach for her, didn't move. He just stood, frozen, as she brushed his lips with hers.

She had expected that kissing him would prove its own antidote, that disgust would quell desire. But it wasn't. It didn't. They were soft, his lips, not hard, not wet and slobbery like the last man who had presumed to make free of her.

Gently, so gently, his hand brushed against her side, not yanking, not grabbing, a feather touch, but something about it made her lean closer, into him, the kiss deepening as he kissed her back, kissed her as though she were the most precious thing in the world, slowly and with infinite care.

She slid her hands across his back and felt the muscles quiver at her touch.

"I—" Mr. Davenant stumbled back, swallowing hard. He touched his fingers to his lips, looking dazed. "We can't do this."

She hadn't intended to, but to be told no made her, contrarily, want him all the more. "I thought you said . . ."

"What I shouldn't." Mr. Davenant held up his hands as though to keep her away, or to keep himself away from her, his face raw with regret. "If we were other than we are, I would court you with poetry and apples. I would take you walking in the gardens, and if you chose to steal a kiss, I would hardly say you nay. But we are what we are. I will not take advantage of a woman who cannot refuse."

"You aren't my master."

"Yes, but under the law—" At her look, Mr. Davenant checked himself. "All right, I won't make a brief of it. You aren't free."

"Because I'm not free, does that mean that I don't feel?" Anger seared through her, anger for everything she had lost, everything that had been stripped from her simply by the circumstances of her birth, the tint of her skin. Something less than human, lower than an animal. "Even the beasts in the fields are allowed to mate as they wish. Would you deny me even that?"

"And if there were a child?"

The words were a knife in her gut. "There won't be," she said flatly. "I cannot bear children."

It had been her father's revenge for the chocolate. He'd tossed her to a visitor, just another amenity of the house, a middle-aged man, a stranger. The potion Mary Anne had procured for her had made her so ill, so very ill. But she wouldn't, she couldn't bear a child to be another weapon for her father to use against her. An asset to be worked or sold, taken from her without a word. Better for it to end in cramps and blood than be a person to toil and suffer, a person with a claim on her heart. She'd made her choice when she was fifteen, a choice made in desperation and fear.

"You need have no fear of consequences. There won't be a child with your face living in the quarters at Beckles." Jenny looked at him defiantly, glaring down his pity. "It's a blessing. Do you think I would want to bear a child to live as I've lived?"

It would have been more impressive if her voice hadn't broken. She hated herself for giving her father that power over her, still.

"Oh, Jenny," said Mr. Davenant, and put his arms around her, not pushing, not grabbing, just holding her, so that her head fit into the curve of his shoulder, the fine wool of his jacket smooth against her cheek. "What did he do to you?"

Jenny shook her head, feeling the warmth of him through the fabric. She wouldn't let her father ruin this too. "That's past." She looked up at him, leaning forward so that her chest pressed against his, and felt a tremendous surge of power as he trembled at her touch. "It's nothing to do with this. With us. If you don't want me, just say so and I'll go."

"But—" Mr. Davenant started to speak and then stopped, struggling for the right words. "How could I know—if it were not of your own free will—that is—I shouldn't wish—"

"If you won't take my word on it, then . . . will this do?"

Jenny took his face in her hands and kissed him, pouring all her anger and frustration into the kiss, all her feelings of loss and yearning, all those years without touch, without affection, sleeping on the floor by her mistress's bed, fearing for her life, guarding her emotions.

Just once. Just once, something to burn away the pain and loss and fear. Just once, something for herself, and her father and Mary Anne be damned.

"Well?" she asked breathlessly, when their lips parted.

Mr. Davenant's lips were swollen, his cheeks flushed. He blinked at her, looking thoroughly dazed, and Jenny felt a savage delight at having deprived him of his eloquence, this man who always had something to say.

"We should—we should meet again," he said. His arms were still around her, holding her loosely. "To plot to bring your mistress and my brother together."

"Only for that?" There was a strange power in demanding what she wanted, only because she wanted it. Never mind that she had come to beg him to marry her mistress; this was her moment now, just hers. Let her go to him because she wanted to, not because her father gave her as a gift or Mary Anne dangled her as a bribe. This was hers and hers only, and she would have it.

"Is that what you wish?" he asked, his voice hoarse and raw.

"No," said Jenny, and reached for his cravat, yanking it free, so that she could see the pulse that beat in his throat. She set her lips to the spot and felt him tremble.

"No," she said again, and freed a button on his jacket, and then another, finding the linen shirt beneath, tugging it free of his breeches, sliding a hand underneath, the skin warm to her touch.

Mr. Davenant stood still as a statue, scarcely breathing. She could hear the rasp of his breath and feel the struggle it took for him to stand so still.

Jenny looked up at him, both hands pressed against his chest. "This. This is what I wish."

CHAPTER THIRTEEN

Christ Church, Barbados
May 1854

"THAT," SAID EMILY, "is pure nonsense. Marry her grandson, indeed!"

"Nonsense, is it?" Adam clasped his hands behind his back, sauntering beside her down the hallway.

"Don't be absurd." Emily picked up her pace. "I'm not nearly aristocratic enough to be a suitable bride for Beckles. You've seen the way Mrs. Davenant talks about Grandfather. And being a parson's daughter seems to be nearly as bad!"

"If you say so," said Adam, undeterred. "As your nearest available male relation, I assume I'll have the honor of walking you down the aisle in the absence of your father?"

"There will be no—oh, never mind. I need to change. Mrs. Davenant has guests for tea."

Adam raised his brows. "Does she? And I assume you're to pour? No, no, you needn't say anything."

And off he went, whistling, leaving Emily wishing she didn't feel the need to be the more mature party. But then, with Adam, she had always had to be the more mature party. *Don't mind Adam.* That had been the refrain throughout her childhood. *It's only Adam.*

It was only Adam, Emily told herself firmly, as she slammed into her own room, submitting to the ministrations of the maid, Katy, who had appeared, as if by magic, to help her out of her habit. Only Adam making trouble, most likely because he was worried about Laura but didn't want to admit it, because heaven forbid he reveal any warmer emotion or human concern.

Yes, that was all. Adam was guilty and cross and making up for it by making trouble. Perhaps he was just a bit offended that he wasn't included in those endless visits by the neighbors. At home, it was Adam, as heir, who was the center of every occasion, while Emily, the poor cousin, sat at the corner of the room in a mended frock.

Here, she was the owner of Peverills, a person of consequence, where Adam was merely a junior partner in a shipping concern. The landowners she had met, Emily had observed, viewed the world very differently. Ships and shares were all very well, but they accounted worth in land, in acres cultivated and crops harvested. Anything else was mere flimflam, and all the Fentys' ships and all the Fentys' ventures couldn't make them gentlemen.

There. Emily splashed water over her face, blotting it with a towel. That disposed of Adam and his insinuations. The idea that Mrs. Davenant was grooming her to marry her grandson . . . It was positively medieval.

Emily stepped into the dress Katy had put out for her, holding out her arms so that the maid could slide the sleeves on. She'd resisted at first, but Mrs. Davenant had remonstrated with her. It unsettled the staff to have her doing for herself what they were meant to do for her. So Emily let herself be dressed like a doll rather than offend Katy or any of the others who accomplished tasks she might easily have done herself.

Katy pressed Emily into a chair and she sat so that the maid might do her hair, twisting it out of all recognition, into a hairstyle far from the simple Psyche knot she would have preferred. Her front hair was bunched into curls on either side of her face, the back elaborately looped and braided and secured by an enameled comb that hadn't come from her own jewelry box.

The dress on her back, the comb in her hair. Neither hers.

Emily looked at herself in the mirror and scarcely knew herself. The dress was of brightly flowered cotton, the wide pagoda sleeves and each tier of the skirt edged with lace to match the fichu that crossed her shoulders, everything flounced and frilled, the material itself painfully impractical, a world away from the sensible, dark stuffs she favored.

More practical for the climate, Emily told herself. That was all. She would swelter in gray twill or black bombazine. It was very kind of Mrs. Davenant to have discovered some old stuffs and made them over for her. All part of the tradition of Creole hospitality, she had been assured; anything for one's guests.

The woman in the mirror wasn't beautiful: her nose was snub and her chin was too strong. But the curls and flowered flounces leant her a sort of determined prettiness.

She looked, in fact, rather like a younger version of Mrs. Davenant.

"Ouch." Emily had, without realizing it, pulled back, leaving a lock of her hair still twisted around Katy's finger. Wincing, she rubbed her aching scalp. "No, it wasn't your fault. It's quite all right, Katy, I've prinked enough."

She smiled reassuringly at the maid, toying for a moment with the idea of ripping out the comb, shimmying out of the dress, and going downstairs as herself, in her own clothes, with her hair pulled into a knot at the back. But what would that accomplish? Katy would only be hurt by it and Mrs. Davenant would have words for her—not for Emily but for Katy.

She closed her hand around the gold of her locket, the one item on her person that was hers, truly hers. It looked wrong on the woman in the mirror, out of place. Which was silly. She was the woman in the mirror. A bit of fabric and a few curls couldn't change the essence of herself.

Not immediately, at any rate. But over time . . .

Emily breathed in deeply, feeling the press of the stays against her ribs. Her own stays, at least. She wasn't going to be cinched into nothingness, even if she was laden down with lace and petticoats. The dress that looked so deceptively light and airy was heavy with the layers of horsehair that held out the skirt, holding her to a slow and stately gait.

I assume I'll have the honor of walking you down the aisle . . .

Emily ignored the gold earrings Katy had set out for her. She wouldn't be decked like a hog for the feast. She wasn't going to the slaughter, thank you very much, whatever Adam might say. Or to the altar.

But it was curious that Mrs. Davenant hadn't once said a word to her about selling Peverills.

"There you are." Mrs. Davenant was already ensconced in her favorite chair in the great room, beneath the portrait of her younger self. Another chair, notably shorter in the seat, was occupied by a woman of late middle age in a truly alarming cap. "Bertha, this is our guest, the new owner of Peverills. Miss Dawson, make your curtsy to my cousin Mrs. Poole. Miss Dawson, you'll pour."

Emily made her curtsy as directed and took up her place beside the tea table. She knew the contours of the teapot by now, the shape of the sugar tongs in her hand. Mrs. Davenant had made a practice of asking her to pour.

Emily wasn't unaccustomed to it; Aunt Millicent liked her to pour at parties, a task given to the least important. But here, in this intimate setting, it was the sort of task that might be taken by the daughter of the house.

Or the granddaughter.

Oh, bother Adam. Emily leaned forward, twitching the lace on her sleeves out of the way. "Do you take sugar, Mrs. Poole?"

Mrs. Poole tittered. "That's not a question you want to ask here, Miss Dawson! We all live by sugar."

"We live by it. That doesn't mean we need to be preserved in it," retorted Mrs. Davenant. "Plenty of sugar for Mrs. Poole. She can't abide anything that isn't sweet as sin."

"Don't be silly, Mary Anne," said Mrs. Poole with dignity. "Just a tiny bit. Well—a tiny bit more than that. So. You're the mistress of Peverills."

She stared at Emily as though trying to read her heritage in her face. Her own was as wrinkled as a windfall apple, and alive with frank curiosity.

"My grandfather left it to me," said Emily, as she had said a dozen times before. "Perhaps you knew him? His name was Jonathan Fenty."

Mrs. Poole didn't seem the least bit surprised. Emily had no doubt everyone in the vicinity knew not only her parentage but the width of her bust and the mole on her left shoulder.

Mrs. Poole nodded vigorously, setting her ribbons bobbing. "Oh yes, I remember your grandfather. It was the talk of the parish when he married that widow."

"My grandmother," Emily reminded her.

"Yes, yes. She'd been married to an Irishman. *Not* a papist. Goodness, but that man could talk. Old, though. When she took up with—well." Mrs. Poole took refuge in a coughing fit as Mrs. Davenant delivered a sharp kick to her ankle.

"Really, Bertha," said Mrs. Davenant. "Haven't you more recent scandals to savor?"

"Was it a scandal, then?" asked Emily doubtfully. Her grandfather she could see having a wild past; her grandmother . . . no.

"Not a scandal precisely," admitted Mrs. Poole reluctantly. "But there was such a short time between the old man dying and their marriage."

"Three years. Mr. Boland died just before my Edward was born. They were with us that Christmas before Mr. Boland died. . . ." Mrs. Davenant's diamond earrings swayed as she set her cup down abruptly. "They hardly married over the funeral meats."

Mrs. Poole took a gulp of her tea. "But weren't they married during the hurricane in the summer of thirteen?"

"No," said Mrs. Davenant with exaggerated patience. "That was that Weekes boy."

"Goodness, it was, wasn't it? Such a horror, the windows smashing during the ceremony. We all thought the roof was going to come off right over our heads." Mrs. Poole shivered with delighted horror. "But it was something dramatic. . . . I remember now. Fenty was wed right after the troubles. Sixteen. That was it."

"Eighteen sixteen?" Emily paused with her teacup halfway to her lips.

"What a year that was," said Mrs. Poole reminiscently. "Who knew when we sat down to supper that we would be fearing for our lives before the sun was down?"

"It must have been someone else you're thinking of," said Emily, looking to Mrs. Davenant. "My grandparents were married sooner than that, I think."

"You're confused again, Bertha," said Mrs. Davenant with grim satisfaction. "Fenty was married from Antigua."

"I know that," said Mrs. Poole comfortably. "Did I say otherwise? It was in the midst of the troubles that he left. That's a time none of us will easily forget, eh, Mary Anne? We lost most of our crop. The house was spared, but, heavens, I'll never forget the stench of that sugar burning and my Horace running out with his uniform only half on. That our own people could do that to us! Base ingratitude, that's what I say."

"Not everyone's people," said Mrs. Davenant with a tight smile. "There's no call to bring up unpleasant memories, Bertha. It's all over and done with long ago."

Ignoring her, Mrs. Poole turned to Emily. "The trials! We were all on tenterhooks until they discovered the ringleaders. There was a renegade named Busy or Barney or . . ."

"Bussa," corrected Mrs. Davenant.

"But some said he was only a scapegoat and the real culprit was a white man. Can you imagine that? Of course, one never knows what to expect from a Redleg, but—"

"More cake, Bertha?" said Mrs. Davenant loudly, and all but shoved a fairy cake into Mrs. Poole's mouth.

Emily set her teacup down. "You don't mean my grandfather, surely?"

Mrs. Davenant looked quellingly at Mrs. Poole. "I understand that Mr. Fenty was a pillar of Bristol society and a credit to the island that bore him."

It would have been more convincing if she hadn't looked as though she were chewing a mouthful of nettles as she said it.

"What a story it made, though!" said Mrs. Poole. "Because who would arrange for a rising on the very eve of his wedding unless the wedding was planned as a distraction to divert people from the rising? And then away on the wedding journey right after . . ."

"Really, Bertha. Trying to untangle your thoughts is like trying to make sense of my work basket after the cat's been at it. Did you hear the rumor that the militia planned the whole rising that they might have the sport of quelling it?"

Mrs. Poole rose like a fish to the fly. "Really?"

"No." Mrs. Davenant snorted, and Emily had to bite her lip to hide her grin. "But you would have believed it, wouldn't you?"

Mrs. Poole drew herself up, bows quivering. "It's not at all the same. No offense to your grandfather, my dear," she added to Emily. "So very long ago, after all . . ."

"Very," agreed Emily, nodding reassuringly to Mrs. Davenant. "More tea?"

Mrs. Poole was clearly muddled in her thinking, Emily decided, as she went through the familiar motions of pouring and portioning out sugar.

The rising might have happened in 1816, but her grandparents' marriage had to have been at least two years earlier, in 1814. Her mother, she knew, had been born in 1815, Uncle Archibald in 1817. It was impossible to imagine her grandmother, with her plain, dark dresses and uncompromising white caps, anticipating the marriage, even for such a charming rogue as her grandfather might have been. Emily had no doubt it was another wedding Mrs. Poole was thinking of, just as she'd confused a rising with a hurricane.

As for her grandfather being involved in a slave rising . . . She just couldn't see it, not at all. Her mother, yes. Her mother would have reveled in organizing secret meetings and striking back against a corrupt system. Her grandfather, no. It was impossible to imagine him as a latter-day Robin Hood. He wasn't nearly civic-minded enough, and a green jerkin would have made him look bilious.

Her grandfather. What would he think of all this? Emily was beginning to feel that he had left her woefully unprepared, that he ought to have left her, at least, a manuscript or a journal detailing the events of his departure from Barbados rather than a locket with a miniature of her mother and a deed to a plantation, both of which were very well in their way but told her nothing of what she was meant to do.

Get on with it. That's what her grandfather would tell her to do. Never mind the events of forty years past.

It was the present that mattered, and, in the present, Peverills was still lying fallow and untended.

When Mrs. Poole finally took her leave, and Mrs. Davenant made to rise, Emily seized the opportunity to say, "May I trouble you for a moment? I had wondered whether we might discuss the arrangements for a lease."

Mrs. Davenant took her time getting to her feet, shaking the creases out of the rich stuff of her skirt. "A lease."

"The southwest corner," said Emily, hoping she had it right. "We had discussed . . ."

"Yes, yes, I know. Heavens, child, what put that in your head now?"

It wasn't precisely the response Emily had been expecting. "We've been here for some time, and—"

Mrs. Davenant cut her off. "There'll be time enough for that once you know which piece of land I mean! I wouldn't want you to make a poor decision out of ignorance."

"I should think an ignorant decision would be very much in your favor," said Emily, surprised into honesty.

Mrs. Davenant gave a bark of a laugh and rose from the chair, walking briskly toward the stair. "You're too wide-awake for that. We'll find time to come to terms soon enough. Now, if you'll excuse me, I have accounts to see to. Go write a letter, take a turn about the garden. I'm sure you can find something to occupy you."

"The ledgers, perhaps?" Emily called after her. Mrs. Davenant stopped, standing very still. "You promised me I might look at the old ledgers from Peverills."

"They're about somewhere," said Mrs. Davenant vaguely. Emily thought of Mrs. Davenant's study, every paper in its place, the ledgers neatly stacked by date. "I'll hunt them up for you when I have time. This is our busiest season, with the cane being harvested and boiled. There's no time for trivia."

But there was time, thought Emily, to entertain guests every day. There was time for George to spend an hour each morning riding with her.

"I don't mind finding them myself," said Emily. "I wouldn't want to put you to any trouble."

"No one goes in my book room without me. If you want occupation, go for a walk." Mrs. Davenant stalked off toward the stairs in a rustle of horsehair. "Where's that useless grandson of mine? Make him show you the rose arbor."

The last thing Emily wanted was a romantic stroll in the rose arbor with George Davenant.

Not that there was anything wrong with George. He was quite pleasant, really. But then, so was blancmange, and she had no desire to marry it. She suspected George had as little desire to marry her, but she had little faith in his resolve. His will was subject to his grandmother's. If Mrs. Davenant told him to propose, he would.

George claimed that his grandmother had arranged his father's marriage to round out the corner of their lands. If she was willing to sacrifice a son for the sake of a field, Mrs. Davenant would hardly balk at bartering a mere grandson for Peverills.

And what was it about Peverills that Mrs. Davenant didn't want her to see? She had given her a glimpse of a ledger—and then taken it away again. Her rides with George had taken her within sight of Peverills but no farther.

That first day, the day Dr. Braithwaite had taken them to see Peverills—what was it that had sent George riding out to intercept them? Curiosity about strangers? Or something more?

The next morning, Emily sent a note to George, making her excuses. Mrs. Davenant might question her, but George wouldn't, especially if she made vague references to wishing to rest. She lurked in her room until such time as one could reasonably expect the others to have left, and then donned her habit and made for the stables.

If her groom Jonah thought it was odd that she wanted to ride out without Mr. Davenant, he didn't say.

"We're riding to Peverills," Emily told him, in a tone that brooked no disagreements, and so they did, past the Old Mill, through a field that might once have held cane but now held only weeds, to the great ruined house at the heart of the plantation.

They passed collections of small houses with untended gardens; a mill and a boiling house from which the scent of sugar had long since gone; stables where no horses whinnied. It was, in a way, worse than the great house itself. That, at least, was an honest ruin, destroyed by fire. These other buildings had been left to rot as they would.

What had happened to all the people who had once worked here? It seemed so strange that everything had just been left, untouched, like Sleeping Beauty's castle in a circle of thorns.

There was no lady in this tower, just a child's doll lying facedown, warped with wind and weather. She knew what it was; she had seen it before. But it still gave Emily a moment's shock, and she had to still the impulse to swing down from her mount and go to the abandoned baby.

Not a baby. Painted wood, she reminded herself. The plaything of a child nearly half a century ago.

Emily turned to Jonah. "Aren't there meant to be other houses on the property? Mr. Davenant said the bookkeeper's house was still standing."

"Time to be getting back," Jonah suggested, "before the sun gets hotter."

"But we've only just got here." Emily looked at him curiously. "Where *is* the bookkeeper's house?"

"Emily!" Hoofbeats broke the silence, sending bits of gravel flying up as George, face flushed, galloped up the drive to her. "If you meant to ride, why didn't you tell me?"

She couldn't very well say that it was because she hadn't wanted him to come with her. "Did you see me in the spyglass?"

"My grandmother did." At Emily's look of indignation, he added, "She was concerned about you. You don't know the country."

"I have a groom," said Emily, indicating Jonah. "And I should think I could visit my own house if I want to!"

"Yes, but—" George glanced sideways at the groom and then said stiffly, "I apologize if I intruded."

It was impossible to be angry with George, especially when one knew he was only following instructions. "Oh, don't be like that. You make me feel like a tartar. It was ill done to take out my bad temper on you."

"Is something the matter?"

A day ago, she would have found his concern touching, would have welcomed his friendship. Now—Emily didn't know what to think of him. She didn't know whether to be annoyed at Adam for the new constraint she felt in George's company or thankful to him for alerting her to a danger she hadn't realized was there.

"If there is anything I might do . . ." George said diffidently.

She couldn't very well tell him she was alarmed at the prospect of being tied to him in holy matrimony. Instead, she looked out at the ruins of Peverills, the jagged outline of the roof, the empty windows, the fields that stretched on and on, withered and dry. "Why *did* your grandfather sell Peverills?"

"Ah," said George. He toyed with the brim of his hat. "He didn't."

"I saw the deed," said Emily, beginning to be annoyed. "It was all quite properly conveyed."

"I didn't mean to question your grandfather's title," said George. "What I meant was that it wasn't my grandfather's to sell. He didn't own Peverills."

"But I thought . . . your grandmother said . . ." What had they said really? That Peverills had belonged to the Davenant family? "What about those portraits in the great room with the pictures of Peverills and Beckles?"

"Ah yes. Those. I suppose you might say that was wishful thinking on my grandfather's part. Or flattery on the part of the painter. My grandfather, he was the younger brother."

This was not at all what she had been led to believe.

"Then Peverills . . ." Emily looked inquisitively at George.

"Peverills belonged to my uncle Charles. He was the one who held it—and he was the one who sold it."

CHAPTER FOURTEEN

Christ Church, Barbados
Autumn 1812

ROBERT DAVENANT AND Mary Anne Beckles were married on a rainy afternoon in October.

The groom wore his militia uniform. The bride wore all her diamonds, cramming them onto her fingers and into her hair, as if to shout to society what they might have had and what they had lost. Beneath the blaze of jewels and the shimmer of silver-spangled gauze over silk, one could scarcely see the bride herself on her uncle's arm.

Standing up in front by his brother, Charles knew the gossips were watching him, searching for signs that he minded his brother snatching the heiress out from under his nose, and could imagine what they would say, that he was putting up a good front.

But it wasn't a front, not at all. As the colonel placed Mary Anne's hand in Robert's, Charles wanted to pump every man in the room by the hand, clap his brother on the back, hug his new sister. This was going to be the making of Robert, he was sure. Mary Anne was freed of the threat that hung over her, and Charles . . .

He didn't dare look at the back of the room, to where Jenny stood with the other upper servants. To do so, he knew, would be to betray himself. The sight of her made him light like a Roman candle, blazing with joy.

They met sometimes in the Old Mill, at other times in the unused overseer's house at Peverills. Charles would need, he knew, to hire a proper overseer to take Robert's place now that Robert was gone to Beckles, but in the meantime the overseer's house sat empty, a perfect place for a tryst. Robert and Mary Anne's courtship had afforded plentiful opportunities; as the courting couple strolled in the gardens at Peverills, Mary Anne had sent her maid away, leaving her free to steal an hour here, an hour there.

Charles longed to bring Jenny gifts, to write her poetry, but anything he gave might be discovered. So he gathered flowers from the fields, bringing her posies of hibiscus and peacock flowers, frangipani and bird-of-paradise. But never oleander. He remembered her distaste for it as he remembered everything she told him, every preference she voiced or, more commonly, indicated with only the slightest gesture.

They walked together, well away from the house and the fields, choosing those rare bits of wilderness where they knew they might not be seen—*might* being the heart of it. He found himself rediscovering the forgotten haunts of his childhood, the caves and gullies in which he had played, so beautiful in memory, even more beautiful now, like another Eden in which they were the only man and the only woman.

But they weren't. There was, inevitably, the moment of parting, when Jenny would disappear again behind her mistress and Charles return to his books.

Charles began to daydream of a world where they might walk together openly. And why not? Once Mary Anne was safely married, once they came back from their wedding trip, why wouldn't Mary Anne be willing to part with her old servant? She would be a married woman, in charge of her own household.

"And what will you do then?" Jenny mocked, when Charles shared his thoughts one afternoon as they lay together in the overseer's house, in a proper bed for once. It was a risk, but Mary Anne was riding with Robert and would, they knew, be some time. "Will you buy me a house in Bridgetown and a pianoforte to play?"

"Would you like a house in Bridgetown?" Charles asked seriously. "I would find a way to buy you one if that was what you wanted, although I would much liefer keep you at Peverills with me."

Jenny raised herself up on one arm, looking down into his face. "As your housekeeper?"

"If you want to call it that." Charles looked up at her, into her eyes, knowing he sounded a fool, but not wanting to lie to her, even by omission. Very quietly, he said, "There are no laws prohibiting our marriage."

Jenny lay back down, resting her head on his chest. "Only because no one has attempted it."

She was right, he knew. It might not be explicitly prohibited by law, but that was only because everyone had, so far, obeyed the unspoken rules. What minister would marry them? And if one did, what would the council do in response? He would find himself embroiled in a prolonged legal wrangle, and Charles was lawyer enough to know the toll that would take, not just on him and Jenny, but on everyone connected to them.

"Fair enough," admitted Charles with a sigh. He stroked her dark hair, the texture and length of it familiar beneath his fingers. "We wouldn't be the first to live together as man and wife without benefit of clergy. When George Ricketts was governor, when I was a child, he had a colored mistress who lived with him at Pilgrim and acted in almost all ways as his wife."

Jenny stirred against his chest. "Almost all?"

"She wasn't permitted to preside at his table." There had been a scandal, he recalled. The governor's mistress had overstepped her place. Ricketts had been reprimanded, perhaps recalled. Perhaps it hadn't been the best example. Charles shifted, settling Jenny more firmly into the crook of his arm. "But I'm not the governor of Barbados. I'm just a private citizen, free to love as I please."

"Don't you mean free to live as you please?" The words were casual but he could feel the tension in her body as she lifted her head to look at him.

"No," said Charles. "Love."

Jenny sat up abruptly, driving an elbow into his chest in her haste. "You needn't make me any pretty vows."

"Ouch," said Charles. "You needn't pummel me into honesty. If I were making you pretty vows, I would do it in rhyme, at least. But this—this is true. Or hadn't you realized that by now?"

"I— This is, what do they call it? Cupboard love." Jenny yanked at her shift, pulling it back over her head. "It will fade in time."

"Not for me." Charles struggled up to a sitting position, propping his back against the headboard. "Does that scare you so? I'll leave you be if that's what you would like."

"No." Jenny moved to sit beside him, her skirts drifting around her as she took his face in her hands. "Don't swear to anything you'll regret later. This—this has been—"

"Yes?" Charles couldn't help but smirk a little.

Jenny swatted him lightly on the shoulder. "You know what this has been. But anything more . . . You have your future to think of."

"Is it so mad that I want my future to be with you?" Charles could feel himself weighing his words very carefully. Go lightly over rough country, his father always used to say, his father, who was so wrong about some things and so right about others. He looked at Jenny, at the familiar lines of her face, the curves of her lips, the tension in her shoulders. "They never loved who loved not at first sight, the poet says, but I never believed it. I still don't. It's not first sight that made me love you, but everything that came after. Getting to know you, getting to know your mind . . ."

"My mind?" repeated Jenny.

Charles wouldn't allow himself to be distracted. "Yes, your mind. Your clever, wary, honest mind. You have a presence of mind I can only envy. If I had half your strength of character . . ."

"Yes?"

"I would tell the world be damned and ask you to run away with me."

She had drawn into herself again, as she always did. She smiled down at him, amused and remote. "And be hunted as a felon? You would be, you know, for defrauding my mistress of her lawful property."

"By Nature's law, you're no more her property than you are mine."

Jenny touched his cheek, very lightly. "That may be, but it's the council's law that rules in Barbados, not Nature's."

Charles refused to be deterred. "Robert and Mary Anne seem well pleased with each other. When they return from their wedding journey . . ."

"Do you think Mary Anne would truly let me go?"

"I have high hopes for the honeymoon," said Charles seriously. "No, don't laugh at me. . . . Or do. I like to hear you laugh."

"You might be right, at that." Jenny looked up at him thoughtfully. "There's a powerful attraction between them. I've seen the state of her linen when they come back from their walks."

"Her linen? Oh. I'm not sure I want to know the details. But don't you see? If they're content—what need does Mary Anne have for you? You stood by her. You saved her life. But the threat is gone now. Almost gone," he amended, as Jenny opened her mouth to protest. "As soon as the vows are said, your father will be away to Jamaica. Mary Anne will be married, mistress of her own house in truth. Would it be so strange for her to free you?"

"Not if you were to argue my case," said Jenny, lifting her brows at him. She paused a moment, and then said, in a very different voice, "And if she were to do so?"

"Then you could come to Peverills and live with me and be my love. Not that you aren't my love either way. You're my love whether you live with me or not. But it would be nice, wouldn't it?"

"Yes," said Jenny.

Just that one word, *yes*. But Charles knew how much it cost her and how much it meant, and in the weeks that followed, the long weeks without Jenny, when Mary Anne and Robert swept off to Antigua on their wedding journey, and Jenny with them, he would remember that *yes* and hold it to him.

It was six weeks before Jenny returned from Antigua, six long weeks, in which Charles applied himself to his neglected duties, interviewed overseers, and attempted to make sense of the accounts Jonathan Fenty set before him.

Charles called at Beckles as soon as was permissible upon his brother's return, and found Mary Anne in the great room, with Jenny behind her.

"Sister," said Charles warmly, doing his best not to look past her, at Jenny. Something was wrong, he could tell. He could read it in the tension in Jenny's shoulders, the closed expression on her face. He pressed a dutiful kiss to Mary Anne's cheek. "Welcome home. You are well, I trust?"

Mary Anne disentangled herself from Charles's embrace. Without preamble, she said, "Your brother has made my uncle a gift of my money." Snapping her fingers, she said, "Jenny! See tea and cakes are brought for Master Charles."

"Yes, Miss Mary Anne." Jenny turned away without meeting Charles's eyes.

"Did you have a pleasant journey?" Charles attempted. This was not at all how he had imagined this meeting.

"Oh, well enough," said Mary Anne. Instead of sitting, she paced back and forth, forcing Charles, out of politeness, to stand as well. "Until your brother decided to make himself free of my money."

"His money now," said Charles, and found himself on the receiving end of a basilisk glare. "As a matter of law, when you married—"

"Yes, I know all that. I asked him to have the money conveyed so that it might remain separate for my use but he said there'd be no need of that, as we were of one mind. . . . One mind, indeed!"

"One body under the law," suggested Charles helpfully. He held up his hands at her frown. "And you do have one object. To make Beckles prosper."

"Oh, I have no objection to Robert using my money to make improvements on my land. His ideas are sound. But how, pray tell, does making my uncle a gift of my money improve our situation?"

Charles was spared the task of replying by the arrival of the cakes. A procession arrived from the kitchen, bearing platters of iced dainties, comfits in sugar, and the tea things, the silver slop bowl polished to a sheen that hurt his eyes. Mary Anne, it seemed, had taken up housekeeping with a vengeance.

Jenny quietly directed the disposition of the tea things, making no sign to Charles.

"You might as well sit down," said Mary Anne ungraciously. "Sugar?"

"Please." He didn't like sweet tea, but it bought him time. When Mary Anne had plunked the cup onto the saucer and sloshed tea into it, thrusting the whole into his hand, Charles asked, "Has your uncle gone, then?"

"Oh yes, back to Jamaica, with enough in his pocket to make this a very profitable interlude, indeed."

"I should think you would be glad to see the back of him," Charles ventured. The tension between them was hardly a secret; that had been there for anyone to see.

"I want to see him poor and starving," said Mary Anne crossly. "I want to see his clothes in tatters and his face covered with sores. Not wealthy and happy in Jamaica!"

"He did make a good job of running Beckles."

"He was stealing from me for years," said Mary Anne flatly.

"Was he?" Despite his best efforts, Charles found himself looking to Jenny, standing like a statue behind her mistress's chair.

"You can say anything in front of Jenny, you know that," said Mary Anne impatiently. "Jenny is my other self. I have no secrets from her."

"Yes, of course," said Charles. He wasn't sure whether to be grateful for her misapprehension or alarmed at the sentiment. "Are you certain? About the money, I mean."

"I can add two and two. I tried to show your brother the books, but he refused to listen. He told me not to enact him a Cheltenham tragedy."

"Perhaps if I have Jonathan look at them . . ."

"Your pet Redleg?"

"He's a very good bookkeeper." Charles didn't want to argue with her. "Can't you talk to Robert about it? I'm sure, once he sees the evidence with his own eyes . . ."

"You talk to him," flung back Mary Anne. "I've talked and talked until I'm short of breath. And when I ask him about my lands—mine!—he tells me not to trouble myself. Does he expect me to sit on a cushion and drink ratafia all day?"

"Er . . ." That was, Charles suspected, exactly what Robert expected of a wife.

"He wants me out of the way. Oh, not like that," she said impatiently, as Charles stared. "He wants me to be a proper Creole wife and stay indoors, with servants to thread my needle and fan my feet. Beckles is my home. *Mine*."

"What's yours?" Robert appeared in the door, fresh from the fields, his stock limp with sweat and his crop still in his hand.

"Nothing, apparently," said Mary Anne, looking crossly at Charles. He wasn't sure what she had expected of him. The law was quite clear on the subject of marital property.

Robert frowned at Charles. "Here so soon, brother?"

"I came to welcome you back home," said Charles, since some sort of explanation seemed to be required. "My new sister kindly entertained me in your absence."

"I'm sure she did." Robert's tone was so acid that Charles had to resist the urge to glance behind him, to see if he'd suddenly grown horns or a tail.

"*If* you will pardon me? Charles." Mary Anne nodded graciously at him and glared at her husband before sweeping from the room, Jenny following behind her.

Charles felt as bewildered as though he'd been too much in the sun. What the blazes had happened in Antigua?

"Did you have a pleasant wedding journey?" Charles ventured.

"What, are you thinking it ought to have been you?" Robert demanded. "My *wife* does."

"You're mistaken," said Charles, unsettled by the unexpected attack. "Her heart was always yours."

Robert flicked the tip of his crop against his boot. "A strange way she has of showing it. All I get are complaints."

"She has a blunt tongue."

"What do you know of her tongue?"

Charles winced. "Nothing like that. I hold your wife in the greatest respect."

"As she does you. She throws you up to me. Did you know that?" Robert adopted a piercing falsetto. " '*If I'd married Charles* . . .' I'm sick of it. I wish she'd married you and had done."

"No, you don't. Not truly." Charles looked at his brother in confusion, wondering how they had come to this in just over a month. They'd seemed well enough pleased with each other when they married; more than pleased, if Jenny was right. "Besides, she wouldn't have had me. She only does it to goad you."

"And how would you know? Oh yes, all those cozy picnics together. She's been cutting up rough because I had the gall to make a gift of money to her uncle. Her own uncle!"

Charles looked closely at Robert. "I understand they don't get on."

"Ingratitude, I call it. He ran this estate for her for well over a decade. Why shouldn't I back him in a little venture? He's a warm man; we'll see the money back. And even if we don't, he's earned it, that's what I say."

"Have you ever asked her why she dislikes her uncle so?"

"No, but you clearly know all about it." Robert looked at his brother with raw dislike.

"Only what I've heard from others," said Charles, which was true as far as it went. Everything he knew came from Jenny's lips, not Mary Anne's. "Think of it. How would you feel if I went about telling people you weren't right in the head?"

"Who's to say that he was lying?" As if realizing he had gone too far, Robert shrugged, dropping the crop on the floor and kicking it away. "She's deuced difficult. She seems to think I should apply to her for permission to use *my* money. What do you say to that?"

"Legally, it certainly is your money. But hadn't you thought . . ." At the expression on Robert's face, Charles gave up the effort.

"If I wanted your advice," said Robert, "I would ask you for it."

There was nothing for Charles to do but take his leave. Jenny met him at the door with his hat and gloves.

"Not exactly billing and cooing," he said softly.

"The Old Mill?" said Jenny in an undertone, as she held his gloves out to him, one by one.

Charles forced himself to concentrate on pulling on the gloves, finger by finger. "I'll be there."

Jenny offered him his hat, head bowed. "Sir."

Behind her, Charles could see Robert, watching.

He rode to Peverills before setting back again to the Old Mill. Just in case anyone might be watching.

The Old Mill was as they'd left it. A little damper, perhaps, after a season of rains, a little greener about the edges, but with the same smells of dirt and loam, bringing back a host of memories. Jenny kissing him for the first time. Lying together. Talking together. That strange pull of flesh to flesh, mind to mind.

She'd been so distant today at Beckles. Charles had a moment's fear that time had dampened her ardor, that she might no longer feel as he did.

But any doubts were quelled when she appeared in the doorway of the mill.

Charles opened his mouth to say something, he wasn't even quite sure what, but he never got the words out. He wasn't sure who moved first, or if they both moved at once, but they came together like raindrops on a windowsill, running together so they blended into one, indistinguishable. She held his face in her hands and kissed him until his lips were raw and the air whistled in his ears. Their clothing only got in the way; piece by piece, rapidly, clumsily, they struggled out of their clothes, pulling each other closer, coming together with more passion than finesse, her cry and his shout echoing together in the damp, dark space.

They made a nest of their discarded garments, snuggling together beneath the breadths of Jenny's chemise. A button from Charles's waistcoat was biting into his back. He shifted, bringing Jenny with him, saying ruefully, "I'd meant to welcome you back in a better way than that."

"I'm not complaining," she said, and rested her head against his chest, just beneath his chin. So softly that he could barely hear it, she said, "I missed you."

"I missed you too," he murmured into her hair. Relief and joy washed through him and he hugged her close, as close as he dared. "I missed you so."

Jenny's fingers traced a pattern in the fine, fair hair on his chest. "When I was away . . . I wondered if I had imagined it all. This."

"No," said Charles fervently. He had no more words for it than that. "No."

"All the time we were in Antigua," she said, not looking at him, "I told myself it was over. That I would come back and you would be a stranger again. That I would see you and feel—nothing."

"If this was nothing, it was a very fine nothing, indeed. Jenny?" All he could see was the parting of her hair. Charles touched her cheek with his finger, trying to think how to put into words what he felt, needing her to know it meant more than that. "I've lain with women before. I've even fancied myself in love. But none of them were anything to this. It's like trying to compare the light of a candle to the strength of the sun. There's no comparison. The one might warm one's hands awhile, but this—this could burn down cities."

Jenny lifted her head to look at him, her eyes troubled. "Isn't that sort of fire dangerous?"

"Some light the fields to make the crops grow," said Charles, running his fingers lightly down her arm. "And there's always the phoenix, emerging triumphant from the flames, born anew with every blaze."

Jenny gave him one of her skeptical looks. He had missed those looks. "The phoenix is a myth."

The little room was very still. Quietly, Charles said, "But this isn't. Is it?"

"No," Jenny admitted. "But how are we to go on like this? Sooner or later, someone will discover us. And Mary Anne—she'll mind. She'll mind badly. She thinks—she thinks if you'd married her, it would all have been better."

"If I had married her, we would have made each other miserable." Scooting up a bit, using the wall as a headboard, Charles asked, "What happened in Antigua?"

Jenny sighed and leaned her head back against the rough stuff of the wall. "It was the colonel. We ought to have known he wouldn't go away without finding some way to spoil things. He went up to Master Robert at the wedding breakfast and told him he'd seen you and Miss Mary Anne together. Intimately together. He said that was why she was so eager to wed."

"But then wouldn't she have wed me? If that had been the case, one imagines the lady's guardian would have something to say about it," said Charles. "Those are the occasions that call for a special license and a hastily planned wedding breakfast."

"The colonel will have found a way to explain it," said Jenny wearily. "That you had a previous commitment or something of that sort."

"I do, as it happens," said Charles, taking her hand. "But that's beside the point."

Jenny cast him a reproving look. "When Master Robert saw us talking at the door, he probably thought I was arranging an assignation for my mistress."

"But wait," said Charles, trying to figure out how they'd got from the promise of the rainy months to this. "Didn't you say the two of them had been—er, anticipating the wedding night?"

"With vigor," said Jenny, smiling a little at Charles's discomfiture. "Oh, he enjoys her appetites well enough. And she enjoys his. But once my father got at him, he started wondering who else might be sharing in those appetites. He threw all those old rumors back at her."

"The ones about her insatiable appetites?" Charles recalled a long-ago discussion with his brother on the balcony at Rosehall. "That's why she wouldn't ride with a groom, only with you."

Jenny nodded. "It's my father's work. It has his signature on it. Poor Mistress Mary. Every time they fight, they end up in bed. And every time they end up in bed, Master Robert invariably ends by accusing her of sharing her charms with others. Mostly you," she added.

"My charms are yours alone," said Charles. "We'll find a way to make it right. If only we can draw your father's poison. Now he's gone . . ."

"Mary Anne can't forgive Master Robert for paying him off," said Jenny flatly. "They've been at each other like cat and dog and it's only getting worse."

"And you in the middle of it?" said Charles. "I'm sorry. I'm so sorry. I had thought if they were happy together—"

"Then we might be too?" There was something so wistful, so vulnerable in the words. It made Charles want to ford oceans and slay dragons for her. Surely, this should be simple in comparison?

"We will be. We'll find a way." Charles wrapped his arms around her, feeling, for the first time in a very long while, as though he'd come home. Which was foolish, since he hadn't been anywhere. She was the one who had gone away. But there it was. "Perhaps once there's a child . . ."

"That may be sooner than you think. Mary Anne's been ill two mornings now."

"But that's of all things wonderful!" Charles said, sitting up straight. "Robert will be pleased, I imagine. He'll have proved his virility and secured an heir. And as for your mistress . . ."

"It will give her someone else to manage?" Jenny finished for him.

Charles felt seized by a sudden surge of optimism. He squeezed Jenny's hands. "You'll see. We'll have it all sorted and you at Peverills by Christmas."

"If you say so," said Jenny skeptically.

"We'll make it so." Nothing could fright him out of his good humor now, not with Jenny home again. "You'll see. Jack shall have Jill and naught shall go ill."

"Until you fall down and break your crown."

"But will you come tumbling after?" Charles kissed her. "There'll be no breaks and tumbles. Once Robert's baby comes, they'll be too pleased with themselves to waste any time on the likes of us. They'll scarce remember we exist."

Chapter Fifteen

Christ Church, Barbados
May 1854

"I HAD NO idea you had an uncle Charles," said Emily. "No one ever mentioned him."

George discovered a deep interest in the backs of his gloves. "Well, they wouldn't. He's been gone for some time now. And my grandmother rather minded his selling Peverills."

It wasn't just that, thought Emily, looking at George's averted face. Mrs. Davenant had gone to some trouble to create the impression that Peverills had been unfairly wrenched from her hands in some hole-and-corner fashion. When, in fact, it had never been hers to begin with. All of it, the paired portraits on the wall, the grand pronouncements, were, if not a lie, then at least a substantial misrepresentation.

"If your grandmother was never mistress of Peverills," said Emily, "then how did she come to have the account books?"

"I wasn't born yet," George prevaricated, "but as I understand it . . . the books were left in the bookkeeper's house, and my grandmother thought it best—that is, she took it upon herself to . . . um, to watch over them for Uncle Charles. While he was away."

In other words, she had stolen them. "I see," said Emily.

"It was all in the family," Mr. Davenant hastened to explain. "Uncle Charles seemed disinclined to marry, so it was expected the estate would come to my father eventually. No one ever expected that he might sell it."

"But why would he go away just like that?" Emily looked out over the blackened gables of Peverills. True, the house was ruined, but there was still the rest of the plantation. If her grandfather had bought the plantation twenty-odd years ago, that still left twenty years that the land had been left untenanted, abandoned. "Even if one hadn't the money to rebuild, he might have gone on farming the land and lived in the book-keeper's house. Or leased the land to someone else. Why leave it all sitting empty like that?"

George glanced at her sideways. "The story I was told was that it was because of the little girl. His ward."

"His who?"

"I forget you don't know. It's all common knowledge here. Well, leg-end, really. I'm not sure how much is true and how much pure embel-lishment, but . . . I'm not telling it very well, am I?"

It seemed churlish to agree, so Emily tilted her head at an expectant angle and waited.

"My grandmother doesn't talk about any of this," George said seri-ously. "I had it from the servants, and the stories do tend to vary rather wildly. But if you boil it all down, it comes to this. My uncle had a ward, a little Portuguese girl. This was during the wars with Napoléon, you know."

Emily nodded. "They went on for some time."

"We're rather proud of our part in it all here," said George. "In any event, the girl was the child of a schoolmate who died on the peninsula. My uncle was very sincerely attached to her, I gather."

Emily remembered the doll lying in the grass, the paint blistered and faded. "What happened to her?"

"She died in the fire."

Emily had expected as much, but to hear it made it more stark, more real. "How dreadful. That poor little girl."

"Uncle Charles was devastated. He'd promised his friend he'd see her safe, and . . ." As one, they both looked out at the fire-blasted stone and fallen rubble. George's Adam's apple bobbed up and down beneath his loosely tied stock. "Can you imagine that? To have made it through a war safely and then to die like this?"

Emily shook her head mutely, trying not to imagine that little girl as she must have been, nearly half a century ago.

"I know such things happen all the time," said George, "that there are fires and children die in them, but this was on our own doorstep, as it were."

Emily looked up at him, her eyes meeting his. "Just because it happens all the time doesn't make it any easier."

"They say she haunts the place, that if you come here after dark, you can hear a child crying, calling out for help that never comes."

There was something about the way George said it that gave Emily a rather shivery feeling, despite the heat of the day.

"What was her name? The little girl?"

George blinked at her. "Do you know, I don't know? Something foreign, I imagine. My grandmother only ever called her the Portuguese ward, so that's how I think of her. The Portuguese ward."

"Is there no grave?" It seemed terribly wrong that a child should die and be remembered as nothing more than a cry in the night, remembered only for the manner of her death and not her brief life.

"I don't believe they ever recovered enough to bury. The fire smoldered for days, my grandmother said. People were afraid to go near it. And by the time they did . . . So many people died in the blaze, and it was all such a muddle, that they never did quite find all the pieces of everyone who was missing. There had been a number of house servants in the building, you see, and some of them had visitors, and . . . well." George grimaced at her. "What a grim topic for a beautiful day. I'm sorry. I didn't follow you out here to regale you with horrors."

"I'm glad to know," said Emily slowly. "It makes it all—not make sense, precisely, but at least I know now why the plantation was sold."

"If you believe the story," said George.

"Do you?"

He thought for a moment. "Yes. I do. My uncle—no one ever speaks much about him, but I gather he had grand plans for Peverills, for reforms and model farms and all that sort of thing. Whatever happened had to be truly wrenching for him to give all that up—and break all ties."

He sounded a bit wistful. "Have you ever wanted to just disappear?" asked Emily curiously.

George smiled a lopsided smile. "Constantly. Haven't you?"

"No." Emily felt a pang of fierce longing for the world she had left, for her grandfather's study at twilight, with the lamps just lit; for Laura's room at Miss Blackwell's, where Laura would read or dream while Emily sewed; for her work at the hospital, where Adam would appear out of nowhere to swoop her off for drives in his new curricle. She missed the life she had built for herself, that busy, useful life. "Where would you go?"

"Rome, perhaps," said George dreamily, "to wander the Colosseum and sketch statues. Or maybe Switzerland to gaze up at the hills and paint my reflection in mountain streams."

"Not Paris?"

"My father is in Paris." George shook himself out of his reverie. "It's just a dream, of course. I'd never go, not really. There's too much to be done here. Shall we go back?"

"I've only just got here," said Emily. "I'd wanted to see more of the estate."

"It's mostly dead fields," said George. "There are some tricky bits toward the east—caverns and ravines as you near the water. You wouldn't want to go there without a guide."

Emily remembered Dr. Braithwaite's warnings. "Are you volunteering?"

"If you'd like."

"Don't worry, I didn't intend adventuring that far," said Emily, amused despite herself at his obvious lack of enthusiasm. "Just to the bookkeeper's house."

"Oh," said George. And then, "Why?"

"Why wouldn't I? It's mine now, isn't it?"

"It's nothing much to see," said George. "Just a house, and not a particularly grand one."

Emily looked up at him curiously, wondering what it was that made him so reluctant to show her that particular corner of the estate. "My grandfather lived there once. I'm curious to see the place that was once his home."

Before he was accused, if Mrs. Poole was to be believed, of sending it all up in flame. But no. She couldn't possibly believe that. It was just malicious gossip, the vicious slanders of those who resented that a poor boy had made good.

"All right," said George reluctantly. "It's not far. But you should know . . . it may not be entirely unoccupied."

"No?" Emily had to concentrate on her footing; what had once been a walkway leading around the house was now crumbled and cracked, roots stretching across to trip the unwary. George offered her his arm as she stumbled. "Thank you. But what do you—oh."

In front of a plain, white-walled house waited a good dozen people, some sitting on the ground, others leaning against the wall of the house. There was a man with a makeshift bandage around his arm and a woman with a child on her back and another in her arms. Three children played a game that involved running back and forth, adding to the din.

They all fell silent as Emily and George approached, and in the sudden silence Emily recognized her own maid Katy, holding a child of two or three, who locked her arms around Katy's neck and buried her head in her shoulder as Emily raised a hand in uncertain greeting.

"Hello?" said Emily, feeling rather as though she'd intruded. She smiled at the little girl. "Good morning."

The little girl ducked her head again. A sister? A daughter? Emily realized with shame that she didn't know and had never asked.

"Is the doctor in?" asked George, a slight edge to his otherwise pleasant voice.

The man nearest the door nodded. He was holding one hand over a bandage stained with red on his right arm.

"How did you come by that, Elijah? Did Ruth come after you with a hoe?"

There was an uneasy laugh all around. "Knife slipped," said Elijah.

"And you came all this way to have it looked at?"

No one answered.

"All right, then," said George. "You don't mind if we slip ahead, do you? We won't keep the doctor long."

"Oh." Emily paused as realization dawned, remembering the last time she had seen Dr. Braithwaite, the words that had passed between them. Slowly, she followed behind George. "Is this . . . ?"

"Yes," said George, leading her ahead of the waiting patients. "Welcome to Nathaniel's illegal infirmary."

He spoke loudly enough that his words preceded them into the room, which had been turned into a makeshift operating theater. A man lay on a well-scrubbed table, flesh gaping from a nasty gash down his leg. Beside him, Dr. Braithwaite was engaged in stitching the wound together. A bowl sat on the floor beside him, filled with reddish water and stained cloths.

"Hardly illegal," said Dr. Braithwaite, without looking up from his work. His stock was neatly tied, his waistcoat of the first quality, but he had stripped to his shirtsleeves, the cuffs folded back to bare his forearms.

"You're trespassing," said George, looking away from the wound.

"Have you come to evict me?" Dr. Braithwaite reached for a pair of scissors. Without stopping to think, Emily leaned forward and placed them in his hand.

"Thank you, Miss Dawson." He looked up and their eyes met.

Emily found herself struggling to find something to say, but her mind was blank.

"If you're planning to assist, you might wash your hands first. You'll find fresh water on the bureau."

"Surely, you're not going to . . ." protested George.

"Wash hands?" said Dr. Braithwaite, deliberately misunderstanding him. "I know a Viennese physician who swears it saves lives. It's a simple enough precaution to take. If there's no value in it, I lose nothing by it."

"Except the cost of the soap," muttered George.

Ignoring George, Emily went to the bureau where there was, as promised, a bowl of water and a cake of soap. Despite the heat of the day, a fire burned on a camp stove, a kettle on the boil.

Wrapping a cloth around her hand to protect it from the handle, Emily lifted the kettle off the hook and poured boiling water into the bowl. The soap smelled strongly of lye. It bit at her skin with the force of memory.

"You didn't mention that you were running your clinic on my land," said Emily as she dried her hands on a cloth.

"I could hardly run it on Beckles land," said Dr. Braithwaite. He glanced up at George. "Could I."

George looked uncomfortable. "Beckles has a physician."

"No, it hasn't," said Dr. Braithwaite. "If MacAndrews has any kind of medical training, I'll eat my hat."

"He attended the University of St. Andrews," said George, without conviction.

"When they were still balancing the humors?" said Dr. Braithwaite, snipping off a thread. "Bandage."

Emily handed him a roll of bandages. "Are you a physician or a surgeon?" she asked, more to change the topic than anything else. As she knew from her time in the hospital in Bristol, only physicians, who assessed and prescribed, were allowed to style themselves doctor. Surgeons, who dealt with the body itself, were mere misters. "Your uncle called you doctor, but . . ."

"Both. On the whole, I find my surgical training the more useful. My uncle, on the other hand, prefers the prestige of the higher degree. You can call me what you will." Dr. Braithwaite tied off the bandage with an expert twist. "There. Keep your leg out of the way of your machete in future."

"Do you sew up a lot of legs?"

"A fair few." Dr. Braithwaite glanced sideways at George as he helped the patient off the table. "It's preferable to lopping them off. Or leaving them until they fester."

Sensing strife, Emily jumped in. "What sorts of ailments do you see? Other than legs, I mean."

"Arms, torsos, scalps." At her look, he began ticking off diseases. "Dropsy, lesions, night blindness, toothache, palsy. On the whole, malnutrition."

George, leaning against the wall, stood up straighter. "We don't starve our workers at Beckles."

Dr. Braithwaite dumped Emily's wash water into a bucket, refilling the bowl from the kettle. "No one said you did. But they hardly receive a varied diet. In case you didn't notice, there's a drought on."

Emily hadn't noticed. "There is?"

"Well, yes," admitted George. "We rely on the rainy season, and this year the rains just weren't . . . well, rainy enough."

"Well said," said Dr. Braithwaite drily, plunging his hands into the steaming water and soaping them briskly.

"But we're surrounded by water," said Emily. "Can't one irrigate?"

"With saltwater?" Dr. Braithwaite shook his hands, looking about for the cloth. Emily handed it to him.

"We've brought in more corn," said George defensively.

"As I said," said Dr. Braithwaite. "Would you eat corn three meals a day?"

"George," said Emily, "is there a well? Would you mind fetching more water? That is, if there is any in it."

"There is," said Dr. Braithwaite. "Peverills has fewer demands on its water supply."

George looked as though he intended to argue, but, instead, he said reluctantly, "I'll have Jonah see to it."

He left the door open behind him. Through it, Emily could see that the yard, which had been full, was now deserted.

"Oh dear," she said, as George made his way across the yard to Jonah and the horses. "I hope we didn't scare away your patients."

"You did," said Dr. Braithwaite.

So much for polite nothings.

"Why *did* you set up your clinic here?" Emily demanded.

"This house," said Dr. Braithwaite, applying a wet cloth to the table, "was conveniently unoccupied. And, as previously noted, there is a well."

"Oh, here, let me. You're only making it worse." Emily took the cloth from him, vigorously scrubbing at a bit of half-dried blood. "I mean, why Beckles? I'm sure there would be many other plantations where your services would be more welcome?"

"Are you?" said Dr. Braithwaite, holding out his hands for her to inspect. He let them drop to his sides. "Would you believe me if I said I did it to annoy Mrs. Davenant?"

"No," said Emily. She thought of those endless teas, the promises Mrs. Davenant had made and hadn't kept. "Although I understand the impulse."

"Like that, is it?"

"She's been a very welcoming hostess," said Emily primly. "You didn't answer my question."

Dr. Braithwaite twitched the cloth away from her, dropping it into the slop bucket. "If you must know, MacAndrews killed my father." As Emily stared at him, he shook his head, as though impatient with himself. "Oh, he didn't take a cutlass to him. But he killed him all the same. My father cut his hand. A smaller cut than the one you saw just now. MacAndrews decided to amputate. My father died."

"But if it was festering . . ."

"It wasn't."

"I'm so sorry." It was so painfully inadequate. "Why does Mrs. Davenant keep him on?"

"Habit?" Turning away from her, Dr. Braithwaite began lining up his implements. "Power, perhaps. She does the real physicking at Beckles. Oh yes. If you want a wound bound, or a powder for a pain, you go to Mrs. Davenant."

"Is she—" Emily waved her hands around, looking for the right word.

"Competent? Yes," admitted Dr. Braithwaite, with the air of someone who would be fair if it killed him. "I doubt she's reading the latest edition of *The Lancet*, but she can clean a cut without killing the patient. She's used to having it her own way. It mightn't suit her to have someone interfering. Or—"

"Or?"

Dr. Braithwaite turned away from her, using a pair of tongs to pass the needle he had been using through the fire. "MacAndrews knows something she doesn't want told."

"You told me, before I came, that there was something wrong with Beckles."

Dr. Braithwaite dropped the red-hot bit of metal into a dish. It clattered against the ceramic. "As I recall, I told you nothing of the kind."

"Not in so many words, perhaps—but you implied it."

"You forget, I've been away these past twenty years. I was eight when I left—when my uncle freed me." He looked up, his expression uncompromising. "I assume you know about that."

"Yes." Emily didn't know where to look or what to say.

Dr. Braithwaite hung up the tongs on their hook. "As you can imagine, it isn't a time I remember affectionately. And no, before you ask, I wasn't hunted with dogs or beaten for sport. One doesn't need to live in Uncle Tom's cabin to resent being chattel."

Emily's cheeks were bright red and not just from the fire. "How did you know I read that?"

"An upstanding member of the Bristol and Clifton Ladies' Anti-Slavery Society?"

"It's done a lot of good, that book."

"I don't deny that. But I don't want you pitying me. Or searching my back for scars."

Emily couldn't help it; she looked at his back, a broad back, cased in linen and wool.

"My point." In a clipped voice, Dr. Braithwaite said, "I've spent most of my life in England. My memories of Beckles are, of necessity, limited. If you ask anyone, they'll tell you that Mrs. Davenant was a good mistress—by the standards by which people judge their own."

Emily felt confused and wrong-footed, and also that she was missing something, something just under her nose. "That isn't an answer."

Dr. Braithwaite sat down heavily on the chair. "That's because I don't have one to give you. Beckles was—is—a thriving place. The people here are fed and clothed as well or as poorly as anywhere else on the island. If I tell you that I found it an unhappy place—I had reason of my own to do so."

She could tell how much it cost him to admit it. He might not bear scars on his back, but that didn't mean he had emerged unscathed.

"No. It isn't just your perception. It is an unhappy place, somehow." The spyglasses, the strange tensions in the great house, the missing members of the family, the ruins of Peverills just visible in the distance. "George—Mr. Davenant, I mean—told me his father ran away."

"Perhaps you'll change all that when you take your place as mistress." Dr. Braithwaite rose from the chair, pushing it back with a screech. "When is the happy day?"

"Happy day?"

"Your impending nuptials." Dr. Braithwaite was at his most clipped. "Two great estates, finally united."

"Oh, not you too," said Emily without thinking. "That is—I have no intention of marrying anyone. If any estates are joined, it will be in exchange for pounds sterling, not my hand in marriage."

"That's not the word among the house servants. An announcement is expected daily."

Emily shook her head and reached for the cloth, busying herself in wiping surfaces that had no need of wiping. "We've overstayed our time at Beckles, my cousins and I. I should have known it would cause talk. It's past time we took our leave."

"If you scrub any more, there will be no table left," said Dr. Braithwaite mildly. "Where do you intend to go?"

Emily surrendered the scrubbing cloth. "Here, eventually. I had thought we might move into this house—or the overseer's house." She could imagine just how much Adam and Laura would approve of that course of action. They would have to be persuaded. Somehow. Emily put that aside to deal with later.

"You'll need furniture. And linens."

"And everything else. In the meantime, I suppose we'll go back to Miss Lee's hotel."

Dr. Braithwaite paused, looking at her as if she were a problem he needed to solve. "If I might give you a word of advice—"

"Which you intend to give me anyway?"

Dr. Braithwaite ignored the interruption. "Stay a while longer. Or if you go, remove to another plantation, not to Bridgetown."

"Why?"

"It's the hot season. There's been a drought. Water supplies are low and increasingly tainted. It's the perfect breeding ground for disease. I don't want to cause alarm, but . . . you're safer in the countryside."

Emily wished she still had the cloth to occupy her hands. Instead, she closed her hand over the locket at her throat. "I'm concerned that my friend—my cousin now, I mean—may have contracted something already."

"What are the symptoms?" Dr. Braithwaite was immediately all professional.

"Retching—to be fair, everyone was ill on the boat, but it hasn't ended since we've been here. It's been over two months now and there's no sign of improvement. If anything, it's worse."

"Anything else?"

"Fatigue. Listlessness."

"No distemper of the bowels?"

"None that I've observed. But I might not know—that is—"

"You're not privy to your cousin's chamber pot."

"Yes."

"No headaches? Body aches? Chills? Fever?"

"No, none of those. But she can't eat. What she does eat, she casts up again. I thought, some variety of tropical distemper . . ."

Dr. Braithwaite's shoulders relaxed. He leaned back against the table. "She's newly married, isn't she?"

Emily nodded. "Yes. But what does that have to do with it?"

"I doubt we're dealing with the beginnings of an epidemic. Not of that sort, at least."

"Do stop speaking in riddles," Emily begged. "You haven't seen her. She's quite genuinely ill."

"I don't doubt that," said Dr. Braithwaite. "Without doing injury to your delicate sensibilities, have you ever considered that Mrs. Fenty might be increasing?"

CHAPTER SIXTEEN

Christ Church, Barbados
December 1812

THERE WAS SOON no doubt that Mary Anne was with child.

Pregnancy didn't suit Mary Anne. Her head ached and her ankles swelled; her stomach rebelled, not just in the mornings, but in the afternoons and the evenings too. Jenny found herself in constant service, called upon to massage Mary Anne's temples with lavender water, to read to her from manuals on estate management, to be Mary Anne's eyes and ears and holder of the slop bucket.

Dr. MacAndrews prescribed champagne, on the theory that the bubbles would settle her stomach. The doctor Robert called in from Bridgetown recommended a reducing diet, which Mary Anne said was all very well, since she couldn't manage to eat anyway, and what in the blazes were they bothering paying him for?

"Only the best for the heir to Beckles," retorted Robert, and Jenny wasn't sure if he meant it as a jibe or not.

Mary Anne took it as her due, and nodded, satisfied, better pleased with her husband than she had been since the marriage. She might chafe at her enforced inactivity, at the weakness that restricted her movements, but she was fierce with pride at the prospect of an heir for Beckles, determined to bring the babe safely to term even if it meant giving up her rides, her walks, the supervision of her estates.

"It might be a girl," Jenny pointed out.

"Don't say that!" Mary Anne pressed her eyes shut, leaning back against her cushions. "Lord, I hope it's not a girl."

"You inherited Beckles," Jenny said soothingly.

"Yes, and look at me." The pink was coming back into her cheeks and lips as the wave of nausea passed. "What I wouldn't give to have been a boy. Do you think I'd wish my situation on my child?"

I can't bring a child into this. That was what Jenny had told Mary Anne ten years ago, and Mary Anne had helped her, even though the loss of the child meant the loss of an asset.

Whenever Mary Anne's demands became too much, when she found herself missing Charles with an intensity that unsettled her, Jenny reminded herself of that. That Mary Anne had stood by her when she needed it, even though it meant the loss of a child for Beckles, a baby whose worth might have been reckoned in dollars and pence.

"There's a difference," said Jenny quietly, easing her mistress back down. "Your child will have you to guide her."

"Yes, I suppose. . . ." said Mary Anne, but Jenny didn't bring up the possibility of the child being a girl again.

At dusk, Robert would stop by her room smelling of the stable and of cane, and Mary Anne would accost him with a battery of questions. What was he doing about the new machinery for the mill? Had he replaced the head driver?

Jenny half expected Robert to shrug and advise Mary Anne to rest. But he didn't. He sat by her bed and expatiated on his doings as day turned to night, like an agrarian Scheherazade. Jenny suspected it was less for Mary Anne's benefit and more because he wanted an audience, someone to impress with his industry, but whatever the reason, the pair seemed better pleased with each other than they had been since the marriage, and Jenny began to cautiously wonder whether Charles might be right, whether the baby might be the making of them.

If Mary Anne survived the process.

If Mary Anne died . . . Jenny repressed the disloyal thought. She was tired, that was all. She felt sleepy and heavy from the long hours of attendance on her mistress, her limbs weighted, her mind prone to wander. Robert had removed to his own chamber, and Mary Anne liked to have Jenny sleep on a pallet by her bed, to be near in the night when she couldn't sleep. In the day, Mary Anne insisted on keeping Jenny close, relinquishing her only for necessary errands.

Mary Anne had always liked to have her with her; now Jenny felt as though she were chained to her. There had been no time to slip away to the Old Mill. Charles, Jenny suspected, had waited for her in vain, more than once. He had finally resorted to sending a gift of fruit to her mistress, a basket of oranges, and, at the bottom, a note bearing only two letters: OH.

Overseer's house.

Doing her best to mask her impatience, Jenny read to Mary Anne and bathed her brow and settled her back against her cushions. "Do you think you can rest a bit? I'll have Queenie sit by you."

Mary Anne cracked open an eye. "Why? Where are you going?"

"To see Nanny Bell." Nanny Bell was officially in charge of the laundry. In reality, she supplied a vast array of remedies and cures. The effectiveness of these, Jenny knew firsthand. Oil of oleander . . . *It's the safest way*, Mary Anne had promised her, holding her hand as she drank. "She's promised me a potion to ease your pain."

"Tell her there's a new dress in it for her if she can stop me casting up my accounts every hour." Mary Anne moved her head restlessly from side to side. "What I wouldn't give to be on my feet right now!"

"Don't," said Jenny. "Rest. I'll be back soon."

Charles was waiting for her at the overseer's house, reading a letter by the light that filtered through the window. He dropped it at the sound of her approach, wrapping her in his arms, holding her, just holding her, for several long minutes.

"I've finally hired an overseer," he said into her hair. "He's to take up residence after Christmas."

Jenny was surprised at the sense of loss she felt. This place, even more than the Old Mill, had been where they had met while Robert and Mary Anne courted, where they could lie together in a proper bed and pretend that this was their home, that they might be together always. But now someone else, a stranger, would be here.

"It doesn't matter," Charles hastened to add. "We won't need this place anymore if all goes well."

"If all goes well," Jenny echoed. She looked up at him, his golden hair, his London tailoring, a storybook hero wandered out of the page, too rich for everyday use. It baffled her still, that they should have come together like this, that when they were together, being with him should feel so simple, so right. It was mad and impossible, but there it was. When she was with him, she didn't have to pretend; she felt as though she'd spent her life in tight lacing only to have the knot slashed open, leaving her to breathe free for the first time.

It made it all the harder to face the prospect of returning to Beckles.

"Robert's invited me for Christmas dinner," Charles said. "He seemed almost amiable. If he's in good temper . . . perhaps he might be amenable to making me the sale of a domestic servant."

"They're to have the Bolands too," Jenny said. Christmas was traditionally a holiday for family, but the Bolands had no family on Barbados, and both Robert and Mary Anne were very eager to claim them as their own. "Master Robert will want to impress Mr. Boland."

"We can find a way to use that to our advantage, I'm sure." Charles moved away from her, fussing with the fall of the drapes at the window. "If all else fails, we'll get them foxed on Christmas punch and conjure Robert's signature onto a bill of sale. He'll never remember in the morning and he'll feel too foolish to disown it."

He meant it, Jenny realized. He meant it and hated himself for it. "You would perjure yourself?"

Charles looked over at her, his eyes very blue. "For you, yes. If that's what it takes. I can't bear—" His voice broke. He shook his head. "What am I doing, telling you what I can't bear? It's you who bears all. But not much longer. We'll find a way to free you at Christmas."

"Don't," said Jenny, crossing the space between them and covering his lips with her fingers, "don't hope too much."

Charles took her hand and pressed a kiss to the palm, a kiss she could feel all the way down to her toes. "If not Christmas, then New Year's."

And Jenny, who had intended to tell him she couldn't stay, found herself lifting up onto her toes to kiss him, wrapping her arms around him, letting him carry her to the old bed that had served them so well.

"Christmas," he promised her as she left, and although she told him not to hope, she couldn't help hoping too.

Somehow, when she was with Charles, all things felt possible. She found herself daydreaming as she never had before, imagining elaborate and impossible scenarios. Her mistress gifting her with freedom as a Christmas gift; her master freeing her to impress Mrs. Boland; proclamations from England freeing everyone.

On Christmas morning, Jenny helped Mary Anne into a new dress, carefully altered to fit the new fullness of her breasts, and placed candied ginger sweetmeats in her reticule to ward off sickness.

"Take them away. The smell makes me sick," Mary Anne declared.

"Nanny Bell said to chew one if you feel the sickness coming on." Her mistress's figure was fuller, but her face was haggard, the skin falling away under the cheeks and dark circles beneath her eyes. Nanny Bell assured her that a sick mother meant a healthy babe. Mary Anne had scowled and said, of course she would say that, but had seemed reassured all the same.

Mary Anne reluctantly took the reticule. "I don't want to embarrass myself in front of the Bolands."

"You won't," Jenny assured her. She doubted the Bolands would care; Mr. Boland had the air of one who had seen it all, and found life, what was left of it, a great joke, and Mrs. Boland was too preoccupied with Mr. Boland's flagging health to care that Mary Anne wasn't in looks.

Mary Anne dropped her reticule onto the dressing table. "It's important that they sign the contract."

"I know," said Jenny, easing Mary Anne into her pelisse, arm by arm. She couldn't let her mistress decide to cry sickness and stay at home. Jenny needed this time, these few minutes of quiet. "They will."

"Not if I cast up my accounts on their shoes," Mary Anne muttered, but she let Jenny clasp her necklace around her neck and thread earrings through her ears. "I hope there's nothing amiss. Robert ought to have been here by now."

There had been a messenger come for the master that morning, and Jenny hadn't seen him since.

"He's most likely waiting for you downstairs." Jenny handed Mary Anne her prayer book. "There. You'll do Beckles proud."

"Hmph," said Mary Anne. And then, to Jenny's surprise, she reached into the drawer of her dressing table and drew out a packet wrapped in brown paper. "Happy Christmas."

"Thank you," said Jenny, trying not to show her surprise.

Mary Anne bit her lip. "Don't think I'm insensible of what you've done for me," she said gruffly. "Go on. Take it. It's yours now."

She didn't wait for Jenny to answer, just thrust the parcel in her hand and left. Jenny didn't follow; she wasn't to accompany the family to church. Her father hadn't believed that slaves ought to be baptized; they were children of Ham, denied salvation.

Jenny looked down at the brown paper parcel Mary Anne had handed her, surprised and touched by the gesture, after the long, difficult weeks that had just passed. She would have her gift later that day with the rest of the servants. It was a tradition at Beckles to give the women a new dress, the men a new smock at Christmas, and a coin to each, with a special gift of money to women who had borne three or more children. Children for Beckles. Jenny's stomach fluttered uneasily and she busied herself untying the wrapping of the package.

Inside was a box, made of local mahogany. Jenny recognized the work of the head carpenter, the delicate carving around the sides. The box opened smoothly on well-oiled hinges, the interior lined with a scrap of satin she recognized as part of a discarded dress.

Inside lay a gold locket. Jenny's gold locket, the one her father had strung about her neck and promised her if she'd be a good girl.

Mary Anne's gold locket, the one the colonel had given her, that she had worn nestled in the hollow of her throat until the day of the poisoned chocolate, when she had pulled it off so hard that the ribbon snapped.

There was a knock at the door. The master was the only one who knocked at the mistress's door. But he had left for the church, some time ago, if the clock was any indication. How long had she been standing here, thinking of times gone by?

Jenny hastily shoved the locket into her pocket.

"Yes?" she said, opening the door a crack.

A strange woman stood on the other side. She wore a well-starched white apron over a neatly pressed dress, but there was something about the curve of her cheeks, the bright fabric of her kerchief, that made her seem like she wouldn't mind the odd rumple in her dress or stain on her apron.

"I'm maid to Mrs. Boland," the other woman said with a warm smile. "I was told I could find thread and needle here. My mistress trod on her dress just before going into church, and I found I had come away with none."

"What color do you need?" asked Jenny, going to get her sewing box.

"Anything will do, if I make the stitches small enough," said the woman cheerfully, "but a dark blue by choice. I'm Nanny Grigg."

"Jenny," said Jenny, rooting about. "Will this do?"

"You're very kind." Nanny Grigg took the spool but made no move to go. She looked at Jenny quizzically. "Are you all right? I don't want to presume. It's just—well, you look as though you saw a duppy."

That was one way of putting it. The box with the gold locket weighed heavy in Jenny's pocket. "It's always a flurry, having guests in the house," Jenny said instead. "And with Christmas and all . . ."

"They get the celebration, we have the work," said Nanny Grigg companionably.

There was a shout outside, and the sounds of hooves and wheels. Jenny couldn't help her neck turning, craning to see out the window. But it wasn't Charles. It was the heavy carriage Mary Anne used for formal occasions, bearing the Bolands and her master and mistress back from church.

"They're back," she said, trying not to sound as low as she felt. It was foolish. It wasn't as though she would be able to speak to Charles anyway, only look at him across the room, which was almost worse than nothing. "Do you need a needle?"

"You gave me one," said Nanny Grigg.

"Oh, of course." Jenny shook her head, feeling like an idiot. Seizing on the first excuse she could think of, she crossed to Mary Anne's writing desk. "I was just remembering that we were nearly out of the puce silk floss. I'll have to add it to the list to buy in Speightstown."

"You can write?" said Nanny Grigg, her eyes lighting up. "I was maid to the mistress of Harrow until she died, and then . . . I used to read her correspondence to her, when her eyes began to fail her. Write for her too."

"My mistress has me write for her sometimes as well," admitted Jenny. "She's with child, and it's been hard with her. Her fingers swell so that it's difficult for her to hold a pen."

"Does she like you to read to her?" asked Nanny Grigg. "I used to read my mistress sermons, mostly. Improving texts, that was what she liked. But she liked Mr. Richardson's works, because she thought they had a good moral sentiment. Have you read *Pamela*?"

"No," said Jenny, trying not to show her distraction too obviously as more hoofbeats sounded from the drive.

"There's a maid in it marries her master," said Nanny Grigg confidingly. "I'll hunt it up for you, if you like. Mrs. Boland doesn't read novels, so she won't ever notice it's missing. If your mistress doesn't mind, that is."

"I don't think she would," said Jenny, although it hit a little too close to home, a maid marrying her master. Not that she thought

Mary Anne would notice or make the connection. Mary Anne didn't read novels.

"My thanks for the thread," said Nanny Grigg, turning to go. She paused in the doorway, looking back at Jenny. "If your mistress can ever spare you, we have Sunday gatherings at Harrow, a few of us. We read the papers from England and share what news we can."

Sunday gatherings were one thing; most masters expected their slaves to go visiting on a Sunday. But reading the papers was another, and dangerous.

"It's all right. Mrs. Boland knows. She thinks it's good that we improve ourselves." Nanny Grigg made a face. "I'm not sure how improving it is, but it's good to have the company, and you're always welcome."

"Thank you," said Jenny, and meant it. She had never joined in the Sunday gatherings before, never gone with the other slaves in groups to dances at other plantations. She had always been held apart, by her father, by her relationship with her mistress. She loved Charles, but there was so much there that was fraught. And as for Mary Anne . . . that was another matter entirely. It would be nice to have a friend, or friends, simple and uncomplicated. Someone to sit and read the papers with on a Sunday evening. If her mistress let her go. "Maybe I will."

"Do. We'd be glad to see you." Nanny Grigg reached out and gave her arm a squeeze. "There'll always be a spot ready for you, whenever you can get away."

She gave Jenny a friendly smile and a nod and let herself out, closing the door behind her.

Jenny's eyes stung. She rubbed them, hard, blinking away tears. It seemed she was always on the verge of crying these days. The long separation from Charles, she supposed. And possibly something else.

The box with her father's locket bumped against her thigh. Jenny drew the box out of her pocket, extracting the locket. Even now, it still made her feel vaguely ill, that scrap of gold, ill with guilt and grief. It weighed heavier in her hand than it ought, like lead instead of gold.

She fit her finger in the clasp. On the interior, her mistress had engraved, "To Jenny, for her good service."

Proof that it was a gift and not stolen. It was a surprisingly thoughtful gesture, if only the locket had been anything but what it was.

Jenny closed her hand over the pendant, feeling the filigree edges biting into her palm. She knew her father would have done what he had anyway. He'd always intended to take her with him; it would have been the same if she'd kicked and bitten and screamed. But she still, even now, felt shame at the sight of the locket, that she'd been tempted into following him, leaving her mother.

Mary Anne didn't know that, though. Jenny forced her fingers to relax. Mary Anne didn't know that, because Jenny had never said. She'd thought she was giving Jenny a gift, an extravagant gift, with title to it written right there for all to see. It was a kindness—and maybe it was, in more ways than one. It was a link, fragile and tainted as it was, to her mother, to those days before. She should think of her mother when she saw it, not her father. It was the only thing she had that her mother had touched. Her mother had helped her string it on a ribbon, helped tie it at the back of her neck.

How had she felt as she had done so? Jenny had never wondered it before, but she wondered it now. Her mother was very much on her mind just now. What had she felt when she bore her? Had she loved her? Feared for her?

To Jenny, for her good service.

Jenny ran a finger over the lightly incised words in their curling script. There was an air of elegy about them, an air of farewell. Recently, Mary Anne had seemed—well, not contented. She was too sick to be contented, too impatient. But as close to contented as Mary Anne could be.

She shouldn't hope too much, she knew. But it wasn't impossible. The threats that had bound them together were gone. There were others who could dress her mistress's hair better than she.

Maybe, just maybe . . . Maybe Mary Anne might be thinking of setting her free.

There was a flurry of activity beneath the window. Another carriage arriving. Something lighter, a gig. The sound of voices, a groom taking the horses, a man's voice, with the flavor of little Scotland. And then another, an English voice, a beautiful tenor with exaggerated vowels that somehow made him sound always amused, even when he wasn't.

Charles.

"CHARLES. WELCOME." ROBERT greeted Charles on the veranda with all the warmth and softness of a hailstorm.

"Happy Christmas," said Charles, although it didn't feel like Christmas at all to him. Christmas was mistletoe and cold so intense it froze the tip of your nose. Christmas was wassail and mummers, velvet and fur. Last year, the Thames had frozen so hard that he had walked on the ice all the way from Battersea Bridge to Hungerford Stairs with two friends from Lincoln's Inn, skidding and laughing and daring each other on.

Here there was no yew and holly, no ice or frost. The coconut palms spread their broad leaves to the sky and the hibiscus bloomed purple and red.

But there was Jenny, Charles reminded himself. And that, somehow, made all the rest indifferent.

"You brought him?" Robert was looking past Charles at Jonathan, who was doing his best to look at nothing at all, his hair still clamped back in an old-fashioned queue, a lace stock the only sign he'd done his best to do honor to the occasion.

"It is Christmas," Charles reminded him. "Our Lord was welcomed into a stable rude."

"Yes, but no one said they had to have the donkey for dinner," muttered Robert. Then, with false congeniality, "Come in, come in. You remember the Bolands, of course."

"Mr. Davenant," said Mr. Boland, struggling to rise from his chair.

"No, no, don't get up," said Charles hastily. The man seemed to have collapsed in on himself, his cheeks flaps of flesh, his coat too large for his frame. "It's a pleasure to see you again. May we join you?"

Robert shouted for more punch, rather more loudly than necessary, cursing the servant who brought it for a lazy jade.

Twin portraits graced the sides of the archway in the great room, the paint barely dry. Jenny was in one, Charles noticed, with a twist in his chest, standing behind Mary Anne. It wasn't a particularly good likeness, but there was something about it that discomfited him all the same, as though she were frozen in the paint, kept forever at Beckles.

"Admiring my wife?" Robert said, an edge to his voice. "I commissioned the paintings to celebrate our marriage."

"And now an heir," said Charles, hoping to soften his brother's mood.

It didn't. Robert looked at him sharply. "What do you know of that? Did Mary Anne tell you?"

The Bolands were politely looking the other way.

"I haven't seen Mrs. Davenant in some time," said Charles carefully, wondering what had sparked this sudden anger. "My man Cuffy had it from one of your maids. You know how news travels. I thought it was common knowledge. If I overstepped, I beg your pardon. I've been wanting to tender my congratulations."

"Consider them tendered," said Robert. He filled a cup of punch from the bowl for Charles, and, as an afterthought, another for Jonathan. His movements, Charles noticed, were not entirely steady, never a good sign. Robert didn't drink for joy; he drank to feed his temper. "Punch? I don't imagine you remember Father's recipe."

"I do, in fact," said Charles, aiming for a conciliating tone. Of Mary Anne and Jenny, he noticed, there was still no sign. "I was wont to mix it for my friends in London. It was much admired there."

"London." Robert raised his brows, inviting Mr. Boland to join in his derision. "What would they know of rum?"

"Enough to appreciate a fine bowl of punch." Charles took a hasty gulp of the concoction Robert had handed him. There was too much lemon and too little sugar; it stung going down. "Just like Father's. It tastes like Christmas. Do you remember sitting on the floor beneath the table while Father mixed the punch? He always gave us a sip or two."

Charles smiled at his brother, willing him to remember the boys they'd been, in short pants and white linen smocks, sitting cross-legged beneath the table, waiting for treats.

"And Mother sliced the great cake," Robert said grudgingly. Charles could smell the rum on his breath. "Before she became too ill."

"There was enough rum in that to fuddle a regiment," said Charles quickly, before Robert could start brooding on their mother. He nodded at Mr. Boland, including the others in the conversation. "The fumes alone could knock a man down."

"In Cork, we'd pudding made with brandy," contributed Mr. Boland. He looked fondly at his wife. "My wife's Christmas was somewhat less bibulous."

"Just because we weren't sotted by noon . . ." countered Mrs. Boland. Her cheeks were warm with punch, and she looked less severe than Charles remembered, not beautiful, but darkly handsome.

"Are you in Barbados long?" asked Charles.

"We've leased Harrow Plantation," said Mr. Boland, as Robert refilled their glasses, clanking the ladle against the sides of the glasses and slopping punch on the floor. "It's a temporary situation. The heir is in England and didn't mind the extra income for a season. My health isn't what it was. I'd like to see my wife well settled among friends."

"Your health will recover," said Mrs. Boland sternly.

"As my wife wills it," said Mr. Boland with a grin. "I'd been meaning to speak to you, Mr. Davenant, about your sugar crop."

Robert straightened, nearly overbalancing. "What about Beckles sugar?" he demanded.

"I've room enough on my ships for both," said Mr. Boland genially.

Robert dropped the ladle beside the punch bowl. "Yes, but how much?"

Mr. Boland pretended not to hear, saying to Charles, "If you've time to go through your books when the holidays are over . . ."

"I'd be delighted to make time," said Charles, looking uneasily at his brother. Mary Anne, he noticed, had still made no appearance. He was beginning to worry. "But if it's numbers you're interested in, I'll have to direct you to Mr. Fenty. He's the one who makes the books balance."

"Splendid," said Mr. Boland. "My wife and I will wait on you in the New Year."

"It would be my pleasure," said Jonathan gruffly, and sounded, astonishingly, as though he meant it.

To Charles, Mr. Boland said confidingly, "My wife will have the business when I'm gone. And she'll run it better than I, I wager. Like your Mr. Fenty, she's the one who understands the numbers."

"Women and Redlegs," muttered Robert. He pushed up from his chair. "Will you pardon me? My lady wife appears to have gone missing."

There was an emphasis on the word *lady* that Charles didn't like.

"In her condition . . ." suggested Charles.

"Don't speak to me of her condition!" Robert exploded, and stormed off toward the stairs, leaving Charles staring after him.

"There's no one so anxious as an expectant father," put in Mr. Boland, trying to ease the situation, but the words were punctuated by a fit of coughing that shook his diminished frame. He touched his handkerchief to his lips and tried to smile over it. "If there's a quiet corner, I might just rest a moment, if I may."

"Let me help you," said Charles, jumping to his feet.

"Thank you," said Mr. Boland, taking his arm without shame. "I'm not as steady on these old legs as I was. We'll leave my Winifred and your Mr. Fenty to discuss pounds and pence."

Mr. Boland kept up an inconsequential stream of chatter as Charles consulted with a maid and helped Mr. Boland up the stairs after her to a spare room, where he saw Mr. Boland settled on a bed with a glass of brandy by him.

"No, no, don't worry about me," Mr. Boland insisted. "Go back and join the party."

Charles intended to do so, and would probably have done so had he not heard Robert's voice, raised in anger, coming from behind a half-open door. "A fine hostess you are."

A servant lurked nearby, ostensibly dusting. At the sight of Charles, she moved away, just as Mary Anne retorted, "Would you rather I cast up my accounts in front of our guests? It's your child that's done this to me."

"Is it?" Robert's voice was so low, Charles could hardly hear him.

"Is it what?" asked Mary Anne impatiently.

There was a crash, the sound of glass shattering. *"Is it my child?"*

"Don't be ridiculous." Mary Anne sounded more annoyed than alarmed. "Of course it's your child! Whose else would it be?"

Charles came to an abrupt halt outside the door, unsure whether to stay or go.

"You tell me." There was the sound of heels on wood as Robert paced the room. "You were awfully close with that brother of mine before we married. Charles this . . . Charles that . . ."

"*That* again?" said Mary Anne.

"Yes, that. Don't you laugh—I know you've been laughing at me, you and my brother both—"

"Robert?" Charles couldn't wait any longer. He pushed the door open, stepping into the room, arresting Robert mid-rant. Across the room, Jenny grimaced at him. Charles ignored the warning and concentrated on Robert. "Mrs. Boland was wondering if you might mix more of your famous punch."

Mary Anne moved toward Charles with thinly veiled relief, her diamond earrings swinging against her dark curls. "I'll do it. Your brother"—she made the words sound like a slur—"always puts too much lemon in."

"Not so fast." Robert grabbed Mary Anne's arm, pulling her into a punitive embrace. "Someone told me they saw my wife's maid at the overseer's house at Peverills last week. What was my wife's maid doing at the overseer's house at Peverills?"

Charles froze. "I have no idea what you're talking about."

"No? If her maid was there, I've a pretty good idea my wife was there too. And do you know who else someone saw going in? You, brother. You."

"Of course I was there," Charles said, trying to keep his voice level. "The new overseer arrives in two weeks. There were repairs to be seen to. . . ."

"And precisely where were you placing the screw, brother?"

"Stop embarrassing yourself and me," said Mary Anne sharply. "I've no idea what you're on about. When was this supposed tryst?"

"Tuesday afternoon," Robert shot back.

"Tuesday afternoon," spat Mary Anne, glaring at her husband, "I was asleep in my bed, alone. Queenie was sitting with me. You can ask her."

"And how would I know she wouldn't lie for you?"

"Would she risk disobliging her master?"

"Oh, am I master here? I thought you'd forgot." Robert folded his arms across his chest, swaying slightly on his feet. "If you were here, then what was your maid doing at Peverills?"

"Whoever told you that was mistaken," said Charles, moving to stand between Robert and Mary Anne. "It was one of the maids from Peverills your friend saw. I had her in to clean for the new man."

Robert regarded him suspiciously. "They said it was Mary Anne's girl."

"One woman in an apron and cap looks much like another," Charles said lightly, the words like glass on his tongue. He was all too aware of Jenny behind him, half-hidden by bed curtains.

Robert looked narrowly at Charles, or as narrowly as he could with his eyes half-crossed. "He said he heard . . . you know."

"Is that so unusual? You've said it yourself, a man would have to be a saint not to take what's offered. I'm no saint, Robin."

That was almost enough to appease Robert. Almost. For a moment, his face lit. "My high-and-mighty brother, sampling dark fruit! The colonel always said you would sooner or later."

Charles resisted the urge to plant a leveler on his brother's chin. "As you see," he said tightly, "your suspicions are unfounded."

It was a mistake to remind him. His expression darkening, Robert turned to his wife. "Whatever it was, I don't like that maid of yours."

Mary Anne's color was high in her cheeks. "Jenny didn't do anything. Didn't you hear Charles? It was a mistake. You're making a fool of yourself and me."

Robert swayed on his feet, his eyes on Jenny. "You're too thick. It isn't right. Someone's got to remember who's master here. Don't like it."

"Oh no." Mary Anne stepped in front of Jenny, facing her husband down. "Jenny is mine. She's mine and you won't take her from me."

"She's mine to sell if I please," retorted Robert belligerently.

This wasn't how they'd planned it, but he'd take what he could. Charles clasped his hands behind his back, trying to hide the sudden racing of his heart. "I'll buy her off you. If you're selling."

"We're not," said Mary Anne fiercely, just as Robert said, "Oh?"

"We could use a new housekeeper at Peverills," Charles said rapidly. "Old Doll is getting on. . . ."

"Not Jenny." Mary Anne clutched at Robert's arm, forcing him to look down at her. "I won't give up my Jenny."

For a moment, no one spoke, all eyes fixed on Robert.

"Please, Robert," said Mary Anne, her voice breaking. Her bosom pressed against his arm; her face was lifted to his in supplication. "You wouldn't."

Robert's lip curled and Charles thought . . . he hoped . . .

Robert shrugged, wrapping an arm around Mary Anne's waist, although whether for affection or to keep from falling, Charles wasn't quite sure. "My wife has spoken. I wouldn't want to upset her while she's with child."

Robert's hand rose, pointedly, to her breast. Mary Anne glanced up at him with slitted eyes, and something crackled between them that was both anger and desire.

Charles looked away, sickened by it all, not sure whether to charge to the rescue or beat a tactful retreat. "If you ever change your mind . . ."

"You couldn't afford the fee. Brother." Robert gave Mary Anne a light shove on the small of her back. "Shall we go down?"

"Yes, of course." Mary Anne looked back over her shoulder. "Jenny . . ."

"Leave her," said Robert sharply, and Mary Anne had no choice but to accompany him, head down, eyes mutinous.

Charles waited until they had gone, and then, softly, closed the door.

They didn't need words; they came together as one, holding each other like mariners in a high wind clinging to a spar, as though that was all that stood between them and oblivion. It was torture to be so close after so long apart, and to know that it was only a moment, that Charles would have to go downstairs and be charming to the Bolands, and Jenny would have to smooth her hair and stand behind her mistress, and neither could give any sign of what they meant to each other.

"We have to be more careful," murmured Charles into Jenny's hair.

"I know. We shouldn't be here together now." Jenny lifted her head, looking at him with a dazed expression that tore his heart to shreds. "Oh, Charles. I had thought, earlier today, that she might mean to free me. But she doesn't, does she? She doesn't mean to give me up. Not now. Not ever."

Charles held her all the tighter. This wouldn't be forever, he promised himself. He'd see this sorted. Somehow. "Not now, no. But we can keep trying." Half-jokingly, he said, "Maybe we can make Robert angry enough to sell you against her wishes. It's only a matter of time."

"What if we haven't time?"

She seemed so defeated, so unlike herself, that Charles grasped her shoulders with alarm, holding her away from him. "What is it? What's wrong? Has he hurt you? Are you ill?"

"No." Jenny's mouth worked as though she was trying not to cry. "I'm with child."

CHAPTER SEVENTEEN

Christ Church, Barbados
May 1854

"WITH CHILD?" EMILY looked at Dr. Braithwaite in surprise. "No, that's—"

Retching. Lethargy. Yes, Laura liked to read novels and daydream, but not like this. So many times, Emily had come upon her with her book fallen facedown on her lap, her eyes closed and head thrown back, as if simply being was eating up all of her resources.

Not being. A being. A baby.

"Yes?" prompted Dr. Braithwaite.

"That's entirely possible," Emily finished weakly. "But why wouldn't she have told me?"

"Natural delicacy?" suggested Dr. Braithwaite. "Or she might not know herself."

Emily remembered the way Adam had shut the door, the way he had told her not to fuss. No, they knew, she was sure. They had simply chosen not to share the news with her, and the realization burned like the handle of a hot kettle, too quickly grasped in a bare palm.

"Maybe," said Emily unhappily.

She was spared further comment by George's appearance. Jonah carried two buckets of water.

"There," directed George, pointing to the hearth. "Is there any other task we might perform?"

"That should be sufficient," said Dr. Braithwaite, politely enough, but there was an edge to it, a tension that crackled between the two men.

Emily had no patience for either of them. "Don't you have patients to see?" she said to Dr. Braithwaite.

"I thought you'd scared them away," said Dr. Braithwaite mildly. He poured more water into the kettle. He nodded to George. "Thank you for the water."

"You're welcome," said George gruffly, and Emily thought she would never understand men. "There was still a patient or two about. I'll send them in, shall I?"

As George poked his head around the door, Dr. Braithwaite said quietly to Emily, "I wouldn't worry too much about your friend. Everything you mentioned is quite common. It won't do her or the baby any harm."

"Yes, I know." Emily's throat felt very tight. Belatedly, she added, "Thank you."

Dr. Braithwaite set down the water bucket. "You never told me: Am I to be tossed out on my ear?"

It felt strange to have such power. Emily wasn't entirely sure she liked it. "Not on my account. I might want the house to use. . . . But I'm sure we can come to an arrangement."

"Financial?"

"Do you charge your patients? I didn't think so." There was a movement at the door. Emily waved a hand. "We can discuss it some other time. At the moment, feel free to carry on."

"Thank you," said Dr. Braithwaite drily. To Katy, who had come in with the little girl, he said, "What seems to be the trouble?"

Not looking at Emily, Katy nudged the little girl forward. After some chivvying, the little girl said, "My throat hurts."

"Open up and let me have a look, then."

Katy murmured something in the child's ear, and the little girl obediently opened her mouth for the doctor.

George shifted uncomfortably. "We should be going. . . ."

"Just a moment. Have you tried a gargle of salt and vinegar with a dash of pepper?" suggested Emily, attempting to peer over Dr. Braithwaite's shoulder. She was rewarded largely with a view of black broadcloth. She moved up on her tiptoes. "Or perhaps a solution of brewer's yeast and honey?"

Dr. Braithwaite stepped back and turned to look at Emily. "Would you like to take over?" His eyes crinkled and the corners of his mustache lifted. "I shouldn't ask that, should I? You would."

Disarmed by that smile, Emily demurred, "I'm not a physician. Or a surgeon either."

"No, but you've certainly done your apprenticeship. Salt and vinegar," he said to Katy. "Come back next week if the throat doesn't improve or if she develops a fever."

He looked at Emily as though challenging her to contradict him. Emily nodded. She was, it seemed, committed to running a free clinic on her plantation.

They left Dr. Braithwaite to his practice. His patients had returned, threefold, the word having spread that the surgery was open. Emily recognized only one or two faces, but she could tell that George knew most. Some greeted him; others developed an interest in the rutted dirt of the yard.

As for George, Emily couldn't tell what he was thinking.

"It's good work he's doing," she said tentatively, as they mounted their horses. After two months of George's tutelage, she was now competent, if not comfortable. She wasn't sure she would ever be entirely comfortable on horseback.

"Oh yes, excellent work," said George. There was a bitter edge to his voice. "Charity work."

You wouldn't need his charity if you had a better surgeon on hand, Emily wanted to say, but couldn't. She felt a wave of pity for her companion, who had all the cares of trusteeship but none of the powers. That the people of Beckles needed better medical attention was plain; that

George couldn't outwardly sanction Dr. Braithwaite's work equally clear. His grandmother would never stand for it, and she was still the real power at Beckles.

Had that been the compromise, then? To know but ignore?

Emily squinted under the brim of her bonnet at George's profile. "Is that why you didn't want me coming to Peverills? Because of Dr. Braithwaite?"

"No one is trying to keep you from Peverills." It would have been more convincing if he hadn't looked away as he said it.

"No?" They had passed the Old Mill. If she wanted to know anything, she needed to ask now, before they were back inside the stultifying atmosphere of the house.

"Peverills is a sore subject. My grandmother . . ."

"Minds that it was sold. Yes, I know." That was beginning to sound thinner and thinner, especially as Peverills had never been hers to begin with. "Those ledgers your grandmother had from Peverills. Do you think you could get them for me?"

"Surely that's a matter for my grandmother?"

"She said I could have them." It wasn't entirely untrue. She had certainly implied Emily could have them. Emily had accepted the invitation to Beckles on the strength of that offer. "You know how busy she is. She just hasn't got around to it yet."

George looked unconvinced.

Through the trees, Emily could see the glint of sun on glass. "You've been lovely showing me about Beckles, but that only goes so far. I won't know what the scope of Peverills should be—could be—until I see what Peverills once was."

"There's truth in that," admitted George reluctantly. "Although I'm not sure how much you'll benefit from that. According to my grandmother, my uncle made a hash of running the place. He had unusual notions."

"Unusual notions?"

"Er, tenant farms and that sort of thing."

"That hardly sounds unusual to me," said Emily.

"Perhaps not in England. But in Barbados, fifty years ago . . . that sort of thing wasn't done. And for a reason. It was a financial disaster."

"It wouldn't need to be, would it?" asked Emily. "Managed properly, there are all sorts of possibilities. Have you heard of Brook Farm?"

"No, I'm afraid I haven't. What do they grow?"

"Hearts and souls, primarily," said Emily cheerfully. "It's a community in Massachusetts of thinkers and farmers." Or had been. Belatedly, she remembered it had failed a few years before. Her father, who had correspondents there, had been terribly disappointed.

"Well . . . Americans," said George, as though that explained that. "The conditions in the northern parts of the United States are quite different, as I understand it. Sugar isn't the sort of crop that responds well to smallholding."

"Oh, I wasn't thinking about breaking up the estate. But if everyone who worked the estate had shares in it, and received back commensurate with what they put in . . ." George was trying to behave himself but looked deeply skeptical. "You see why I need the ledgers? I don't know the slightest thing about the exigencies of sugar production. Perhaps seeing it all in ink, as it were, will cure me of utopian notions."

"I should think living with Grandmother would do that," said George. They trotted sedately into the stable yard. George dismounted, then held out a hand to help Emily. "All right. I'll see what I can do about those ledgers."

When Emily went upstairs, there was hot water waiting for her, but no Katy. She had, she realized uncomfortably, become accustomed to the strange alchemy by which water was available for washing, food for eating, clothes for wearing, ink for writing, before she ever knew she needed it. Over two months at Beckles, she had grown to take these things for granted, and the people who provided them.

In the place of Katy was Mrs. Davenant's own maid Queenie, the lace on her cap a sign of her elevated office. If her pride was hurt at being sent to see to a guest, she didn't show it, only undid the buttons of Emily's habit, helping her out of the damp and clinging wool.

"Does Katy have a daughter?" Emily asked, emerging gasping from a faceful of hot water.

Queenie efficiently stripped Emily of her soiled shift. "Katy has four children." She produced a clean chemise, smelling of sunshine and soap. "Three girls, one boy."

"Oh," said Emily. She stood still as Queenie tied the tapes of her petticoat around her waist, raising her arms as an apple-green cotton day dress was lowered over her head. "Four children."

She thought of the late nights Katy waited to undress her for bed, the early mornings when Katy was there to direct her toilette.

Queenie sat Emily down, brushing out Emily's sweat-damp hair with smooth, even strokes. "My grandbabies," she said.

"You're Katy's mother?" Emily turned her head to look and found her head being gently but firmly pushed back into place.

"Grandmother," Queenie corrected her. "My daughter was maid to Miss Julia, Master Edward's wife. Someday Katy will be maid to Mr. George's wife."

With neat movements, she sleeked Emily's hair into two loops, one on either side of her head.

"I see. How nice. You don't look much like Katy," she said, in an attempt to exonerate herself and to avoid thinking of what it meant that she'd been given the maid designated for Mr. George's future wife.

"She takes after her father," said Queenie, securing an enamel comb over each loop. "He's head joiner."

Aristocracy of sorts, Emily gathered. She felt like the lowest sort of crawling creature for never having realized the family relationships inside the house. No fraternizing with the servants, that was Aunt Millicent's rule, but Emily had always prided herself on asking anyway, being aware of who had a sister in service or a cousin in the poorhouse or a little brother in want of a trade.

She ought to have asked. Why hadn't she asked?

It was Beckles, she decided. Her mother had written about the moral rot of slavery, sinking into the soul one luxury at a time, and Emily could feel her own soul in the balance, a decaying thing tricked out in lace and gold bangles.

Yes, she knew what Dr. Braithwaite had said about Bridgetown in the hot season, but it was hot here as well, as far as she could tell. The sooner they left, the better. Surely Adam and Laura must be bored by now?

"Thank you," she called after Queenie, then lifted her beribboned skirts and went to find Laura.

Laura wasn't in her room or lying on the veranda. Emily finally found her in the garden, in a shaded bower where bright-petaled flowers grew and vines had been trained over a trellis overhead, creating a fragrant canopy.

George sat at her feet, still in his riding things, a book in his hand, his hat discarded beside him.

"*I love thee to the level of every day's / Most quiet need, by sun and candlelight. / I love thee freely, as men strive for right.*"

"Laura?"

George stumbled to his feet, stepping on his own hat in the process. "Oh, hullo. We were just reading."

Laura sat in the shade of the bower, one hand, Emily noticed, lying lightly on her stomach. "It's a book called *Sonnets from the Portuguese*. By a lady," she added.

"Why from the Portuguese?" asked Emily.

George looked to Laura. "I'm not sure, really. Do you know?" Without waiting for an answer, he scooped up his maltreated hat and set the small volume reverently beside Laura on the bench. "I'll leave you. I've a dozen tasks left undone."

"You'll find me those ledgers?" Emily prompted.

"The . . . ? Oh yes, certainly." George took himself off in a flurry.

Laura, without comment, scooted her skirts closer to her, making room for Emily on the bench.

Emily settled herself beside her, disconcerted by the familiarity of it all. How often had they sat together like this, Laura with a volume of poetry in her hand, closed over one finger, as Emily held forth about this and that? But now Emily found the words stunted on her lips; she felt strangely uneasy in the company of her best and oldest friend.

"Did you have a good ride?" Laura asked as the silence lengthened.

"It was very hot," said Emily. "Dr. Braithwaite is running a surgery from Peverills."

"I should think you would enjoy that," said Laura, looking at Emily tolerantly, and, for a brief moment, everything was as it had been again.

Emily twisted the locket on its ribbon around her throat. "Well, yes. But I'd rather thought we might stay in the bookkeeper's house while I dealt with putting the plantation back into order, and if Dr. Braithwaite has his surgery there . . ."

Two fine lines appeared between Laura's brows. "Stay at the book-keeper's house?"

It wasn't how she'd intended to broach the topic. "We've rather overstayed our welcome at Beckles, haven't we?"

Laura sat upright, the poetry book forgotten. "Has Mrs. Davenant asked us to go?"

"No! Quite the contrary. She seems perfectly happy to have us cluttering up her drawing room until the sound of the last trump. But you know what Grandfather always said, 'Neither a borrower nor a lender be. . . .'"

"That was Polonius," said Laura flatly. "In *Hamlet*. Your grandfather's whole business was built on borrowing and lending."

"Not his whole business. . . ." Emily shoved her carefully arranged hair back behind her ears. "I'm sorry. I didn't mean to distress you."

"I'm not distressed," said Laura, in a voice that, to Emily, gave the lie to the statement. Others might see Laura as reserved, but Emily knew all the little tricks of her tone, the silences that spoke louder than words. Laura was very distressed, indeed.

"It was just a thought. I—I've been worried about you. You haven't been yourself." Emily looked hopefully at Laura, willing her to say something. "Are you sure you're quite all right?"

"Quite." Laura stood, putting out a hand against the trellis to steady herself. A few petals drifted down about their heads. "Shall we go in? I should like to rest."

As far as Emily could see, Laura's day was one continuous rest, but it was clear that the topic was closed. "Do you know when Adam will be back from Bridgetown?"

"Adam will return when he sees fit to return." Laura's hands tightened on the volume of poetry. "Why?"

"No reason. I had something I wanted to ask him. It's not important."

And it wasn't, she told herself. The words George had been reading weren't his; they were a lady's, possibly translated from the Portuguese. Adam and Laura had passage booked back to England in June. They would leave and their stay at Beckles would become nothing but a memory, a story to be told of their tropical sojourn in chill drawing rooms in Bristol.

Emily retreated to her room, where she found, to her surprise, that the desk of the escritoire in the corner of her room had been lowered and an untidy stack of clothbound ledgers dropped on it, spilling one over the other.

Laura's delicate condition could wait. Emily seated herself eagerly at the table, set out some blank paper, dipped her nib in ink, and began.

Men and women, horses and oxen, bushels of feed and bolts of cloth. The Peverills that had been unfurled across the page in her grandfather's strong hand. The land that she had only seen laid waste came back to life, a busy, bustling place, with carpenters and seamstresses, cooks and housemaids, wheelwrights and joiners, and everything else one could imagine. It was all there, down to the tiniest detail.

Some made Emily squirm uncomfortably in her seat.

The slave trade had been long since abolished by the time her grandfather had taken over his wife's shipping company. He had traded in sugar, rum, and molasses; in cloth and tools and timber. Never in flesh. But here. This. This was how the sugar his ships had carried had been planted and harvested, with the sweat of men and women whose lives were not their own. And her grandfather, as book-keeper, had noted it, without criticism or comment, bonuses for the women who bore children, the value assigned to each man, woman, and child.

Thank goodness for people like her mother, then, Emily told herself determinedly, and forced herself to concentrate on the practical aspects, the numbers of barrels required, the repairs to machinery.

The numbers involved seemed very large to her, but she could tell why Mrs. Davenant had shaken her head over the management of Pe-verills; however large the revenue, the outgoing receipts were nearly as great, leaving little in the way of profit. She could see where econ-omies began to be made, household stuffs cut down, the number of candles and amount of tea queried and then reduced.

Her grandfather's salary was in there with the rest, and then— Emily blinked, thinking she must be misreading. No. Her grandfather's hand was remarkably clear. Payments to a Rachel Fenty, for fine sewing.

There were no fewer than eight seamstresses on the plantation.

Rachel Fenty . . . Vaguely, Emily remembered her grandfather speaking of his sisters. He'd been youngest of six, six who lived, that was. It was a story he loved to tell, the poverty and loss in sharp con-trast to the well-lit room with its polished brass fire irons and Axmin-ster carpet. Yes, he'd mentioned his sister Rachel, closest to him in age and temperament.

It wasn't surprising that he might have found her employment on the plantation. What was surprising was the sum. Emily flipped for-ward, her pen resting forgotten against the blotter. There it was, once a month, starting in July of 1813. Rachel Fenty: fine sewing, two dollars.

A special project of some sort? Needlepoint chair covers or brocade drapes? It would have to be very fine, indeed, to merit the sum.

The payments stopped, abruptly, in January of 1815.

Emily set aside the 1813 and 1814 ledgers, an uneasy feeling in the pit of her stomach. There were other payments to tradesmen outside the plantation. But nothing like that, nothing so regular.

Her grandfather thought the Peverills owed them, Adam had said. It would be like her grandfather to settle the score by any means possible. If he believed he was owed the money . . . it wouldn't be stealing.

She was, she realized, chewing the end of her pen and staining her fingers with ink. Emily hastily set down the pen. She was being fanciful. It was that ridiculous Mrs. Poole, that was all, going on about Redlegs and sabotage and goodness only knew what. The payments to Rachel Fenty for fine sewing were probably just that, payments for fine sewing.

Emily returned to the 1815 ledger, forcing herself to concentrate. She was beginning to note the patterns in the ledgers now, the regular rhythms of the plantation year. Her grandfather had separate sections in the book for agrarian and household expenses, although the two sometimes blurred, as her eyes were beginning to do. Her stomach grumbled, reminding her she'd had only a hasty bite to eat before riding out to Peverills that morning.

She glanced at the clock and was amazed to realize that she'd missed luncheon; she'd been bent over the ledgers for hours. Emily hunched her shoulders, stretching as much as the closely stitched fabric of her bodice would allow.

She was ready to close the 1815 book when a new entry caught her eye. *Cot for Carlota.*

There was also an order of law to make Carlota underthings, leather to be given to the cobbler to make her shoes, muslin for her dresses, and ribbons for her hair.

He had a ward, George had said. A Portuguese ward, without a name, without a grave.

But here she was. Here was her name. Carlota. Carlota in a sprig muslin dress with blue ribbons for her plaits, put to bed in a cot made for her by the most senior of the plantation carpenters, a cot with carved finials, and a small rocking chair made to match.

Another page in, her name came up again.

One doll (Paris).

Wooden ark and animals (Dresden).

The estate carpenter must have been capable of making playthings. These were the very cream of their kind, imported from England and France, Italy and the German states.

One gold bracelet, for Lottie. She was Lottie now, Emily noticed, with an ache in her chest for this little girl in her ruffled lace panta-lets and sprig muslin dress, her hair tied back with silk ribbons, Italian leather slippers on her little feet, kneeling by her German Noah's ark, her French doll in her arms, a gold bracelet from the finest goldsmith in London on her wrist.

That poor, poor child. Whoever she was, wherever she had come from, she had settled in to Peverills, been loved, cherished. She could feel it even in the ledger, the extra care her grandfather had taken with the entries for Lottie, the writing careful and clear, the letters just a bit larger than usual. There was a doll's house made for her in March of 1816, and then, just one month later, nothing. All entries ended, the pages blank.

Can you imagine that? To have made it through a war safely and then to die like this? George's words echoed through Emily's mind.

Emily shivered and started to shut the ledger—when something struck her, forcibly.

Eighteen sixteen. Peverills had burned in 1816. Poor little Lottie, Carlota, whatever her name was, had died in 1816. Everything had ended in 1816, including her grandfather's entries in this, the very last ledger for the accounts for Peverills Plantation.

She had been so caught up in the pathos of the little lost girl that it had taken her a moment to realize the oddity of it all, these entries in her grandfather's unmistakable hand.

Her grandfather had left Barbados when he married and never come back, that was what Emily had always been told. By April of 1816, her grandparents were two years married, her mother over one year old, and Uncle Archibald on the way, or nearly.

What, then, was her grandfather doing keeping accounts for Peverills in 1816?

CHAPTER EIGHTEEN

Christ Church, Barbados
December 1812

"ARE YOU CERTAIN? I thought you said . . ."

"That I couldn't bear children. That's what Nanny Bell told me." Jenny took a step back, wrapping her arms around herself. "I could be wrong. It might be nothing."

"Or Nanny Bell might be wrong." An ebullient grin spread across Charles's face as he swept Jenny into an exuberant embrace. "Just think of it. Our child. Our *child*."

His joy was infectious. But only for a moment. Jenny wiggled to be set down. "Not just our child. Your brother's chattel."

"No." She'd never seen Charles's face look so hard. "I won't allow it."

"How? It doesn't matter if the child is yours or not. If it's mine, it's his." She had lain awake night after night, uneasily feeling the tenderness in her breasts, telling herself it must be something else, that her courses might be late for any number of reasons. Not Charles's baby.

Their baby.

Charles's lips set in a determined line. "If I told Robert—"

"That it's yours?" Jenny stared at him. "Do you really think that would help?"

"No. You're right," Charles said slowly. "Of course."

He was staring at her, and Jenny realized she'd wrapped her arms around her stomach, as though already protecting the child within.

Flushing, she dropped her arms and made a flapping gesture at Charles. "Go. You'll be missed. We don't want anyone asking questions."

"No. Not now." Resting his hands on her shoulders, Charles kissed her as carefully as if she were made of fine porcelain. "We'll speak of this more later. Is there anything that you need?"

"Nothing you can give me." Too late, Jenny realized how it sounded. Rising on her toes, she pressed a quick kiss to the corner of his lips. "If there's anything, I'll tell you. You know that."

"Do I?" said Charles. He looked at her very seriously. "We'll find a way to see you free before the child is born, I promise."

Don't, Jenny wanted to say. Don't promise what you can't achieve. It was almost worse to have the hope of something knowing it could never be. But she couldn't say that to Charles, not when she knew that he meant it truly, that he would do anything in his control to make it happen.

It was just a pity there wasn't terribly much within his control.

"I know," she said instead. "Go."

It was only when he had gone that she allowed herself the luxury of sinking down on Mary Anne's chaise longue, pulling up her legs until her forehead touched her knees. She would have cried, but what good would tears do? She had learned that all those long years ago on the ship from Jamaica, when she had cried for her mother, and her tears had brought her nothing but threats.

"You won't have to cry for me," she promised her baby, and felt ridiculous for speaking to someone who couldn't hear.

Mary Anne wasn't Jenny's father. She wasn't cruel, at least, not intentionally. But Master Robert? That was another story entirely. He had the viciousness of the weak, flaring out in temper, hurting for the sake of hurting. It was, in its way, almost more alarming than the calculated cruelties of Jenny's father. One could predict those.

Jenny didn't think Mary Anne would sell her child away from her—but Master Robert might. Especially if he knew or suspected it was his brother's child.

There was the oil of oleander. She'd thought of that when she'd first missed her time, when she'd begun to feel the fullness in her chest, the weariness in her bones.

But then she'd thought of Charles and known she couldn't. Last time, she'd had no qualms, but this child, their child . . .

Fool, she told herself. Sentimental fool.

But she couldn't help picturing the child all the same. A little boy with her face and Charles's mop of curls, holding a hoop and stick. She thought of that day in Bridgetown, the house Charles's father had bought his lover, the little girl learning to play the pianoforte.

He'd find a way, he promised, and she believed he meant it. Her Charles, with his lawyer's brain and his belief in the fundamental goodness of man. Jenny lifted her head, rubbing her aching temples. Well, she was cynic enough for both of them. Together . . . together they'd think of something, she promised the unknown creature in her stomach.

But when she met with Charles the following week, in the shadows behind the icehouse, his face told its own story.

"I spoke to Robert after the militia meeting," he said, without preamble. "Don't worry—I didn't mention you by name. I just asked again whether there were any upper servants at Beckles who might make a likely housekeeper for Peverills."

"And?" asked Jenny, although she already knew the answer.

Charles shook his head.

Jenny swallowed her disappointment, amazed at how much it hurt, this loss of something she'd never expected to have. "You knew he wouldn't sell you a cat you wanted," she said, trying to keep her voice matter-of-fact. "Not now."

She could have cried for their own foolishness, for that ill-fated tryst where she'd been seen. But for that . . . No, she couldn't think that way. There was no point in looking back, only forward.

In a low voice, Charles asked, "Was it selfish of me to refuse to wed Mary Anne? If I had . . . I might have freed you. You might be free now."

"And chained yourself?" Jenny shook her head reluctantly. She knew him now, knew the workings of his conscience, so different from her own. He would torture himself over a scruple, break over the loss of an ideal. "You couldn't have done so in honor. And—"

"Yes?" Charles's feelings were written all over his face.

Jenny turned her own away, unable to bear it, to be so bare. What could she say? That if he'd married Mary Anne, they would never have had this? It scared her how much these moments meant to her, how she craved his company, his touch.

"There's no point in sighing over what might have been. There's only the road ahead."

"So there is." Charles squared his shoulders. "What about the Bolands? Robert doesn't want to offend Boland. If Boland were to buy you for his wife . . . Perhaps she needs a maid."

"She has one," said Jenny, remembering Nanny Grigg, with her borrowed spool of thread and her English papers. She had liked Nanny Grigg, liked her instinctively.

"I could ask Boland to buy you as a favor. If I explained the situation . . ."

Jenny stiffened. "And if he told the master?"

"He seems like a good-hearted man."

Jenny squeezed his hand, as if she could squeeze some sense into him. "He didn't build up a shipping business by being good-hearted! Are you willing to stake our child's well-being on seeming?"

"No." Charles lifted her hand absently to his lips, toying with her fingers as he thought. He looked up, his eyes very blue. "We could go away together. You'd be free in London."

"How?" asked Jenny skeptically. "If I were still your brother's property . . ."

"That doesn't matter. Lord Mansfield declared it years ago, in Somersett's case. The air of England is too pure for a slave to breathe in."

Charles's shoulders straightened, his chin lifted; Jenny could almost hear the trumpets playing. Sheepishly, Charles dropped his chin. "Well, Mansfield himself didn't say it—the man who spoke for Somersett did—but it's accepted as dictum all the same. And Mansfield himself decided it. As soon as Somersett set foot on English soil, he was set free, and not another enslaved man has remained in chains in England since."

To be free. She stared at Charles, seeing her own wonder and delight mirrored in his face.

But only for a moment.

When something sounded too good to be true, Jenny knew, it generally was.

"Once we set foot in England, I would be free. But what of you?" She put a hand to his lips, forestalling his answer. "I would be free, but you would be branded a felon. Everything you had would be forfeit."

"Not forfeit, precisely," began Charles, and broke off at Jenny's look. "I'd be charged a fine, most likely."

"You wouldn't be able to come back." He didn't deny it. "You would be a criminal and, worse than a criminal, a traitor."

"But I would have you and our child." He sounded as though he were trying to convince himself.

"And Peverills?"

Charles looked away, and Jenny knew, with a sinking feeling, that they wouldn't be going anywhere, least of all to England.

"Perhaps I should just sell it all to Robert," said Charles, with an attempt at lightness. "He has the blunt to hear him tell it. We could take the money and sail away."

"If you sold it to your brother, he would abandon all your plans. Everything you've worked for would be torn up within a fortnight."

"It might take him slightly longer than that. A month, at the least." When she didn't return his smile, he abandoned the pretense. "Yes."

It hurt more than anything she had ever done, to give up that dream of England and freedom. But how could she be the cause of Charles's misery? "You have people who depend on you."

"Would you force me to be honorable at your expense?"

Jenny gave a strangled laugh. "I can't force you to be honorable. You are. It's in your bones. You would hate me, by and by, if you gave it all up for my sake alone."

"Not for your sake alone."

"And if I were to miscarry or our child were stillborn? Such things have been known to happen. There would be no going back." Every part of her being recoiled from the words, but she forced herself to say them anyway. "Wait a while yet. England will still be there if it comes to that."

The relief on his face cut through her like a knife. Eagerly, too eagerly, Charles said, "I've been corresponding with Henry Brougham—he was a member of Parliament, although he's out of office at the moment. He says sentiment in England is changing. Emancipation is coming—he's willing to stake his career on it."

"Is it?" She didn't want to ruin his dreams, but, from where she was standing, it sounded like so many empty words. "Mary Anne thinks it's all nonsense."

"Trust me," said Charles. "No one thought they'd abolish the slave trade, and yet that happened."

Jenny rested her hand on her stomach, still flat beneath the thin fabric of her dress and chemise. "And how long did that take?"

Charles looked slightly abashed. "You're right. We need action, not dreams."

"I like your dreams," said Jenny softly. And she did. She loved him for dreaming them. Attempting to cheer him, she said, "Who knows? If my mistress makes the master angry enough, he might sell me just to get back at her."

"Will you tell her about the child?"

"I'll have to. If she discovers it without hearing first from me, she won't like it." Jenny put a hand on his arm, trying to sound as reassuring as she could. "Don't worry. I know how to manage my mistress."

Or she had once.

Mary Anne's moods were erratic, her temper uncertain. Jenny

weathered the storms and bided her time, knowing that, sooner or later, someone would comment on her lack of bloody cloths, and Mary Anne's temper would be touched by her silence. It wasn't enough for Mary Anne to own her body, these days, she needed to own her mind and heart as well, channeling all her fear and discomfort into a fierce possessiveness, clinging to Jenny as she hadn't since those first, horrible days after the incident of the poisoned chocolate, when their world had collapsed around them.

It was in March that Jenny finally broached the subject with her mistress, as she massaged what had, at one point, been Mary Anne's ankles. Mary Anne wasn't quite six months gone, but her feet and ankles had all but disappeared in swollen flesh; it hurt her to walk, so she was carried about on a palanquin laden with cushions, squinting against the light. Jenny had smuggled her the accounts to try to cheer her up, but she complained the words shifted and blurred on the page.

Jenny had consulted Nanny Bell, who told her only that it took women that way sometimes and brewed a pot of dandelion tea for the swelling.

Mary Anne drank it without seeming to notice what it was, and looked for more. "Is there any water left in the jug? I'll have to use the chamber pot again, but I don't care. I feel I could drink an ocean and still be thirsty."

"Here." Jenny poured her a glass of well water and watched as her mistress guzzled it down, drops falling on her dress. When Mary Anne had finished, Jenny said, "I've something to tell you. I think—I'm fairly sure—I'm with child."

Mary Anne set down the empty glass very, very slowly. "How?"

"The usual way." She knew what Mary Anne was really asking. "There was a man I met in Antigua. Do you remember the dance at Fairview? The one the Bolands gave in your honor? He was a guest."

"A white man?" Jenny nodded, trying to read Mary Anne's thoughts beneath her hooded lids. Mary Anne turned her head restlessly against the cushions. "Did he force you?"

"No! He was . . . very charming. And I—I was lonely." The words spilled out, half truth, half lie. "I'm happy for your marriage, Mistress Mary, don't think I'm not, but it's always been us together, the two of us. And now you have Master Robert and the baby and I . . . He was kind."

As she said it, she could almost believe it, the handsome stranger at the dance, sweet words in the garden, a moment's lapse.

Whether Mary Anne believed it was another matter. "What was his name?"

"Henry." It was the first to pop into Jenny's head. "He never told me his last name. He was visiting, from the Carolinas, I think he said."

Mary Anne pushed herself up against the pillows, looking a bit more like her old self as she calculated. "If it was the dance at Fairview, then you'll be due in . . . late July."

"First babies sometimes come late, that's what Nanny Bell always says."

"This one had better not," said Mary Anne grimly, looking at the curve of her stomach. "I've had enough of him already. Ah, well. That's one good thing to your condition. He'll be a companion for my boy."

Jenny knew better than to point out that one or both might be girls. Mary Anne was determined to bear a male child, and if she said it, so must it be.

Mary Anne's face was gray with fatigue and pain. "Your child and mine. History repeats itself."

"But not in all ways," Jenny said hastily.

"I hope not." There was an abstracted expression on Mary Anne's face, as though she were working out a particularly knotty sum, and one whose result didn't please her. "Bring me my writing desk. And call Queenie. I want to send a letter."

"Shall I carry it for you?"

"No." Mary Anne softened the harsh negative by saying roughly, "Bearing a child is miserable. I need you to take care of yourself."

This, for Mary Anne, Jenny knew, was an effusive expression of concern.

"Thank you," she said quietly, her expression calm, her emotions in turmoil, resentment and affection, all jumbled together. She would leave Mary Anne for England in a moment if the chance arose. But she would also feel guilty for it, as absurd as she knew that to be.

Mary Anne turned her face away, uncomfortable at being caught out in a kindness. "How will you attend me if you don't? Weren't you meant to be fetching Queenie?"

Jenny never did see what Mary Anne wrote, but Charles did. The letter came to him as he was in conference with the head driver, mapping out a new constellation of tenant farms. Making his apologies, he traded his stained buckskins for pantaloons, hastily tied a fresh cravat, and took horse to Beckles.

Mary Anne received him in the garden, where a special chair had been arranged for her in the shade of the arbor, well supplied with cushions.

It had been some months since he had seen her—four to be precise—and the change in her was as alarming as it was sudden. Her face was puffy, her hands and fingers so swollen that her wedding ring was all but lost in the reddened swell of flesh. She looked like a caricature of herself drawn by Gillray, the greedy Creole swollen with sugar proceeds, lolling on cushions and being served iced drinks by a waiting slave.

Charles dropped to his knees beside her chair, horrified. "Miss Be— Mary Anne. I had no idea it was so bad."

"There's no need to wring your hands over me," she said irritably. "I'm with child. It's hardly an unusual condition."

"No, but—" Charles felt entirely at a loss. His knowledge of pregnancy was hardly extensive, but he'd had enough friends with sisters and wives to know that this was something out of the ordinary. He seized on a vague memory from a drawing-room discussion in London. "Has Robert called for an accoucheur? It's quite commonplace now in London, to have a specialist for childbirth."

"As if any man could know more than Nanny Bell. Who do you think delivers your slaves' children?" Charles was caught wrong-footed. He knew, of course, that there were children who were born

and midwives who cared for them, but other than ratifying the distri-
bution of extra provisions and monetary gifts to the new mothers, he
had little to do with it. Mary Anne took advantage of his confusion
to say, "That's what I wanted to talk to you about. No, not my child.
My maid's. Jenny's."

Charles sat down abruptly on his heels. "Oh? Is your maid with
child? If you need a new maid, I'm the last person to be of assistance."

"It's not that." Mary Anne drank deeply from her water glass, then
held it up for the slave standing behind her to refill it, never once looking back as the water magically poured into the glass. "She claims the
father was a Henry from the Carolinas."

There was a slave behind her with a water jug, another with a
palmetto fan. Mary Anne seemed entirely unaware of either. Charles
glanced nervously from them to his sister-in-law. "Do you have reason
to doubt it?"

Mary Anne thrust out the cup for the boy behind her to take. "I
thought—Robert."

"Robert." Charles didn't have to feign his surprise. Relief gagged
him, making him gape at her. "Robert?"

Mary Anne scowled at him. "Yes, Robert. Well?"

"You know I'm not in Robert's confidence," Charles said carefully. "I
haven't noticed any signs of partiality."

"No. Not partiality. Revenge." Mary Anne looked up, and Charles
thought that he'd never seen her look so vulnerable. He was accustomed
to thinking of his sister-in-law as indomitable, but now she looked very
lost and very young. "If he wanted to hurt me . . . Jenny is the one person in the world who is completely mine."

It gave Charles a sick feeling, to hear Jenny spoken of so, like a
jewel one might put in a case and lock away. "Have you ever thought
of freeing her? In reward for her service to you."

"Why would I do that?" Mary Anne looked at him as though he
were mad. "Did Robert put you up to this? He wants me to give her up.
He thinks she keeps secrets for me."

"I haven't spoken to Robert since Christmas." Charles pressed his eyes briefly shut. Jenny had been right and he had been wrong, all along. "Are things so bad, then, between you and Robert?"

"He thinks I cuckolded him with you. But you know that."

"Yes." He had caused this, without intending to. All of it. "I don't know how to convince him otherwise."

"Find a wife," said Mary Anne. She made to rise, but stopped, her face contorting with pain, her hand going to her stomach.

"Mary Anne?" Charles grasped her by the elbow.

She shook him aside, her back hunched, her breathing ragged. "It's nothing. It happens—just a pain."

"Let me take you inside." For a moment, all Charles's other worries were submerged beneath the immediate emergency. Whatever she claimed, Mary Anne wasn't well. He nodded to her attendants to bring her palanquin. "And don't worry about your maid's child. I'm sure Robert has nothing to do with it."

"He's keeping a woman in Bridgetown. A mulatto girl. He thinks I don't know, but . . ." She lifted her hand to her temples, pressing hard. "She's welcome to him."

Charles held her arm to steady her as she lowered herself onto the sedan chair her attendants had brought for her. "I'm sorry."

"I'm not." As they lifted her in the air, Mary Anne looked down at him, chin jutting out. "I should have married you."

"You don't mean that." To the nearest slave, Charles said, "Please give my compliments to your master and tell him to call on me if I can be of any assistance at all."

He watched, with concern, as Mary Anne was carried back along the path into the house, looking strangely small slumped in her litter. He thought he caught a glimpse of Jenny, standing by the veranda, but he couldn't be sure and didn't want to risk coming closer to the house. The risks were too high for them all.

Instead, he went home and wrote letters to friends in London, to Brougham, to Wilberforce, to Lord Grenville. He wrote to Lord Liverpool, the prime minister, and to Lord Castlereagh, the secretary of state for foreign affairs. He wrote to Lord Bathurst, the secretary of state for the colonies, and to Henry Bunbury, his undersecretary. He had little sway with them, he knew; they were Tories and his father had been a vocal Whig, and they were preoccupied with the war with France besides, but someone, someone had to care, to be struck by the injustices being perpetrated under the aegis of the Union Jack.

Charles threw himself into the work of the estate and his letter-writing campaign, permitting himself to wait at the Old Mill not more than once in a week. It was a pointless indulgence, he knew. With Mary Anne as she was, Jenny couldn't get away, and to walk that far, in her own delicate condition—Charles grimaced himself. He'd seen his own slaves in the field holing the ground and chopping cane while carrying a baby to term. Jenny wouldn't balk at the walk. It was he who worried for her. It was torture being unable to see her, being forced to rely on the odd glimpse as he rode past on trumped-up errands.

He forced himself to go hat in hand to his brother, under pretense of asking for advice about Peverills in light of Robert's greater experience, praying for a glimpse, at least, of his Jenny.

Robert was gratified but suspicious. Charles dragged out the meeting as long as he could, accepting the punch Robert offered reluctantly, because hospitality demanded it, trying to give Jenny time to hear and find a way to visit.

"Aren't you going to ask about my wife?" Robert demanded, as Charles finally took his leave.

"You must think me rag-mannered," said Charles with a forced smile. "How does Mrs. Davenant?"

"Well," said Robert, in a tone that forbade further questions, just as Jenny slipped into the room. Charles's heart twisted at the sight of her. Her face was thinner, her features more defined, but she didn't look like Mary Anne, he saw with a surge of relief that nearly unmanned him, only like a more tired version of herself.

"Master Robert?" She didn't look at Charles, but Charles couldn't quite stop himself from looking at her, at the curve of her belly beneath her apron where their child grew. "My mistress was asking for you."

"Shall I pay my respects?" Charles inquired carefully. Anything to draw out this moment, to drink in the sight of Jenny and his child.

"No need," said Robert. "I'll let her know you were inquiring after her."

Reluctantly, Charles took his leave. His last sight of Jenny was the sway of her skirt as she climbed the stairs behind Robert.

Charles went home and tried to begin another letter, but his pen stalled and stuttered, spilling blots on the page. What use was the pen? It was nothing here. All his hopes, all his beliefs were mere airy nothing, powerless against the force of law and custom that kept his lover and child from him.

He rested his head against his desk, despair making him weak. What in the devil were they to do? Wait a while, Jenny had urged him, and that was all very well, but what happened when the time passed and he had no better plan than before? And every moment, their child's birth drew closer. If he failed to free Jenny, he failed their child as well. His own child, who would be born his brother's slave.

Mad ideas chased around Charles's head. Kidnapping, deception. The stuff of Monk Lewis's novels.

Shaking his head at himself, Charles did the only thing he could do. He crumpled up the soiled sheet of paper and began again.

My dear sir . . .

When the letter came from England in May, Charles knew it was too soon to be a reply to his petitions. He knew, but he tore it open eagerly anyway, cursing himself for disappointment when he saw that it was in Septimus's hand, his old schoolfellow and one of his closest friends. It was a long letter, two sheets closely written and crossed.

Situated as you are, you won't have heard about Hal. He died bravely, they say. . . .

Harold St. Aubyn. The heat and sounds of the plantation receded, jalousies gave way to shutters, the barking of the dogs to the cries of small boys. Hal had been his first friend at Eton, his champion, the one to stand against the bullies all too eager to debag the little West Indian whelp. *Are his balls made of gold?* they'd jeered. But Hal had come out of nowhere, taking Charles's part.

Hal and Septimus and Arthur, his closest companions, his true brothers. He'd always assumed that no matter how far they all roamed, they would still be ready at a moment to come together again, connected by shared memories and ancient affection, present even in absence.

But Septimus was in Northumberland, trying to sort the finances of an estate he'd never expected to inherit and didn't know how to run. Arthur had taken orders and was serving his flock somewhere in Cornwall, already engaged to the daughter of the local squire, growing fat on pasties and clotted cream. If they thought of Charles at all, it was in the same way, a part of their pasts, tinged with the exotic, sugar and rum and coconut trees.

And Hal, the best of them all, was dead, fighting the French in Portugal and Spain.

The waste of it all ate at him. How many like Hal were gone? How many lives lost? What had his last moments been like, in that strange and foreign country? He'd formed a connection with a Portuguese woman, Septimus wrote. His family hadn't approved. Septimus had sent money to the woman, by a trusted intermediary. Money, Charles didn't need to be told, that Septimus could ill afford to spare.

He would have to write and offer to make Septimus whole. He would write . . . and say what? That his heart was breaking? That he was about to have a child he couldn't acknowledge, whose body could be broken or bartered by his own brother?

Maybe Hal was the lucky one, after all. At least he had died with honor, fighting to keep England free.

Free. The word was a mockery.

"Yes?" He'd asked not to be disturbed but the door had burst open, revealing Robert, disheveled and reeking of rum punch. "Robert?"

"I've had a son." Robert swayed on his feet, catching at the cane back of a chair. "Hadn't you better congratulate me?"

"Congratulations," said Charles sincerely, or as sincerely as he could. He was still half at Eton, a boy again, chasing with Hal along pathways that existed only in his memory. "Isn't it early?"

"Yes. But you'd never know it. The boy's big. Strong." Robert stumbled forward, resting both hands on the desk, crumpling Septimus's letter. "His eyes are blue."

It took Charles a moment to realize what he was getting at. "All babies' eyes are blue! And even if they stay blue, Father's eyes were blue. What color are Mary Anne's eyes?"

Robert looked uncomfortable. Or perhaps it was simply that he was bilious. "They're not blue," he said belligerently.

They were gray, the same gray as Jenny's, but Charles couldn't say that. "They're not black, either."

"And how would you know that?" Robert was spoiling for a fight.

Charles couldn't take it anymore. He rose to his feet, kicking back his chair. "Because she's my neighbor. Because I have eyes." Relenting a bit, he asked, "How is she?"

"Not good," said Robert. "Nanny Bell's with her. That maid of hers chased Dr. MacAndrews off, wouldn't let him bleed her. Said there was enough blood already."

"Shouldn't you be with her?" Septimus's letter. Mary Anne. Death compassed Charles about. He could hear it like a roaring in his ears, like waves coming to claim everyone around him. "She needs you. Your son needs you."

Robert glowered at him. "If he's my son."

"I don't believe your wife played you false," Charles said shortly. "I can tell you for certain that she didn't play you false with me. You have a choice, as I see it. You can let jealousy poison everything you touch, or you can welcome your son into the world and cherish him."

Robert blinked at the onslaught of words. "And if he's not my son?"

"He is," said Charles. "But if he weren't . . . who's to say what makes a man himself? You're Father's son, but you're not the least bit like him. In looks, yes. But not in spirit."

"Mother had the raising of me." Robert's eyes narrowed and Charles could tell that what little ground he had gained was about to be lost. "Father was too busy writing letters and tupping Mother's maid."

Charles cut him off before he could revisit old slights. "There you have it. Whatever this boy's blood—and I tell you now, it is yours— you can decide whether or not you want the raising of him, whether you want him to share your thoughts, your feelings. You can leave him entirely to your wife. Or you can go home and bend the knee and give thanks that you have a healthy baby in the cradle."

He could feel his anger rising like flame, pure and hot, that Robert should have a child and deny him when all he wanted was the right to call his child his own.

What had Hal fought and died for if not this? The fundamental principles of England, a man's right to his own hearth and home.

"Go home," he said. "Go home."

Robert looked as though he might argue.

Charles lifted Septimus's letter, holding it up in front of Robert's face. "I've just had word that my closest friend is dead. He was fighting Bonaparte in the peninsula. He can't hold his child."

There was no child, as far as Charles knew; at least, Septimus hadn't mentioned one. But he was angry, at Robert, at the world, and it seemed a shame to let facts get in the way of rhetoric. And why not? Hal might well have had a child by this unknown Portuguese woman.

"I'm sorry," mumbled Robert.

"So am I," said Charles, and turned his back on his brother, his muscles tense and shaking with anger and something else.

The dawning of an idea.

CHAPTER NINETEEN

Christ Church, Barbados
May 1854

EMILY DIDN'T KNOW what to think.

But there it was, in front of her, in black and white, her grandfather's hand, recording barrels of sugar and tuns of rum and a silver-backed mirror for Lottie in spring of 1816, long after her grandparents were meant to be married and gone to Antigua.

The very last entry read: *One silver tea service, to Jonathan Fenty, for good service, on the occasion of his marriage.*

One silver tea service. She could picture the silver pot, the matching creamer and sugar, all engraved with her grandfather's initials. It was the tea service her grandmother had always used, gone now to Aunt Millicent, who had never liked it, because the lines of it were too plain, too simple, too much of the style of the early part of the century.

Emily leafed slowly back through the entries, as though she might find a clue among the barrels and tuns. If her grandfather had first married in 1816, then what did that make her mother?

A mistake—not in these dates—but in her mother's birthday? But no. Uncle Archibald had been born in 1817; her mother was the older by two and a half years. These were the commonplaces of life, the things she knew without knowing how she knew them.

Which meant that her mother had been born at least two years prior to her grandparents' marriage.

"Shall I dress you for dinner?" Katy appeared, holding freshly pressed linens and an evening frock boasting tiers of apple-green muslin.

Emily hastily slammed the ledger shut, as though caught out in something illicit. "Yes, thank you. Your little girl . . . she's well?"

"Just a touch of ague." Katy busied herself with Emily's buttons, letting the dress drop so Emily could step out of it.

"If you need— If she needs you, I can dress myself," Emily offered.

"She's all right," said Katy, tying the tapes of an impossibly wide petticoat around Emily's waist. "Her father's with her."

Father. Fathers and daughters. Emily submitted to Katy's ministrations while her mind returned again to her mother, her grandfather's pet. That was what Aunt Millicent claimed when Uncle Archibald wasn't listening. Uncle Archie had been baffled by his older sister, by her causes, by her passions, but he had loved her with a little brother's unquestioning love. It was Aunt Millicent who complained on his behalf.

But if they had only married in 1816 . . . Her grandmother had been married before. Emily knew that. He had died—what had Mrs. Davenant said? Three years before her grandparents' marriage.

If her grandmother had borne a posthumous child—Emily didn't like to think it, but the timing was right, or close enough.

Uncle Archibald looked like Grandfather, with his red hair and bright blue eyes. Emily's mother had taken, she had always thought, after her Welsh mother, with darker skin and hair. Her eyes were blue, but a paler blue, the misty blue of the sky after rain. Emily remembered so little, but that she remembered, her mother's eyes, which looked far-away even when she was close.

"There," said Katy, and Emily realized that she was waiting for Emily to say something, that her hair had been dressed and her earrings tied on and her locket nestled in the hollow of her throat while she brooded and brooded.

For a rarity, Laura was at supper, ethereal in blond lace. Emily looked at her uncertainly, feeling the rift between them, unsure, for the first time, of her best friend's feelings. Ordinarily, she would have gone to Laura with her concerns about her grandparents, as she and Laura had spoken, long ago, about the loss of their mothers, Emily's to disease, Laura's to continental spas, but there was a gulf between them marked by everything that had been left unsaid since their arrival in Barbados.

Emily smiled, tentatively. Laura smiled back, but as quickly ducked her head and let Adam hand her into her chair.

The fare was largely European; Mrs. Davenant, she was learning, brought out the more exotic varieties of local cuisine to terrorize European visitors and, occasionally, the hapless Dr. MacAndrews.

Once the soup had been ladled from the great tureen, Emily asked Mrs. Davenant, "I've been meaning to ask: Were you at my grandparents' wedding?"

She tried very hard to make the inquiry sound casual, moving about the bits of turtle in her soup without actually making any effort to eat them.

Mrs. Davenant took a long, slow sip of her wine, which had been watered until it was barely pink. "No. They were married from Antigua, as I recall. Your grandmother owned a property there."

"And then they sold it and went on an extended wedding journey through the southern bits of America." Emily grasped at straws. "Did he come back in between?"

"Not that I know," said Mrs. Davenant. She held her glass in the air but didn't drink, the light winking off the intricate patterns in the cut glass. "The last time I saw your grandfather was on Easter Day in 1816. I remember it, because that was the day the troubles started. We were at table at Peverills when the news came. The men ran to join the militia. In the confusion . . . I believe your grandfather left to join your grandmother in Antigua later that week. I couldn't say."

"Might they have been married already?" Emily asked hopefully.

"No." Mrs. Davenant seemed to come back from far away. "If they were, I wasn't informed."

"Yes, of course." Emily looked across the table at Adam, a red-haired, fair-skinned Fenty, his face blotchy with heat. "My grandmother was married before. Did she have any children in her first marriage?"

Mrs. Davenant paused before answering. "Perhaps. She might have done. I didn't know them well."

George choked on his claret. "I thought Mrs. Boland stood god-mother to my father."

"And look how that turned out," snapped his grandmother. As if it ended the matter, she said decidedly, "The Bolands weren't a Barbados family."

George raised his brows at Emily behind his napkin, inviting Emily to share his amusement. Emily wasn't feeling terribly amused. "I know my grandmother was older than our grandfather, by some years."

Adam gestured to one of the servants to refill his glass. "If she'd had another child, wouldn't we have known? It's hardly the sort of thing one would keep secret. Unless you think our aunt or uncle met some deep and dismal fate."

"You're right." Emily forced a smile. "It's just that my grandparents rarely spoke of their courtship. There's so little I know of their lives before Bristol."

Adam looked at her incredulously. "That's hardly true. What about all the stories about laboring in the hot sun?"

"I thought you claimed those were more morality tales than true histories."

George smiled at Laura. "If you want family histories, I can tell you about my mother's great-great-grandfather, the privateer."

"Oh, not that nonsense," muttered Mrs. Davenant, but she resumed eating again, albeit slowly, her eyes on Emily all the while, watching, measuring.

"A privateer?" asked Laura, blissfully unaware of undercurrents.

"Yes, pillaging the Spanish for the sake of the Virgin Queen," said George with a smile. "It began in Dorset. . . ."

The servants removed the soup course, moving silently among the guests with platters of meat and poultry, sweetbreads, and stewed mushrooms. Emily let George's words drift around her, pretending to eat, making the correct responses at the correct times, caught in her own thoughts. There was something Mrs. Davenant knew, something she was hiding.

Perhaps. She might have done.

Not a no. Emily found herself watching her own hands as though expecting them to have changed, to belong to someone else. It was almost a surprise to find them exactly the same, with a sunburst of freckles on her right wrist, almost exactly in the shape of a star, and the scar on her right index finger from a forgotten accident as a child.

She had always been Jonathan Fenty's granddaughter. That was as much a part of who she was as the curl of her hair and the shape of her chin. She knew nothing of her grandmother's first husband, the mysterious Mr. Boland, only that he was Irish, and older, and rich.

No. Emily sawed at her chicken. She was getting ahead of herself. There might be another explanation.

"What?" George was talking to her.

"I said it's dead already," said George. "The chicken."

"Oh. Yes." Emily set down her knife and fork. "How far away is the part of the island where my grandfather grew up?"

"Scotland?"

"No," said Emily, "he was born in Barbados."

Mrs. Davenant gave a dry laugh. "Scotland is in Barbados. It's a portion of the parish of St. Andrew."

"It's not terribly far." Ever chivalrous, George jumped in to save Emily's pride. "It's considered a great place for a picnic. It's very picturesque. We could ride there next week if you like."

"If we took the carriage, Laura and Adam could come," suggested Emily. "What do you think, Laura? You could bring your sketchbook."

"The terrain is rugged and wild," Mrs. Davenant said. "You'll do better to go on horseback."

"You can sketch it for me," said Laura, adding, as a precaution, "In words."

"I can draw a straight line," protested Emily, feeling an inexplicable surge of relief, as though she'd been forgiven for a trespass she hadn't realized she'd committed.

"Yes," agreed Laura, looking more herself than Emily had seen her in weeks. "It's only all the other ones that are the problem."

"I was the despair of our drawing master," Emily confessed to George.

"But the French mistress adored you," said Laura. "And that poor woman who tried to teach us geography."

She smiled across the table at Emily, and Emily smiled back, feeling as though the last few months had disappeared and they were themselves again.

"I'll bring you back flowers to press," she promised. "And you can come next time."

Emily approached Adam after dinner, when the men had returned to the great room after the ritual passing of the port. They seldom lingered over their tipple; Adam found George tedious and George preferred the company of the ladies. "Will you come to Scotland?"

"Are you afraid young Davenant intends to make his intentions plain?" Emily frowned at him; George was just on the other side of the room, turning the pages while Laura played the pianoforte. Adam held up his hands. "Don't look to me. I have a meeting in town."

"Surely, you can do without your visit to the icehouse for one day!"

"I'm not going to the icehouse! I have a meeting with a man named Montefiore. He's a merchant." Adam's mouth twisted. "I know what you think of me, coz, but believe me, this is business, not pleasure."

"What sort of business?" Emily asked suspiciously.

"Fenty and Company business." Lowering his voice, Adam said, "London Turner hasn't renewed his contract. I'm sure—well, he says it's just waiting for his clerks to produce the documents, but don't you think if he wanted the documents ready they'd have been ready by now? I don't know if he's just enjoying making me cool my heels or if he has other irons in the fire."

Emily glanced over her shoulder. George and Laura were lost in their music. But Mrs. Davenant was watching them. "I suspect the former."

"But what if it's not? What if he's seen his chance to strike a better bargain elsewhere? I've been searching out other business. This man Montefiore isn't as big a fish as Turner, but he's a man of some property, with warehouses in town. If Turner leaves us empty-handed, it would be something to take home to Papa." Adam tugged at his cravat pin, looking like the boy he had once been. "I can't go back and tell them I've made a hash of everything."

Emily put a hand on his arm. "You haven't made a hash of everything."

"Haven't I? I insulted Turner's nephew. He hasn't forgiven that. If someone had only told me . . . But never mind. I'm determined to make it right."

"Would you like me to speak to Dr. Braithwaite?" She certainly knew where to find him on Thursdays.

"No! That is, I mean, it wouldn't do any good. I don't believe Turner lets his nephew have anything to do with his business. Truly, Emily. Don't meddle. This is my own mess. I need to fix it myself."

"All right, then." It had been a long time since they had spoken so frankly with each other, as they used to. It was on the tip of Emily's tongue to tell him about the ledger and their grandparents' marriage— but what would Adam think? Would he look at her differently if she wasn't their grandfather's grandchild?

"Do I have a spot on my chin?" Adam demanded. "You're staring like you've never seen me before."

Emily shook her head and said the first thing that came to mind. "Is Laura with child?"

Adam looked at her incredulously. "That's my Emily, delicate and tactful."

"Why didn't you tell me?" It was a relief to focus on something so relatively simple, to allow herself the luxury of hurt feelings.

Adam waved a hand. "Laura said she didn't want you fussing over her."

"I don't fuss," Emily protested. She looked over her shoulder at Laura, ethereal in the light of the candles in their brackets on either side of the pianoforte. "She should be drinking beef tea to build up her blood. Can you tell her? It doesn't need to have come from me."

"MacAndrews is looking after her," said Adam carelessly, turning to rejoin the group.

"MacAndrews? He's about as much use as blancmange!" Flushing, Emily lowered her voice. Mercifully, Laura and George were in the midst of a mournful ballad, caught in their own music.

> *In the Hazel Dell my Nelly's sleeping,*
> *Nelly lov'd so long!*
> *And my lonely lonely watch I'm keeping,*
> *Nelly lost and gone!*

A little shiver ran down Emily's spine. Sweat, she told herself. It was the hot season, and while the evenings were cooler than the day, the multiple layers of chemise, corset, and bodice felt uncomfortably hot and rather itchy.

"He can hardly physic himself!"

> *The silent stars are nightly weeping . . .*

Adam shrugged. "That's not what Laura says. But suit yourself. You always do. Mama always said I got Grandfather's looks but you got his character."

> *Now I'm weary, friendless, and forsaken . . .*

Did character travel in the blood, or was it something that could be imparted by gift? Her grandfather had raised her as his own, had loved her as his own, she was sure of it. But if she wasn't his, not truly, what did that make her?

Not like this child, Adam and Laura's child, who would know exactly who he was and where he came from.

Emily stepped back, feeling suddenly very flat. "I won't meddle. With you or Laura. Is that what you wanted to hear?"

"Don't take on, Emily. Coz—"

Emily batted blindly at his outstretched arm. "Good night, Adam."

"Are you all right?" The music had ended and George had walked over to join them.

Emily wrinkled her forehead. "Just a touch of the headache. I think I'll have a quiet day tomorrow. I was too much in the sun today."

It might even be true. The ride to and from Peverills was longer than she was accustomed to. The day had taken on a kaleidoscope quality, too much happening at once: Dr. Braithwaite's surgery, Laura in the garden, the entries in the ledgers.

Emily spent the next few days quietly at home; she sat with Laura and Mr. Davenant in the garden, although only briefly. Her presence was too clearly a constraint. She accompanied Mrs. Davenant to church in Oistins, sitting in the box reserved for the Davenants. In short, she was exceptionally well behaved and half-mad with trying to avoid her own thoughts by the time George broached their proposed trip to Scotland. She accepted so enthusiastically that George stammered something about seeing to the picnic and disappeared, while Mrs. Davenant watched approvingly from behind her coffeepot.

Emily still found riding an awkward exercise at best, but there was no denying the relief of passing through the gates. When George suggested they canter, she agreed, feeling as though she were breathing for the first time in days as Beckles receded behind them, even though she knew she was going to pay for it in bruises on her backside later.

"Well done!" said George. His cheeks were flushed with the exercise, his eyes bright, and Emily realized what a constraint was on him too in his grandmother's house. "You've come some way since we began."

"I had a good teacher," said Emily neutrally, and shifted a little in her saddle as he looked away.

As they rode, the landscape began to change around them, the even fields of cane giving way to an uneven terrain of hills and hidden valleys where oleander and aloes, cacti and Scottish heather grew in the lee of the rocks. Even the very color of the dirt beneath their horses' hooves was different from the soil to which she'd become accustomed at Beckles.

"I'm told by visitors that it's very like Scotland," said George, as they walked their horses carefully up a rocky incline. "I've only their word on it, though. I've never been off this little island."

"Until I came here, I'd never been more than a day's journey from Bristol," said Emily. "We can be ignorant together."

"The men who settled here came mostly from Scotland and Ireland," said George. "I've often wondered if they came here, to this part of the island, because it reminded them of home."

"My grandfather's family was Scottish, I think," said Emily doubtfully. "He said his ancestors came over as indentured servants and were promised fifteen pounds and land if they completed their service."

"Many came as prisoners of war," said George. He had that faraway look he got when he started on about Cavaliers and Roundheads. "Captured in the risings against Cromwell. They were brought here in shackles, to an inhospitable land, and forced to survive as best they could under the burning sun."

"It sounds like something by Daniel Defoe," said Emily.

"Or Sir Walter Scott?" said George, with a sheepish smile. "It might sound like a tale, but such things did happen."

In earlier, less civilized times, perhaps. But this was the year 1854. Emily didn't quite understand romanticizing a time when life had been poor, nasty, brutish, and short.

It was the more recent past she was interested in. She saw huts scattered along the slope, perched upon outcroppings of rock, gardens scratched into the stony ground. Trees grew thick around them, breadfruit and custard apple, trees bearing oranges that were nothing like the carefully cultivated orange trees that grew in pots in Laura's father's conservatory.

"There's a pretty prospect from the next rise," said George. "We could set out our picnic there."

Emily glanced back at the houses. "I was hoping we might speak to some of the people who lived here. I had thought that maybe someone would remember my grandfather."

"We can ask. Shall we make inquiries first and picnic later?"

"If you'd rather eat first . . ." The problem with people like George was that one felt the need to be nice in return.

"No, no, that's quite all right. The cold collation will keep."

"All right, then. Thank you." Emily wasn't sure what it was about his unflagging helpfulness that she found quite so irritating. He was being all that was kind. She should be grateful. But his very diffidence made him opaque; it was impossible to tell, beneath those flawless manners, what he was really thinking.

George swung down from his horse and held out a hand to help her down. Gesturing to the groom to take charge of their mounts, he said, "Shall we inquire here?"

The dwelling in front of them was scarcely a house, just a box made of rubble and lime, with crudely cut squares for windows. Shutters of sorts had been fitted to them, but one had come loose, and through it Emily could see a single room, crowded with pallets, a well-worn table in the middle of the room. The hearth was in a sort of stone cairn a few feet away.

A woman was working in the garden, yanking at weeds on her hands and knees, a baby strapped to her back, another, wearing only a cloth around his waist, playing in the dirt, minded by an older child with a soiled kerchief around her head, who couldn't have been more than four.

Another woman was feeding damp stalks into a mill of sorts, turning the handle round and round to squeeze out a pale juice. She didn't bother to look up as Emily and George approached.

"Hullo," said George, with a winning smile. "Do you know where we might find the Fenty house?"

"Fenty?" The woman slowly straightened, scrubbing her palms against the skirt of her dress, and Emily realized she couldn't be much older than herself, was younger perhaps, but her skin was grained with dirt and freckled from the sun, two teeth missing from her mouth. "I don't know any Fentys."

Her accent was a thicker version of Emily's grandfather's. It was strange, so strange, to think of her urbane grandfather here, in these hills, his nails dark with dirt.

"Is there perhaps someone who's lived here quite some time?" Emily asked hastily. "My grandfather came from these parts and I was hoping to find someone who knew him."

The woman clearly found this rather eccentric behavior, but was willing to humor her. "You might talk to Old Betty." She indicated the far end of the ridge. "She live above the mile tree."

"For your trouble," said George, and produced a coin, which disappeared rapidly into the woman's bodice. To Emily he said, "I believe that's the mile tree she means."

It was a large tree, with bunches of thin green leaves like the bristles of a broom. Emily picked her way carefully down the rocky path. She felt as though she'd stepped into a different country. After the bustle of Bridgetown and Beckles, the isolation and silence were almost eerie. "What was she growing?"

"Arrowroot and eddoes. There's not much will grow in this soil. But the rents are low." He paused in front of the house the other woman had indicated. There was no need to knock. A woman had opened the slatted doors. Her skin was impossibly weathered and wrinkled, her back stooped, her thin gray hair pulled into a knot.

"Are you Betty?" Emily inquired, tactfully leaving off the "Old."

She was beginning to think that it might have been better to simply picnic and go home. "We were told you might have known my grandfather. Jonathan Fenty?"

She opened her mouth to speak and Emily saw that she was missing most of her front teeth. Those that remained were blackened and crooked. A stream of incomprehensible syllables emerged.

"I'm afraid I didn't catch that," said Emily apologetically.

"She said that she knew your grandfather from when she was a girl," George translated. The woman interjected. George bent his head to listen. "I beg your pardon, she knew your grandfather's sisters. Your grandfather was grown and gone to Peverills. He didn't come back much."

"You were younger than my grandfather?" That would make her around Mrs. Davenant's age, but Emily would have thought Betty at least two decades older.

Betty was looking at Emily as though she thought her rather slow. Emily tried to remember what she'd meant to ask. "Did you know Rachel Fenty? My grandfather's sister? Do you know—did she take in needlework for Peverills?"

The woman gave a rusty laugh. "My lady," she said tolerantly, and then something else that Emily didn't quite get, although she thought she was beginning to discern the shapes of words.

"She says that would be a fine thing," said George. "Rachel Fenty was the sloppiest seamstress in the parish."

The woman added something.

"And besides, she was mostly busy with the children."

"Her children?" That was something else Emily had never considered, that there was a whole branch of the family tree elsewhere. She knew that her grandfather's sisters had moved to the Carolinas, that he had seen them settled there with some of his wife's money, but it had never occurred to her to wonder if they had families of their own. Her grandfather's world had narrowed to Bristol.

George leaned his head close to listen. "Her child and the child her brother paid her to look after."

"Aye, my lady." The woman put her hand on Emily's arm, speaking simply and clearly so that Emily could understand. "'Ee gi' 'ee outside trild to 'ee sister."

Emily looked up at George. "Outside child?"

George tugged at his white stock. "His, er, natural offspring."

The woman nodded, unimpressed. "'Ee bastard."

CHAPTER TWENTY

Christ Church, Barbados
June 1813

"I'VE BEEN THINKING about our child," said Charles.

Jenny rubbed her aching back, trying not to think unkind thoughts. He might have been thinking about their child, but she'd been doing the work of carrying it.

The only mercy was that she was spared from doing her usual work. Mary Anne lay in a twilight state from the laudanum Dr. MacAndrews had prescribed, drifting in and out of consciousness. Robert, frightened into contrition, sat by his wife's side, reading to her from manuals on estate management. Queenie and a series of undermaids bathed their mistress and changed her linens, leaving Jenny, for the first time in months, with time on her hands and no one to watch where she went.

"Have you now?" she said neutrally.

Charles was too lost in his own thoughts to notice. "What if . . ." he began. "What if the baby were to be born dead?"

Jenny could feel herself stiffen, turning to salt like the woman in the tale. "Is that what you want?"

"No! Quite the contrary!" Charles looked so genuinely horrified that Jenny let herself relax, but just a little. Instead of leaning into him, she stayed upright on the stone they were sharing in the Old Mill, moving just a little away from him. He looked at her earnestly. "What I meant was, what if the baby were to appear to be born dead?"

How had they come to this? From promises of manumission to mad schemes. Jenny put her hand on her stomach, on the mound that was their baby, and felt the child squirm within her.

"Are you planning to whisk it away in a warming pan?" Jenny asked wearily.

Charles had the grace to look sheepish. "Something like that. Not the warming pan, perhaps, but what if your baby—our baby—were to disappear?"

"And be raised by someone else?" As if feeling her distress, the child undulated, making ripples against her dress. "Where—where would you send him?"

Jenny tried to control her emotions, to think of the baby and not of herself. What was better, to keep her child with her in captivity or see him free and a stranger? Her child might grow up in England, that land where even the air conferred freedom. He might grow up ignorant of her past, thinking himself the equal of any man.

He might grow up among strangers, never knowing his mother.

At least she'd had her mother, even for a short time. She could re-member what it was to be loved.

Yes, Charles loved her, she knew that. It seemed strange to say that, to believe in his love, when a year ago she would have sneered to think that such a thing existed. But it was a different sort of love, a balancing of personalities, not the simple, fierce love of a mother for a child. She'd known that love; was it so wrong she wanted her child to know it too?

Or was it for herself she wanted it?

Perhaps it was crueler so. Perhaps her child would be happier for the not knowing her, not having to bear the pain of losing later.

Charles took her hands, all contrition. "I'm making a muddle of this, aren't I? I don't mean our child to be sent to strangers, not permanently, at any rate. I had a letter last week, from an old schoolfellow. One of my friends, one of the best men I knew, died on the peninsula."

Sometimes, she felt she and Charles had lived like this forever, known each other forever, but at times like this, she was reminded how much of his life she didn't know. Charles might give the impression of being an open book, but there were whole chapters he kept closed. "Are you all right?"

"I don't quite believe he's dead. Perhaps if I were in England, perhaps if the war were over, it might seem possible, but as it is, I keep thinking he must still be somewhere in Portugal, and the whole thing a mistake." Charles recalled himself with a visible effort. "But that isn't the point. What if Hal were to have left a child?"

"Did he?"

"Not that I know of, but what if he had? What if that child—that Portuguese child—were to be sent to be raised at Peverills?" Charles's blue eyes were intent on hers. "No one would question such an arrangement. I was Hal's closest and oldest friend. It isn't beyond reason that he would entrust his natural child to me. If he should be dark skinned . . . well, everyone knows the Portuguese are dark. The child could be raised at Peverills, with every honor and advantage."

"And where would I be in this?"

She saw Charles's eyes flicker away and knew she'd hit the problem. "With us, as soon as we can win your freedom."

"But not as his mother. His mother would be an unknown Portuguese woman."

"I wouldn't be able to claim him as his father either. Only as his guardian."

Jenny wanted to shake him and shout that it wasn't the same. But she suspected he knew that already. "What of the midwife who delivers the child? Even if we pay her off, there's no guaranteeing she'll hold her tongue. Where's the child to live until your friend's child arrives from Portugal?"

"I hadn't thought of the former, I confess. But I do have some thoughts on the latter. I know it's not perfect. But it would be a way to keep our child with us, free." Sensing her resistance, he said, "It's a damnable coil. If I could think of a better way, I would. We could smuggle the child abroad—"

"No!" To transport a child so young would be a death sentence.

Charles held up a hand. "Or all go away together. Or we could let fate take its course and you can have your baby at Beckles, with Nanny Bell, and we can pray that Parliament will do what they ought and free you both."

Jenny's throat felt very dry. "I have more faith in warming pans than prayers."

"It will happen, eventually. But I find I can't risk our child on eventually."

"What if the deception were to be discovered?"

"How would they prove it? It would be Robert's word against mine. He'd sound mad for forcing the point. The truth would be nearly impossible to trace. I have friends in England who would help create a false trail for us if need be. . . ."

Bringing more and more people into the conspiracy, more danger of discovery. Jenny put her hands protectively over her stomach. "And where will our child live when he's meant to be traveling from Portugal? Who will nurse him?"

Charles sat a little straighter. "Jonathan Fenty has a sister with a new baby." His lips twisted in a half smile. "I know because I had our housekeeper give Jonathan a rattle and some old dresses for the baby. They live in St. Andrew, in an area so remote that many never even get so far as Speightstown. If a child were to be fostered there, just for a year, there would be no tattling tongues to bear word back to Beckles."

Jenny thought of Fenty, with his hair clubbed back in a queue, his hard face, his watchful eyes. "Do you trust him so far?"

"Absolutely," said Charles, without hesitation. "What reason would he have to betray us?"

What reason did anyone have to betray anyone else? And yet people did so all the time, for money or love or sheer ill temper.

"How do we know his sister would care for our child?"

"Because I would pay her," said Charles. "And we'd have Jonathan to keep an eye for us. No one could find it strange that he wanted to visit his family once a fortnight."

"Have you broached this with him yet?"

"No. I wouldn't without speaking to you first. If you mislike it . . . we'll think of something else."

He'd already said he could think of no other way.

"I mislike everything," said Jenny, letting herself lean against him. She was so tired, so very tired, their growing child sapping her strength, weakening her resolve.

Charles smoothed the hair back from her forehead. "We could still go away together."

Jenny shook her head. "It's too late for that. I'd as lief not have our child born with fins."

"We'd be on a ship, not in the water," pointed out Charles, but he didn't argue the point.

Jenny lowered her face so he couldn't see her expression. It wasn't fair to resent him for not wanting to throw everything away for her and their child. He had offered, after all. It was more than most would have done. What did she expect? She was lucky he was standing by her so far, she knew that.

But it stung a bit, all the same.

"I don't trust Nanny Bell to remain silent," she said. They both knew it was a capitulation.

"If I can find a midwife . . ." With sudden decision, Charles rose from their seat, holding out both hands to help Jenny up. "Will you come speak to Jonathan with me? If he refuses, we'll know we need to find another way."

"Now?" She wasn't sure she liked this. But then, she didn't like anything right now. Her emotions were all out of joint.

"Why let 'I dare not' wait upon 'I would'?" Charles abandoned Shakespeare for plain prose. "I'm afraid if we stop to reflect we'll decide it's mad."

"It is mad," said Jenny, falling into step beside him. She couldn't help but notice how he shortened his stride to accommodate her new bulk.

"If the world is mad, maybe to be mad is to be sane. It's not sophistry, or even philosophy; I mean it. I'd always thought that there was a remedy for everything in law, but when Nature's law conflicts with positive law, I hold it no breach to maintain the right."

When one's own self-interest demanded it. There might be a child at this very moment being born into bondage on Charles's own land, a child who would call him master. How was it Nature's law when it was his own child, but the law of the land when it was someone else's?

Jenny swallowed the thought. For one, she knew that Charles was well aware of it, and if he hadn't manumitted his people yet, it was because he hadn't the resources to do so without plunging everyone into poverty. For another, in this case, the contradiction was in her favor. Let Charles dream of universals and the rights of man. She would fight to protect her own.

They found Charles's bookkeeper at his desk in the little room that served as book room and office, bent over his accounts. The door was open, but Charles knocked on it all the same.

"Jonathan? Might I trouble you awhile?"

"It's your house," said the bookkeeper, thriftily tapping the excess ink off his pen before setting it down. He made to rise, but checked at the sight of Jenny, straightening slowly. "Is something amiss at Beckles?"

"Yes and no." Charles regarded Jenny, half pride, half bemusement, looking for a moment like any father-to-be. "Jenny and I are expecting a child."

"Felicitations." Whatever he truly thought, Fenty didn't betray his emotions by so much as the flicker of an eyelash. "Does Mrs. Davenant know?"

"No. We'd like to keep it that way, if we can." Blindly, Charles took Jenny's nearest hand in his, holding it so tightly that she could feel the bones crunch together. "Both of us are determined that our child not be born a slave."

Jenny could see Fenty take in their linked hands. "I'll do my possible, such as it is. I assume you don't mean me to beat Mr. Robert into submission?"

"Tempting as that is . . . we were thinking more of theft than battery. If that would cause you troubles with your conscience, we can stop the conversation here and you can pretend none of this was ever said."

"Oh, my conscience isn't so delicate as that. There's no love lost between me and Beckles. They wouldn't hesitate to do me a mischief, so why shouldn't I return the favor?"

Jenny could feel Charles's surprise, but he did his best not to show it. "Why, indeed?" he said gamely. "You should be paid for your trouble, of course. In coin, as well as the moral satisfaction."

"What precisely did you have in mind? Do you mean to make Miss Beck—Mrs. Davenant's maid disappear?"

"No," said Jenny emphatically, before Charles could say anything at all. "Miss Mary Anne would raise the parish looking for me. But she won't care about one child born dead."

"Ah," said Fenty, as though a complicated sum had just come right. He gave a small nod. "Babies die all the time. Die and are buried and never seen again?"

"We'd thought your sister might be willing to foster an orphan child, a baby sent from Bridgetown. She'd be generously paid, of course." Charles looked meaningfully at Fenty. "It's only for a year or so, until my old friend Hal's child arrives from Portugal to be raised at Peverills."

Fenty snorted. "When you contrive, you don't go by halves! All right, then, let me see if I have this aright. In a year—or so—the baby goes back to its family in Bridgetown, and I'll be sent to fetch a foreign wean from a ship in Carlisle Bay?" He grinned, a pirate's grin, all teeth and trouble. "I'll do it, devil take me if I won't."

"It is theft," Charles cautioned. "The child is the property of the Beckles estate."

"It's not theft if they can't prove it happened," said Fenty, with a glint in his eye. "That may not be in your books, but that's the law as I've seen it."

"Won't you need to ascertain your sister's willingness?"

"My sister knows what side her bread is buttered. It's easier to nurse a babe than squeeze starch out of arrowroot. As long as she's paid for her trouble, she'll nurse the babe as tenderly as her own."

"Well, then," said Charles, looking helplessly at Jenny, as though trying to figure out what to do next. "All that's left to do is discuss terms."

"Not quite all," Jenny interjected. Where did they think this child was planning to appear from? "There's one difficulty."

"Only one?" said Fenty, and Jenny found herself smiling back despite herself. Fenty had a strange charm, but it was charm all the same.

"The midwife," said Jenny. "I don't trust Nanny Bell not to betray us."

Fenty looked to Charles, who shook his head. "I can't vouch for our people at Peverills. They're accustomed to answering to Robert, even if he is master of Beckles now."

"Well, that's soon enough mended. My sisters have more than enough experience between them." His accent grew thicker, Jenny noticed, when he spoke of his family. "Who do you think delivered their trildren? Becky's brought a dozen trildren into the world. Some of them have even lived past infancy."

Charles looked a little uneasy at his gallows humor. "If she would . . ."

"But wait," said Jenny. "How is she to be brought to me? Or am I to be brought to her? Won't someone question her presence at Beckles?"

"To bring Becky to you is no great obstacle. I'm assuming you wouldn't mind if I were to offer my widowed sister the hospitality of this house for, oh, a fortnight or thereabouts?" Without waiting for Charles to answer, he went on, briskly taking charge. "You can't have the child here. There are too many people about. And it's too far for you to come in your condition. You'll have to send a message for Becky to come to you. A prearranged phrase, something that will seem innocent to anyone else."

"Have you silk floss to spare?" Jenny suggested ironically.

"That will do well enough. Have it sent to me by my groom London. He's a likely lad. He won't ask questions." Fenty moved quickly on. "You can't have the child at Beckles. If they see the baby, they'll want a body. Develop a habit of taking walks or visiting elsewhere. Do you have friends on other plantations?"

Jenny was about to say no when she remembered Nanny Grigg. "Yes, at Harrow. I've been invited to stop there of a Sunday evening."

Fenty grinned. "Better and better. And you'll give my respects to Mrs. Boland while you're there?"

"It's true," said Charles thoughtfully. "Even if Robert were to notice, he'd never stop you going to Harrow. He needs Mrs. Boland."

Mrs. Boland had been widowed in the spring. While she stayed close to home in her hired house, mourning her husband, Robert had grown increasingly anxious over whether the widow would honor the promises made by her husband.

"Go two or three times, perhaps," suggested Charles. "Enough to establish a pattern. That way, if you're not at hand, everyone will assume you've gone to Harrow."

"If the baby has the consideration to come on a Sunday," pointed out Jenny with some asperity. "And where am I to go in truth?"

For once it was Charles who took the lead and not Fenty. "The Old Mill," he said decidedly. "It's close enough for you to walk and far enough that we won't be overheard."

The baby, in the way of babies, didn't oblige by coming on a Sunday.

The first pain struck on a Tuesday afternoon in early August, while Jenny was reading to her mistress from an old book of poetry.

It didn't matter much what she read; Mary Anne wasn't listening, not really. There were times she was almost herself again, frustrated at her own weakness, and other times when she turned her face to the wall and demanded her medicine, refusing to look at or hold her child, her longed-for heir.

So Jenny picked the books herself. Her father, whatever his other sins, had been an educated man. The library at Beckles was well stocked with volumes with his signature on the flyleaf. She had chosen poetry because it made her feel closer to Charles, Charles who so earnestly believed that the world could be made beautiful.

She found it an unexpected consolation as she sat in the unnatural twilight of the shuttered room, her body heavy and slow, letting the words wash over her. This was her gift to her child too, that he should be learned like his father. She wanted to wince away from the reality of what they planned to do, but that wasn't in her nature: so she forced herself to face it head-on. That if they were lucky, if they were clever, she would give her child up so that he could have this: calf-bound volumes and tutors in Greek and Latin, all that careless erudition that Charles took so for granted but was so much a part of him, and a hallmark of his world, where even the most indifferently educated could quote Latin tags in his cups.

"*Sweetest love, I do not go, / For weariness of thee,*" she read softly, and knew she was speaking to her child, not to Mary Anne, inert in her bed. "*Nor in the hope the world can show / A fitter love for me.*"

She felt it then, a cramping pain. But she'd had pains before, in her hips, her belly, her back, so she stayed where she was and kept on reading.

"*Let not thy divining heart / Forethink me any ill. . . .*"

It came again, harder now. Jenny sat very still, half-afraid to move. All these months, fretting, planning. Now that the moment was here, she found herself frozen like an animal caught out in the open.

Breathe. Breathe. She finished the poem. "*They who one another keep alive ne'er parted be.*"

Silently, she closed the book and set it down on the bedside table. Mary Anne's eyes were closed, her breathing shallow but regular.

Another pain took her, stronger now, as though her child were growing impatient with her.

"All right, baby," Jenny murmured, and shook off the thought that this might be her last chance to talk to her child.

She knew what she needed to do; the men might assume the baby would come obligingly on a Sunday, but she'd prepared her own contingency.

The clock on the mantel said it was gone five. Jenny closed the door of Mary Anne's room behind her and hailed Queenie, who was coming up to sit with Mary Anne. "She's sleeping. But she's asked me to mend her Pomona gown and I can't find the green floss. Will you send to the seamstress?"

"Now?" asked Queenie.

Jenny glanced over her shoulder at the closed door, biting her lip in exaggerated concern. "You know how she is these days. If she says she wants the gown, I'd best have the gown for her. Even if she's most like to have forgot she wanted it by suppertime. But then again, she might not."

"Green?" said Queenie.

"Pomona green. You know how particular she gets. If the seam shows, I'll never hear the end of it. Didn't we use the last of the Pomona green floss sewing the trim on her pelisse?"

"Oh no," said Queenie with feeling. She was so young and eager that Jenny almost felt bad about gulling her.

"Never you mind," said Jenny quickly. "You sit with her. I'll go to Harrow. Mrs. Boland has a dress of the same color. I'll wager Nanny Grigg will have the right shade in her sewing box."

"But it's so far and so late—it will be past dark by the time you get back!"

"When has that ever bothered anyone?" Jenny tried to sound jaunty, but it was ruined by her wince as another pain struck. At the alarm on Queenie's face, she said, white-lipped, "Don't you worry. This baby's not coming yet. All the same, though, maybe send to Peverills and see if they've the thread there? There might be some left from the old mistress. Paris!" She snagged one of the boys who ran errands and delivered messages. "Go to Peverills and ask Mr. Fenty's groom London to see if they've any Pomona green silk floss. Tell him the mistress wants it without delay."

"Yes, ma'am." Paris and London had been born in the same year, victims of her father's fancy to name all the children after cities.

What would Charles name their child? Jenny wondered, and then dragged her mind back to the present, to Queenie holding tight to her arm.

"Maybe you should go to Nanny Bell instead of Harrow?"

"Don't be foolish; it's not that far away. And if I'm taken there, well, Nanny Grigg's as skilled as Nanny Bell. Only don't let her hear you say that." Jenny forced a smile. "Don't you worry about me, Queenie. Just go sit by our mistress and make sure she's not alone when she wakes."

The sun was already setting when she set off down the road in the direction of Harrow, just far enough to confound anyone watching. She didn't, at least, have to worry about the spyglasses; her mistress was too fuddled to use them, and Master Robert was away at what he said was a militia meeting but Jenny knew to be a tryst with his mistress in Bridgetown.

The cane had been felled months ago; the first gang had finished turning the ground and had just begun holing the cane, breaking the fields into large squares, with two young plants in each. Jenny missed the protection of the mature cane, those long fronds shielding her.

The pains were stronger now. She found herself sinking to her knees in the newly turned earth, breathing in the scent of dirt and manure as she struggled not to cry out. She forced herself up to her feet, taking advantage of the space between pains to get as far as she could as fast as she could, her shoes sinking into the soft earth, stumbling and catching herself again, pausing again, nails biting into her fists, her body feeling as though it were breaking apart.

Dimly, she was aware that there was dirt on her face and knees. In between pains, she felt herself again, ashamed of how she gave in to the agony, let it turn her into an animal, stripping her of reason and dignity.

She'd heard Mary Anne shouting and crying, had seen her frenzied writhing. How had she not realized it would come to her too?

Because she'd thought herself stronger. But she wasn't strong, not now, and the pains were coming closer now, closer and harder.

It felt like years before she made it to the mill, a lantern shining through the ruined door. She'd wanted to greet them with dignity, but the pain hit again, rendering her insensible, and she was only aware of arms grasping her forearms, holding her up, arms around her. She shook them off; she hurt, she hurt, to be touched only made it worse. But then the pain was past and it was Charles there, Charles frantic with worry, chafing her hands, her wrists, hugging her as close as he dared, helping her over the threshold, to where a makeshift bed had been prepared with blankets upon blankets. Water boiled over a campfire, and beside it stood a strange woman with Jonathan Fenty's red-gold hair tucked up underneath a kerchief and some of his brisk and businesslike manner.

Jenny gave herself into the strange woman's hands, hiding her face as another pain took her, hating anyone to see her like this, hating Charles to see her like this.

"—nothing to worry about," she could hear the woman saying to Charles. "It takes all women like this."

"I don't like this," Jenny managed.

She heard an earthy chuckle and felt a brisk pat on her side. "My lady, nobody does. It's the curse of Eve and we all have to bear it."

Jenny had some choice thoughts about that, but the pain was on her again and there was nothing but the rending of her body, light dancing crazily at the corners of her eyes, the crackling of the fire subsumed under her own moans. She tried to stop the cries, to stop herself, but they came all the same.

"Don't fight it," the red-haired woman said, and Jenny snarled at her, actually snarled, baring her teeth, and the woman poked at her stomach and did something undignified to her legs and told Charles to hold her hand or get her some water but at any rate to do something useful and not just stand there blocking her light.

"Push," the woman told her, and then again, more loudly. "Push. Now."

Charles was holding her hand and murmuring something to her, but Jenny didn't hear it, she was crying and struggling and pushing, panting with the effort, and then there was a cry that wasn't her own, a cry of triumph from the midwife.

"Now! Again!"

With one last, gasping, panting push, Jenny felt the tension release, and before she could quite realize that it had happened, that it had truly happened, the midwife was holding up a red and wrinkled creature covered in slime and blood.

The midwife cut the cord and expertly wrapped the baby in a blanket, delivering it into Charles's arms. "A girl," she said. "Hold her while I deliver the afterbirth."

Jenny craned her neck, trying to see her child, irrationally anxious that Charles should be holding her—what if he took her away?

"Mind on your work, my lady." The midwife was massaging her stomach, pumping and palpitating. "You'll have your wee one soon enough."

"Here." Charles knelt down, holding the bundle out so Jenny could see her.

Jenny stared at the little scrunched face blinking skeptically up at her. She reached out a finger, very tentatively, to touch her soft, wrinkled cheek.

"It's our baby," she said, not quite believing it, not quite believing this little creature, this little person, had come from her, had lived inside her all these months, and here she was, alive and whole and rather displeased at being born.

"Our little girl," said Charles, reaching out a finger gingerly, so gingerly. Their daughter clamped her hand around it. He looked at Jenny with delight. "She's a grip like a land crab!"

"She's strong," said Jenny softly.

"Like her mother," said Charles.

"She'll be wanting to eat now," said the midwife, and Jenny realized that while they'd been staring at their child, Jonathan Fenty's alarmingly competent sister had made a pile of cushions and blankets against the wall.

Helping Jenny up off the soiled clothes, she led her across to the improvised bed. Jenny's body felt strange and sore, a mass of aches, but she was only just aware of them, all of her attention focused on the bundle in Charles's arms.

"Nah, nah, baby, you'll not be getting anything from him," said Miss Fenty, and transferred the baby neatly from Charles to Jenny. The baby began rooting blindly at her chest, nudging the nipple with her nose.

"Like this," said the midwife, and expertly guided the baby's mouth to Jenny's breast.

The child sucked for a few moments and then dozed off, mouth open, head lolling back in the crook of Jenny's arm. Charles sank down against the wall next to her, his arm around her shoulders, both of them quiet, watching their child.

In the background, Jenny was vaguely aware of the midwife, industriously tidying, piling up the bloodied sheets.

"You won't mind if I take these?" she said to Charles.

"Have them," said Charles, not taking his eyes off the baby. "Have anything you want."

Jenny was tired, so tired. Charles's shoulder and the cushions were soft, the weight of the baby warm against her. She found herself drifting in and out of sleep, Charles's lips brushing her forehead, her arms locked around her baby. Every now and then she would start awake and blink at her child, at the wrinkled eyelids, the fine tufts of dark hair, the crumpled little mouth.

She came awake again to see Charles standing, staring out the door of the mill. The sky had begun to turn from black to gray. Jenny felt a chill steal across her heart and held her baby tighter.

"What time is it?" she asked, her voice raw.

Charles didn't need to consult his pocket watch. He must have already looked. "Nearly gone five," he said. "We'll have to go soon."

"No." She didn't mean to say it, it just came out. "Please, can't we wait a little more?"

It was the midwife who answered, her supplies neatly packed, the fire banked, the pot that had sat upon it gone cold and stowed in a straw basket. "It's time," she said.

Jenny's lips tightened; she blinked hard against a frightening rush of tears, holding her baby close, resisting the urge to hit out at anyone who came near her.

But to what end? She knew it as well as they. If she refused now, if she took her child back to Beckles, her baby would be marked, forever, as chattel. If they liked, Robert and Mary Anne could take her away from Jenny, give her to another family to raise, sell her, starve her.

Mary Anne wouldn't—Jenny didn't think. But it was so hard to tell with Mary Anne these days.

"All right," she said reluctantly. And then, delaying the moment as long as she could, she said to Charles, "What shall we call her?"

"I had thought . . . Carlota. Since she's meant to be Portuguese. We can call her Lottie."

"But we'll just call her Baby," said the midwife, kneeling down to take the child.

"Wait." One-handed, Jenny reached up to her neck, yanking so hard that she tore the frayed old ribbon. She tried to tuck the locket into the folds of the baby's blanket, but her hand fumbled and failed. She could have cried with frustration. "I want her to have this."

She had nothing of her own mother, not even her looks. When she looked into the mirror she saw her father. What would it have been to have something to hold, to remember?

"That's Mary Anne's locket."

"She gave it to me. You'll see. It says, inside. You can change it, take off the filigree, cover the inscription. Just so long as she has it."

"That's easily done, isn't it?" said the midwife, looking meaningfully at Charles. She reached for the baby and scooped her expertly up, and this time Jenny didn't fight her. "Up you get, little one."

Jenny's arms fell to her sides, numb. Her stomach and her arms felt empty, desolate.

Charles rose, pressing a kiss to the baby's forehead. "Good-bye, sweetling. We'll be with you again soon."

Jenny stuffed her fist into her mouth, trying not to cry out.

The midwife glanced down at her, not without compassion. "My sister Rachel will nurse her with her own. Don't worry, she'll be fed and cared for."

"And free." Charles's voice was hoarse. He knelt down next to Jenny, holding her hands; it felt less like an embrace and more like a restraint. "Remember that. She'll be free."

Jenny stared up at him, almost hating him at that moment, wanting to snap at him, to push him away.

"It's only for a time," he said softly, as the midwife, with a nod, disappeared silently out the door. "We'll have her back, I promise you that."

Promises, promises, what were promises? He had promised so much and done none of it and her stomach was empty, her baby gone, farther away by the moment, and it didn't matter right now that she had been a part of this, that she had agreed; her baby was gone.

Jenny turned her head into Charles's side and wept, great, ugly, gasping sobs that soaked through his shirtfront and dripped down onto his buckskin breeches.

He held her and murmured nonsense to her, as though she were their child, the child they had lost. "Hush, hush, my love. Hush, hush. It's only for a time . . . for a time . . ."

Light-headed and hollow, Jenny pushed away at last. "I'd best go back," she said flatly. She felt like a husk, emptied of everything.

Charles smoothed the hair back from her face, looking at her with such concern and love that her stomach cramped, guilt and love and resentment mixed all together. "You'll go to Nanny Bell straightaway?"

"Straightaway," Jenny lied. It was so hard to hate him when she knew that he was suffering too. But she did, just a little. Hated him and loved him and wanted to hold him close and push him away, all at once.

"I wish I could see you back."

"Oh, and no one would comment on that," said Jenny, pushing up to a sitting position, even though it made her head swim. She looked down at her soiled skirt. "I'll tell them the baby was born dead, on the road to Harrow. There's no reason for anyone to doubt me."

Charles wrapped his arms around her, holding her tightly, so tightly that Jenny wasn't sure who was meant to be comforting whom.

"I'll call on your mistress tomorrow," he said, standing and reaching down to help her up.

"Don't," said Jenny. It wasn't just that Master Robert wouldn't like it. She wasn't sure she could bear it, not right now, to see Charles and not be able to go to him, knowing their daughter was with strangers, far in the hills of St. Andrew. "Please."

The walk back to Beckles felt endless, her legs like lead, her stomach cramping, blood seeping from between her legs. Step by step, she made her way, the sunlight blurring in her eyes. She hadn't meant to take Charles's advice, but she found herself going not to the house but to Nanny Bell's hut.

"My baby—she was born dead," she managed, and fainted, ungracefully, on Nanny Bell's stoop.

When she woke, Nanny had a strengthening posset for her. Nanny didn't ask any questions; no one did. Babies died, some by accident, some by design, and it was always better not to inquire which.

It was night by the time she made her way back to the big house, to her mistress's chambers. The candles had been blown out in Mary Anne's room, and Jenny was grateful for that. All she wanted was to strip off her soiled dress, curl up on her pallet, and drift into oblivion.

She was creeping across the room when a hazy voice came from behind the netting of the great bed. "Where were you? I wanted you. I called and called and only Queenie came."

Jenny had thought she was beyond tears, but they came all the same, clogging her throat, making her voice thick. "My baby died."

"Oh, Jenny." She could hear Mary Anne pulling herself up against the pillows, her voice thick with sleep and laudanum. "You're not hurt?"

Not hurt? She felt like she'd been flayed, her emotions raw and aching. "Nanny Bell says I'll heal."

"Thank goodness for that," said Mary Anne, with real feeling. Clearing her throat, she added, "Well, there's one good thing to come of this. You can nurse Ned."

Jenny stood there, in the middle of the room, grateful for the darkness that hid her. The idea of holding another child, nursing another child . . . it made her whole body recoil.

The cruelty of it took her breath away. She'd known her mistress long enough to know that nothing was by chance and no slight went unpunished; she was being sentenced for bearing a child without her mistress's approval, for daring to risk her life in childbirth.

"Master Ned has a nurse," she said carefully.

Mary Anne dropped back against the pillows. "I don't like that nurse Robert found. She's slovenly." Drowsily, she added, "They say babies take their character from their milk. I'd rather have Neddy be like you. At least it's all in the family."

It was the first time Mary Anne had acknowledged her relationship and Jenny knew it was only because of the opium, loosening her tongue, making her say what she would otherwise hide.

By rote, she went to the side of the bed, smoothing the pillows for her mistress, pulling the coverlet up around her shoulders, trying not to let her anger show in her motions. "I'll do my best by Master Ned."

"Jenny." Mary Anne reached up, covering one of Jenny's hands with her own. In the dark, her eyes looked black, the pupils fully dilated. "I am sorry. About your baby."

Jenny let her hand lie still beneath Mary Anne's. Tears pricked at the backs of her eyes. "Thank you," she managed.

Mary Anne let go, lifting her hand to smother a yawn. "Such a pity. . . . He might have been a companion for Ned."

Jenny stared at her cousin with disbelief, disbelief and something that felt very much like hatred.

"She." Jenny yanked the mosquito netting back into place, her knuckles white around the floss, fighting the urge to bring the whole edifice crashing down on Mary Anne's head. "She was a girl. A little girl . . ."

CHAPTER TWENTY-ONE

St. Andrew, Barbados
May 1854

"What was the child's name?" Emily asked urgently.

George cocked his head, listening. "She says they just called her Baby."

"Her? The child was a girl?"

Old Betty chuckled and said something that made George's cheeks turn red. After a moment, he relayed, "She says all babies look alike in skirts. But she changed that child's swaddling more than once, and she can vouch it had the, er, correct parts."

Emily might have been amused if her attention hadn't been elsewhere, on the baby she hadn't known existed. "What happened to her? To the child? Did she go to the Carolinas with my aunties?"

"No." George cleared his throat. "She says that Fenty—er, your grandfather—took the baby away well before that. How long? A year or so, she thinks. Before the troubles."

"That would be sixteen? The troubles, I mean?" A child born at least two years before the troubles, before her grandparents' marriage. A child her grandfather took away with him.

No. It couldn't be. She was refining too much on the disordered memories of a poor old woman, who might very well be telling her a tall tale.

But why this tale? If she were going to spin stories, why this particular story?

Emily put her hand to the locket at her throat. Inside, on one side was a lock of her grandfather's red-gray hair and her mother's dark brown plaited together under glass, on the other a miniature of her mother as a small child, a replica of a miniature her grandfather had kept on a little stand in his study.

A little girl with dark brown curls and blue eyes, and a warm skin that her grandfather sometimes put to her mother's Welsh heritage, and other times, with a chuckle, to a gypsy somewhere in the family tree.

Or to an unknown woman who bore her grandfather a bastard child.

It made far more sense for her mother to be a child of her grandmother's first marriage. And yet . . .

She didn't want to ask in front of George. Not when it was probably all nonsense.

"Do you think we might offer her some of our picnic?" Emily asked George in an undertone. "I'd like to give her something, but I don't want to offend her with money. . . ."

"I don't think she'll be offended," said George.

"Please?" asked Emily prettily, doing her best to pretend to be Laura. "How often do you think she gets to taste meat?"

"Not often," admitted George. "All right. I'll be back presently."

"Thank you," said Emily, with real feeling. She waited until he'd picked his way back along the trail before turning back to Old Betty. She flicked the catch on the locket, feeling the two sides release. It was rather an awkward position, but she didn't want to remove it from her neck, so instead she leaned forward, holding out the locket on its ribbon as far as it would go. "Is this the child?"

"Gih muh dah day." Old Betty reached out and took the locket, angling it toward her faded eyes. She turned it this way and that, forcing Emily to crick her neck at a decidedly uncomfortable angle.

"This child is older, I know," said Emily breathlessly, trying not to breathe into the woman's face. "She would have been three or four here. I know babies don't look much like anyone yet, but . . ."

"I in know." Old Betty released the locket. "Mi' be."

George came back, directing Jonah, who was laden with comestibles and looking distinctly discomfited at being forced to deliver packages to a Redleg. Emily hastily stuffed the locket back into the collar of her dress.

George cleared his throat, directing Jonah to hand the basket to Old Betty. "For your troubles," he said. He held out a coin. "For your troubles as well."

When she took it and bit it, he looked pointedly at Emily.

"Thank you," said Emily, feeling subdued. There was so much she wanted to ask, but she knew she wouldn't understand the answer and didn't want to draw George into it. As an afterthought, she added, "Do you know where my grandfather took the child?"

In the stream of words that followed, only one was clear. Peverills.

"She says, where else would he take her but Peverills?"

"Yes, I got that, rather. Thank you," she said again, and they followed a rapidly retreating Jonah to the horses as, behind them, Old Betty began to explore the bounty of the basket. "I hope that wasn't the whole of your lunch."

George smiled down at her looking a bit strained. "No, there's plenty. Shall we have that picnic? There's a lovely spot not far from here."

"Yes, let's." She wasn't terribly hungry, but eating was something one did. She allowed George to help her up onto her mount, not really noticing where they were going, other than that it was steep, and the terrain seemed to require all of her companion's attention, for which she was grateful.

She had assumed that her mother must be the child of her grandmother's first husband. But no one had said anything to make her believe such a child existed. Mrs. Poole had believed them childless.

And here, here was another child. Her grandfather's child.

It was a family commonplace that her mother had been Grandfather's favorite, Uncle Archie her grandmother's. But what if it was more than a question of temperament? What if her mother wasn't her grandmother's child?

Would her grandmother have taken in another woman's baby? The answer was immediate and unequivocal. Yes. Not merely because her grandfather had asked her to, but because her stern Calvinist conscience would accommodate nothing less. But that didn't mean she had to like it.

Emily remembered the tension between her mother and grandmother. Young as she was, Emily had been old enough to mark the discord between them. But she had always taken their arguments at face value. Her grandmother had disapproved of her mother's passionate pursuit of causes, adjuring her to be more circumspect; her mother had retorted that her grandmother ought to do more to serve her Lord than sing his praise. Ungoverned, said the one; hypocritical, said the other.

But there had been affection in it too, hadn't there?

They had looked alike. Everyone said so. Or was it only her grandfather who said so?

"Mind how you go there." George took her bridle. Clearing his throat, he added, "It wasn't uncommon, you know."

"What?" She had no idea what George was on about. "Did you say something?"

"Your grandfather—many men back then had, well, outside children." Emily looked at him in surprise, nearly causing her horse to stumble. "You shouldn't be ashamed of him. It was really quite common."

"And does that make it right, that it was common?" Emily was too distracted to be tactful.

"You know what they say, *autres temps, autres moeurs.*" When Emily only stared at him, George added hastily, "My grandmother's never said, but I gather my grandfather kept a colored woman and her children in Bridgetown. They even call themselves Davenant."

He made it sound like a vast social faux pas. "It seems to me they've a right to the name, don't you think? They're your cousins."

"Not really. These other families, they, well." George looked up with relief as they reached the end of the steep and winding path, the vista opening up before them to reveal a broad beach, edged with scrub and studded with crags. "Ah, here we are. They call this Bathsheba's pool, from the Bible, you know. The story has it that Bathsheba bathed in milk to keep her skin fair. When you look at these waters, you can almost believe they're milk, can't you?"

Emily was still feeling prickly and unsettled, but it was easier to let him change the subject than pick a fight on a subject on which they were clearly not going to come to an accord. She let Jonah take the bridle and slid down from the horse onto the rough grasses at the verge of the beach. Pebbles prickled through the soles of her boots. "Do you think it will do anything for my cousin's freckles? My aunt used to blister his nose with lemon juice."

"People do bathe here," said George, taking her pleasantry for a genuine inquiry. "But I'm not sure I would advise it. It's rather rocky."

"Less so than Weston-super-Mare." Taking pity, she said, "You needn't worry. I've no intention of plunging into the surf. It is cooler here, isn't it?" A wind from the sea seemed intent on disengaging her hair from its pins.

"We're on the windward side of the island," said George apologetically. "If you don't like it, we could—"

"No, it's fine." The last thing Emily wanted was to prolong the outing. All she wanted was to go back to Beckles and—what? Adam knew as little as she. Whatever Mrs. Davenant knew, she wasn't telling.

For a mad moment, Emily wondered if Mrs. Davenant might have borne her grandfather a child. They did say that hate was first cousin to love—or some sort of relation, at any event. There were all those questions Mrs. Davenant had asked Adam about her mother and when her mother was born, the interest Mrs. Davenant showed in Emily . . .

But Mrs. Davenant had been married. If she'd borne a child, she'd have had no need to smuggle it out to St. Andrew. She would simply claim it as her husband's.

One assumed?

Emily used to feel quite comfortable assuming. But here, everything she thought she'd known had turned on its head, not once, but again and again. All of the assumptions that seemed sturdy as masonry one moment were revealed as hollow reeds the next.

What had her grandfather been doing sending her here? That he had sent her, that he had intended this, she had no doubt. Why leave her Peverills, else? He must have known that, once in Barbados, she would see the discrepancy in the dates and realize that her mother couldn't be the child of her grandparents' marriage.

But then who was she? And why hadn't her grandfather simply *told* her? Emily felt a surge of rage and grief, for her difficult, domineering, puckish grandfather who liked to make everyone dance to his tune. She'd never minded it before, but that was most likely because they'd always played in harmony; he'd given her her head, encouraging her in hobbies her aunt found unladylike, egging her on at her most outspoken, most forthright. Adam might complain about her grandfather controlling him by pulling on the purse strings, but he'd never, ever tried to bend Emily to his will.

Well, with the one exception. When he wanted her to marry Adam. But he hadn't pressed her. When she'd demurred, he'd shrugged and accepted it, even if the light in his eye had told her he hadn't given up the fight just yet. But it had become almost a joke over time. Or, at least, it had suited Emily to treat it as a joke. She wondered, now, uneasily, if her grandfather had felt the same. And what else he had kept from her.

He needs you, he'd told Emily, of Adam. *The boy's a flibbertigibbet. He needs someone to keep him in line.*

I've no desire to be my cousin's keeper, she'd told him, and he'd flicked her nose and told her not to be pert. *I only want to see you settled.*

Everyone wanted to see her settled, it seemed. Mrs. Davenant, because she came with Peverills. Her grandfather—because he loved her?

Or because he knew something about her past and felt the need to see her truly and legitimately a member of the Fenty family?

But her legitimacy wouldn't be in doubt if he hadn't sent her here. If he hadn't left her Peverills. If she'd stayed in Bristol, she might have been what she was, Jonathan and Winifred Fenty's granddaughter, the child of that daughter, you know, the one who ran off with an impoverished minister and wrote all those tedious tracts about the rights of man and injustice of slavery and goodness only knows what else.

There had to be other people in Barbados who had known her grandparents. The danger was, if she asked too many questions, she might start other people asking them too.

Did she mind? Not for the sake of the Mrs. Davenants of the world. But she would mind Adam looking at her differently, as somehow less, less a cousin, less a member of the family.

"Are you cold?"

"What? No. I rather like it." Emily dragged herself back to the present with an effort. Jonah had set out a rug on the scrub, weighting it down with porcelain and crystal and enough food to feed half of St. Andrew.

"Would you prefer chicken or ham?"

Looking at the piles of cold chicken and plates of dainties, Emily thought of that exhausted woman working her small field of arrowroot, her children barefoot and bony. "It seems rather obscene to have all this when the people in St. Andrew have so little."

"It's the way of the world," said George, helping himself to a slice of ham. "Was it so different in Bristol?"

"No," Emily had to admit. The gulf between Aunt Millicent's table and her father's parish had been hard to stomach. But there, at least, she had felt secure in her ability to do some good. Here, she felt at a loss, lost between worlds, neither Redleg nor planter, neither native nor foreigner.

Above them, the crags stretched high overheard, harsh and hilly. It seemed impossible that there were people living up there, on those cliffs, that her grandfather had been born there, eking out a living until he was able to snatch his opportunity and make his escape.

"It is majestic, isn't it?" said George, entirely misunderstanding what she was thinking. He toyed with the fringe of the rug. "I'm glad to have a chance to speak to you. I suppose you realize my grandmother would like to see us make a match of it?"

"I gathered as much. She hasn't precisely been subtle." Why did he have to broach this now? Emily forced herself to focus on George, although the cliffs lurked above her, taunting her with secrets. "You needn't mind it. I don't."

"I don't mind it either." George attempted to muster a smile, but it came out wobbly. He tried again. "What I mean is, I wouldn't mind it. Would it be so dreadful, to be married?"

Oh no. Not now. Not here. Emily stared at him, trying, very hard, not to sound as irritated as she felt. "I think that would depend on the person, don't you?" she said, with false brightness.

George failed to take the hint. "I do like you, Emily. Quite a lot. I think we might rub on well together."

"You do, or your grandmother does?" said Emily, and then wished she hadn't.

"I do," said George, not entirely convincingly. "Truly. I've enjoyed our rides together. We do get along, don't we?"

Yes, like brother and sister. Or really, more like distant cousins. But she couldn't say that without hurting his feelings. "I'm truly sensible of the honor you do me," said Emily, falling back on the phrase they had all practiced at Miss Blackwell's, in anticipation of hordes of importunate suitors. "But I'm not sure I mean to marry."

"Now? Or ever?" He tried to make a joke of it, but he looked nervous, like a puppy waiting to be kicked.

"I don't know," said Emily honestly. She thought of Adam and Laura, whose courtship had been so romantic, so passionate; they had scarcely two words to say to each other.

She'd always thought her parents had been the epitome of romance.

It had been a byword that her father had been lost without her mother. But if her mother was the great love of his life, why allow himself to be so entirely annexed by Hester? She'd begun to suspect that her parents' marriage had been less a great love story and more the attraction of the stronger character for the weaker, her mother dragging her father along in her wake.

She didn't want to be someone's prop. She didn't want to run two plantations while George painted pretty pictures and read Sir Walter Scott.

If she ever married, she wanted it to be someone who wanted her more than he needed her, someone who loved her because he was strong enough to appreciate her and not because he needed her strength.

Like her grandparents, equal partners in everything, each balancing the other.

But what did she really know of her grandparents, after all?

"I don't know," she said again. George looked so worried, so distressed, that she reached out and squeezed his hand. "But I do know that you ought to marry someone who loves beauty as much as you do, not someone who can't tell a sonnet from a sestina."

"I'd be happy to teach you," offered George.

"But I," said Emily, withdrawing her hand, "have no interest in being taught."

George looked down at his gloved hands, then back at Emily. "Is that a no, then?"

"If it would make you more comfortable," said Emily, "you might tell your grandmother that I am deeply flattered but still too unsure of my circumstances to make any plans for my future."

"Would you believe me if I told you that I was asking for myself, not my grandmother?" he asked quietly.

A moment ago, she would have said no, but the words stalled on Emily's lips and she found herself uncertain, unsettled by his earnestness.

"May we discuss this another time?" Emily said in desperation, grabbing at the hat that was trying its best to free itself from its pins.

"Of course," said George immediately, all solicitude. "I apologize if I've caused you any distress. Have you had enough to eat?"

"Oh, more than enough." This was the problem. He was so very good. She would never know what was genuine and what was politeness. She doubted he knew himself, so eager to please others that he fooled himself. Maybe he did truly think he cared for her?

Emily pushed aside the tangle, falling back on the scenery, letting George lead the conversation back into more general terms as they took the smoother coast road back south, leaving the shadow of the hills behind them. They discussed the local pottery, the chalk industry, the fishermen dotted among the rocks in the water. It was all very pleasant.

George was very pleasant. He'd doubtless make an entirely complaisant husband. For all of his comments about men keeping other families, she doubted he himself would stray. Not in body at any rate. It was far easier to imagine him writing lovelorn sonnet sequences to an unknown dark lady while coming meekly home for supper every night, treats for the children in his pockets. He would be a good father, she had no doubt, or, at least, a loving and indulgent one. Rather like her own father, who had always been more child than father.

She didn't want to have to be parent to her husband.

Yes, George was very pleasant, but if she married him, she'd have poetry read to her in which she'd no interest, and watercolors painted of her that she'd no time to sit for. She'd grow impatient of his good nature and frustrated with his kindness. It wouldn't be fair to either of them.

And who would she be? She could see herself turning into Mrs. Davenant, bullying her offspring and organizing her workers, always meaning to make changes, to do the sort of work her mother would have approved of, but mired in traditions of someone else's making. There was something about Beckles that sapped one's will, bent one to its routines and expectations.

It made one wonder if Mrs. Davenant had always been Mrs. Davenant or if she too had once been someone else, but found herself twisted into what she was now, her entire life bent to the service of her estate, husband dead, son fled, grandson too scared to voice an opinion.

"Thank you for taking me all the way to St. Andrew," said Emily, as they dismounted in the stable yard.

George pressed her hand. "The pleasure was mine. As always."

Light glinted from the direction of Mrs. Davenant's book room, sunlight on a telescope lens.

Emily murmured something conventional and fled into the house. Looking back, she could see Jonah leading the horses away, to be rubbed down, fed, and watered after their long ride.

Goodness only knew what Jonah had overheard, what stories he was telling now in the servants' quarters. Emily rubbed her temples with a gloved hand that smelled strongly of horse. Aunt Millicent always did say that servants knew everything, and here more than most, especially a groom, who would know all of one's comings and goings.

What was it London Turner had said? He had been the boy who held her grandfather's horse.

His groom.

If her grandfather had stashed a child in the hills of St. Andrew, who would have gone with him? His groom, of course.

Emily felt her lethargy slough away like the dust of the road. How foolish not to think of it before. If anyone knew what had become of that child, her grandfather's child, it would be London Turner.

And then she would leave it, she promised herself. Once this mystery was solved, she would stop dwelling on the past and decide what to do about Peverills.

She just needed to speak to London Turner first.

Emily pounced on Adam as he was about to go down to supper. "Do you have more meetings in town?" she asked without preamble.

"Why?" Adam fell into stride with her on the broad staircase.

"I'd like to come with you. I need to see Mr. Turner—about Peverills." It was, after all, about Peverills, even if in a roundabout sort of way.

Adam's lip twisted. "One doesn't just see Mr. Turner. One attempts to make an appointment and hopes for the best."

"I suspect he'll see me," said Emily thoughtfully. There was something between her grandfather and Mr. Turner. "If not, I'll do some shopping."

"Suit yourself. I'm seeing Montefiore Tuesday week." Adam scuffed the heel of his evening shoe against the polished treads of the stairs. "The man's a nigger and a Jew but I'd work a deal with the devil if it meant not going home empty-handed."

"And you're the grandson of a Redleg," retorted Emily. Adam looked at her blankly. "Oh, never mind. I'll send to Mr. Turner and see if he can see me Tuesday week."

"Don't hold out hopes," said Adam. "I've been banging on his door for weeks now."

Chapter Twenty-Two

Christic Church, Barbados
Christ Church, Barbados
August 1814

THE BANGING ON the door grew louder. "Let me in, damn you!"

Jenny cradled Neddy closer, covering his ears with the crook of her arm, rocking and rocking. His body gave a startled jerk at another flurry of knocks, and Jenny began to sing to him, mindlessly, tunelessly, less of a song and more of a chant, to blot out the shouting and the clatter.

"I saw a ship a-sailing, a-sailing on the sea . . ."

"You can't keep me out forever, Mary Anne!"

"And it was deeply laden with pretty things for me . . ."

Neddy yawned and burrowed closer, pushing with his legs against the side of the chair. He was getting big now, so big, too big to be held like this. He only resorted to the breast now late at night or very early in the morning, or when something scared him.

"There were comfits in the cabin, and almonds in the hold . . ."

"Don't think this is an end to it!"

A final rattle and the sound of booted feet pounding off down the corridor. Jenny felt the tension in her shoulders release but she kept rocking, rocking and singing, as she had night after night, month after month, as Robert and Mary Anne shouted and ornaments smashed and Neddy cried from confusion and rooted at her breast for comfort.

"The sails were made of satin, the mast it was of gold . . ."

There were times, in the forgiving androgyny of infancy, when Jenny had pretended that the child at her breast was her own, that the hair on her child's head had lightened from that dark birth hair to Charles's tow, that this was her little girl, snuggling boneless into her embrace. This was her little girl and they were sailing away together in a ship made of satin and gold, far away to a land beyond the horizon, where they would feast on comfits and almonds and never be apart.

Jenny stood, taking care not to jostle the sleeping baby in her arms. He was quite an armful now, big and solid. The older he grew, the harder it was to pretend, except in those wee hours of the morning when it was dark in the nursery and she was muzzy with sleep.

It was strange to think of a baby, still in skirts, as masculine, but there was something distinctly male about Neddy's peremptory shout when he wanted food, or his broad grin as he learned to sit up by himself, to reach for a toy without toppling over, to pull himself up to standing against the side of a chair. His legs stuck out over the side of her lap, too long now to fit comfortably, and he squirmed to be set down, to be free to toddle and fall and stick unsuitable things in his mouth. It was only in sleep that he relaxed against her, burrowing close, his face falling back into the roundness of babyhood.

Was her own little girl toddling now, on plump, unsteady feet?

It was her baby's birthday today. August 4. Today she was one year old, and Jenny found herself fighting hard, so very, very hard, to remember the shape of her infant features, those wrinkled cheeks and squinting eyes, the curve of her hand around Charles's finger.

What did she look like now? Was she starting to speak, as Neddy was, a word here and a word there?

Neddy called her "Ma-Ma."

Mary Anne had brushed it off, but Jenny knew she'd minded. Not that Mary Anne would ever say, but Mary Anne had her own way of making her displeasure felt.

"I need you," she'd declared, just that morning. "Queenie hasn't half your hand with hair. Isn't he old enough to be weaned?"

She'd announced that Jenny would be coming with them to Peverills tonight, to stand in attendance behind Mary Anne, to carry her fan and drape her shawl and be there with pins in case a flounce should tear.

"You know that Dutchess is perfectly capable of taking care of Neddy," she'd said, hauling Neddy, protesting, from Jenny's arms. "From the way you take on about that child, you'd think he was your own."

She hadn't forgot her own.

Did Jenny's little girl call Rachel Fenty "Ma-Ma"? She both hoped so and hoped not at the same time. She wanted her to be loved, yes, but she also wanted there to be space left for her, for Jenny.

But why should there be? Her daughter had never known her. Only for those few short minutes, and those nine long months when she'd been all in all to her baby, the entirety of her world.

There were folds on her stomach that hadn't been there before, folds that attested that she had once been great with child. Sometimes, Jenny had to look at them to remind herself that her little girl had been there, that she existed.

"We'll see her again," Charles said, but he didn't seem to realize how quickly they grew, these little ones, how soon they became people, with thoughts and opinions and preferences. Her daughter's affections and tastes were being shaped by someone else. By the time she came to them again—and not to them, to Charles, only to Charles—she would be a stranger already, and they strangers to her.

But how could she explain that to Charles, who hadn't spent every day holding a baby, nurturing a baby, watching him grow by startling leaps. He was a handsome baby, Neddy, with a shock of gold curls and Mary Anne's stubborn chin and gray eyes. Jenny's gray eyes.

There were times when Jenny couldn't help delighting in Neddy, and others when she could scarcely look at him, hating him for being here, for being acknowledged, when her own child was far away, being raised by strangers.

Charles promised her all was well, but Charles—Charles tended to believe what he wanted to believe.

Sometimes, Jenny fantasized about setting off down the road to St. Andrew, wandering into the hills, climbing and climbing until she found that village, the village where her daughter was being raised.

And for what? To bring their plans crashing down around them? They had come this far. If there were any suggestion that the child from Portugal were Jenny's, it would all be for naught.

But it hurt, it hurt so very much, to stay away.

Carefully, Jenny laid Neddy down in his cot, watching as he thumped his legs three times in his own strange fashion before settling.

Mary Anne kept him in a room adjoining her own, more, Jenny suspected, to annoy Robert than for any other reason. Although perhaps she was being unfair. The older Neddy grew, the more interest Mary Anne took in him, watching him with a fierce, possessive love that expressed itself more in directives than in cuddles.

"This is *my* boy," she said, and Jenny wasn't sure if she was defending her rights against Jenny or her husband. Or possibly both.

Her boy was to be raised in her image, as she saw fit. Her boy would learn estate management at her knee.

Her boy was only fourteen months and still in skirts. But Jenny couldn't tell her that. Mary Anne was even less amenable to advice than she had been in those long-ago days when they had lived in fear of the colonel. Whatever they had once shared was gone. There were days when Jenny could scarcely bear to touch her mistress, to brush her hair and pretend to smile. She went through the old motions by rote.

Shutting the door softly behind her, Jenny passed through into Mary Anne's room, where her mistress sat at her dressing table, dressed in Nile green satin, her hair wrapped in a matching silk turban, moodily dabbing a hare's foot into a pot of rouge.

"Where were you? Queenie had to help me dress."

Mary Anne knew perfectly well where she'd been. "I was feeding Master Neddy. The noise disturbed him." Mary Anne had painted two red circles on her cheeks, but beneath them her face looked pale and haggard, her lips thin. "Are you all right?"

"Perfectly. Why wouldn't I be?" Mary Anne shoved the rouge pot away. "That *husband* of mine thought to take me unawares while I was dressing. Apparently, I'm denying him his *rights.*"

Taking the hare's foot away from her, Jenny began quietly blending the rouge on Mary Anne's cheeks, trying to give her more the appearance of health and less the look of a French dandy of the previous century.

Mary Anne wafted Jenny away. "He can perfectly well comfort himself with his doxy. Does he think I don't know about her? I've provided him an heir, what more does he want?"

Acknowledgment. That was what Master Robert wanted. Acknowledgment that he was master here. That was the one thing, in bed or out, that Mary Anne refused to cede.

"Would it, perhaps, be less trouble to be seen to accede?" Jenny suggested. She found the pot of lip rouge, massaged a bit into her mistress's lips.

"I'm not having another child," Mary Anne said indistinctly. She smacked her lips together to equally distribute the rouge, looking up at Jenny in the mirror. "I won't go through that again. I'll die if I do, and then who will look after all this?"

There was no answer to that. If her mistress would only tell the master her fears—it probably wouldn't do any good, thought Jenny wryly. They'd come too far down this road for there to be either understanding or compromise. Nothing short of total conquest would suit either.

"What I meant," said Jenny, "was that perhaps if you were to give the impression of eagerness, he might be less insistent? Men do tend to want what they're told they can't have."

"Perhaps that was my mistake," said Mary Anne grimly. She was silent, and Jenny could see she was chewing the problem over. "No. No. I can't. If he gets me with child again . . . I won't. I can't. Get me my diamonds, Jenny. No, not the diamonds. Mrs. Boland is always so plain. The cameo set."

Obediently, Jenny fetched the cameos, fastening them around Mary Anne's throat, in her ears, around her wrists.

"Is the dinner for Mrs. Boland?" She knew already, of course. She and Charles met when they could, complicated by Jenny's obligations to both Neddy and her mistress. Mary Anne had clawed her way back to lucidity, but with that had come an anxious possessiveness; Mary Anne needed to know that her allies were around her at all times. It was hard, at times, especially when Jenny had been up half the night with Neddy and her wits were slow, to remember what she was meant to know, and where she was meant to have been.

"She's out of mourning and taking up her late husband's business." Mary Anne made no effort to hide her jealousy. She adjusted the cameo necklace, making faces at herself in the mirror. "Perhaps Robert will come up sweeter if our business prospers. He can buy his whore another bauble."

Robert greeted his wife with exaggerated politeness, as though he hadn't been threatening to break her door down less than half an hour before. The strong smell of smuggled French brandy made clear what had occupied him in the interim.

Jenny sat on the box with the coachman, her mistress's belongings clasped in her lap, her hands cold despite the heat of the day. Jonathan Fenty would be there tonight—Mrs. Boland, she knew, had requested it specially. She knew, because Charles had told her, that Fenty went to St. Andrew once a month to visit his sister and her children.

Yes, she had accounts from Charles, but they were secondhand. She craved word of her child the way she had once thirsted after Charles's embrace.

Was she well, was she happy, was there someone who cradled her in the night?

From the box, she could see Fenty, dressed in his best suit of clothes, a tall hat jammed on his old-fashioned queue, crossing through the lime hedge to the house. Jenny followed after Mary Anne and Robert toward the house, but, as the carriage began to rattle away to the coach house, she made a moue of distress.

"I've forgot the pins," she whispered to Robert's man Derry. "I'd best fetch them."

She hurried down the path, making sure to collide with Mr. Fenty, dropping her mistress's fan in the process.

"I beg pardon," she said anxiously, and then, in an undertone, "Is she well?"

She shouldn't be doing this, she knew. It wasn't that Charles had explicitly forbade it, but they both knew it was safest if there was no connection between her and Jonathan. But today was her baby's birthday, and, with each day, her child felt further and further away, a dream she had once had.

"You've dropped something." Fenty leaned over, his hat tipping. "She's the cleverest puss in Christendom. And her smile! She could make a saint do her bidding. She knows it too, the minx. She'll grin at you, so, and hold up her arms to be picked up. She's got everyone running circles around her."

Jenny blinked back sudden tears, the affection and fondness in his voice making her feel even more bereft.

"Thank you," she said hoarsely, taking the fan from him. She wanted to ask him more, whether she ever laughed, if she called Rachel Fenty "Ma-Ma," if she looked like Charles or Jenny or neither, did she like to sleep with the covers or did she kick them off at night. But the yard was swarming with servants and anything more would be noted. "When next you go, will you kiss her for me?"

Fenty took a moment to straighten his hat, squinting into the sun, away from Jenny, as though he weren't aware of her presence. "Don't you fret yourself. You'll be able to kiss her yourself soon enough."

He walked briskly away, toward the house, limping slightly in his smart new evening shoes with buckles, leaving Jenny scrambling to gather her wits about her, hurrying off to the coach house to discover the pins that were tucked safely in her pocket.

The party was seated at table by the time Jenny returned, sweaty and breathless. Mary Anne frowned at her and Jenny held up the packet of pins, rolling her eyes in silent apology. Jenny hurried to pick up the shawl her mistress had allowed to fall to the floor, and drape it over her mistress's arms.

Charles was seated at the head of the table, Mrs. Boland on his right. He didn't lift his head or look at Jenny, but she knew, without being told, that he was aware of her presence, was watching her without looking, just as she watched him.

With a smile, he disengaged himself from whatever conversation he had been having with Mrs. Boland and looked down the table. It was a small group by local standards: Mr. and Mrs. Poole were there; a floridfaced captain from the militia and his skinny wife; someone's maiden cousin, visiting from England.

Charles held up his glass to a footman, who filled it with claret, deep red in the candlelight.

"Oy," said Robert, clicking his fingers and holding up his own glass.

Charles cast a look at his brother but didn't comment. Instead, he raised his glass and said, "Thank you all for joining me this evening. I've a bit of news to share."

"He's marrying the widow," slurred Robert.

Fenty's hand tightened so hard on his glass, Jenny thought the stem would break. Mrs. Boland didn't deign to acknowledge the comment. She had a quiet dignity about her, the granite-hard dignity of a Roman matron.

"A good friend gave his life on the peninsula, fighting Bonaparte."

There was a ragged chorus of "Here, here!" and a "Damn the French!" from the florid captain that earned him an elbow in the ribs from his wife, causing his cheer to end in a hiccup.

Charles turned the glass around and around in his fingers, as if he might distract his audience with the glow, like a gypsy with a glass ball. "He leaves behind him a daughter, by a Portuguese woman. The child is now doubly an orphan, with the loss of her mother." For a moment, his eyes met Jenny's, behind Mary Anne's chair, and then flinched away again. "It seems that he expressed a wish that I raise the child."

"Doesn't the man have family of his own?" inquired the maiden cousin, lifting her lorgnette.

"They were estranged," said Charles briefly.

"Don't wonder," murmured the captain, "if he was consortin' with Portugee beauties."

"Were they married?" demanded Mrs. Poole avidly. She was only just a wife herself, wearing a plunging décolletage with all the recklessness of new maturity.

"I believe so," said Charles cautiously.

"If a marriage to a papist can be accounted a marriage," said the captain's wife, in a voice that carried.

"The child," said Charles, raising his voice to be heard above the commentary, "will be taking ship from Lisbon as soon as the winds are favorable. I look forward to welcoming Carlota St. Aubyn to Barbados, and hope you will too."

Robert lifted his glass. "The more the merrier, what? Portuguese brats and Redlegs. What next? Shall we open the dining room to the slaves and have 'em to supper?"

"Robert," Mary Anne hissed. To Charles, she said, "How old is the child?"

"I don't know precisely," said Charles apologetically. "Communications from Portugal have been, as you can imagine, hurried and fraught. She's quite little, I gather. One or two years old? But that's all I know."

"How do you know it's not a hoax?" Robert demanded. "Zounds, anyone with a sad story could touch you for cash and you'd open the coffers for them."

"I trust you will believe me when I say that I have investigated the claims with the resources at my disposal and found nothing amiss." Charles betrayed no signs of anger but Jenny had noticed that he sounded more and more like a lawyer the closer he was to losing his temper.

"Ha! Just hand out the family silver, why don't you?"

"If I wanted to," said Charles quietly, "it would be within my gift."

"Well, I think it's lovely that you're taking in a poor little orphan," said Mary Anne brightly. "She can be a companion for Neddy."

"If you think I'm letting my son—" Robert broke off, wincing, as Mary Anne's foot connected with his shin.

"Christian charity is always to be lauded," said Mrs. Boland seriously. "Those of us who have much have a duty to those who have little."

Mrs. Poole played with her emeralds. "Yes, but so many have so little. If one started like that, where would it end, I ask you?"

"With no one hungry?" said Mrs. Boland.

"Mrs. Boland," said Mr. Fenty, speaking for the first time, his voice warm with admiration, "has made a gift to the parish council to see assistance given to all worthy families in want."

Mrs. Boland nodded to him in acknowledgment, and a look passed between them, plainer than words. "One does what one can," she said.

"They bring it on themselves," said Robert, draining his glass again, his eyes darting from one to the other. "Shiftless, that's what they are. Begging and scraping instead of doing an honest day's work."

"What work? What work is there for them?" asked Charles.

"There's a little man who goes from plantation to plantation peddling," offered Mrs. Poole, her silks and jewels glimmering. "I think most of it is stolen, but one does have to admire the dedication in all that walking from place to place. He hasn't any shoes either."

Charles glanced at Mrs. Boland. "That's another piece of news. Mrs. Boland has been kind enough to join me in a pet scheme of mine. A model plantation. Our workers will be paid for their time, with the option of staying on as tenant farmers."

"You plan to have Redlegs plant sugar?" Robert demanded.

"Some Redlegs, yes. But also slaves." Charles met his brother's eyes. "Their wages will go to purchasing their freedom. Mrs. Boland has agreed to advance the sum for the sugar. We believe there are those in England who will be glad to buy sugar grown so."

"Are you mad?" Robert half rose from his seat, staring at Mrs. Boland with a combination of scorn and rage. "I thought you were buying Beckles sugar!"

"Mr. Davenant made a compelling argument," said Mrs. Boland firmly. "I've looked at the books, and I believe there's promise in it."

"Oh, the *books*," said Robert. "Is that what they're calling it now?"

"Robert," said his wife flatly. "Stop."

"Do you realize what this means?" Robert seemed to have lost all awareness that there were other people at the table. "We've half the crop with nowhere to sell it! All because some jumped-up bogtrotter's widow fancies my idiot brother."

Mr. Fenty pushed back his chair with a scrape. "Take that back."

The other men all half rose, but Charles was there first, clamping a hand on Jonathan's arm. "He's drunk."

"The wine is in and the wit is out!" offered the captain.

Mrs. Poole giggled.

"He's insulted a worthy lady."

"Lady, is it?" Robert tried to push back from his chair and almost managed to send it over with himself still in it. "With a complexion like that, you have to wonder just where old Boland picked her up."

"That's enough, Robert." Charles had one hand on Fenty's shoulder, holding him in check. "Apologize."

"To whom? Your pet Redleg? Or *her*?" He made no effort to hide his scorn. "This is what happens when women play at men's business."

"Get out." Charles's voice was clear as breaking glass, each word sharp-edged. "You are no longer welcome here."

Robert looked at him incredulously, his blond hair flopping in front of his eyes. "You can't throw me out of my own home."

"It's not your home," said Charles, and Jenny could see how much it cost him, how hard it was for him to repudiate his own blood. "It's mine. And I cannot have my guests insulted."

Robert looked like he might have argued, but Mary Anne rose from her chair, gathering up her gloves and fan. With a put-upon sigh, she reached for her husband. "Come along, Robert. Let's go soak your head in a trough."

"Get off me, you harpy." Robert pulled away from her and went sprawling. He struck out at his hapless manservant, who bent down to help him up. He staggered to his feet. "I don't need you. I don't need any of you. I'll go where I'm wanted."

There was a horrible silence as he lurched from the room, Derry jogging behind him, grabbing him as he stumbled.

A moment later, they all heard the sound of retching from the veranda.

"It's the brandy does it," said the captain virtuously. He held up his glass to be refilled. "I make a practice of never drinking but claret and good Barbados rum punch."

To Mary Anne, Charles said, "I'm so sorry."

He was, Jenny knew, apologizing for more than just the evening.

Mary Anne smiled determinedly at him. In a carrying voice, she said, "Is there any more treacle tart? You must have your cook send to mine with the receipt. When ours attempts it, it always comes out looking and tasting like molasses mixed with mud."

Mrs. Poole, looking for hysterics, looked greatly disappointed. Following Mary Anne's lead, the conversation became general, although there was still a tense set to Fenty's shoulders and a troubled look to Charles's eyes.

When the guests had taken themselves off, earlier than usual, Charles seized the opportunity to speak to Mary Anne.

"I'm so very sorry. For everything. I feel responsible."

Mary Anne shrugged, turning her back to Jenny so Jenny might wrap her in her shawl. "You know how he gets. We'd counted on the Boland contract."

"I didn't think. I ought to have realized . . ." Charles looked at Mary Anne with concern. "Beckles sugar is justly famed. Surely you can find another buyer?"

"Easily," said Mary Anne, lifting her chin, although Jenny knew that it wasn't going to be as easy as that.

"Would you like to stay the night at Peverills?" Jenny frowned at Charles over Mary Anne's shoulder. He wasn't meant to know of the fights between Mary Anne and Robert; she had told him in confidence. Charles checked himself, adding quickly, "Robert's not pleasant when he's in a temper. I'd hate to see you suffer for my thoughtlessness."

"He'll be less pleasant if I'm seen to be spending the night here. Unless you mean to keep Mrs. Boland as chaperone? No. I'm not afraid of Robert." Mary Anne's eyes narrowed. "I've a strong lock on my door."

But Robert was already there when they got back, sitting on the chair beside Mary Anne's bed, a half-empty decanter beside him.

"If it isn't my beloved wife," he said, lifting the decanter.

"Mistress." Jenny tugged on her dress. "Come away."

"What in the devil were you thinking?" demanded Mary Anne, advancing into the room, ignoring Jenny's entreaties. "Insulting Mrs. Boland! In front of the Pooles! Do you want to be shunned by every sugar trader from Bridgetown to Bristol?"

"You want to talk to me about being shunned?"

In a sudden, violent movement, Robert lurched to his feet, flinging the glass decanter so that it exploded against the wall behind Mary Anne's head. Crimson trails of claret trickled down the pale-papered wall like blood. Jenny put her hand to her arm and realized she was bleeding, a shallow, stinging cut where a shard had grazed her.

Robert advanced on Mary Anne, glass crunching beneath his boots. "Talk to me about a wife who locks her door."

A sharp wail rose from the next room, Neddy roused from sleep, angry and frightened.

"Shut that brat up," said Robert. As Jenny paused, caught between her mistress's need and the baby, he shouted, "Go, damn you! Who's master here?"

Mary Anne nodded to her, and Jenny ran to Neddy, whose wails had doubled in volume as he discovered that he was wet as well as awake, and it was dark and people were shouting, and no one was picking him up even though he was calling and calling.

As Jenny hastily jiggled him, she heard behind her, through the open door, "Is he mine, Mary Anne? Or is he my brother's? Have you been sneaking off to Peverills behind my back?"

"Oh Lord," snapped Mary Anne. "Not that again. If you had any brains that weren't in your cock, you'd know better."

"You want me to show you my cock?"

There was the sound of a chair overturning, cloth ripping, grappling, muffled cries.

"—my wife," Robert grunted, and then grunted in pain rather than pleasure as Mary Anne landed a knee between his legs. Jenny could hear him scrabbling, cursing, crying out as he landed in some broken glass, and then Mary Anne's cry of distress as he grabbed her, forcing her back against the wall. "—show you—"

Jenny clutched Neddy, trying to decide what to do. To come to her mistress's aid would be an offense punishable by death.

She could hear a thump as her master pushed her mistress back against the wall. Mary Anne didn't cry or cry out; Jenny heard her sobbing pant, her master's noises of satisfaction, and then a loud and horrible cracking noise, followed by something heavy tumbling to the ground.

There was silence.

Neddy let out an exploratory series of grunts and grumbles. Jenny clutched him to her chest and hurried into the bedroom.

Mary Anne was holding her mahogany writing box in both hands, lifted above her head. Her hair was down around her back, half in her pins, half out. There was a bruise on one cheek, another on her collarbone where her dress had been torn away. One cameo earing still dangled from her ear; the other had fallen on the carpet, lying next to a limp male hand.

Robert lay sprawled on the floor, his pantaloons undone, his shirt billowing around him, his blue eyes as glossy and still as the glass of the decanter. Blood seeped beneath his head, unfurling like crimson cloth.

"He's dead." Jenny pressed Neddy's head close to her chest, ignoring his mumfle of protest. "He's dead."

Slowly, Mary Anne lowered her arms, setting the writing box down carefully in its spot on her escritoire.

"Get Dr. MacAndrews," she said. "My husband's had an accident. Did you hear me? He's had an *accident.*"

Chapter Twenty-Three

Bridgetown, Barbados
May 1854

"Forgive our disarray. My wife and daughters have left for the country and I am to join them in a matter of hours."

Mr. Turner received Emily in the same room to which she had first been escorted four long months ago. It felt more like four years. The fossils were still in their places in the curio cabinets, the works of philosophy and theology on the shelves, but there was already the slightly sleepy air of a house abandoned, the dust motes dancing lazily in the sunshine, the furniture waiting only for the guest to depart so the holland covers could be set over them.

Tea and cakes had been set out, but it was a bachelor effort, not the bounty Mrs. Turner might have commanded. It didn't matter; Emily wasn't terribly hungry. She was feeling rather foolish about the whole affair, but having come so far, she knew there was no turning back.

"I hope you didn't delay for my sake," said Emily.

"Not at all," said Mr. Turner, in a way that implied just the opposite. "I sent to Beckles this morning to cancel our appointment, but my message must have missed you. Have you come to discuss the sale of Peverills? If so, I would advise that you wait. This isn't a good time to sell."

"No. No, it's not that." Emily worried at the clasp of her net bag, the one Laura had worked for her a hundred years ago, back at Miss

Blackwell's, adorned with fat cabbage roses and extravagant green vines. "You mentioned, some time ago, that you had once been my grandfather's groom?"

Mr. Turner leaned back against the settee, propping one ankle against the opposite knee. Emily had an impression of leashed power, a tiger being kind to a kitten. "Yes?"

"I made a visit to St. Andrew, to my grandfather's people. There was an old woman there, Old Betty." Mr. Turner's attention never wavered, but she could tell he was waiting for her to get to the point. Emily took a deep breath. "She told me my grandfather kept a child there, an 'outside' child, she called it."

"Ah," said Mr. Turner.

"Is there—do you—that is, could you tell me anything about that child?" Emily linked her fingers together, leaning forward. "I need to know, *was* it my grandfather's child?"

Mr. Turner looked at her, taking her measure, her old dress and sensible hat. She hadn't wanted to wear Mrs. Davenant's borrowed finery to go to town. It was one thing to play make-believe at Beckles, but she had felt, somehow, that to take that person, that Emily, to Bridgetown would be to cross a line she couldn't cross back.

"I suppose there's no harm in telling you now," said Mr. Turner at last.

Emily waited, painfully aware of every noise around them, every hoofbeat in the street, every tick of the clock. "You knew her, then?"

"The child? Yes. I didn't bring her to Scotland, but I went with your grandfather when he visited. The fiction, then, was that she was your grand-aunt's child. Rachel Fenty," he amended. "Everyone there knew otherwise, of course, but it was what your grandfather told strangers."

"What was she like? The little girl."

"A baby," said Turner. His lips spread in a smile at Emily's obvious disappointment. "I was a boy of eight. I had no interest in babies. One looked much like another. Your grandfather doted on her, though. We never went up that cliff without treasures in the saddlebags. Embroidered linens and wooden toys. There wasn't another child in St. Andrew so pampered. His sisters didn't mind it, though," he added pragmatically. "Their children got the leavings. And the money for keeping her."

Emily's hand closed around the locket at her throat. She'd pinned it to her collar like a broach, a talisman. "So it was true, then. The child was my grandfather's."

"What? No." Mr. Turner shook himself out of the past.

"I don't understand," said Emily, feeling very stupid and very slow. "I'd thought they said——"

"That's what the people there believed, of course, and it didn't do to disabuse them. But the child—no." Mr. Turner regarded her expressionlessly, and she had the sense he was doing sums in his head, weighing his options. "The child that your grandfather brought to Scotland wasn't his. She was the child of Charles Davenant and a slave, Mary Anne Davenant's maid Jenny."

"Oh," said Emily, feeling her brain go blank with surprise. She'd been prepared to show the miniature of her mother, to grapple with the reality of her parentage, but it wasn't her parentage at all. Her grandfather had been doing a kindness for someone else. She had stumbled into someone else's tragedy.

"You see their problem," said Mr. Turner conversationally, politely giving her time to recover her wits. "The girl belonged to Mrs. Davenant. So would the child. So they hid it."

"The woman in St. Andrew—she said my grandfather took the child away again?"

"Yes. I was with him for that," Mr. Turner said reminiscently. It was, Emily thought, more than a space in time for him. He had been a different person then, a boy, a slave, a world away from the man of property he had become. "We brought the child to Peverills. The story put out was that she'd come from Portugal."

"The Portuguese ward." Emily didn't realize she'd spoken the words aloud until she saw Mr. Turner looking at her. "So she wasn't Portuguese at all?"

"No more than you or I," said Mr. Turner gravely. "Your grandfather never spoke to you of it?"

Emily shook her head. "I only learned of it from Mr. Davenant."

Can you imagine that? To have made it through a war safely and then to die like this? George had said. There had been no war, but it was almost worse, what the child had survived; to be wrested from slavery only to perish in a rising meant to free those like her.

"That poor child," said Emily with feeling.

Mr. Turner considered a cake and set it down again, uneaten. "There is a bit more to the story."

"Mr. Davenant abandoned Peverills, I know. I can't wonder at it. The poor man." To engage in so much subterfuge to extricate his child from the toils of slavery, only to see her die in a fire. No wonder Mr. Davenant had fled from Peverills and never returned, never rebuilt. Emily thought of the shadowy figure behind Mrs. Davenant in the portrait at Beckles. "Whatever became of the mother? Jenny?"

"She was also lost in the fire," said Mr. Turner. "Like her child."

"Uncle? Shouldn't you be—" Dr. Braithwaite checked at the sight of Emily, comfortably ensconced on a Louis XV chair. He regarded her with unmitigated horror. "What are you doing here?"

"I came into town to see your uncle," said Emily, not a little offended. She had thought they had parted on friendly terms.

"Well, get back out again," said Dr. Braithwaite. Prowling around her chair, he snapped out a series of questions. "Did you go anywhere else? Did you see anyone? Take food with anyone?"

"I came from Beckles this morning. The carriage brought me straight here. Are you quite well, Dr. Braithwaite? Do I need to make you a tisane?"

"You need to get back to Beckles." Dr. Braithwaite pressed his fingers to his temples, breathing in deeply. "Did no one tell you? It's not safe in Bridgetown. The Board of Health is posting the notices today. Asiatic cholera."

Emily's skin prickled; she could feel the cold sweat forming beneath her arms. "How many dead so far?"

"We don't know for certain. There are a dozen dead already in Lightfoot Lane, six of them in the Goodrich house alone. And more in Jemmott's. But it's moving. It's moving. And so had you better," Dr. Braithwaite said, turning to his uncle. "Aunt Ada would never forgive me if I let you come to grief."

"If you let me?" said Mr. Turner, amused. "I'm master of my own destiny, my lad."

For a moment, Dr. Braithwaite grinned at his uncle, and the resemblance between the two men was startling. But his amusement quickly faded. "Not with the cholera in the town. With cholera, no man is master of anything but a wooden box in the ground."

"Always so lyrical," said Mr. Turner mildly. "Miss Dawson, may I offer you a ride from town? I go to St. Philip. I pass by Beckles on my way."

Emily shook her head. Her lips felt numb. "I need to wait for my cousin. We came by carriage from Beckles. He was to see a Mr. Montefiore. . . ."

A look passed between the two men. Reluctantly, Dr. Braithwaite said, "I attended on Mr. Montefiore yesterday."

He didn't need to tell her what he meant. "Oh no."

Dr. Braithwaite lowered his chin. "Stomach cramps, evacuations of the bowel."

Emily's throat felt very dry. "I know. I've seen it before. We had it in Bristol, in forty-nine. There was so much death. . . ."

Whole families dead. Babies, alone in the world, crying next to the bodies of their dead mothers. There had been so little she could do, so little to stem the tide. She could still smell it, in the back of her nostrils, the cologne of the handkerchief she had tied around her face mingled with the putrid stench of death. She could smell it in her dress, in her hair; she could taste it at the back of her throat, after all this time.

At sixteen, she had, secretly, been a little in love with the young doctor who had worked so indefatigably for the poor of Stapleton Work-house. Until he had died too. "Even Dr. Williams died. He died tending to his patients."

"I don't need to tell you how dangerous it is, then." Dr. Braithwaite made to hustle her out. "Go with my uncle. Get away while you can. I'll find your cousin."

"Are you talking about me?" There was a heavy tread on the floor of the hall and Adam tumbled through the door of the study, catching at the doorframe to steady himself. With the exaggerated dignity of the inebriated, he said, "My apologies, sir. There was no one at the door."

"I've sent the servants ahead to the country," said Mr. Turner.

"Adam," Emily said, rising from her seat. "Adam, you should know—"

"It's the strangest thing, Emily," Adam interrupted. He scrubbed a hand over his eyes and Emily realized he had lost his hat somewhere, leaving him bareheaded, his red hair disordered and darkened with sweat. "He's dead. Montefiore's dead."

"He was a good man," said Mr. Turner soberly.

Adam didn't seem to hear him. "I went to his store on Swan Street and they told me he'd never come in, so I went to his home and there was a little boy crying and they were hanging black cloths over the mir-rors. They told me he died just this morning. Went into convulsions. One minute he was alive, the next he was gone."

"Adam," Emily said urgently. "Adam, we have to get away. There's illness in the town."

Adam swayed on his feet. His forehead glistened with a sheen of sweat in the half-light of the shuttered drawing room. "'S hot today." He tugged at the knot of his cravat. "I'm feeling the heat. Lord, how do people live in this?"

Emily caught at her cousin's arm. She smelled rum on him, on his clothes, on his breath. "Did you come straight here?"

Adam's eyes shifted away. "I might have stopped at the icehouse first. Don't look like that. I only had one cup—spilled some of it. It was very distressing!"

"I'm sure it was," said Dr. Braithwaite. "Uncle—"

"All right, all right." Mr. Turner rose. He bowed courteously, but Emily noticed he kept his distance, making no attempt to shake hands. "Mr. Fenty, Miss Dawson, if you'll forgive me? I've overstayed my time. Nathaniel—"

Dr. Braithwaite stepped back, away from him, holding up a hand to ward off contact. "Give my most sincere expressions of affection to Aunt Ada and my cousins. Tell them to drink no water that isn't first boiled."

"We'll hardly have to worry at Belle View. But yes, I'll tell her. She can blame you when the servants leave us."

"Tell them they'll be glad for it by and by. Better to sweat and live."

"Emily?" Emily's attention was abruptly wrenched back to her cousin as he tugged at her sleeve. "I might—I might have had one too many."

Emily regarded Adam with dawning alarm. "I thought you only had one cup."

"I'm not—I'm not feeling so clever."

Adam's face looked more green than pink. Doubling over, he sprayed the contents of his stomach all over Mrs. Turner's Aubusson rug.

Emily started forward, but Dr. Braithwaite flung out an imperious arm. "Don't. I'll see to him."

"It might just be the rum."

Dr. Braithwaite made an attempt to hold her back. "Would you stake your life on that?"

Emily pushed him impatiently aside. "If that's what it is, I've already been exposed." She knelt by her cousin, feeling his head with the back of her hand, supporting him with her arm. "Adam? Adam, how are you feeling?"

Adam groaned. "I've been sick, haven't I?"

"All over the rug," said Emily, with a cheerfulness she was far from feeling. Outside, she could hear the cry of Mr. Turner's coachman, the crack of the whip, the clatter of hoofbeats as Mr. Turner's carriage rattled away, fleeing the sickness. "Just like the time you gobbled all the jam tarts, you big greedyguts. We're going to get you cleaned up and get you to bed."

She looked to Braithwaite, and he nodded. "You'd best keep him here. I've my rounds to make, but I'll attend him when I can."

"The servants . . . ?"

"All gone to Belle View except for one kitchen maid and a boy to tend my horse and gig." Sliding an arm under Adam's shoulders, Dr. Braithwaite said, "Come along, Mr. Fenty. Do you think you can stand?"

"Dizzy." With Dr. Braithwaite's help, Adam lurched to his feet, wincing in pain. "Christ, my stomach."

"Let's get you upstairs."

Emily looked back over her shoulder. "The rug—"

"I'll burn it." At Emily's expression, he added, "My uncle can afford another."

Together, they managed to get Adam out of his coat and boots and into a bed in a small bedroom at the back of the house, away from the street side.

They stood looking at each other across the foot of the bed. Dr. Braithwaite said, "It's no use to try to persuade you to go, I imagine."

Emily shook her head. "What would be the point now?"

"You're not concerned about your reputation?"

"If I were to put my reputation before my responsibilities, then I would be a poor character, indeed," said Emily warmly. "I don't care what busybodies think, but I do care for my own good opinion."

Dr. Braithwaite raised his brows. "There's no possible answer to that. I'll leave laudanum for you. It will help him rest—and it does seem to do some good. I'm not sure why, but it does." He looked at Emily's vomit-splashed skirt and jabbed a finger at it. "Burn that too. Or at least boil it."

"And wear what?" Emily looked down at her own maltreated frock. "I wasn't intending to make an extended visit."

"I have to get back," said Dr. Braithwaite, beating a hasty retreat. "Help yourself to anything you need from my aunt's wardrobe."

Emily remembered Mrs. Turner's gown, a miracle of French fashion. Aside from being entirely impractical for tending sickbed, it most likely cost enough to rebuild the roof of Peverills.

"I'm not emptying slop buckets in your aunt's Paris dresses!" Emily called after him, horrified.

Dr. Braithwaite paused on the landing. "Why not?"

"If you don't know why not . . . Oh, never mind. I'll find something." Emily went off to raid the wardrobes of the upper servants, supplying herself with two plain calico dresses and a variety of brightly colored head scarves to tie up her hair.

The housekeeper was stouter than she; the dresses hung loosely, but that was all to the best in the growing heat, which haunted the corners of the house, rising with the day. It was decidedly hotter in town than it had been at Beckles. Emily found herself grateful for the scarves that kept her hair off her face and neck, and began to wonder if she ought to have lodged Adam in a downstairs room as he lay in his shirt on tangled sheets.

Emily scoured the pantry, searching for suitable foods for an invalid. She ruthlessly raided the chicken coop, sacrificing a fowl for the pot, wringing its neck, scalding and plucking it with her own hands while Adam dozed, fitfully. She would have to find some way, later on, to thank Mr. Turner for his unwitting hospitality. In the meantime, the only object could be to get Adam on his feet again.

"You can cook?" Dr. Braithwaite came in as Emily was hovering over the soup, trying to fish out a recalcitrant sprig of greens.

"Not like your aunt's cook," said Emily, poking at the chicken with a wooden spoon. "But I can do you a good, strong broth, or a milk pudding."

"Your talents never cease to amaze me."

"Don't say that until you've tasted it." The steam from the pot warmed Emily's cheeks. She thrust her spoon at Dr. Braithwaite. "Does this need more salt?"

She fed Adam broth, alternately bullying and cajoling him into taking a spoon here and a spoon there, letting him rest against the pillow between sips, mopping his brow with a damp cloth.

Adam moved restlessly against the pillow. "Do you ever think we ought to have married?"

"You're talking nonsense. Hush."

"That was what Grandfather wanted, you know."

"Grandfather wanted what Grandfather wanted." Emily touched a gentle finger to Adam's sunken cheek. "You'll get better and go back to Laura and your baby and be very glad we didn't marry, I'm sure of it. Now have another spoon of soup."

Sometimes he thought they were in the nursery again, that Emily's mother had just died. "Don't worry, Cousin Em'ly, we'll have a jolly time, I promise. Nurse is an old fussbudget, but she's all right if you know how to get around her."

And Emily would thank him and pretend to be that long-ago girl, until he drifted again into sleep.

There were mumblings about debts and moneylenders, women and French letters, horses that ran too fast and horses that didn't run fast enough; there were times when he carried on conversations with cronies that weren't there and others when he argued with imaginary adversaries.

But it was the adversary inside him whom Emily was determined to fight.

When his bowels emptied, soaking him and the sheets in foul-smelling liquid, Emily stripped the bed and sponged Adam clean, clothing him in a shirt and unmentionables filched from Mr. Turner's own wardrobe, boiling the sheets in a giant kettle in the yard, before hanging them out to dry in the brilliance of the noonday sun. Her arms ached with the effort and her hair was lank with sweat, but she felt a sense of triumph at the achievement, that she had done it herself, the kitchen girl having wisely made herself scarce. Gone to visit an aunt, she told Emily, and never returned, leaving Emily in sole command of the house.

There were more sheets to boil, more noxious liquids; there were days when Adam scarcely moved at all and others when he moved restlessly and convulsively on the sun-scented sheets and Emily had to struggle to dose him with laudanum. The Board of Health offered lime to afflicted households, to scour away the sickness. Emily scrubbed the yard and the house, the astringent smell burning her nostrils, her hands red and chapped, then went back inside to slip chips of ice between Adam's cracked lips, to bathe his brow with water and oil of lavender, and coax him to swallow a bit of laudanum.

Dr. Braithwaite was right; the laudanum did seem to give him some ease, not only helping him sleep but slowing the pace of the disease.

"Hadn't you better find me a proper doctor?" rasped Adam, in one of his lucid moments.

"Don't be an ass," said Emily sharply, lifting the tray she had brought. "Dr. Braithwaite is a proper doctor. Be polite or I'll send you back to Dr. MacAndrews."

By the sixth day, Emily had begun to hope that Adam might make a recovery. His color seemed clearer; he had obediently sucked the ice chips she had given him.

"He's getting better," she said to Dr. Braithwaite. "I'm sure he is."

Dr. Braithwaite took the glass of sherry she handed him. They'd fallen into the habit of having a glass of sherry in the drawing room of an evening, a moment of peace between the difficulties of the day and the looming demands of the night. "It's a good sign when they're sick," he said seriously. "It's the cases where there's no, er, effluvia, where there's the least chance of recovery."

"He seemed more lucid today. And he took some water. Boiled," she added. Her companion was adamant that they follow Dr. Snow's directive that all water be filtered and boiled before use.

Dr. Braithwaite slumped down on the settee. "We'd another forty deaths today. And those are only the ones that were reported."

"Is it getting worse?"

"Much." He closed his eyes, resting his glass of sherry on his stomach. "They're to close St. Leonard's Church. The smell from the graveyard has become too overwhelming for services to be held. Anyone who lives downwind is seeking accommodation elsewhere. The governor is looking to buy land for a new graveyard. Something that can accommodate death in the thousands."

"I'll keep boiling water," said Emily. "If it doesn't do any good, at least it can't do harm."

Dr. Braithwaite opened his eyes and regarded her ruefully. "It's damnable of me, but I'm selfishly glad you're here. I should wish you back at Beckles, for your own good."

"If I were at Beckles," said Emily matter-of-factly, "then the cholera would be too. So there's no point in wishing me away."

Dr. Braithwaite peered owlishly over the top of his glass. "Are you telling me you're cursed?"

It took her a moment to realize he was joking. "Ha," she said. "No. It's just that if Adam weren't here, he would be there, and he'd already been exposed. We can't tell when he contracted it."

"No, we can't." Dr. Braithwaite turned his glass of sherry around and around, letting the liquid catch the lamplight. "What will happen to Fenty and Company if your cousin doesn't pull through?"

"He will," said Emily stoutly. "I'm sure of it. But should anything happen to him . . . My uncle was never much interested. If Adam weren't about to carry on the legacy, I expect Uncle Archibald might sell the company, and invest in a country estate, and pretend to be a gentleman."

"Pretend?"

"We're not, really, you know. We're only a generation removed from those people in the hills in St. Andrew, with dirt grimed beneath their fingernails. We haven't a genteel bone in our bodies." It belatedly occurred to her that she wasn't entirely sure what sort of bones she had in her body, other than the fact that they all ached right now. Her quest to find her true parentage seemed very far away right now and rather silly. The threat of death did tend to concentrate the mind on the essentials.

"When Adam delved and Eve span, who then was the gentleman?" recited Dr. Braithwaite. He sounded drunk, although Emily suspected it was fatigue rather than the sherry, which he had touched not at all. "Don't look to me. I'm just a jobbing surgeon."

"If you're angling for compliments, I'm not going to provide them," said Emily. She decided she liked looking at her sherry more than drinking it. She admired the amber hue, and then set the glass down on the table. "When we first arrived, the night your uncle made you agree to take us to Peverills—"

Dr. Braithwaite groaned. "You're not going to throw that up at me, are you?"

"Oh, I don't blame you for not wanting to go. Especially since you'd been trespassing." She looked pointedly at her companion, who assumed an air of exaggerated innocence. "No, what I wondered about was what your uncle said that night, about the obligation you owed my family."

"Oh, that," said Dr. Braithwaite. He let his head fall back against the wooden frame of the sofa, which couldn't have been comfortable, as it had been carved into a stylized and rather pointy design.

"Yes, that," Emily said.

"Your grandfather gave my uncle the money to buy his freedom." There was a pause. Dr. Braithwaite slowly wiggled himself back up into a sitting position. "If you must know, he also arranged for my freedom. Of course, if my uncle had waited a year, he could have saved himself the money and your grandfather the trouble. But they didn't know, then, that emancipation was so close. And there were the apprenticeships, so there was that."

"Wait," said Emily. "I don't understand. Couldn't your uncle just buy your freedom?"

"That assumes my mistress would have been willing to sell." He grimaced, as though the words had a sour taste, and took a swig of sherry to wash them away. He coughed a little, as the alcohol hit his throat, and then said, his voice hoarse, "As you may have noticed, Mrs. Davenant doesn't like to let any of her people go."

Emily thought about George, about the spyglasses, about the son run off to Paris. "No," she said.

Dr. Braithwaite leaned forward over his sherry glass, cupping it in both hands. "Your grandfather had a hold over Mrs. Davenant." He held up his hand before Emily could speak. "I don't know what it was. I only know that whatever it was, it was enough. Of course, the next question is what hold my uncle had over your grandfather. But that, you'll have to ask him."

"I think I might know," said Emily slowly, thinking of the little Portuguese girl who wasn't. She was so tired that even the one or two sips of sherry had made her feel worn through, as limp as an old dishrag. Rising, she stretched her arms as far as her dress would allow them to go, stifling a yawn. "I'd best go up to Adam. He's been very quiet."

Dr. Braithwaite caught her hand. The motion was so natural, so completely unconsidered, that it took both of them by surprise.

He dropped it as though he'd been burnt, saying rapidly, "Are you getting enough rest? You won't do him any good if you work yourself into a decline."

"I haven't time to go into a decline." Emily stared down at her own hand, as though expecting to see the imprint of his fingers branded into her wrist. She gave her head a little shake. "Truly. I'm in the pink of health."

"I can see that." Dr. Braithwaite leaned back against the couch, self-consciously holding his sherry. "The kerchief suits you."

Emily wrinkled her nose at him, trying very hard to conjure the easy, comfortable tone of a few moments before. "I'll look one out for you," she promised. "After I've looked in on Adam."

Adam was sleeping soundly, very soundly. Emily didn't like to wake him. The room was dim, lit only by Emily's candle. She shaded it to keep it from falling too harshly on Adam's eyes, but something about the slackness of his wrist arrested her attention and she moved closer, holding the candle aloft so she could see his face.

"Nathaniel." She didn't even realize she'd called him by his first name as his uncle did. *"Nathaniel."*

"What is it?" She could hear him taking the steps by twos. He was in the room in two bounds, coming up hard behind her.

"It's Adam. He's not— I don't think he's breathing."

She stood there with the candle, feeling painfully helpless as Dr. Braithwaite lifted Adam's wrist to feel his pulse, then very gently reached out to pull his lids down over his eyes. "I'm so sorry."

Emily shook her head, unable to make sense of it. "He was getting better! He *was*."

Nathaniel took the candle from her hand, setting it down on the table. "Miss Dawson—Emily. Come away. There's nothing more you can do for him."

"There must be. There must be *something*."

Nathaniel took her gently by the shoulders, turning her away. "Emily. He's dead."

CHAPTER TWENTY-FOUR

Christ Church, Barbados
August 1814

"DEAD?"

"An hour since. Dr. MacAndrews is there now. He gave her something to help her sleep." Jenny shivered, wrapping her arms around herself. "I had to tell you now, before you heard the news from someone else."

"Dead," Charles repeated.

He couldn't quite get his mind around it, that his brother, whom he had seen alive only hours before, earthy, fleshy, reeling with drink, brimming with life, was still and cold. He thought of the little brother he had known, stumbling behind him in skirts, the sun shining off his golden hair. His mother's arms, cradling a baby. *This is your brother, Robert.*

"I ought to have kept him here. I ought to have made him sleep it off." He'd known he ought, but he had been thoroughly fed up with Robert and his grievances. He'd wanted rid of him. But not permanently. Not like this. "Did he fall from his horse? Did he do himself an injury?"

"In a manner of speaking."

Something of Jenny's strange stillness penetrated Charles's grief. Not simple respect for a death, but something more, something that stank of secrets. "What happened?"

"He was waiting for her when we came back. He was in his cups. He tried to force her." There was something terrible about the flat, uninflected narrative. Jenny looked him in the eye, her face set, and Charles had the awful feeling that she was seeing him, not as himself, but as a stranger, an enemy. "He had her against the wall."

Maybe he was dreaming. Maybe this was all a nightmare. He'd dreamed the whole awful evening, the fight, its sequel. "What did she do?"

"She hit him. With the writing desk. She didn't mean to kill him. Just to stop him. But he fell—so hard."

"Oh God." Charles stared at her in horror.

Jenny's calm slipped for a moment. "There was so much blood."

"Head wounds do bleed, you know," said Charles, gaining hope. "They always look worse than they are. He might be alive yet."

Jenny shook her head. "Dr. MacAndrews has been."

"The man wouldn't know a corpse from a fowl cock!"

"Charles." Jenny put a hand on his arm. "He held a mirror to his mouth. There was no breath."

Cases of men who seemed dead and then revived, men in their coffins, terrifying their family by knocking to be let out . . . All these bubbled up in Charles's throat, a hundred arguments against death. But Jenny was watching him, watching him with pity and no little impatience.

"She can't know you know. Do you hear me?" He was aware she was speaking, but only just. Grief and disbelief blinded him, choked him. "I only told you because—because you deserved to know. Dr. MacAndrews says it's an apoplexy. Master Robert hit his head as he fell. There's no one who knows otherwise. Only me. And you."

"But— That shouldn't be for us to determine," said Charles dazedly, thinking of the little boy he remembered, the little boy lost beneath the angry young man.

There were so many Roberts who would never be, now. Robert in comfortable middle age, Robert the patriarch.

Grasping for something, anything, Charles fell back on his legal training. "It was self-defense. That's manslaughter. But there's only her word." Not Jenny's. A slave couldn't testify in a trial. And Mary Anne was a woman, a wife, which complicated matters. "There's no legal concept of rape in marriage. In the eyes of the court, there was nothing for her to defend against. Which makes it murder. But I can't imagine any jury wouldn't take into account—"

"Are you mad?" Jenny grabbed Charles's arm, hard. "She'll deny it. And then she'll say that I was the one who did it, that she was protecting me."

"Surely, she wouldn't. . . ."

"Wouldn't she? If it were me or she, she would abandon me in a moment. She'd say he made advances and I attacked him. They'd put me in the Cage, and then they'd kill me. Or worse." She didn't need to say. They could both imagine it. Whippings so severe they tore the flesh from the bone. She might be chained, left without water, raw, bleeding, a living meal for bird and beast. "*Charles*. I'm the only one who saw. I'm the only one who knows."

Charles blinked, trying to shut out the image of Robert, sprawled lifeless on the floor, Robert, in his white smock and golden curls, calling his name. "Will she . . . try to silence you?"

He remembered the day Jenny had told him about her father, the mix of horror and disbelief that such things could happen in a Christian household, in the nineteenth century. But they had. And Mary Anne Beckles had been trained at her uncle's knee.

Jenny shook her head, white-lipped. "Not if her account goes unchallenged. Not if she thinks she's safe. She'll keep me close, but she won't hurt me. I don't think."

"Oh God," Charles said, lifting his hands to his head.

"She doesn't trust me anymore. Once, perhaps." Jenny looked at him, all her feelings written on her face. "She offered me the position of housekeeper. The keys to the household and the choicest cuts of meat.

I told her it was enough to me to serve her. I don't know whether she believed me or not."

Charles sat down heavily on a bench. "We did this to her." It had seemed such a grand idea, in the endless summer of new love, to play at being Cupid. What harm could it bring? They were doing both a favor, that was what he had told himself. "We did this to him. We killed him. If they'd never married—"

"He might have drunk himself to death or plunged his horse over a cliff or run away to Jamaica. What does it matter? The truth can't come out. Not if you love me." She searched his face, and whatever it was she saw there made her drop her hands and step away. "I shouldn't have told you."

"No!" Charles hastened toward her, running his hands up and down her arms, drawing her close, as much for his own comfort as hers. They'd sacrificed so much; how could they lose each other? "Not that. Never that. You can always tell me anything. We have no secrets from one another. We should have no secrets from one another."

Jenny stood like a statue in his embrace. "Why didn't you tell me about the baby coming to Peverills?"

"I—I would have done." It had seemed a grand idea to announce her to the world. It should, he realized, have occurred to him to tell Jenny first. "I should have done. When Carlota comes . . ."

"Carlota." The name resounded from her tongue like the sack of a city, all destruction and ash. "You've made my child foreign. You've made my child foreign to me."

Charles scrambled to try to understand her grief. "Jenny. Jenny." He slid a finger under her chin, lifting her face to his, trying to make her see. "She's not really foreign. It's just a name, only a name. You agreed to it."

"Because I had no choice!" Jenny wrenched away from him, her face a Medusa mask of despair. She pressed both hands to her face, holding them there for a long moment, and then said, in a voice as dry as the cane, "I'm sorry."

"No. I'm sorry." Charles held out his hands to her, and this time, slowly, she came to him, pressing her face into that spot in his chest that seemed to have been made just for her. Charles stroked her hair, taking comfort in the repetitive motion, in her presence. "I'm so sorry. For all of this. I'd only meant to make things better. If I'd known . . ."

If he had known, what then? Could they have done any differently?

"*I am more an antique Roman than a Dane,*" Charles quoted, looking out over Jenny's head at the midnight gardens, so carefully laid out by his mother, the gardens where he and Robert had played as children, innocent and unknowing. "But I'm not. I'm neither. I'm an Englishman. I'd always thought it overblown, all that ancient Greek palaver about rushing into one's fate by seeking to avoid it, but now—I wonder. *As flies to wanton boys are we to th' gods; / They kill us for their sport.*"

Robert. They had killed Robert. Or had Robert killed himself? Fate or free will, divine judgment or the mere consequence of one choice leading to another and another and another, until the weight of those choices collapsed on one, bearing one down?

Charles could hear his own voice, as distant as the moon. "I'd thought we lived in an age of reason, that man might make his own destiny. Is it all a snare? Do we create our own doom, or are we mere actors in a drama of someone else's devising?"

"Charles," Jenny interrupted. "Charles. When is the child coming?"

History, poetry, natural philosophy, all tangled together. Anything to put off thinking about the immediacy of it all. Charles dragged his attention back to Jenny. "Soon. Six months, perhaps a year?"

Jenny pulled back, staring up at him. "Another *year*?"

"We have to make it look right, like she's really coming all the way from Portugal," Charles said earnestly. "There would be arrangements to be made, passage to book, a nursemaid to be hired. . . . It all takes time."

"She'll be nearly two by then." The grief in Jenny's voice tore at Charles's heart.

He wanted to promise to produce the child immediately, to thrust her into Jenny's arms, but he couldn't, not now, not without doing violence to all their plans.

How had they come to this? So much grief, so much grief caused with the purest of intentions. He'd thought to see Robert and Mary Anne happily married; he'd wanted his and Jenny's child safe and free, close at hand. It had all made sense at the time.

Choice piled upon choice upon choice.

But this wasn't Athens. It was Barbados. And he was neither an antique Roman nor a Dane. Robert was dead, but they weren't.

"Do you remember anything from that age?" said Charles, attempting to cheer her. "I don't. In France, they send their babies out to the country and only bring them home when they're an age to reason. We're only in keeping with the fashion."

Jenny looked up at him, her gray eyes nearly black in the darkness. "Don't you want her back?"

Did he? The truth was, Charles wasn't quite sure how he felt about it. In theory, yes, she was his child. But he had a strange reluctance to see her. It was as if this child was his failures made flesh. He'd thought to be better than his father, but his father, at least, had contrived to free his lover and child.

It was almost easier to pretend she was what he claimed, the child of a friend, whom he could welcome with open arms and every affection, for Hal's sake.

But he couldn't say that, so, instead, he said, "Don't worry. She's being raised with every care. Jonathan wouldn't stand for less. I would suspect Jonathan of extending the arrangement to keep the fees but for the fact that he spends most of it on gifts for her."

Jenny wasn't amused. "He doesn't want to give her up. Have you seen the way he looks when he speaks of her? As if she were his."

Charles rubbed her arm consolingly. "He's hardly going to run off with her. Don't worry. We'll have our girl home soon."

"You'll have our girl home," said Jenny, so softly that Charles could scarcely make out the words. But he did, and he knew she was right.

"We'll find a way," he said again, but even to his own ears, the words sounded thin.

"Yes," said Jenny politely, and turned to go.

"Wait!" Charles put out a hand to her. Speaking rapidly, he said, "There's a seat opening on the council. I mean to have it. It will mean spending some time making up to red-faced planters and their narrow-minded wives, but . . . you were right. Writing letters to London only does so much. If I can work here, from within . . ."

"Oh, Charles." Jenny put a hand to his cheek. Charles wasn't sure why, but it felt like good-bye.

Taking her hand, he turned it and pressed a kiss against the palm, trying to put all the strength of his love into that kiss. "Please, don't give up. I haven't. We've come this far."

Standing on her tiptoes, Jenny pressed a kiss to the corner of his lips. "I need to get back."

Charles watched her go, seeing his mother, Robert, everyone he had failed. But there was only Jenny, stepping lightly across the freshly hoed fields, disappearing into the gloaming. Jenny, who was his future, he promised himself, not his past.

It would all come right. He would make it right.

Once he had his seat on the council, once their child was come to Peverills . . .

"Soon," he promised Jenny, his whisper traveling on the wind like the sound of the cane. "Soon."

Christ Church, Barbados
July 1815

IT WAS NEARLY a year before Charles Davenant's Portuguese ward came to Peverills.

Ructions in Europe had caused difficulties in getting a ship from Lisbon. The girl's nursemaid had taken fright at thought of the journey and abandoned her post at the harbor, causing a delay as a new nursemaid was found. The stories were vague, but no one really demanded much in the way of details. No one cared. All thoughts were concentrated on Napoléon's escape from Elba, his triumphal march on Paris, the new war in Europe.

Carlota St. Aubyn slipped into Barbados society hard on the heels of the news of the Duke of Wellington's victory at Waterloo.

She benefited from the general elation and a vague sense of warmth that extended to all things related to the duke, Portugal included. Gossip, predisposed, in this case, to be positively inclined to anyone connected with the late victories, elevated her parentage, endowing her mother with the fictional rank of first *contessa* and then *marquesa*, creating a dramatic and doomed love story between the persecuted noblewoman (resisting the lustful advances of the French conquerors) and the noble English officer who had rescued and married her, only to succumb, tragically, to a Frenchman's sword.

That there wasn't a word of truth in it didn't bother anyone in the slightest. By the time Carlota had been at Peverills for a week, half the island believed it, and the other half deemed it impolitic to disagree.

"Not that it matters," said Mary Anne, donning a new round gown of ruby merino, trimmed with sapphire velvet and Valenciennes lace, utterly impractical for the climate, but made to model from a batch of slightly wilted fashion papers come from England on the same ship as word of the duke's victory over Bonaparte. It was, Mary Anne had decided, close enough to a year that the lilac of half mourning could be abandoned, and she intended to do so with a will. "The child is Charles's ward, whether she's the daughter of a countess or a Lisbon doxy."

She seemed to have no suspicion that the child might be anything other than the daughter of Charles's old school friend, and for that, Jenny was grateful.

Not that Jenny would know if Mary Anne thought otherwise. The old days, when Mary Anne would speak whatever was on her mind, were gone.

Sometimes, Jenny would catch Mary Anne watching her, eyes narrowed and lips pursed. There were tests, seemingly casual comments, designed to see if Jenny could be tricked into referring to the events of that awful night. Jenny, who had thought the skill gone with her father, rediscovered the art of turning to stone, presenting a blank countenance when pressed.

But Mary Anne wasn't satisfied.

Jenny wasn't sure what would satisfy her. To bring it up, openly, and swear fealty? But to voice it would be to acknowledge it, to acknowledge that Mary Anne had killed her husband and suborned the nearest physician; it would be like plunging her hand into a fire to grasp a hot coal, like a medieval saint praying for a miracle.

Jenny didn't believe in miracles, only in survival.

Mary Anne adjusted her high-crowned bonnet with the white ostrich plumes. "Is Edward ready? Call Dutchess. That girl, I swear, she spends half her time making eyes at Johnny Cooper."

"There's no need to bring Dutchess. I can manage Master Edward." If she was playing with Neddy, it would give her an excuse to approach Carlota. No one ever minded the nursemaid. Not that she would say anything to Carlota. She wasn't that foolish. She just wanted to see her, to compare the living child to that tiny creature in her memory, whom she'd so briefly held in her arms.

"No," said Mary Anne flatly, and Jenny knew she'd gone too far. "You'll attend me."

"Yes, mistress," said Jenny, and knelt to help her mistress into her gloves.

When they arrived at Peverills, Neddy ran ahead, calling, "Unker Charles! Unker Charles!"

Uncle Charles was a great favorite, largely because he allowed himself to be climbed upon and his hair to be pulled.

"Welcome." Charles didn't look at her. One wouldn't, at a slave. He extended an arm to Mary Anne as Neddy raced ahead, very much at home in his uncle's house. "Come and meet my ward. She's in the garden."

He took them through the house and out the back, where the ground sloped away in the gardens planned by Charles's mother. By a trick of topography, one could see the sea in the distance, but not the cane closer by. A clever arrangement of walls and terraces created a world apart.

Beneath the shade of a tamarind tree, a little girl in a white gown was playing. Her shoes were of red morocco, her hair a cluster of soft, dark curls around her face that she shook back as she tried to spin two cups on a string, tossing them up into the air, and then tossing them again. Scattered around her were two brightly painted tops, a cup and a ball, and a quaintly carved doll in a miniature gig.

"Go on, then," said Charles to Neddy. "I've got her a diabolo but neither of us can quite figure out how to work it. Would you like a go? I'm sure Carlota would be happy to share."

Nothing loath, Neddy raced out to join her. Carlota yanked the diabolo behind her back and, her little tongue between her lips, selected a top for him instead, which Neddy took gladly.

She was so much smaller than Neddy, but she didn't look little, somehow. With a pang, Jenny realized who the child reminded her of. Not herself, but Mary Anne. There was something in her self-possessed determination, in the set of her chin.

But Charles was there too, in the flash of those blue eyes, the ready humor as she laughed at Neddy as he jumped for the flying bobbins.

Here, Jenny willed her daughter. *I'm here.*

But it was to Charles their child looked for approval as she cast the diabolo into the air, with such a look of satisfaction that Jenny had to stop herself from reaching out. She was, she realized, holding Mary Anne's Kashmir shawl so tightly that she'd practically caused a rent in the fabric.

"Where's your shadow?" Mary Anne asked Charles, wearying of nursery matters.

"Jonathan? He's discussing some matter of business with Mrs. Boland. She's made rather a good thing of her husband's business, I understand."

"She's not the only one to take up the reins," pointed out Mary Anne, with some asperity. "Has she seen the child?"

"Not yet," said Charles mildly. "I'd thought you might like to be the first to officially greet her. As an honorary aunt of sorts."

Jenny felt as though she'd swallowed a mouthful of pebbles. What was he playing at? Or was she merely distressed because everyone but she was entitled to stake a claim to her child?

Losing interest, Carlota abandoned the diabolo to Neddy, skipping away with one of the tops. She moved with the uncoordinated energy that came with being not quite a baby anymore, but not yet a child, limbs and face still rounded with baby fat, ready to conquer the world and occasionally fall on one's bottom.

"Jenny, Jenny, Jenny!" Neddy rattled the diabolo at her. "Jenny, Jenny, look, look, look!"

Bless him, she'd been staring and she shouldn't. At least Mary Anne would assume all the wrong things, as she always did. Jenny smiled at Neddy, trying to hide her pain. All those nights she'd held him and pretended he was her daughter, and now her daughter was here and didn't know her.

What had she expected? A magical pull of like to like?

Not to be outdone, Carlota waved, her gold bracelet glinting in the sunshine, shouting out, "Unker, Unker, Unker!"

Charles waved back. "I told her to call me 'Uncle,'" he explained. "It seemed simplest, under the circumstances. 'Mr. Davenant' is such a mouthful. And 'Papa' . . ."

"You don't want to raise expectations," said Mary Anne, regarding Carlota with a critical eye. "You'll need to find her a good nursery governess. Goodness only knows what she was accustomed to in Portugal."

"I had wondered . . ." Charles's eyes were on the children, but Jenny noticed how he shifted from foot to foot, the movement of the fingers of his right hand, as though he were mimicking holding a pen. He did that when he was nervous, as though the act of writing brought him ease. "Mine is a bachelor establishment. You have a nursery, with nursery maids who know what they're about. Carlota and Edward are of an age. Might you consider having Carlota at Beckles for a time? If it wouldn't be too much trouble."

Jenny was grateful she was standing behind them, as a good servant should. All she could see was the back of Charles's head, but she knew him, knew exactly what he was doing, foolish, honorable Charles. He was trying, the only way he knew how, to give her her daughter back.

It was a noble gesture, but it was far, so far from what he had promised her all those years ago. Oh, she knew he'd meant it, every word of it, but that didn't mean she didn't want to scream and rage.

"It would be that much trouble," said Mary Anne sharply. "I'm not in the habit of taking in unknown orphans."

"I'd pay for her keep, of course," Charles said hastily. "I'm not trying to shirk my responsibilities. But it's lonely for a child in a house without other children."

"I didn't mind it," said Mary Anne. She stopped to consider the problem, having decided, now that she'd made her point, that she could be generous with her advice, if not her home. "But then, I had my Jenny. Have you thought of acquiring a young girl to bear your Carlota company?"

Charles shook his head. "It never occurred to me. I haven't the first notion of how to get on. Which is why I had hoped you might——"

"I'm happy to advise, of course," said Mary Anne firmly, "but it would hardly be right to take on the rearing of a strange child. What if she and Edward didn't get on? No. She's welcome to come visit at Beckles whenever she likes, but I have more than enough on my hands."

"I know it's been hard for you, with Robert gone," said Charles sympathetically.

Mary Anne looked over her shoulder, a quick, furtive glance at Jenny. "It's terribly hot today, isn't it? I'm perishing for something cool."

"I'll have someone bring you a drink," said Charles quickly.

"Don't trouble yourself. I know you've a bachelor establishment. Jenny can go. Jenny!" Turning back to Charles, she said, "Yes, it has been terribly hard, but I don't know that I would want to hire an estate agent. One can't trust them, can one?"

Dismissed, Jenny made her way toward the kitchen house, not permitting herself to look back at the children at play, at Neddy and Carlota. Carlota. Not her daughter. A stranger named Carlota. Her eyes stung and she blinked back stupid, inconvenient tears.

Fool, she told herself. Didn't she know by now that crying did nothing? She'd cried for her mother and look what that had got her.

Her nails were digging holes in her palms; bile rose in her throat.

"Jenny!" Nanny Grigg was outside the kitchen, drinking blackstrap with Charles's cook. She folded Jenny into an embrace that smelled of soap and sunshine. Jenny breathed in that comforting smell, trying to compose herself. "You look like you lost a dollar and found a penny."

"I forgot." Jenny mustered a smile. "Master Charles said Mrs. Boland was visiting. It's good to see you."

"You haven't visited in months," said Nanny Grigg, putting a companionable arm around Jenny and leading her away toward the chicken coop.

"My mistress was in mourning," Jenny prevaricated. She'd wanted to see Nanny Grigg, she had. She'd missed those evenings at Harrow, Jackey the head driver puffing away on his pipe, Nanny reading aloud from the papers from England. But Mary Anne had been leery of letting Jenny out of her sight, as if afraid she might betray her at any moment. It had been all she could do to get away to Peverills to see Charles. The thought of Charles made her chest clench. Charles, who had brought Carlota home, but not to her. "My mistress needed me."

"Is that what's making you look so low?" asked Nanny Grigg, pausing to throw a bit of corn to the chickens. "Or is it the master here?"

"Why would it be? What has he to do with anything?"

Nanny chuckled. "Don't fret yourself. No one's said anything. It's just I know you. I remember that first day I met you, at Christmas, and you looking out the window like you were waiting for the king himself to walk through the door. Nearly three years ago that was."

"That was a long time ago." Back then she'd still believed Charles when he promised he'd see her free and with him. Castles in the air, all. Nanny Grigg was watching her, her head cocked expectantly.

"You're telling me it's over, then?"

It was easier to tell a half-truth. Jenny turned away with a shrug. "All right. It's true. But you can't tell anyone. My mistress wouldn't like it. He'd thought he might persuade Master Robert to sell me, but . . ."

"If you were free, do you think he'd keep you?"

"Yes," said Jenny, without hesitation. "But my mistress will never part with me."

Nanny Grigg glanced back over her shoulder and lowered her voice. "She might have to. Have you heard talk of the registry bill?"

"The what?" said Jenny.

Charles hadn't said anything. Or rather, Charles was always saying things, so many things that she had ceased to listen. She had grown impatient of his promises of the world that was to come—when? When all men were good and virtuous? His dreams were pretty, but they were all ink on paper, sound without substance.

"It's early days yet," said Nanny Grigg, keeping her eyes on the chickens as they fought for the grain. "But it's that Wilberforce man, the one who ended the slave trade. He wants every slave owner in the Indies to make a list of all their slaves—and why would that be, do you think? So that we might be freed. That's what the English papers say."

"Papers say all sorts of things." Jenny looked at her friend, not wanting to get her hopes up. "They could say that day was night, but that doesn't mean we'd believe it."

Nanny grinned at her. "You should see what a clucking there is! Letters from plantation owners protesting that we ought to be grateful for a bed, but you can tell they're scared. It's the beginning of the end for them."

"If it is . . ." The words trailed away.

Never to have to answer to Mary Anne again. To be able to live, openly, with her child.

And with Charles, she reminded herself. But Charles faded into the background in her imaginings. Her love for Charles had long since ceased to be a fiery, all-consuming thing. It was a soft blanket she wrapped around herself, somewhat frayed around the edges. She loved him, yes, but it was her child who consumed her thoughts, for whom she planned and schemed.

Her child, who had seen her today and never known her for who she was.

Jenny made a face at the chickens. "I'll believe it when I see it."

"Come to Harrow of an evening. . . . I forget. We're called Simmons now. The new master likes the sound of his own name. It's all one, whatever it's called." Nanny Grigg gave Jenny's arm a squeeze. "Come to Simmons and I'll show you and you can read it for yourself. Seeing as you can."

"Thank you," said Jenny slowly. "I think I shall."

"The new master, he doesn't like us reading the papers, but we get them all the same. Those of us who can read have been spreading the news to those who can't." Nanny Grigg's cheerful face turned serious. "You might think of doing the same here. I wouldn't trust any of them not to try to cheat us out of our freedom."

"Not Charles," said Jenny automatically. Had he said anything about the registry bill? She couldn't recall. She'd stopped listening.

"Eh," said Nanny Grigg, and then looked at Jenny, struck by a thought. "We've only the papers, but your Master Charles—he'll have better news, wouldn't he? With his place on the council? And with all his fine friends in London?"

"He's always writing," said Jenny carefully.

"If you hear anything, you'll tell us? We've missed you for your own sake—but it would be good to have news. As you say, you can only trust the papers so far."

"I'll see what I can find," promised Jenny.

"There," said Nanny Grigg. "That's put the color back in your cheeks. We'll wait for the word."

CHAPTER TWENTY-FIVE

Bridgetown, Barbados
June 1854

EMILY DREADED THE thought of sending word of Adam's death to Laura. And to Uncle Archie and Aunt Millicent.

"There has to have been some mistake." They had retreated to the hallway, away from the specter of death. Emily craned to see over Nathaniel's arm. "Check again. Maybe he was breathing. Maybe you missed it."

"Emily." Nathaniel took her by the shoulders. "Emily, there's nothing to be done."

"He took a little broth this morning. He sat up against the pillows!"

"It takes people like that sometimes," said Nathaniel soberly. "We don't know enough yet about the course of the disease."

"But he was getting *better*."

Even as she said it, she knew Nathaniel was right. Hadn't she seen it herself? People who seemed perfectly well, dead two hours later. Horrible cases recovering, unexpectedly. The supposedly convalescent suddenly struck down. They didn't know. There were times when she wondered if it wasn't natural at all, but God's retribution, smiting as he saw fit.

Her father, she knew, wouldn't appreciate such thoughts. Her father's God was a God of love, a God of patience and kindness. She had seen the strength of her father's faith during the affliction of '49 and knew her own to be a pale thing in comparison.

Emily lowered her head, staring at Nathaniel's waistcoat buttons. They were very nice waistcoat buttons, brass, incised with a fleur-de-lis. "I don't know how I'm going to tell them. And the baby—" Emily drew in a deep, shuddering breath. She had to take control of herself. There were practicalities to be dealt with. A funeral. The idea of burying Adam, so full of life, of mischief, seemed insane, obscene. "There's no question of sending the body home to England."

"No." Nathaniel left it at that. "I'll make the necessary arrangements."

Emily blinked, hard. "Thank you," she said, in as steady a voice as she could muster. "I think—I think I shall go to bed now."

There wasn't any reason to stay up, no Adam to check on in the night.

Nathaniel looked at her with concern. "Can I give you something to help you sleep?"

"No! No, thank you. I don't—I don't like to blur my wits." The helplessness of it terrified her, the idea of lying there in a stupor as death flew over the rooftops.

Nathaniel looked for a moment as though he might argue, but said only, "If you need me, I'll leave my door open. Don't worry about waking me."

The house had a curious emptiness to it as Emily walked down the hall to the room she had claimed as her own. Everything looked strange and unfamiliar, the bed with its netting tucked to the sides, the brush and combs on the dresser. She had lived here for seven days now, but it felt as though she had never been here at all. The silence pressed around her, unnatural silence, and Emily clutched her knees to her chest in the great bed and lowered her cheek to her knee and allowed herself to imagine that it had all been a dream, that Adam was still there in the next room, stirring restlessly against the pillow, about to demand why she was feeding him invalid food when what he wanted was meat.

But the bed in the next room was empty.

She was alone in the house with Nathaniel. The thought struck her like a blow. She couldn't stay here. It had been bad enough with only a sick male cousin for chaperone, but now—she would have to go back to Beckles. Her entire being recoiled at the thought of going back to Laura and confessing how she'd failed.

Emily woke twice in the night and found herself by Adam's bedside before she realized where she was. The bed was empty, the sheets stripped, all trace of Adam gone.

The second time, she saw a figure silhouetted in a doorway and knew Nathaniel was there, watching over her.

"I'm all right," she said to the shadows, and shut the bedroom door.

He was gone when she woke in the morning, after a restless sleep haunted with dreams. There was a note left in the drawing room, informing her that he would be at the hospital, but would be back by early afternoon.

Of Adam, there was no sign, and it struck Emily like a knife in the chest that Adam had been carted away to be buried alone, with no one to mourn him, no service, no words beside the grave, no widow in black. Nathaniel would have done it properly, she knew. Between his conscientiousness and Mr. Turner's influence, a coffin would have been secured, no matter how scarce coffins might be. There would be a place in a graveyard for Adam, a shallow one, perhaps, but still a grave.

This wasn't where his bones were meant to be. He was meant to be buried in Bristol, by the hideous memorial of a weeping angel that marked their grandfather's grave. He was meant to grow old and sport ludicrous whiskers and develop a paunch and a taste for tartan waistcoats and tease his children with stories of his youth. Not this, bleached bones in a mass grave on an island far, far away.

Emily took up pen and paper, but she couldn't write.

Dearest Laura . . .

She tried again.

My dear Aunt Millicent . . .

She couldn't do it. Part of her, the cowardly part, said it would be kinder so. Kinder to let them believe Adam was alive a little longer, his red hair shining under a tropical sun, grinning that rogue's grin, scheming and plotting for the greater glory of the House of Fenty.

He had so wanted to make a success of this trip.

Emily flung the pen aside. Good, vigorous, mindless physical exercise, that was what she needed. There was nothing left in the house to scrub. She would go for a walk. Walking always cleared her mind.

It felt strange to struggle into a walking dress, to tie the ribbon of a bonnet. She had worn nothing for days but the oversized gown she had borrowed from Mr. Turner's housekeeper. Mrs. Turner's gowns were too fine for her, but she had no other choice. Her own dress, the dress in which she had come into Bridgetown over a week ago, had long since been burned.

Her shoes, at least, were her own.

Emily squinted, her eyes dazzled by the light as she let herself out the door she had entered eight days before. How long had it been since she had last been farther than the yard? Emily lifted a hand to shade her eyes, thought of going back for a parasol, and decided better of it. Adam might twit her about burning brown, but . . .

No. Adam wouldn't twit her about her complexion. Ever again.

Emily bit down hard on her lip and plowed forward, not caring where she was going, so long as it was away. Her borrowed bodice was damp with sweat, her hair sticking in curls to the back of her neck where it had escaped the knot in which she'd bound it. One foot, then another. One foot, then another.

He had been getting better. He had. What had she been thinking, having sherry in the parlor with Nathaniel? If she'd been by his side . . . might she have done something? Called for help? Or would death have come all the same? What had she missed? What symptom, what sign? It takes them that way, Nathaniel had said, but it was easy for him to say, it wasn't his family, his cousin. She knew she was being unfair, but she didn't care.

Why hadn't she taken more care? If she had sponged his head

again . . . If she hadn't fed him soup that morning . . . Maybe the act of digestion had overtaxed his system? If she had given him a larger dose of laudanum . . . If, if, if, a thousand ifs. If they had never come to Barbados, if she had never heard of Peverills, if their grandfather had left well enough alone, if Uncle Archie had come to Barbados instead of Adam, and always, always, at the end of it, if she had been more vigilant, more careful, more competent. All those years ago, she had been too young to nurse her mother properly, but she had worked and worked and learned and learned, and had thought, now, at last, she might change the ending. She would bring Adam triumphantly home, weak but on the mend.

But she hadn't.

She had failed Adam. She had failed Laura. She had failed everyone.

A cart rattled past, piled high with empty coffins. That was all. Coffin upon coffin, some cobbled together so carelessly that Emily could see the spaces between the slats, the nails only half-hammered. Her steps slowed as she began to be aware of her surroundings, to realize how eerie was the stillness of the street. There were no vendors, no cries to buy this or that, to patronize this icehouse or that haberdashery. The shops on Swan Street and Roebuck were still and shuttered. The statue of Nelson in Trafalgar Square stood sanctuary over a desolate and abandoned landscape.

A dog prowled past, dragging something in his mouth. Emily jumped back, almost tripping over the hem of Mrs. Turner's dress as she saw fingers trailing behind. It was an arm, a human arm.

A woman passed her, moving rapidly, head down, a basket on her arm.

"Where are you going?" asked Emily.

"Shops open at half eight," the woman said shortly. "You're out of luck if you want brandy or blankets. Can't get them for love or money."

Emily wandered through the empty streets, discovering pockets of civilization. A Wesleyan minister standing on an empty barrel preached to a congregation of several hundred people. *"The voice said, Cry! And he said, What shall I cry? All flesh is grass . . ."*

A group of men reeking of rum and cigars reeled past, laughing at the congregants. One of their number fell in the street and lay still, his fellows fleeing.

Emily ventured closer, but when she saw it was drink, rather than the disease, she left him be to sleep it off.

A street away, a harried government official was doling out rice, bread, arrowroot, and candles in prearranged parcels.

"Do you have your certificate?" Emily heard him ask a petitioner. "You've got your share already this morning, I remember you."

A phaeton, the sort Adam had driven back in Bristol, lurched past, nearly overset by its awkward burden. A coffin protruded from one side, listing farther and farther until it fell, hitting the street with a crash, the corpse rolling free. The horses came to a halt, and the driver dropped down, using his whip to disperse the dogs, who had leaped forward, snarling.

A girl of not more than six held a toddler balanced on her hip. "Are you all right?" Emily asked. "Do you have anywhere to go?"

The girl regarded her warily but answered easily enough. "Auntie."

"I'll see you to Auntie," said Emily, needing to do something, anything.

From a house, someone shouted to the driver behind them, "Hey! Bring your cart! There's dead here!"

But there was an auntie. Emily delivered the two children and admired a baby kicking his fat feet in the yard. "What a handsome boy you have," she said politely.

"No, ma'am," said the auntie. "He's not mine. I saw this one sitting on the floor in an empty house. With the help of God, I'll care for it."

"God bless you," said Emily, wishing she had her father there, with his calm certainty of faith. But surely, if God would bless anyone, it would be someone like this?

She found her way back to the house on Bay Street, past the silent wharves where no sailors plied their trade, the smell of death and the sea in her nostrils.

"Where have you been?" The door was open before she was half down the walk. "I was ready to start searching the streets!"

The dimness of the hall after the sunshine made everything seem rather vague. Or perhaps it was the combination of the sights she had seen, the horrors upon horrors that stalked the silent streets.

"I went for a walk," said Emily, untying the strings of her borrowed bonnet and setting it carefully down on the hall table.

"A *walk*?" Nathaniel made a visible effort to contain himself.

"Yes, it's what one does when one doesn't take a gig." Emily abandoned the pretense of normalcy. "You didn't tell me how bad it was."

"You had enough to bear." Adam might have been gone, but his presence was a tangible thing between them. Nathaniel turned away, saying, "Carts and horses are in short supply. I've sent to my uncle to see if we can find a way to get you back to Beckles."

"No. What I saw today— I met a woman who had children and relations of her own, but had still taken in a child she found alone in an empty house. If she can do that, what excuse have I? I'll hand out parcels of food or boil water or wash floors. But I have to do *something*." The memory of the empty bed upstairs haunted her. She looked up at Nathaniel, feeling raw and bare. "Unless you think I'd be more harm to the patients than good."

"You did everything you could for your cousin. Do you understand me? There wasn't a doctor from here to London who could have done more." The hallway echoed with the force of his words.

Emily blinked at his vehemence. "Thank you."

"Don't thank me," said Nathaniel brusquely. "You did what you had to do. It's done. That woman you saw today, this is her home, these are her people."

"But they're not mine?"

"No," he said bluntly. "You can walk away, leave it. This isn't your fight. You accused me of not telling you how bad it is? It's bad. It's worse than you can imagine. I was called out to the Asylum for the Destitute today. Every last inmate is dead. Mrs. Kennedy, the keeper's wife, died this morning. Her husband died last night. There's not a criminal left in the gaol. They were assigned grave-digging duty and brought the disease back with them. It took three days, Emily. Three days to kill near eighty men. All gone. Every one. And don't think you'll be spared by virtue of your station. They're dying at Government House. It was His Excellency's orderly this morning. His sister's maid died last week. It's killing the doctors. I attended on Dr. Springer's wife this morning and found him unconscious beside her corpse. Bascom and Brereton were taken last week. There were three hundred deaths yesterday—and that's only the deaths that were recorded by the Board of Health. There may well have been more, rotting undiscovered. Do you understand what I'm saying? No one is safe, Emily. No one."

"I know that." Her mother, her resolute, indomitable mother had been taken off by a disease that took some and spared others, with no reason to it. "I know I'm not proof against it, any more than any other man. But if I were to die, what of it? Would it be so very dreadful? I have no husband, no children, no brothers or sisters to mourn me. At least I would know I had done what was needed."

"I would mourn you." The hall felt suddenly very small and very close, the air warm and heavy. Clearing his throat, Nathaniel added, "And I'm sure Mr. Davenant would shed a tear. He might even write you an ode."

"Thank you," said Emily with some asperity. "Do you rate my value so low? I'd hoped for a sonnet sequence at least."

Nathaniel didn't rise to the challenge. "I rate you higher than you think. That's why I need to make you understand. You don't know what you're offering. I know you saw the cholera in Bristol. But the climate— it's different there. I don't think you understand the effect the heat has on the spread of the disease. Or if not the spread, at least the smell."

"Will you let me be the judge of that? I promise not to swoon on you."

"I never expected you would." Nathaniel seized on another line of attack. "Have you thought that there might be an objection to your staying here alone in my uncle's house?"

"But I'm not alone," said Emily. "You're here."

Nathaniel raised a brow. "My point."

Emily grimaced at him. "Do you really care what evil-minded people think? Besides," she added impatiently, "anyone who has seen the work you do would know you haven't the energy to go about ravishing people!"

Nathaniel put his face into his hands and snorted, shoulders shaking with helpless mirth. "I don't know whether to be comforted or insulted."

"Don't make me dose you with laudanum for your nerves."

"My nerves are beyond laudanum." Lifting his head, Nathaniel blinked away tears of laughter. "My, er, stamina aside, evil-minded people will talk if an unmarried man and woman share a house. Not during the height of the panic, perhaps, but afterward."

Emily had to acknowledge the justice of that. "I could go back to Miss Lee's, I suppose," she said doubtfully.

"Good Lord, do you think I want to sign your death warrant? The Lord only knows where she gets her water. I could take lodgings—"

"There is one obvious solution," pointed out Emily. "We could bring patients in."

"You want me to turn my uncle's house into a hospital."

"If you put it that way—yes." Seeing that he was wavering, she added reasonably, "We could limit it to women and children if you like. Surely, no one could object to *that*."

"No one, indeed," murmured Dr. Braithwaite.

"They'll be too sick to steal the silver. You've said yourself, you're not allowed to house them in the hospital because of the rules regarding infectious diseases. Besides," she added, "it's only fair. I let you use my house as an infirmary."

"For broken arms," said Nathaniel. "Not the bowel death."

But he found two nurses from the hospital and installed them in the servants' quarters and arranged for cots and pallets to be delivered and set up in bedrooms and along the veranda. Word was sent to Belle View. London Turner sent back his approval and an elderly relation to serve as chaperone to Emily. He asked only that they not burn the house down in his absence, and that they save all receipts.

Cousin Bella wasn't terribly much use as a practical nurse, but she told wonderful stories, sitting and knitting and talking as Emily plunged yet another load of soiled sheets into the kettle in the yard or splashed lime across the floor.

"Trust my uncle not to miss a trick," said Nathaniel darkly, when Cousin Bella arrived, sitting on a cart piled high with blankets and rolled mattresses and even a squawking crate of poultry.

"I like her," said Emily firmly, and she found that while Cousin Bella wasn't much for mopping up sick or changing soiled nappies, she was a wonder with the young children, many of whom had lost their parents and siblings, and found themselves weak and sick in a strange house with echoing high ceilings and stern-looking portraits on the walls. She never wearied of telling endless stories about clever spiders and thwarted witches, each more fantastical than the last, keeping even the sickest children spellbound as Emily bustled about changing sheets and swaddling cloths, feeling brows and emptying bedpans.

A public fast day was held on June 14, but both Nathaniel and Emily were too busy to attend the service at the cathedral. Nearly three hundred died that day in Bridgetown, and as many again were taken ill. Word had spread that London Turner's house had turned infirmary, and even Cousin Bella had her hands full, admitting those they could admit, turning away those they couldn't, helping to set up a tent in the yard to make room for more beds, more babies. Cots marched in lines down the veranda. Mrs. Turner's prized silver and china were locked away and the great mahogany table turned on its side to make room for more beds in the dining room.

The days took on their own strange pattern as they battled death.

June boiled into July. The house was divided into sections, one for cholera patients, one for children who had lost their families. Nathaniel grumbled that he'd never anticipated running an orphanage, but Emily just thrust freshly boiled coffee at him and told him to drink up and not to think she didn't know about the sweets in his pockets, and could he please stop inciting riot among her younger patients?

They took great delight in scoring points off each other, the one bright spot in otherwise grim days, days of relentless heat and hideous smells. There were recoveries, but there were deaths too, and Emily found herself having to spend some time in the airing cupboard to hide her damp eyes from the other nurses.

"You shouldn't be ashamed of mourning them," said Nathaniel, who discovered her when he came in for clean sheets.

"It's not terribly productive, is it," retorted Emily, wiping her nose clumsily on the back of her hand. "Do you weep every time you lose a patient? But oh, I had such hopes of her!"

"Courage." Nathaniel produced a clean handkerchief from his waistcoat pocket. He paused at the door of the airing cupboard, his face in shadow. "It doesn't get easier, you know. No matter how many patients one treats. I was called to the Reverend Bannister's home this morning. His youngest died yesterday. The idiot man not only kissed the baby in his coffin but encouraged the boy's sister to do the same."

"Oh no," said Emily, the handkerchief crumpled in her hand.

Nathaniel nodded, his mustache failing to mask the grim line of his mouth. "Oh yes. There was nothing to be done for her by the time I got there. I did what I could for Mr. Bannister, but he was in a bad way." He looked down at his hands, dark against the white of his cuffs. His face was tired and strained in the half-light. "That's one thing about the plague. People will take whatever physician they can get, regardless of color."

Emily looked at him sharply, wondering, for a moment, whether he'd heard Adam's comment about getting him a proper physician.

She bit her lip. "I hadn't thought," she said lamely. "I'd forgot."

And she had, mostly. It wasn't something she thought about when they were together. It was only now, when he said it, that she remembered Adam, and felt as though she had been somehow complicit. He didn't mean it, she wanted to say, but it felt odd to defend the dead to the living. And, she suspected, he had meant it.

"I'd have been shown the door a month ago. Now . . ." Nathaniel rubbed his brow with his knuckles. "One woman—an Englishwoman—asked me if I knew any native cures or local magic. She wanted me to find an obeah man for her. She didn't believe me when I told her I didn't know any. I told her I had laudanum, and I hoped that was magic enough."

"I'm not surprised people are looking for magic," said Emily ruefully. "There are times when it seems surer than medicine."

"No. Give me good, sound science over hocus-pocus any day. We'll defeat this yet. Just not," he admitted wearily, "soon enough."

Emily shoved his handkerchief up her sleeve and took him firmly by the arm, pointing him in the direction of his room. "Get some rest. We'll add you to the death toll, if you don't."

"Yes, ma'am," said Nathaniel, but he went meekly enough, objecting only to the threat of having Cousin Bella sent in to make sure he stayed there.

Emily went back to the yard and boiled sheets until she felt more like herself. Her own hands, on the wooden wash paddle, looked strangely pale. It was, she realized, because she'd got so used to the fact that everyone around her bore some degree of African blood. Her own hands looked somehow wrong.

Hands were hands, and hers were good enough to soak a sheet. Emily shook her head at herself and went back to her work.

By the first week of August, they were able to fold up the tent in the yard. A week later, the cots were taken up off the veranda. As beds emptied, through either recovery or death, they weren't filled again. Cautiously, cousins and aunts and grandparents began to appear to claim orphaned children. The dining room emptied, and then the bedrooms. Cousin Bella found her audience shrinking, and began to make noises about returning to Belle View.

"There were only thirty-two deaths today," said Nathaniel, coming back from his rounds to an almost empty house. He took the glass of sherry Emily handed him and absently drank from it. "Lord, listen to me. *Only* thirty-two."

The parlor had been reclaimed for its proper use, the curio cabinets set back in their place. Only the absence of the carpet, on which Adam had been ill, proclaimed the ravages that had taken place.

Nathaniel was standing in the same spot, in the same pose, as the first night she'd met him. It might have been six months ago. But it wasn't. He was different; they were both different.

"Thirty-two makes an improvement over three hundred," said Emily matter-of-factly, getting a grip on her thoughts and her sherry.

"It's getting worse in the countryside," warned Nathaniel, setting his glass down on the cabinet. "It's bad in St. Lucy, they say, and beginning to move through St. Andrew. But yes. It seems to be dying down in the town. I was beginning to be afraid it would never stop, that it would rage on and on until there was no one left to claim."

Emily looked at him in surprise. "You never said."

"What would have been the good? It's my job to fight death—even when death seems to be playing with loaded dice." Taking up his glass again, he added, looking at the sherry instead of her, "I know I ought to have insisted you return to Beckles, but—I don't know what I would have done without you here."

"Slept from time to time?" suggested Emily, more touched than she cared to admit. "It can't have been much help, having your home given over to patients."

"Can't it have been? No matter what happened, you were there, with that infernal pot in the yard and your bucket of lime. Any challenge that arose, you met it with a mop and a bowl of broth. You never despaired, and you kept me from despairing. Without you . . ." Nathaniel made a brusque gesture, nearly oversetting his sherry. "Oh, for heaven's sake, will you just take my thanks and leave it at that?"

He seemed so uncomfortable, so unlike his usual assured self that Emily found herself at a loss for tart comments.

"I'll accept your thanks if you'll take mine," she said, before she could think better of it. "In truth, I think I would have gone mad if I hadn't had something to do after—well, after."

"Your cousin?" Nathaniel toyed with his sherry, pushing the delicate cut-crystal glass this way and that on the top of the cabinet. "I'd wondered, a long time ago, if you had feelings for your cousin."

"Of course I did. He was my cousin. Oh, you mean like that. No." There had been a time she'd been comforted by the notion that Adam was there to marry if she ever really wanted to marry someone, but that had been the extent of it. For the most part. "He would have complained that I bullied him."

"You mean the way you bully me?"

"I don't—" Emily broke off as she realized he was teasing her. "You don't let me bully you."

His eyes were a deep, deep brown. She had never noticed that before. She had never noticed the small scar just above his right eye, or the softness of the skin beneath his mustache. But she noticed it all now.

"That's because I have the good sense to acknowledge when you're right," said Nathaniel.

"And when I'm wrong?" Her voice sounded very strange to her ears, as if coming from far away, from someone else's throat.

Nathaniel's eyes crinkled at the corners and Emily wondered that she had never noticed that before or the particular shape of his hair against his brow. "You haven't led me astray yet," he said. And then, "Emily . . ."

The sun was setting, the light fading. No one had thought to light the lamps. The room was dim and cool, the house quiet, the city outside the windows quiet. After so much pain and strife, there was, here, peace, and Emily found herself answering without words. Her arms knew what they wanted to do without conscious thought from her brain. They wrapped around his neck as if that was where they'd always meant to be.

At some point or other in his life, Nathaniel must have kissed someone. Quite a few someones. He certainly seemed to know what he was about. That was the last thought Emily had before she gave up on thinking entirely as a waste of valuable energy that could be better spent kissing him back.

All the tension, all the fear of the past two months, all the relief that it was finally over, it all found an outlet in this, transmuted into a mad sort of passion. Her hands were in his hair, his fingers on her face, her hair, her back. She'd never understood girls who ruined themselves before, but she did now, as she wiggled closer, impatient with the layers of cotton and poplin and lace, horsehair and whalebone and wool.

"Ahem?" Cousin Bella gave a discreet rap at the door and Emily jumped back, putting a hand to her hair, which was rather less neatly arranged than it had been a moment before.

Nathaniel backed up, bumping inelegantly into the curio cabinet. "Yes?" he said shortly.

Emily bit her lip to still a slightly hysterical giggle. She put her hand to cover her lips, which felt swollen and strange.

"There's a letter come from Beckles," said Cousin Bella peaceably. "For Miss Emily."

The mention of Beckles was enough to dispel any lingering giddiness. "Thank you, Cousin Bella."

Cousin Bella handed the letter to Emily and sat down on the settee, looking as though she intended to stay there for quite some time. Emily glanced at Nathaniel. She wasn't entirely sure which of them was being chaperoned.

Until five minutes ago, she wouldn't have thought they had any need to be chaperoned.

But now . . .

"Aren't you going to read it?" asked Nathaniel, his voice as clipped as it had been six months ago.

Emily looked uncertainly at him. "Yes."

It wasn't from Laura. She knew her hand, her penmanship the envy of the other girls at Miss Blackwell's.

"From George Davenant, I take it?" said Nathaniel. "I know the seal. I'll leave you to read your correspondence in private."

"No. There's no need." She'd fallen once into a pond in winter. She felt the same way now, shivering with the suddenness of the chill. "There's nothing in it that can't be shared."

She saw the hostility on Nathaniel's face change to concern. "What is it?"

Emily passed him the note with a hand that shook, ever so slightly. "The cholera is in Christ Church. It's come to Beckles."

CHAPTER TWENTY-SIX

Christ Church, Barbados
November 1815

WHEN CHARLES BROUGHT his ward to Beckles to visit with Neddy, Jenny wasn't included in the party.

She would hear about it from Dutchess, trying not to look like she was asking, trying not to crane for a glimpse of her daughter as she climbed into the Peverills carriage, lace on her petticoats and red leather shoes.

"You'd never guess she was younger than Neddy," Charles said proudly, in one of their rare meetings at the Old Mill. The rainy season ought to have been almost past, but the humidity in the air made Jenny's dress cling damply to her skin and the hair prickle at the nape of her neck. Another storm was coming, or thinking of it. In the mood she was in, Jenny was ready for it to unfurl with wind and rain, blowing away everything in its path. "She's so much quicker than he. He follows wherever she goes."

"Oh?" said Jenny flatly.

Charles didn't seem to notice. "I've hired a Frenchwoman to come twice a week and speak French with Lottie. She can say *bonjour* and *comment ça va*."

"*Magnifique*," said Jenny, who had learned French with Mary Anne, or what passed for French in her governess's estimation.

"Are you all right?" said Charles, lifting himself on an elbow, and Jenny didn't know whether to hit him for his obtuseness or weep onto his chest, or possibly both.

"It's the weather," she said.

It was no use telling him that every word he told her about Lottie was a dagger in her heart, because then he might stop, and she didn't want him to stop. She wanted to know. But it hurt. It hurt so badly to know she was there, so close, growing bigger every day, every day another day that she didn't know her mother.

She held to what Nanny Grigg had told her, this promise of intervention from abroad, from the king and queen, who valued them as their masters didn't. Wasn't it what Charles had been saying for years, and she hadn't believed him?

Jenny sat up, yanking her dress back up around her shoulders. "Has there been any word from the assembly about the registry bill?"

Charles blinked up at her. "About the . . . Why do you ask?"

Jenny busied herself braiding her hair back into order. "Someone told me that there'd been papers sent from England, that we're to have our freedom by the New Year."

Charles levered himself into a sitting position, looking at her with some concern. His shirt was open, his cravat discarded nearby. "Who said that?"

"Oh, just talk." Jenny turned her back to him. "Could you pin up my hair for me?"

Charles obediently began coiling the braid around. "The way Alleyne was going on about it in the council, you'd think he was about to be stripped of all his property tomorrow," he said indistinctly around the pins in his mouth. "I thought the man was going to have an apoplexy on the spot. And he's not the only one. They've resolved against the bill and mean to tell Parliament so."

Jenny jerked her head around, wincing as her hair pulled. "But—if the king in England says—"

Charles patiently put her hair back up, sticking the last pin in place.

"The king in England might say—or, in this case, Mr. Wilberforce in Parliament—but the planters of Barbados do not." Rooting about on the ground, he found her kerchief and handed it to her. "It will come back again, I've no doubt. It's not nearly so radical as they claim. It's their own fevered imaginations that make it so."

Jenny looked at him, the kerchief in her hand. "What will happen?"

Charles shook his head. "A great deal of jabbering and angry editorials in the *Barbados Mercury*. All sound and fury signifying nothing."

"Nothing," repeated Jenny.

All of that and then nothing. Jenny felt a stab of fear; she had held to the idea that there was a greater power, a power that could step in and free them, but if the law of England couldn't prevail, what could? She felt as though she were back under the regime of her father, where rules changed at his whim, and nothing and no one was safe.

Instead of going back to Beckles, Jenny walked north instead, to Simmons. Mary Anne was dining at Rosehall and had taken Queenie with her. She had a few hours, at least.

She found Nanny Grigg in the slave yard, sitting with Jackey, the head driver, and King Wiltshire, a carpenter from Bayleys, who was, she thought, married to one of Jackey's sisters, who had been sold away to Bayleys. Jackey's children were playing a game with buttons while Jackey and King Wiltshire looked on and offered advice.

Nanny raised a hand in greeting. "Jenny! You're here late."

"I've just come from Peverills." She looked at the children playing at their game, with their much-mended smocks, their feet bare. Their father was an important man on the plantation, so if they were lucky they might be apprenticed to a trade by and by instead of set to hoeing cane, but they would live on Simmons and die on Simmons unless they were sold away. The wrongness of it smote her like a fist. "They've refused the registry bill. The assembly. Mr. Davenant just told me."

"They can't do that." King Wiltshire came to his feet, stepping heavily on one of the counters.

"You've broken it!" protested Jackey's oldest.

"Hush," said Nanny. "He'll find you another. Run along. There's grown-up business at hand. Go to your mother in the kitchen. She'll give you a piece of cane to suck."

The children looked to their father. "Go on," Jackey echoed.

King Wiltshire kicked the cracked bits of ivory away. "I heard that there's a black queen in England and she means us to have our freedom, and it's Mr. Wilberforce who's to give it to us."

"I heard that too," said Nanny. "It was in a paper Will Nightingale showed me. He had it from Washington Franklin over at Contented Retreat, and if he wouldn't know, no one would. He's a freeman—his father freed him as he lay dying, and his brother too. They go where they please and read what they will."

"Nice for those who can get it," said Jenny. She didn't know where her father was now. Jamaica, most likely. But he'd certainly never thought about freeing her. "I don't know about the queen or Mr. Wilberforce, but I do know what I heard from Mr. Davenant, and that's that the council and assembly mean to deny the bill."

"They're keeping our freedom from us." She'd never seen Nanny look so, her pleasant-featured face stiff with anger. "They've stolen it. They've stolen our freedom."

"The queen won't stand for it," said King Wiltshire reassuringly, putting a hand on Nanny Grigg's arm.

She shook him off. "And what's the queen to do in England when we're here? I was a fool to think they'd let us go. We'll never have our freedom unless we fight for it."

"But how?" said Jackey. "They'll have the militia on us."

"I don't mean tonight, you great goathead. We'd need to work, to plan. . . . They did it in Saint Domingo, didn't they?" Nanny started pacing back and forth, her hands moving with her thoughts. "People don't *know*. Once they know, once they know what's being kept from us, they'll rise up and demand it. Why do you think they keep so many of us from reading and writing? To keep us ignorant. To keep us low. But we're not."

"I could spread the word at Bayleys," said King Wiltshire. "There are like-minded souls there. They'd help."

Nanny Grigg nodded and looked to Jackey. "Your friend Franklin. He'd help us?"

"A few years past, an overseer—a white man—broke into his house and tried to rob him. Franklin beat him off. Franklin got six months in the gaol. You know what the overseer got?" Jackey looked around the little group, his face grim. "Whatever he wanted from Franklin's house. He'll help us, all right."

"Jenny." Nanny Grigg turned to her, all business. "Who at Beckles would help?"

"I don't know." She wasn't sure what she thought about all this. Her old instinct, to keep her head down and avoid trouble, warred with a burning sense of injustice, a furious need to do something, anything. Seeing the way they were looking at her, she added quickly, "I'm not trying to shirk my share. The old master, Colonel Lyons, he liked to set people against each other. I wouldn't trust anyone not to tell the mistress."

Nanny thought for a moment, and then said decisively, "There's Davenant. You'll be our eyes and ears in the council. Whatever he says, whatever papers he has from England, you bring to us. The more we know, the better. We'll spread the word."

"Charles—Mr. Davenant—said they'd have it back again, the bill, I mean," said Jenny.

"And what will they do?" said Nanny. "The same. No disrespect to your Master Charles, but if we wait for him to argue them into sense, we'll all be dust and our great-grandbabies yet in chains."

Jenny thought of Lottie, in gold bracelets and red leather shoes. Lottie, who, at the wrong word, would be clapped in irons and hauled back to Beckles, stripped of her lace and ribbons and set to work digging weeds and watering cattle.

She could feel the features of her face set in a hard mask, echoing Nanny's. "Whatever's needful, I'll do it."

Nanny nodded. "We'll have the island in arms by Christmas."

But it wasn't Christmas; it was nearly Easter by the time the ground-work had been laid. The papers buzzed with news of the registry bill and its rejection; planters sent petitions to Parliament and angry screeds to the *Spectator* in London and the *Mercury* in Bridgetown.

"You see this?" Nanny said. She read aloud from the *Spectator*: "'The vulgar are influenced by names and titles.' Oh, it's the names that are the trouble, right enough. If I were a rose, I'd smell sweeter. 'Instead of SLAVES, let the Negroes be called ASSISTANT-PLANTERS; and we shall not then hear such violent outcries against the slave trade by pious divines, tender-hearted poetesses, and short-sighted politicians.' Assistant planters, is it? If they want to visit Simmons, I'll show them who's short-sighted. Let them spend a day being an *assistant planter*, and see how they like it."

Slowly, quietly, their network spread. A slave named Bussa, at Bay-leys, took charge of finding arms. Two freedmen, Cain Davis and John Richard Sarjeant, joined the cause. Davis was free, but his children were still slaves. With no master to answer to, he was able to circulate through the fields, conveying the intelligence that the queen was to free them but the assembly had denied them, and if they wanted their freedom they must fight for it.

The leaders of the conspiracy were to meet at the River Plantation for a dance on Good Friday to finalize the details.

"A dance at the River?" Mary Anne eyed Jenny askance in the dress-ing table mirror.

"Do you need me tonight?" Jenny asked, trying to look as if it didn't really matter. They would go ahead without her, she knew, but it would look bad. And she wanted this. She wanted a hand in it; she wanted to bring it about herself, for herself, for Lottie, for Charles.

"Don't I always need you?" said Mary Anne absently, rooting through her jewel box. She looked up. "Is it a man?"

"A man?" Jenny didn't have to feign her surprise.

"I wasn't born yesterday, you know," said Mary Anne. "You're constantly at Simmons. Yes, yes, I know you like exchanging recipes with Nanny Grigg, but if you haven't learned to get claret stains from silk by now, you never will."

"There might be," Jenny said slowly. Better for Mary Anne to think her infatuated than seditious. "He's a driver, at Bayleys, but he often calls at Simmons."

Mary Anne closed her jewel box with a snap and looked up at Jenny in the mirror. "If you must go courting, let me find you someone at Beckles. Johnny Cooper, perhaps. He has a good leg."

Jenny found herself smiling despite herself. "Queenie would have something to say about that."

Mary Anne didn't return her smile. "It's not her place to say anything," she said smartly. "Would you like to be married? I could arrange it, if you liked. You could have a house in the yard. A baby."

A baby to add to the rolls at Beckles. Increase of slaves, one infant, out of Jenny. Value sixty dollars. "I haven't forgot my last baby."

Mary Anne turned in her seat, and her hand rested briefly on Jenny's. "Babies die," she said matter-of-factly. It was, Jenny knew, her idea of comfort. "My mother lost three before she had me. It's sad, but there it is. You can't mourn the rest of your life. It isn't healthy."

Would she be saying the same if it were Master Neddy? "No, Miss Mary," said Jenny. "About the dance . . ."

"Go. I can't have you looking like death."

"Thank you, Miss Mary." Jenny began to walk away, not going too fast, not wanting to look like she was hurrying.

"Wait." Jenny stopped at the door. Her mistress was looking at her speculatively. "If you tell me who it is, I'll see about buying him. It's little enough to keep you happy. If he's a good worker."

"Mistress," said Jenny, trying to muster the correct degree of wonder and gratitude. Mary Anne looked so pleased with herself, so delighted with her own generosity. Jenny would have laughed if her nerves hadn't been so tightly wound. "Thank you."

"You've been with me a long time." Mary Anne checked her hair in the mirror. "It's time we saw you settled."

Settled and breeding. Jenny knew the way her mistress's mind worked. More babies for Beckles, a price tag attached to each one.

Only two days more. Two days more and she would be free.

Or dead.

As she hurried toward the River along the road, joining scattered groups from other plantations heading in the same direction, she allowed herself to imagine Charles's reaction. Shock, of course. But, she thought, in the end, relief. He'd wanted this too. It was just that their methods were, of necessity, different. He'd failed with the pen; now it was her turn to try the sword.

The dance was well under way in the slave yard at the River by the time Jenny arrived.

"You're late. In here." Jackey hurried her back to one of the huts at the very edge of the yard, well removed from the festivities.

"What kept you?" demanded Nanny, from the shadows.

Jenny blinked as her eyes adjusted from the brilliant light of the bonfires to the dimness of the hut. She could just make out Nanny Grigg, Cain Davis, Washington Franklin, and King Wiltshire and Bussa from Bayleys sitting around a square of fabric.

"I thought my mistress wasn't going to let me go. She's worried I'm forming an attachment."

Nanny snorted. "That'll be the least of her worries in another two days. We've just done the flags," she added, gesturing to the cloth.

"Every army needs a flag," said Bussa, grinning at her in the darkness. General Bussa, the others had begun to call him; of them all, he was the most involved in the military aspect of their plans.

Jenny looked down at the flag on top. The king and queen, conspicuously dark skinned, sat on either side of a black man wearing a tricorne and holding a musket as a royal warship sailed to his aid. Below them, a well-dressed black man and woman held hands, looking imploringly to the king and queen for their liberation.

Scrolled across the bottom of the flag, the legend read: *Happiness ever remains the endeavour. Britannier are always happy to help all such sons as endeavour.*

Jenny recognized the elegantly curved hand as Washington Franklin's.

"We'll get what they wanted for us," said Jackey, touching his fingers to the figure of the queen. "Who knows? Maybe they'll send to our aid when they hear."

"I heard there might be troops coming from 'Mingo," said King Wiltshire. "Frenchmen come to help us."

"God saves those who endeavor for themselves," said Nanny firmly. She bundled the flags out of the way. "We can't rely on anyone but our own selves. They'll bring the militia out on us, so we'll have to act fast and make sure we act together. There'll be fires to signal the time. Bussa's to start at Bayleys."

Bussa nodded. "Sunday at sunset." He drew a map in the dust, using buttons for landmarks. "First Bayleys . . . then Rivers . . . Mapps . . . the Thicket . . . Three Houses . . . Golden Grove. As soon as I light the cane trash, the others will follow."

"I've a great pile of corn in my garden ready to light," said Cain Davis. "I've spread the word as far as I can; I've gone from house to house. We're as ready as we'll ever be."

"We'll have half the island in flames before they realize an ember's been sparked," said Jackey, with satisfaction.

"They'll wake in the night to the smell of their cane burning," said Nanny, with grim satisfaction. "That'll wake them up all right."

"And then to arms," said Bussa quietly. "On the first night, they'll cry *water*, and on the second night, they'll cry *blood*."

"Not Peverills." The words were out before Jenny realized she'd spoken them. "Whatever you may think, Charles Davenant's a good man. He means us well."

Jackey folded his arms across his chest, leaning back against the rough wood wall. "He didn't mean us well enough to give us our freedom."

"He's one man among many in the council. What was he to do?"

Jenny looked around the circle, from one to the next. "Peverills is one plantation among many."

"It's one of the oldest," said Franklin thoughtfully. "It will mean something to see it burn."

"But not one of the richest," Jenny argued. "There are better targets. If you want to make them quake, you'll fire St. Nicholas Abbey or Sunbury."

Jackey looked at Franklin, then at Bussa, who nodded slightly, and then back to Jenny. "All right. Peverills for your loyalty."

"We don't need to buy her loyalty," said Nanny, moving to put an arm around Jenny's shoulders, like a mother hen taking her chick under her wing. "Jenny is with us, aren't you? She's been with us from the first, and I won't hear a word against her. If she wants us to leave Peverills be . . . well, there are plenty of other fields to burn."

"What about Beckles?" asked Bussa.

Mary Anne and Neddy were to go to Peverills to eat their Easter dinner with Charles and Lottie. She would, Jenny decided, make sure they stayed there, if she had to break the axle of the carriage with her own two hands.

"Burn it," she said. "Burn every last cane and sow the ground with salt, and I'll come and dance on the ashes."

Christ Church, Barbados
Easter 1816

"I WISH YOU'D let me hold a proper celebration for you," Charles said to Jonathan. "A dance, perhaps."

They were back from Easter services, still trailing the odor of sanctity about them. Carlota had been carried off to bed, protesting, by her nursemaid. Neddy had fallen quietly asleep in a corner of the pew and been borne back to Beckles. The adults sat over their supper, a farewell supper as well as an Easter one.

"With rum punch and everyone whispering about how I'm marrying above my station?" Jonathan looked pointedly at Mary Anne, who very deliberately pretended not to notice. "No, thank you. I'm just as happy to slip off quietly. I'll come back when I'm too important to ignore."

"Don't forget us once you're grand," said Charles.

"Forget my Lottie? Never." Jonathan took a hearty swig of his claret, the good claret, which Charles had brought out in honor of the occasion. "I'll visit to make sure you're taking care of her proper."

"I think I can manage," said Charles, trying not to betray his annoyance. Yes, he was delighted to see Lottie enveloped in affection, but Jonathan contrived to make him feel unfit. It didn't help that Jenny was standing behind Mary Anne's chair. She did her best to hide it, but he knew she felt he'd failed her. "You go and enjoy your honeymoon. You're bound for Antigua?"

"We're to be married from Antigua and then sail for the Carolinas." Jonathan's rather harsh-featured face lit when he spoke of his bride. Personally, Charles didn't quite see it, but he was delighted that Jonathan did.

Jack shall have Jill; / Nought shall go ill. Charles wished it were as simple as that, that there were a deus ex machina out of a Shakespeare comedy who could sprinkle fairy dust on them all and make it all come out right, everyone with his proper mate.

His mate was there, standing just behind his sister-in-law, but he couldn't acknowledge her, not by a word, not by a smile.

Was it worth it? Sometimes Charles wondered. He was proud of the changes he'd made to Peverills, but they were so small, so little in the grand scheme of things. Change, if it came, wasn't going to come from men like him, tinkering on their plantations, but from men like Wilberforce, holding forth in the House of Commons. They might have run away together years ago, been together with their child, sailed away like Jonathan and his bride, Jonathan, who was beaming like he'd made the very earth and found it good.

It was the claret, making him maudlin. Charles caught himself just before he looked at Jenny and made himself smile at Jonathan instead.

"I wish you very happy," said Charles. He raised his glass. "A toast to you and your bride. May you have long and happy lives together."

"I'll drink to that," said Jonathan.

"You don't drink to a toast in your own honor," protested Mary Anne.

"There's no need to stand on ceremony. We're all family here." Charles nodded at Jonathan. "I account Jonathan family. I couldn't have held Peverills without him and I don't know what I'll do when he's gone."

"Run it all into the ground within a year," said Jonathan with a grin. His face changed, and he lifted his head, sniffing. "What is that smell?"

Now that he mentioned it, Charles could smell it too, like caramel, a burnt-sugar smell that singed the nose and clung to the back of the throat. "I hope Cook isn't attempting French tarts again. We had burnt pears for days."

Mary Anne rose from her chair, her fork still in her hand. "That's cane. That's cane burning."

Jonathan's groom London came running into the room. "There's word come from Bayleys. There's plantations burning all across St. Philip!"

"What?" Charles stared at the boy, uncomprehending. The last revolt on the island had been so long ago, it was out of all memory, in the days when there was still a Stuart on the throne of England and men wore wigs that fell in curls past their shoulders. "It must be some mistake—cane trash burning that got out of hand. . . ."

"No mistake, Master Charles." London's eyes were bright with excitement. "There's men marching under banners. They're headed straight here. Simkin from Bayleys said."

They weren't supposed to be here. Behind Mary Anne's chair, Jenny stood, disbelieving. They weren't supposed to be at Peverills. Jenny knew the plan, knew it down to the minute. Beckles, yes, but not Peverills. They had agreed.

"Excuse me," said Jonathan, and pushed away from the table, hurriedly leaving the room.

The sounds of the mob were growing closer now; Jenny could hear the shouting. Through the window, she could see the red glow of torches, brighter and brighter.

Charles stood up, the candlelight turning his features into something out of a storybook, a knight about to go into battle. "I'll go speak to them."

"Don't be a fool, Charles," said Mary Anne, looking at her fork in confusion and then flinging it down. "If you ignore them, they'll shout a bit and go away."

There was the crash of broken glass from the front of the house, followed by a shout.

"I won't be a moment," Charles said, and his eyes met Jenny's. "Don't worry."

Don't worry? She had to get them out of here, she had to get them all out of here. Where would be safe? The mill? They would burn the mill. The bookkeeper's house? Maybe. Beckles? She'd told them to burn Beckles, to burn Beckles and sow the ground with salt. Peverills was supposed to be safe. Lottie was supposed to be safe.

"Lottie." Jenny's throat was dry, her hands cold. She dropped Mary Anne's fan and shawl and bolted for the door.

"Jenny! Where do you think you're going? Jenny!"

Peverills wasn't like Beckles; it hadn't been built to a simple plan. There were rooms off of rooms, stairs that led up and then down. Lottie's room was in one of the wings.

"Fire!" someone shouted, and another anxious voice took up the cry. Outside, people were running to and fro. Jenny heard the high and anguished whinny of a horse run wild. "Fire!"

Mary Anne grabbed her by her arm. "For heaven's sake! Don't lose your head. Come away. We'd best get back to Beckles—if we still can."

She could hear the crackle of fire, timbers burning, stone crumbling. Charles was in the fields, and Lottie, Lottie was in her bed, in the back of the house, in the back of the house where the fire was raging.

Oh God. What had she done? Not Peverills, they'd promised. Not Peverills.

"Lottie!" she shouted, hoping against hope that she would see a little body in a white nightdress stumbling toward her. Her words disappeared into the howl of the flames and the cries from outside.

"Jenny!" Mary Anne tugged at her arm. "This way. Now."

"Let go!" Half-mad with fear, Jenny yanked away so hard she sent her mistress stumbling. "My baby—I have to get my baby."

Without looking back, she ran toward the rear of the house, toward the fire.

Mary Anne's shout and a rending noise were the only warning she had before the flaming beam came hurtling down, straight toward her head.

CHAPTER TWENTY-SEVEN

Christ Church, Barbados
August 1854

EMILY'S ROOM AT Beckles was waiting for her, just as it had been.

One would never know that only an hour away, thousands of people had died; one would never know that they were dying even now. The furniture smelled of lemon oil and beeswax. Her brushes and combs were on the dressing table, silver shining with polish. The mirror glittered in the sunlight that slanted through the jalousies.

There had been water left for her in the washstand. Emily found herself eyeing it askance. "If it wouldn't be too much trouble," she asked Katy, "could you see that my wash water is boiled?"

She could tell that the maid thought it a rather eccentric request, hot water in the heat of the day, but she took the pitcher all the same.

"How is your little girl?" Emily called after her, but Katy must not have heard, because she didn't answer.

Emily began to unpin her cuffs, feeling out of place and out of sorts. As soon as the message arrived from Beckles, it was taken as a given that she would go back; there could be no reason for her to stay in Bridgetown now. Cousin Bella had helped her to pack "her" things, although precious little of them were hers. Emily had felt, discomfitingly, that she was being chivvied away.

There had been no time to speak with Nathaniel alone, and Emily wasn't sure whether to be annoyed or relieved by that.

What was there to say?

On the other hand, it was far more disturbing to think that there might be nothing to say, that that kiss had been nothing more than relief, relief that the death toll had slowed, that the plague had lifted.

It was hardly a romantic thought.

But what else did she expect? What could possibly come of it?

"Emily?" Laura poked her head around the door. "They told me you were back."

"Oh, Laura." Emily jumped out of her seat, and stopped, unsure of herself. It was the color that struck her first, or, rather, the absence of it, the black of Laura's widow's weeds blending with the black of her hair, contrasting with the translucent pallor of her skin. "I'm so sorry. I'm so very sorry."

"Thank you," said Laura.

"I wouldn't blame you if you blame me," said Emily miserably. "I did try, you know. I thought he was getting better. He seemed to be getting better. It was so sudden, in the end."

Laura stepped inside, closing the door behind her. She had reefed up the top hoop of her dress, but it did more to emphasize than hide her condition. "I'm sure you did everything you could."

Emily tried very hard not to stare. "I would have come back sooner. I would have told you about Adam myself and not by letter. But I didn't want to bring the infection back to you. Not in your condition."

"You knew?" Laura looked ruefully down at her bulging belly. "I suppose Adam told you."

"No. Nath—Dr. Braithwaite guessed." Emily choked over his name, feeling, obscurely, that she hadn't the right to use it anymore, not unless he explicitly granted it to her. Not after the kiss. Turning her attention back to Laura, she asked, "Why didn't you tell me? Adam said you didn't want me fussing over you."

Laura shook her head, drifting over to the dressing table, where she fiddled with Emily's silver brush, moving it from one side of the table to the other. "That wasn't it." She looked up at Emily, looked at her directly for the first time in months. "I didn't want to tell you because if I told you, it would mean it was real, that I was married, and—and having a baby."

"But you are married and having a baby," said Emily, thoroughly confused. "It's not as though you weren't married and having a baby. I was at the wedding. Unless—don't tell me there was some irregularity?"

"Irregularity?" said Laura. "Oh no, nothing like that."

"Oh good. I wouldn't have put it past Adam to have married a barque of frailty and then tried to hide it to make Aunt Millicent happy, or just pretended it never happened." Remembering to whom she was speaking, Emily abruptly broke off. "Not that he would have done such a thing. What I mean is—"

"No," said Laura eagerly. "What you mean is exactly what you meant. You used to speak your mind to me, you know, before I married Adam. But then it changed everything. You looked at me differently. As though I weren't myself anymore. And Adam—"

"I didn't mean to shut you out." Emily stared at Laura in confusion, the past nine months running through her head in a jumble. "I thought you didn't need me anymore. You were a married lady and I—I was just a spinster cousin."

"You're *his* cousin. And you were always so close." Laura sat down heavily on the little chair in front of the dressing table. "What could I say to you? I couldn't tell you how unhappy I was. It would have put you in an impossible position. How could I tell you? You would have gone straight to Adam."

There was no denying that. She had put Laura's distance down to the constraints caused by the new gulf in their circumstances. It had never occurred to her that Laura might be unhappy, that Laura might need her. "Well . . . yes. But mightn't that have helped?"

"Or made it worse." Laura pleated her fingers together against the black stuff of her skirt. "I'm not sure how to explain it. He wasn't . . . unkind. But once we married, it was as though he became someone else entirely. Anything I found interesting bored and frustrated him. I bored and frustrated him. When we were courting, Adam seemed so *sure*. He was sure enough for both of us."

"You never said," said Emily softly. She felt awful. She had prided herself so on her ability to judge character, and yet she had misjudged Laura so entirely, had misunderstood everything that had passed between them.

"I didn't expect him to be tied to my skirts." Laura looked up at Emily, delicate purple circles under her eyes. "I didn't need him to share my interests. But for him to pretend to it and then . . . At least, you never pretended."

"Laura—"

"Truly, I never minded that you had no patience for poetry and no ear for music," said Laura earnestly. "You never claimed otherwise."

"Thank you?" said Emily. She'd always thought she sang rather nicely, but now wasn't the time to quibble about her ability to carry a tune, not when Laura was baring her soul.

"You had your interests and I had mine and we each respected the other for it. If Adam had told me honestly . . . But it was as though, once he had me, he wanted me to be something else entirely, and I wasn't sure what it was or how to be what he wanted. I'm not sure I know how to be anyone other than myself."

"I wouldn't want you to be."

"Adam did. Everything I wore, everything I said, was wrong. He was so concerned that I might make a poor impression on the Turners, that I sounded too rich or not rich enough." Laura took a deep breath, letting it out in a gusty stream. "I was so unhappy. I think he was too."

"He had other worries," said Emily, remembering Adam's frantic attempt to make good, his determination that he wouldn't go back to Bristol empty-handed.

"But he didn't share them with me," said Laura. She paused for a moment, and then said, with difficulty, "I felt so guilty about you. It haunted me, that I had stolen him from you. I know your grandfather always intended you to marry. If ours was a great love, then it was all for the good. But if it wasn't . . . I had wronged you to no purpose."

"That was Grandfather's project, not mine." Emily knelt by Laura's chair. If Laura could be honest, so could she. "It was comforting to think that Adam was there should I need someone to marry. Had it come to that, I don't think either of us could have gone through with it. We knew each other too well. I always knew Adam would marry someone else one day."

"One day," said Laura, and Emily didn't need her to say more to know what she was thinking.

"I didn't mind that Adam had married. I minded that it was you." It was something she hadn't even admitted to herself. In a rush, Emily said, "I knew I should be glad that the two people I cared for more than anyone had found happiness with each other. But—I didn't think you would suit. And I minded that I didn't come first with you anymore."

"You were right. We didn't suit." Laura's voice was very small. She stared down at her wedding ring. The polish had already worn off; it looked battered and dim. "Poor Adam. He deserved better."

"For what it's worth, he was very proud of having won you. Even if you had nothing to say to each other in private, he liked to have you on his arm. He boasted like anything about you." Emily pulled herself up to standing. "I suppose you'll go back to Bristol now?"

Laura put her hands protectively to her stomach. "I couldn't possibly go anywhere until after the baby. And then . . . I wouldn't want to risk the child in travel. In a year, perhaps. Or two."

"I shouldn't want to live with Aunt Millicent either," said Emily frankly. "I suppose I should find our hostess. Do you know where she might be?"

"In the pest house." Laura grimaced. "I mean, the infirmary."

"*Pest house* is probably about right at the moment," said Emily.

Laura took the hand Emily offered her and hauled herself out of the chair. "She's been there since the sickness started. She's had her meals sent and won't let any of us near her."

"She'll let me," said Emily.

Laura's lips twitched. The smile started small and then spread against her friend's thin face, transforming it. "Oh, Emily, I have missed you."

"I've missed you too," said Emily. All the weight of everything she hadn't told Laura pressed around her. Nathaniel, her grandparents, Nathaniel. But there was sickness at Beckles and Laura was with child and had just lost her husband and there could really be only so many revelations in one day. "I'll just go see what I can do to help. Is there anything you need?"

"No, I'm quite all right. You will take care?"

"You don't need to worry about me," said Emily firmly. "It can't possibly be as bad as Bridgetown."

It was worse. Or, at least, the smell was. The pest house had never been designed for such extensive or extended occupancy. It was a one-roomed hut, of the sort the servants lived in. Under ordinary circumstances, it was equipped as a sort of consulting room–cum–infirmary, with a single cot, a table, a chair, and a row of deeply outdated medical texts, including Buchan's *Domestic Medicine*, which attributed cholera to the unhealthy habit of eating cold cucumbers.

The smell assaulted Emily as soon as she stepped inside, not just the normal putridity of excrescence but an acrid aroma that seemed to strip the inside of her nose.

A woman was standing in between two tightly jammed rows of cots, her hair wrapped in a kerchief, her gown swathed in an apron. Emily would never have recognized her, but for the diamonds in her ears.

"So you're back, are you?" Mrs. Davenant rasped.

Emily scrubbed at her eyes with the backs of her hands. She couldn't blame Mrs. Davenant for sounding like that; her own throat was stinging. "What on earth is that smell?"

Mrs. Davenant came to join Emily in the doorway, leaning heavily against the wall. Her face was gray beneath her brightly patterned kerchief. "Turpentine wraps to induce a sweat. If they sweat they live."

Emily peered over her shoulder. "Is it cholera?"

"No, it's dyspepsia. Of course it's cholera. MacAndrews was the first to succumb, the useless old fool."

There were aprons hanging on a hook by the wall. Emily helped herself to one, tying the straps behind her back. "How bad is it?"

"We've had ten deaths. Mimbo, Hannah, Joe Horner, Hagar, Rose . . . I saw them all born. Mary Frances, that's Johnny Cooper's girl. Little Henry, Quasheba, Philly Ann, Charity. And we've twelve more sick." She turned away, but not before Emily saw the tears seeping from her eyes, tears of exhaustion and loss.

"What have you done, other than turpentine?" asked Emily briskly.

Mrs. Davenant drew a rasping breath and then straightened, painfully. "Pomegranate skin, to check the effusions. A decoction of Christmas bush. You pound the leaves in a clean cloth and mix it with salt and a little rum—Nanny Bell taught me. But you wouldn't know Nanny Bell. She was before your time."

"I've found laudanum helps, a little." Emily moved past Mrs. Davenant into the room. There were patients in all stages of the disease, including, she noticed, with a tightening of her chest, Katy's little girl, who was curled on her side, clutching a rag doll. "You've a fire lit to boil water?"

Mrs. Davenant had been sagging against the wall. At Emily's comment, she drew herself up. "Why would I do a fool thing like that?"

"If you've read Dr. Snow's 1849 paper," said Emily, moving from bed to bed, checking heads and making notes of sheets to change, "*On the Mode of Communication of Cholera*, he advises boiling all water before use, on the grounds that—"

"Stop. I'll light a fire to boil water; it's little price to pay to prevent you quoting learned authorities at me. I've more faith in Nanny Bell than any doctor in Christendom but if a little boiled water will make you happy, boil your water. It can't do nearly as much harm as MacAndrews's remedies." Mrs. Davenant got the words out with difficulty; there was a sheen of sweat across her forehead.

Emily moved quickly toward her, afraid she might faint. "You don't look well."

Mrs. Davenant pushed her aside, swaying on her feet and nearly overbalancing. "I'm perfectly all right."

"You're not perfectly all right." Emily took her arm to steady her, and this time Mrs. Davenant didn't object. "Your face is flushed."

"We're in the tropics." Mrs. Davenant winced with the effort of speaking, half doubling over. "Queenie laced my stays too tight."

Emily didn't let her waste more breath. "I'm taking you back to the house. No, don't argue with me. If you'll like, we'll scrub everything you touch, but you're going to your own bed, and you're going right now, and I'm calling in the doctor—a proper doctor."

Queenie took one look at Mrs. Davenant and took charge, getting her mistress into a nightdress. It was a sign of Mrs. Davenant's growing weakness that her protests were decidedly pro forma. Emily saw her settled in bed with a dose of laudanum she staunchly refused to take and left her under Queenie's care while she first sent an urgent message to Nathaniel and then, tying her apron strings about her, returned to the pest house to do what she could, feeling very small and very alone.

She hadn't realized, back in Bridgetown, just how much she had relied on Nathaniel. Not to care for the patients—she was perfectly capable of caring for the patients—but to be there. His caustic humor had bolstered her, had kept her going through the losses and the fear.

If he got her message, would he come? It was selfish of her, she knew. He had patients of his own in Bridgetown. And he had his own reasons not to love Beckles or its mistress.

She wouldn't blame him if he didn't come. Day turned to night, the sun flaring out with the sudden sunset of the tropics. Emily lit a lantern and circulated among her patients, doling out boiled water and broth, and little dribbles of laudanum to those in the worst case. The turpentine wraps she discarded.

George came and called to her from a safe distance. He seemed relieved when his only instructions were to bear Laura company.

"Do you need anything?" he called, in the tone of one who hopes the answer will be no.

"You'll let me know if Dr. Braithwaite comes?" It was too late now, Emily told herself. It was dark already. No one would attempt the drive from Bridgetown now. There had been rioting of late; gangs of frightened men robbing shops and plantations in St. Lucy.

"You've called Nat?"

"He's the best doctor I know," said Emily. He was also the only doctor she knew, but that was beside the point.

It was full dark when she heard the sounds of hoofbeats. Emily ran out from the pest house to see the twin lights of carriage lamps bobbing their way toward the house. Emily yanked her apron over her head, dipped her hands in a basin of steaming water, and bolted toward the house, ducking through the gap in the lime hedge, catching him just as he was climbing down from his uncle's phaeton.

"You came."

"You're not with Mrs. Davenant?"

"There are twelve sick in the pest house. Mrs. Davenant had Queenie to look after her." Emily ran out of words and simply stood, staring up at him. The buttons on his waistcoat glimmered faintly in the torchlight, and his high-crowned hat made him seem very tall. "Thank you."

"I could hardly say no, could I?" He sounded rueful, and rather weary, and Emily wasn't quite sure how to take it. She curled her hands into fists and tucked them behind her to keep from reaching for his arm. "You'll bring me to the patient?"

"This way." Emily led him into the house, through the front door, which opened for them as it always opened, as if by magic. Up the stairs they went, to Mrs. Davenant's room, dimly lit by a rose-shaded lamp.

Queenie came to the doorway.

"Is she sleeping? I've brought the doctor."

"As awake as you or I," said Queenie grimly, and stepped aside to let them through, although Emily saw her subjecting Nathaniel to a long, inquisitive look.

Mrs. Davenant stirred against the pillows, her voice like the rustle of old, dead leaves. "I remember you. Nat Cooper, you were then."

"That," said Nathaniel, setting down his bag, "was then. Any vomit? Diarrhea?"

"No," said Emily, hovering by the bedside. "But you know, the more virulent cases sometimes don't."

"Sit up, please," said Nathaniel to Mrs. Davenant. He took a stethoscope from his bag, a tube of polished wood with an elegant ivory earpiece and chest piece. He saw Emily looking at it and said, shortly, "A gift from my uncle upon my graduation. It's the latest model from Paris."

"Am I to have French treatment, then?" rasped Mrs. Davenant.

"Breathe in, please," said Nathaniel, placing the bell-shaped piece against her back and his ear to the other.

Mrs. Davenant breathed in, flinching at the pain. "I don't see the reason for this. I'm just tired, that's all. You'd be tired too."

"And out," said Nathaniel.

"Cholera's not in the chest," said Emily. "It's in the bowels."

"This isn't cholera," said Nathaniel, frowning over his stethoscope.

"I could have told you that," said Mrs. Davenant. "It's the grippe, that's all."

Nathaniel ignored her. "Breathe in."

Mrs. Davenant took a shallow breath that turned into a fit of coughing that made her whole body shake. When she could speak again, she whispered crossly, "What did I tell you? *La grippe*. Nothing to make a fuss about."

"You can lie back now." Nathaniel straightened, looking grim. "It's not *la grippe*. It's winter fever."

Mrs. Davenant was not impressed. "It's summer. With all your education, I think you'd know that."

Nathaniel packed his stethoscope back in its velvet-lined case. "Lung fever, then, if you prefer."

"I don't. I don't have lung fever. I *refuse* to have lung fever." Mrs. Davenant tried to sit up, and, with a cry, fell back again against the pillows.

Queenie rushed over to help settle her, casting Nathaniel and Emily a reproachful look.

"Ow," said Mrs. Davenant.

"You have lung fever. Denying it won't make it otherwise." To Emily, Nathaniel said, "There's not much to be done other than what you already know. Rest, quiet, beef tea, if she'll take it."

"Caroline Davenant died of lung fever." Mrs. Davenant's voice drifted up from the great bed, so faint that Emily could hardly hear her. "Robert and Charles's mother. She'd been sick for as long as I could remember, but it was the lung fever ended her. Robert told me. Not that he said it that way. He thought it was his father's neglect that killed her. He didn't love her anymore. His attention wandered. And she died."

"*Men have died . . . and worms have eaten them, but not for love.* There's no medical precedent for dying of a broken heart," said Nathaniel harshly. Opening his bag, he took out a phial of laudanum. "You'll want something to help you sleep. Miss Dawson can give you four drops of this in a bit of wine."

"No! They gave me laudanum before, after Edward. I won't have it. I won't have it."

"Shhhh." Emily went to her, settling her back against the pillows. "I'll make you up a posset. Don't worry. No spirits of wine."

Mrs. Davenant grabbed at her shoulder, staring up at Emily, her face skeletal in the uncertain light. "She was like you. Answer for everything."

"Who?"

Mrs. Davenant let go. "Jenny, of course."

"It takes people this way sometimes," said Nathaniel in an undertone. "The lung fever. It makes their minds wander."

"I'm not wandering!" Mrs. Davenant's voice broke, her protests lost in a fit of coughing. "Don't you think I knew who you were from the first? I knew. As soon as you came, I knew."

Emily wrinkled her brow at Nathaniel. "Don't distress yourself, Mrs. Davenant. Queenie will sit with you and I'll be back with that posset before you know I've gone."

Mrs. Davenant subsided against the pillows. "You've come to be a judgment to me. Or to put things right. One or the other. Unless they're one and the same."

"I've come to help you rest," said Emily firmly.

Leaving Queenie in charge, she went out with Nathaniel into the hall. "Thank you for coming all this way. I would never have guessed that it might be lung fever."

"So there are some benefits to all my education, then," said Nathaniel.

For a moment, they stood looking at each other in the dim hall, a candle guttering in its holder on the wall, the air between them charged with memory.

Feeling like a coward, Emily ducked away, saying quickly, "I know it's late, but would you mind seeing to the patients in the infirmary before you go? Mrs. Davenant was subjecting them to the most bizarre treatments, turpentine wraps and Christmas bush. . . ."

"She might not have been far wrong with the Christmas bush." Nathaniel's voice was brisk, doctorly. "I'll stay the night and go back in the morning."

"I'll have someone make up a room for you."

"There's no need."

"There's every need. I won't have you going into a decline."

"Do I look as though I'm going into a decline?"

Men have died . . . and worms have eaten them . . . Emily covered her confusion by saying primly, "You need to look after your own health. They need you back in town."

"Not as much as they used to. It will be over soon. There were fewer than ten new cases today."

"So you don't miss the extra pair of hands?" She sounded, she realized, as though she were fishing for compliments.

"I didn't say that," said Nathaniel.

"Jenny!" There was the sound of thrashing from Mrs. Davenant's room, and a thud. "Jenny!"

Emily seized on the excuse. "I'd best go to her. You'll be at the infirmary?"

"I'll see you in the morning before I go," said Nathaniel. "We can talk then."

"The morning, then," said Emily, and escaped into Mrs. Davenant's room, where she occupied herself in changing sweaty nightdresses, mixing possets, and other mundane tasks. He wanted to talk about the disposition of the patients, of course. That was all. Just as they had once before.

What else was there to talk about?

Emily wrestled a pillow into a fresh case with unnecessary force and took out her feelings in shaking out the eiderdown.

Mrs. Davenant slept fitfully, waking often. There were moments she was lucid and knew Emily and fretted about her patients back in the pest house, but, more often, she called out for Jenny or argued with her dead husband, her voice rising so that Emily was afraid that anyone would think she was torturing her.

Despite her patient's instructions to the contrary, she measured out some laudanum and tricked her into drinking it, and finally saw Mrs. Davenant fall into a proper sleep. A drugged sleep, but a sleep all the same.

Emily meant to stay awake and keep watch, but the day had been long and the night even longer and she found herself drifting into sleep and waking with a jerk of the neck, until exhaustion took her and she slept as soundly as though she had been drugged instead of Mrs. Davenant.

When Emily woke, it was dawn, the thin light stretching through the breaks in the jalousies.

Her patient was already awake, lying against her pillows, staring at her. "You're very like her. Not in looks. Not in looks at all. She was beautiful, did you know?"

"I take after my father," said Emily. She rubbed her eyes, still muzzy with sleep. "No one has ever praised him for his beauty, but it's generally agreed he has a beautiful soul."

"Souls, piffle. My uncle was a handsome man." Mrs. Davenant coughed into her hand, her chest rattling painfully. Her eyes glittered strangely, darting around the room, as though she were seeing people who weren't there. "We all knew she was his daughter. He told me when he gave her to me. 'I give you my own child,' he said. Of course, that was before I knew him for what he was. A snake. He'd as soon eat his young, if it suited him."

Distracted, Nathaniel had said. Emily rose painfully from her chair, shaking out her crumpled skirts. One leg had fallen asleep under her and she had a crick in her neck.

Hobbling over to the bed, Emily put the back of her hand to Mrs. Davenant's head. "You're burning up."

"Bring me my wrap, Jenny. It's cold. I'm cold." Emily went to look for a blanket, but Mrs. Davenant clawed herself upright, calling, "What are you doing? Where are you going? Jenny!"

"Shhh, Mrs. Davenant, don't fret yourself." Emily wrung out a bit of cloth in the basin, bathing the older woman's forehead.

After a few moments, Mrs. Davenant's eyes opened. She blinked, and then blinked again. "Miss Dawson," she said slowly. "Miss Dawson?"

"Yes, Mrs. Davenant. You're ill but you're going to get better," said Emily, with the practiced cheer of the sickroom.

"Did I tell you that I know who you are? I guessed right away. What I didn't know was whether you knew. At first, I thought you might."

Emily nodded and dipped the cloth into the water, letting the patient ramble. She'd heard stranger things. She leaned over to put the cool cloth on Mrs. Davenant's forehead. The older woman was shivering and shaking with the fever.

"You think I'm distracted, don't you? I'm not. I remember everything." Mrs. Davenant pointed at Emily's locket, which had come out of her bodice and was swinging on its ribbon. "That's a pretty bauble you've got there. Give it here. I want a look at it."

Reluctantly, but not wanting to upset her further, Emily untied the ribbon and handed Mrs. Davenant the locket. Her neck felt very bare without it.

"This," said Mrs. Davenant, holding it up triumphantly, "used to be mine. My uncle gave it to me."

Emily instinctively reached to take it back. "I'm afraid you're mistaken. This was my mother's."

She was too slow. Pressing hard on the locket, Mrs. Davenant flicked open the catch, and, before Emily had time to protest, stuck her nail beneath the miniature of Emily's mother, prying it from the back.

"Stop!" Emily protested, but it was too late; the tiny piece of vellum had come loose, the glue on the back old and dried.

"See?" rasped Mrs. Davenant. She pointed with a trembling finger at the gold center of the locket. "*To Jenny, for her good service.* I gave it to her. I should know. And she gave it to her daughter. There."

Emily rescued her mother's miniature, grabbing miniature and locket and pressing the former haphazardly back into its place. "That was my mother," she said, trying not to show how shaken she felt.

Mrs. Davenant stared up at her, her gray eyes all but black. "Yes, your mother. Lottie."

"No," said Emily, beginning to lose patience. "My mother was Lucy. Lucy Fenty."

"Lucy, Lottie. Jonathan Fenty's girl. Only she wasn't. First they said she was Portuguese and then they passed her off as Fenty's. I'd like to say I knew, but I didn't. Not until the day of the fire, when Jenny . . ." Mrs. Davenant's face twisted with pain and grief. "My Jenny."

"My mother was Jonathan Fenty's daughter," said Emily. Never mind that she wasn't sure whose child her mother was. Augustus Boland's, most likely. "She can't have been the little Portuguese girl. Lottie? She died in the fire. George told me."

"And how would George know? He knows only what he's been told. He wasn't there." Mrs. Davenant grasped Emily's wrist, her fingers surprisingly strong. "I was there. I was there."

"I don't understand," said Emily. Mrs. Davenant's fingers encircled her wrist like a manacle.

"Don't you think I didn't know who you were from the first?" It ought to have sounded mad, but it didn't. Beneath the fever glow, Mrs. Davenant's eyes were clear, clear and intent on Emily's face. "I was there. I was there and I saw. I saw Jonathan Fenty steal her away. . . ."

Chapter Twenty-Eight

Christ Church, Barbados
April 1816

"Jenny!" There was no answer from within, only the crackle of the flames. "Jenny!"

Mary Anne darted forward but the flames were licking up, catching onto the wood panels of the walls, making the canvas of old portraits sizzle. She couldn't see Jenny through the flames, couldn't see if she had been hit or had made it through.

Outside, she could hear the shout of "Fire! Fire!"

Mary Anne hesitated a moment, and then gathered up her skirts and ran out the front. People were running about, some with buckets, some with silver, some throwing water on the flames, others fleeing.

Mary Anne grabbed at the first slave she came across, pulling at his arm. "My maid—she's in there."

The man didn't so much as pause.

Mary Anne tried grabbing at someone else. "I order you to—"

But the man yanked away, hurrying with his bucket toward the blaze.

There were doors in the back, she knew, somewhere, doors on the garden side, doors out to the veranda, doors, doors, doors, more and more being engulfed in flames as the futile trickles of water did little to damp the rapacity of the fire. Ash blew on the wind, stinging her cheeks and hair, making her bat at the embers on her dress. The scent of burning cane singed her nostrils and made her cough into the fold of her shawl.

"Jenny!" She couldn't be gone, not Jenny, her Jenny. Mary Anne ran around the side of the house and saw Charles hurrying toward her, toward the house, his face haggard, a gash over one eye.

"Charles!" The word came out a sob of relief. "Thank goodness. My Jenny—she's in there. She might be hurt. Please, please, send someone in for her."

"Jenny?" To her dying day, she would never forget the look on Charles's face, horror, stark and dreadful.

Without another word, he turned and plunged toward the house, into the flames.

"Charles! What are you—" He was gone, through what had once been a door and was now a gaping maw to hell, spitting ash and fire.

The flames flared up; stones fell from one of the great gables, landing with a crash on what once had been a flagstone terrace. Mary Anne felt as though her world was collapsing around her in the same way, stone by stone, tumbling to the ground, as a horrible suspicion overtook her, clear as day in the light of the fire, in the memory of Charles's horror-struck face, of Jenny's agitated cry.

My baby, she had said. *Lottie. My baby.*

And Charles . . . Charles . . . running into the fire . . .

A window burst from the flames, glass exploding across the lawn, and Mary Anne turned and ran, ran for the stables, for her carriage. The air was bright with flame and dark with soot; the smell of burnt cane was smothering. She lowered her head into the crook of her shawl, fighting her way through to the stable yard, where she was met by the sound of confusion.

A horse reared by her, hooves pawing the air, before plunging madly off, nearly missing kicking her.

The stable boys were running this way and that, trying to calm the horrified horses, but to no avail.

Mary Anne got a hold of herself and grabbed at a bridle. She was a good rider, wasn't she? She'd ride back to Beckles. Beckles and Edward. Fear seized her, but she refused to acknowledge it. Her people would stand fast, she was sure of it. Well, mostly sure of it.

The horse flung back his head, snatching the bridle out of her hand, scoring the skin. Mary Anne barely noticed. She launched herself blindly at another and found herself staring at a booted foot.

She looked up, her eyes streaming in the smoke, and saw Jonathan Fenty, holding the reins in one hand, the other arm clamped around a blanket-wrapped bundle from which emerged a pair of wide blue eyes and dark curls tied up in blue ribbons.

"Where do you think you're going with her?" Mary Anne grabbed at his boot, saying the first thing that came to mind. "That's my property you're making off with."

Fenty's riding crop flicked down, not hard, just enough to make her snatch her hand. "Don't you dare," he said, bringing his horse back under control with effort.

"Unker Johnny . . ."

"Hush, lamb," he said.

Anger boiled up in Mary Anne, anger and fear and loss, all mixed together, bubbling and poisonous. "She's not your lamb," she said sharply. "She's my property, and she's coming back to Beckles with me."

Fenty tucked Lottie's head into his arm, shielding her. "Stay away from her."

The horse sidled and a boy grabbed it, Fenty's groom, one of the slaves she'd leased to Charles, Paris or Rome or something of that sort.

She couldn't be outfaced like this, not in front of one of her own slaves. Mary Anne grabbed at the stirrup. "Don't be absurd. Get down from there and give me the horse and the girl and I won't have you up for theft."

"You won't have me up for anything, you poisonous hag. Not unless you want everyone to know the truth about you." Mary Anne couldn't help it, she stiffened, and saw the triumph in Fenty's eyes. "I'll do it too."

"I can't imagine what you're talking about." He was bluffing, bluffing, he had to be. Robert, lying in a pool of blood. The writing desk heavy in her hands. Jenny, clutching Edward. "You're bluffing."

"Do you want to take that gamble?" Behind Jonathan, the night was orange and black. The horse reared in fear, the boy, with difficulty, holding him steady. "I didn't think so. We'll be going now."

"No!" Mary Anne was too angry to think clearly.

This was Jenny's girl, her Jenny's girl, Jenny, who had lied to her, had kept secrets from her. Jenny owed her this. Oh God, Jenny. And beneath it all, the gnawing worry. Would Jenny have told? It was only a Redleg's word against hers, but rumors had a tendency to spread. And who knew what MacAndrews might say in his cups if pressed?

"Charles went in after her, did you know that?" Mary Anne tossed at him. "They're both dead."

That hit him. He closed his eyes for a moment and held the girl a little tighter. "A bad end to a bad business. And it would none of it have happened if you'd shown a little human kindness."

"Me?" Human kindness? This was her fault now.

"We're going now. If you follow us, if you make any trouble for us, I'll blazon your secrets to the world." Fenty glanced over his shoulder, at the house, which was burning merrily. "I'll make you a deal. You leave us alone, I'll leave you alone. And hi! London!"

The boy stood to attention. "Master Jonathan?"

He's not your master, Mary Anne wanted to spit. He's just a jumped-up bakkra. But her throat was gritty with smoke and her eyes were sticky with smuts and there were no words, no words at all.

Fenty looked down at the boy, his smoke-grimed face and low-brimmed hat giving him the look of a pirate. "What would you say if I told you I was bringing my sister's child to Antigua with me?"

"I'd say it's good to care for family, Master Jonathan."

Fenty extracted a purse from his pocket and tossed it to the boy. To Mary Anne he said hoarsely, "I'm buying his freedom. That will cover his price and the manumission fees. You're free now, boy. And not a word of this to anyone. You'll see it done?"

She hated him. She hated him more than she'd hated anyone. But the boy, London, was watching her, his eyes bright, clutching that purse for dear life. "I'll see it done," she said, her voice choked with smoke and rage. "Now get out and take that foreign brat with you before I call the law on you."

"The law is busy tonight," said Fenty, and he had the nerve, the absolute nerve, to tip his hat to her in passing, as the horse cantered away, out of the stable yard, her Jenny's daughter, her property, snuggled neatly in the crook of his arm.

"You!" Mary Anne snapped at London. "What are you looking at? Get me a horse! Now!"

"Yes, mistress," he said, and, miraculously, he found her a horse and helped her mount.

Mary Anne spared a thought for Charles, but it was too late for him; the towers of Peverills were toppling, generations gone in a moment. She leaned hard over the mane of her horse and rode as she hadn't ridden since she was a girl, her silk skirts hitched up around her knees, riding without saddle or bridle, the smoke in her nose and her hair, the sound of shouting in her ears.

She kept her eyes trained for plumes of smoke, but the air grew clearer as they rode south. Lights blossomed in the house as she pounded up the drive, and she could have cried to see that they were the normal light of candles, not great gusts of flame.

"Rioters at Peverills," she said shortly to Prince Robert, the steward, as he came hurrying out, fuddled with sleep. "See the silver's hidden and the household ready to take arms, if need be."

For a moment, she wondered, if they took arms, would it be for her? But no, that was absurd. Of course they would. Wouldn't they?

"The vandals have torched the cane fields," she said shortly. "The militia's out. They'll make short work of them."

Just in case anyone had any ideas. She wasn't sure whether the militia was out or not, but they ought to be.

She spared a thought for Robert, Robert who had been so handsome in his militia uniform once upon a time. How he would have loved this. He would have donned his brass-embellished coat and flung himself on his horse and gamboled off, delighted with the chance for action. His portrait seemed to smile at her, forever young, forever handsome. On the opposite wall, there was Jenny, holding her shawl and her fan, Jenny, always behind her, always waiting.

Mary Anne sank down into a chair and buried her head in her knees. All her hopes, everyone she had ever cared about, all turned to ash, all gone, all dead.

She hadn't meant to hurt him. She had never meant to hurt him. But when he grabbed her like that, when he pushed her—what else was she to have done?

And Jenny. Jenny.

The tears dripping down onto her hands were black, black as shame. Mary Anne touched them with a trembling finger, half wondering if this was a sort of judgment, before realizing that it was soot, soot from the fire, that her face and her dress were caked with it, that it was matted in her hair and caught beneath her nails.

The reality of it, that ash, hit her like the falling stones of Peverills, and she lowered her face into her hands and let the grief and sorrow take her. Robert and Jenny and Charles and Lottie . . .

"Mistress?" A hand touched her back, and for a moment wild hope surged through her, Jenny, escaped from the fire, Jenny, returned to her, and she'd make it right this time, she'd scold her for lying, of course, but she'd tell her she was forgiven and they would start over again, together, and she'd find Jenny a nice husband, a good husband, and maybe, maybe, she would even free her if she liked, if she would stay close, just so long as she was alive, alive and unharmed. "Mistress?"

But it was only Queenie, looking anxious and very, very young, and, most important, not Jenny.

Mary Anne pressed her hands to her mouth, choking a howl of grief. "It's Master Charles," she managed. "Peverills is burnt, and Master Charles with it."

Let them think she was crying for Charles, not Jenny, oh Jenny. There was a jagged hole where Jenny had been, all blighted earth and scorched ground. She couldn't remember a time when there hadn't been Jenny, standing behind her, brushing her hair, offering her counsel she was too proud to take.

She wanted to crush the face of the clock, to take the hands and turn them back, to make everything right, to bring back Robert in his militia uniform, Charles, with his absurd dreams, but, most of all, Jenny, her Jenny.

"Mistress, come away," said Queenie, and Mary Anne let herself be led away, hunched and hobbling like an old woman, ash in her hair and in her mouth.

She let Queenie help her into the bath, and watched as the soot sluiced down around her, rinsing out of her hair and off her face, turning the water gray, then black. She stood as Queenie dried her, and held her arms up so that Queenie could put a clean shift over her head, and submitted to being led into the bed she had once, so briefly, shared with Robert.

Gone, gone, all gone.

She slept badly, and her dreams were dreams of riot and flame. Beckles was burning and Edward in it and Jenny only stood there and watched and watched and when Mary Anne reached for her she was gone.

She woke with the taste of soot in her mouth, her throat so raw she could hardly speak.

Mary Anne dressed in a red day dress, banded with blue, and set about the motions of living. She ate a breakfast that tasted of nothing and reviewed books that seemed to be composed of jots and squiggles. Reports came from other plantations. There had been deviltry in the night. Thousands of slaves were up in arms. The cane fields were burning. Martial law had been declared. The militia was out, rounding up the perpetrators. Rum, sugar, wine, corn, jewels, and plate had been looted and discarded, strewn about the roads.

But Beckles, Beckles had been spared. The trouble had passed Beckles by. Mary Anne tried to take comfort in that. But her eyes stung, all the same, and her hand shook too badly to hold her pen.

"I'll see myself in." Mary Anne's head came up at the sound of the voice, raw and smoke-stung though it was.

"Charles?" She would never have known him. His clothes were little more than rags. There was a raw and ugly burn on one arm. His hair was gray with soot, adding twenty years to his age. He looked as though he'd come from the siege of Troy, and it had gone ill with him. Mary Anne stumbled from her seat and hurried to him. "Your arm! I've a salve for that."

Charles shook his head, as though his ears were still ringing. His voice was the merest rasp. "I've come to beg a bed and a bath. Peverills is gone."

Mary Anne's chest felt very tight. "And Jenny?"

"Gone. The east wing burned to the ground."

Mary Anne's fist pressed against her lips. It wasn't true; she wouldn't let it be true. "Did they find—was she—are you sure?"

"There were so many—so many trapped— Their bodies— Oh God." Charles's voice broke. "Lottie was sleeping in there."

"Oh, Charles." Mary Anne put a hand on his arm, not sure what to say. Last night, she'd thought Charles dead. Fenty—he was probably already gone to Antigua. What good would it do to get him back now? "Oh, Charles. I'm so very sorry."

"Why didn't I go to her? I ought to have thought—I didn't think. I never thought they would fire the house. I thought I could talk to them—reason with them—" His eyes were very blue in his soot-grimed face. "Someone told me—someone told me that they were meant to be burning Beckles and sparing Peverills. But the message got garbled."

"Oh," said Mary Anne, feeling an overwhelming surge of gratitude for the incompetence of the insurgents. If Edward had been caught, asleep . . . It wasn't to be thought of. "Oh, Charles. You know you can stay with us at Beckles as long as you like."

Charles buried his face in his hands. "I killed her, Mary Anne. My baby. My Lottie."

Mary Anne put a hand on his arm, feeling deeply ineffectual. Now was the time to tell him that she knew, that she'd guessed. Now was the time to tell him that Lottie was alive and safe, with that thief and bully Jonathan Fenty.

But instead, she said, "Charles. Charles. There's nothing to be done now." He looked up at her blindly, not seeing her, and Mary Anne said, with more confidence, "You'll start again. Don't they say something or other rises up out of the ashes? Maybe it's a blessing?"

"A *blessing*?"

The thought of Jenny smote her, but she pushed on. If Jenny and Charles hadn't lied—well, none of this need have happened. Lottie would have been safe at Beckles, learning the art of cleaning silks and doing hair. And really, it was for the best for Charles. If he knew Lottie was alive, he would go after her, and how would he forget Jenny then? He hadn't really known Jenny, not like Mary Anne had.

It was absurd for him to wear the willow over her, but that's what he would do unless he was pushed to abandon his grief and make something of himself. That's the sort of man he was. If she had to take it on her own conscience to see him free of the past, that was what she would do.

Besides, she didn't trust Fenty not to make good his word. Not that she really thought he could bring a case against her for murder, not now, but it wasn't something she particularly wanted to test.

"You're young yet," said Mary Anne bracingly. "You can rebuild Peverills. You'll marry, have other children."

Charles flung away from her, looking at her with undisguised loathing. "Peverills can rot. It's brought me nothing but misery."

It brought him thousands of dollars a year, but Mary Anne didn't think Charles would necessarily appreciate that observation, not in the mood he was in.

"A little time away might do you good," she said, doing her best to sound supportive and understanding, even if she did think a stronger man would stand and face his losses and not go running away to be coddled and consoled with port and beef dinners. "You'll want a good manager for Peverills while you're gone, and you'll need to leave instructions about rebuilding. . . ."

"I'm not rebuilding," said Charles shortly. "I mean it, Mary Anne. I'm done."

It was on the tip of her tongue to say something about Jenny, about knowing. But Edward came running in, the end of a hobby horse bumping against the floor behind him. He'd recently graduated from dresses to a skeleton suit, in blue serge with a white collar, his golden curls shining around his face.

"Mama, where Jenny?" he demanded imperiously. "Want Jenny."

A choking sound emerged from Charles's throat.

Edward looked from one grown-up to the other, confused. He tightened his stranglehold on the hobby horse's neck and sidled over to her, tugging at her skirt.

"Mama. Mama, why Uncle Charles cry?"

CHAPTER TWENTY-NINE

Christ Church, Barbados
August 1854

DRIED TEARS MADE tracks down Mrs. Davenant's cheeks as she slept.

Emily heaved herself up from her chair, every muscle in her body sore. Her dress was sticky with old sweat; her eyes felt fusty. The woman in the bed was sleeping now, her breath rattling in her throat as she fought to breathe around the sickness in her lungs.

Lung fever made the elderly wander, Nathaniel had said. For a wandering person, Mrs. Davenant had come back, again and again, to the same story. There had been justifications and arguments; there had been moments when Mrs. Davenant knew her and others when she had called her Jenny and alternately berated her for lying and pleaded with her for forgiveness, with rather more berating than pleading. The shade of Charles Davenant had been with them; Mrs. Davenant had carried on one-sided conversations with him, some cajoling, some defensive. But all had, in the end, come to the same thing.

A child had been taken away, and Mrs. Davenant had lied about it and pretended that the child had died.

Not just a child. Lottie St. Aubyn.

Lottie. Lucy. Lucy. Lottie.

Emily's stomach grumbled, and she realized it had been some time since she had last eaten. She had partaken of bread and cheese in the carriage on the way to Beckles. Had it truly been that long? Her stomach thought so.

Food. She would get some food and a nice strong cup of tea and then she would go and do something useful in the infirmary, where there were people, real people, sick people, who needed her.

But she paused, all the same, looking down at Mrs. Davenant, at that willful face, slack with sleep, and felt a combination of pity and horror, so strong that it choked her.

To carry something like that, all one's life . . . How could one do it?

But perhaps, Emily thought numbly, having the lives of hundreds of souls in one's hands numbed the conscience. Perhaps it was something about the institution of slavery that made the impossible possible and the horrible mundane. If one regularly traded in people, what was one more child separated from her parents?

She put her hands to her temples. Food, she reminded herself. And a clean dress. She was still wearing the same dress she'd put on yesterday morning to come from Bridgetown. It was one of Mrs. Turner's, sadly worn and stained now. She would have to try to make it good, although she doubted Mrs. Turner would want it back now, no matter how she scrubbed at the stains.

Queenie was waiting to take her turn at Mrs. Davenant's bedside. Mechanically, Emily apprised her of the patient's progress. It was easier to think of Mrs. Davenant as that, as the patient.

Emily's clothes were in the wardrobe where she'd left them. Emily selected one of her own dresses, plain gray serge, entirely inappropriate for the climate, but hers.

She looked at herself in the mirror, a different person from the girl who had last stood at this same glass, almost three months since. Thinner, her face drawn, the cheekbones more prominent, the eyes shadowed from long nights and care. The face of a woman, not a girl.

Was it her imagination, or did she look more like her mother? She'd always had her father's coloring, his mid-brown hair, his hazel eyes, his round cheeks. But the past month had whittled away at her, leaving hollows in her cheeks that hadn't been there before, making her eyes seem larger, her mouth wider.

Or maybe it was just the expression on her face that made her think of her mother, a watchful determination.

She had always thought her mother looked like her grandmother—or the woman she'd believed her grandmother. Or maybe she'd only thought it because she'd been told so many times, or from the simple fact of their both having dark hair, similarly dressed, and an air of command. Their voices too had been the same, even when they argued; they had the same pitch, the same turns of phrase.

It had never occurred to her to doubt that they might be mother and daughter, any more than she would have doubted her own parentage.

But now . . . Now there were patients who needed her.

Emily hastily pinned on her collar and cuffs and made her way downstairs. She would scrounge a bit of bread and then find Nathaniel in the infirmary. She hoped he'd slept, although she doubted he had. He was too proud to take a bed in the house where he had once been a slave.

If her mother truly was who Mrs. Davenant said, Emily might have been born a slave at Beckles. She might have lived here as a child in one of the huts that made up a village behind the house, as Nathaniel had.

She certainly wouldn't be sleeping in one of the great bedrooms upstairs, waited upon and pampered.

Emily went down the stairs, meaning to go out to the infirmary, but she paused and retraced her steps across the great room, to the portrait of her hostess that hung on one side of the arch that led into the dining room.

It wasn't Mrs. Davenant she looked at, but the woman behind her, the slave, Jenny.

It was nearly impossible to make out anything of her features. She had been painted in a white kerchief and apron. The artist had an uncertain grasp on perspective, but she seemed to be of middle height, taller than Mrs. Davenant, and gracefully built. The artist's technique wasn't good, but he had captured something. There was a dignity about Jenny that even the artist had grasped, just as he had grasped the pugnacious tilt to Mrs. Davenant's chin.

Just beneath Mrs. Davenant's chin, Emily saw something she hadn't noticed before. The glimmer of gold. It was a locket, tied around her neck with a ribbon. A locket, edged in filigree. A locket, in fact, very like the one around Emily's neck.

To Jenny, for her good service . . .

A coincidence. An accident. Maybe her grandfather had taken the locket. Adam had said he'd stolen something, hadn't he? Or might have stolen something.

But if her grandfather were to steal anything, why a locket?

Why a child?

At that rate, how did she even know the woman in the picture was the mysterious Jenny? George had said it might not be anyone at all, might just be the idea of a servant. It was madness to stare at her, searching for some similarity of feature. It was mad, all of it.

Emily held tightly to her locket, striving for reason. She had been prepared to believe that her mother was the child of an unknown Irishman. Why should this be any more incomprehensible than that?

Because her grandmother had been married before, Emily told herself. Because it was perfectly plausible that there might have been a child of that first marriage. This story Mrs. Davenant had told her was a regular mare's nest of lies and subterfuge, as improbable as a princess letting down her hair for a prince to climb up or a maiden dancing all night on a shoe made of glass.

Sometimes the strangest stories were the truest. It was the plausible one had to mistrust, not the improbable.

Emily stared into the face of the woman in the picture, a sick feeling in her stomach, a corrosion that came from within. It wasn't about logic or reason or likelihood. The truth was that she didn't want to believe that might have been her grandmother in the picture, in kerchief and apron. It was one thing to go to a lecture and account herself enlightened, or to host a sewing circle for our brethren in chains, but quite another to imagine oneself in shackles, her will subject to others, bought and sold because of the color of her skin.

Emily looked down at her hands. Her skin looked just the same as it always had. A little redder, perhaps, from all the boiling, with a few shiny spots where she had burned herself and the burn had begun to scar.

But that wouldn't have mattered, not before the emancipation bill. She knew that. It didn't matter if she was as black as coal or as fair as Laura; if her mother had been a slave, she would be too, a lesser being, to be looked down upon and ordered about.

She might have been mocked for her poverty by the girls at Miss Blackwell's, but she had never been looked down upon, not really. She had always been the vicar's daughter, supreme in her domain, Jonathan Fenty's granddaughter, with the aura of a great fortune about her, even if her dress was twice turned.

"Emily!" George hurried across the room, arms out as though he intended to embrace her. Emily took an automatic step back and he checked, reaching for her hands instead, giving them a quick squeeze of welcome. "We were terribly concerned about you, especially after we had the news about Mr. Fenty. I'm so very sorry for your loss."

"Thank you," said Emily. Adam's death felt very far away, something that had happened in another life. Emily was horrified at herself, at her own callousness. Quickly, she said, "I had hoped to spare you at Beckles the infection."

"But the infection came to us all the same." George looked at her anxiously. "My grandmother— Is it the Asiatic cholera?"

"No," said Emily. She could give him that much comfort, at least. It felt so strange to be back at Beckles, back with George, as though no time had passed at all, as though last night, as though all the weeks in Bridgetown, had been nothing but a fever dream. Here, nothing had changed; the room smelled of lemon and wax, not the putrid stench of death.

An illusion, Emily reminded herself, pinching her palms. Death was here. It waited in the pest house, shoved out of sight. It was as though everything around her were a stage set, the painted scenery they had made for their theatricals at Miss Blackwell's, paper thin, with emptiness behind.

George didn't seem to notice anything amiss. "Thank goodness," he said fervently. He looked up at the portrait, seeing only his grandmother, not the dark figure behind her. "I don't know what I'll do once she's gone. It's impossible to imagine Beckles without her."

Emily looked at him, at the closely shaven chin and aristocratic nose. He looked very little like his grandmother, which meant he probably took after the Davenant side. It struck her that they were cousins. His grandfather and hers would have been brothers. If it was true, that was.

He was, she realized, looking at her. "Do I have something on my chin?"

"No," said Emily. And then, "You do love her, don't you?"

"She raised me," George said simply. "She was more a father to me than my father ever was."

Emily turned away, not wanting him to see her face. "We're doing our best, you know. She has the lung fever. It's . . . not good. But she has a strong constitution."

"The strongest," said George, smiling painfully. He grasped her hand, clutching it so hard the bones rubbed together. "Thank you."

"Miss Dawson? Mr. Davenant." Nathaniel stood in the doorway, his hat in his hand.

"Nathaniel—Dr. Braithwaite." Emily retrieved her hand with rather more force than necessary. It seemed, suddenly, imperative to be away from George and the portrait behind her. Her worlds had bumped into one another; she wasn't sure what to do with Nathaniel in the great room at Beckles, any more than she would know what to do with George in the drawing room at Mr. Turner's. Her head ached from lack of sleep. "It was so very kind of you to come all this way. I didn't know what to do with the doctor gone."

"Burn his books and bury his remedies? I saw that butchery he called an infirmary." He waited for a response from Emily, and, when none came, Nathaniel said, in a more dignified tone, "I'll look in on Mrs. Davenant, and then I need to be getting back to Bridgetown."

"You're going?" A moment ago, she had only wanted him gone; now she hated the thought of his leaving.

"Unless you need me to stay." He looked steadily at her, his expression so unguarded that it hurt Emily to look at it.

She dropped her gaze first. "You should have something to eat before you go," she murmured, telling herself it was for Nathaniel's own good, that she shouldn't keep him, that he looked exhausted.

"I can have Cook wrap something up for you," George chimed in cheerfully.

"Yes, that would be best, wouldn't it?" Nathaniel set his hat on his head, looking, suddenly, very remote. "I'm needed in Bridgetown. And you have enough to occupy you here."

"You need a nap," said Emily, stricken with guilt. In contrast to George, he clearly hadn't shaved, or bathed, or slept. His chin was lightly stubbled and his cravat wilted. He had come running all this way for her, and now she'd snubbed him without meaning to. "You look dreadful."

"Thank you," said Nathaniel. He rubbed his eyes with the back of his hand, only succeeding in making them redder. "Don't trouble yourself. I can sleep in the barouche."

"And drive yourself into a case of lung fever or worse? Don't make me come and nurse you."

Nathaniel's weary face lightened a little. "Is that a promise or a threat?"

"A threat," said Emily, trying her best to achieve their old bantering tone. "I'll persecute you with mustard plasters and torment you with castor oil. Truly, you're no use to any of your patients if you fall ill. It was selfish of me to summon you—but I didn't know what else to do."

"It was very good of you to come," said George, moving to stand next to Emily.

"You know you can always call on me," Nathaniel said briskly. "And now, if you'll excuse me . . ."

"Wait!" The word had come out rather too forcefully. Emily modulated her tone, forcing a smile. "Won't you come to the infirmary with me before you go and show me what I need to do to go on?"

"I'll just see Cook about making up that parcel," said George, and departed with a nod for Emily and a slight twitch of the head to Nathaniel, the recognition one gave an old playmate who had been one's slave and who now didn't fit into the social order anywhere at all. Like a dust mote one might flick away.

Is that how Aunt Millicent and Uncle Archie would see her if they knew? As someone less than herself?

"Come along, then. I took the liberty of moving your patients," said Nathaniel, as they moved toward the slave yard and he directed her instead along a side path. "This was the estate manager's house, once."

"When you lived here." It was a spacious white-walled building, built with Georgian simplicity, Beckles in small.

"When I was a slave," Nathaniel countered. He walked forward, his head down, concentrating on his footing. "What happened in Bridgetown . . ."

He seemed to be waiting for her to respond. Emily's mind felt numb. Bridgetown. A lifetime ago. Yesterday. She wanted to be back there with a force that alarmed her.

"What happened in Bridgetown?" she echoed.

Nathaniel's step faltered. He paused, one hand on the veranda rail. Quietly, he said, "The circumstances were unusual, to say the least. You needn't think I'll presume."

The kiss, she realized. He had kissed her. Or she had kissed him. Or a bit of both. Her cheeks colored at the memory and she bit her lip, at a loss. "Presume? I don't— That is—"

"I take it that it wasn't a memorable occurrence." Nathaniel gave her a twisted smile. He plunged ahead, into the house. "That's one way, I suppose. Least said, soonest mended, isn't that the phrase? I've put the men in the old front room. Women and children are upstairs. There's water on the boil in the old kitchen. Come along. Katy's daughter is this way."

Emily stopped him at the foot of the stairs. "Nathaniel, wait. I—"

"Yes?" There was a grandfather clock at the turn of the stair, but it had long since stopped, the hands permanently set at half past three, the pendulum still.

She was bone weary, jittery with exhaustion and confusion, and, for the first time in her life, she had no idea what she wanted. To sleep, perhaps. To be back in Bridgetown, with Nathaniel's arms around her, back when people were dying by the dozen and everything was simple and plain. To be back, before all of this, in Bristol, at her father's hearth, where she was who she was, Mr. Dawson's daughter, Jonathan and Winifred Fenty's granddaughter, with none of this doubt and uncertainty.

I might have been a slave, she could say. But would his face change when he looked at her?

"I should put on an apron," she said lamely.

Nathaniel's face went blank. "Don't worry. This won't take long. I wouldn't want to keep you from Mr. Davenant."

Emily frowned at him. "What is that supposed to mean?"

"I had heard," said Nathaniel, "that there was an understanding. But in Bridgetown, I had thought . . . Never mind."

"An understanding?" She was echoing everything he said like a parrot. She felt slow and stupid, which did nothing for her temper. "You don't think I would have kissed you if—"

He did. He did think that. She could tell, and it horrified her, that he might think that of her.

"They were unusual circumstances in Bridgetown," said Nathaniel, as though he were trying to exonerate her, to explain away a crime that had never occurred. "It's not every day one watches a city collapse around one."

"Do you think my word is such a poor thing as that? If I had pledged myself to Mr. Davenant, I wouldn't have betrayed him for all the crumbling walls of Jericho! No, not for all the plagues of the Bible. But I'm not pledged to Mr. Davenant, I never have been, and I never will be. And what's more, I've told him so."

"You have?"

Emily glared at him. On this, at least, she was on solid ground. "He proposed, I refused. It's as simple as that."

"Is it?" Nathaniel made a jerky gesture with his hands, never taking his eyes off her. "You might be mistress of all this."

"I don't want to be mistress of all this! Which you would know if you had bothered to ask—or if you knew me at all, which you *ought* by now." Emily felt her temper rising, her jangled nerves finally snapping. "And if you thought I was to marry Mr. Davenant, what in heaven's name were you doing kissing me?"

"I wasn't thinking," said Nathaniel honestly. "That is— Oh, bother."

He had kissed her because he wasn't thinking. Emily was rather sure she had just been insulted. She clung to anger, the one emotion that made sense at the moment. "You weren't thinking? That's all you can think to say to me? That you weren't thinking?"

"What was I meant to say? That I love you?" Nathaniel snapped, and then froze, staring at her with an expression of raw panic. "Don't tell me you would have welcomed such a declaration."

Would she? Emily felt frozen, panicked. She hadn't thought about the kiss. She had been busy; there had been cholera, lung fever. . . . She admired Dr. Braithwaite; if she was being honest, she desired him. She had seen enough in her father's parish, had heard enough, to know there was more to married life than thinking of England, but she had never felt it, that burning in the blood, until yesterday, until their kiss.

But would she have welcomed a declaration?

"That wasn't your decision to make for me," Emily said fiercely. "You don't know whether I would have welcomed it or not, because you never made it."

Nathaniel stared at her. "And if I were to tell you I loved you?"

The words were soft, but they seemed to echo around her. Emily's ears were ringing and there were little black spots in front of her eyes that might have been dust motes or might not.

Emily grabbed the banister, feeling the reassuring solidity of mahogany beneath her palm. *If I were to tell you*, he had said. Not *I love you* but *if*.

She took a deep breath and said stringently, "Then I would tell you that I can't reason in hypotheticals. If you loved me—*if* you loved me—you would have the courage to say it, not dance around it like a Frenchman at a ball."

Nathaniel looked at her bemusedly. "A Frenchman at a ball?"

That was what he chose to notice? Emily flapped her hand distractedly. "You know what I mean, all mincing and capering and, oh, I don't know! People are dying, Mrs. Davenant is dying, and you're talking in riddles. If you decide you have something to say to me, you know where to find me."

"People are dying," said Nathaniel, his voice low. Emily wasn't sure whether he was reasoning with himself or her. "Your cousin is dead, Mrs. Davenant is ill. Your emotions are disordered. . . ."

He made her deepest feelings sound like a drunken doxy on a spree at the public house. "Don't you dare presume to lecture me on the state of my emotions. You have no idea what they are. You don't even know your own." It was a case of pot and kettle, but Emily was too angry to acknowledge that. "If you loved me—*if* you loved me—you wouldn't let conventions stand in your way."

"Emily . . ."

She couldn't bear it a moment more. "Don't Emily me. That's Miss Dawson to you, Dr. Braithwaite. I wouldn't want to *presume*." Turning in a fury of starched petticoats so he wouldn't see her tears, Emily said thickly, "Now, if you'll excuse me, I have patients to see to. You can . . . go to Bridgetown."

She stomped up the stairs, leaving Nathaniel standing behind her, trying very hard to contain her mouth, which had an unfortunate tendency to quiver. She dashed the back of her hand against her eyes, feeling like an idiot.

She paused outside the makeshift ward, waiting for the clatter of footsteps behind her. But there were none. Instead, she heard a faint click as the door of the house was closed, very, very softly.

CHAPTER THIRTY

Christ Church, Barbados
August 1854

EMILY FELT AS though the inside had been scooped out of her like a melon.

She folded against the wall, her forehead scraping against the whitewash, her chest convulsing in silent sobs, the tears sliding down her cheeks no matter how much she screwed up her eyes to try to stop them.

All of that, every bit of that miserable, painful scene, had been her own fault. She could blame Nathaniel all she liked, with his hypotheticals and his *if I loved you*, but the truth of the matter was that she had sent him away, because she couldn't bear to admit to herself that she didn't know her own mind.

Would she have welcomed a declaration? The question haunted her. A day ago, in Mr. Turner's drawing room, she thought she would have said yes. In fact, she was almost sure of it. But that was a different day and a different woman. That was Emily Dawson, who knew her own mind.

And heart? Did she know her own heart?

Hearts were more trouble than they were worth. She had, not so very long ago, smiled benignly upon those giddy souls who spoke of falling in love as though it were an infection, who did foolish things and claimed they couldn't help it.

She had hurt Nathaniel. She had hurt Nathaniel and it clawed at her gut because she knew it wasn't his fault but her own. She had called him here, heedlessly, selfishly, and then she had pushed him away because she felt like a porcelain figurine that had been smashed and put back together again with the pieces in all the wrong places, and, if she were being very honest, part of her was angry at him for not being able to see that, for professing to care for her but not being able to look at her and diagnose in a glance the trouble that ailed her, and cure it with the strength of his own surety.

If he loved her.

She wanted him to love her so madly that it wouldn't matter. She wanted him to sweep her doubts away, to be sure enough for both of them.

Emily lifted her head from the wall, a sick taste in her mouth. She had heard that phrase before. It was Laura who had said it, that Adam was sure enough for both of them. Until he wasn't.

How could she expect Nathaniel to know what she wanted, when she didn't? He was never, she realized with a catch in her throat, going to make her decisions for her. That was part of his charm.

Of course, he would never make her decisions for her if she never saw him again.

Drawing in a hiccupping breath, Emily scrubbed her face roughly on her skirt. Bother Nathaniel Braithwaite, bother Mrs. Davenant, bother everybody. She had basins to empty.

Emily threw herself into her work. There was no time for brooding when there was refuse to be dealt with, some so foul that even a cologne-soaked handkerchief wasn't enough to stop her retching quietly behind the old manager's house. But even the satisfaction of hard labor failed to distract her.

Mrs. Davenant had sunk into insensibility, her wasted frame shaking with coughs, shivering despite the heat. Emily left Mrs. Davenant to Queenie as much as she could, spending her time in the old overseer's house instead, where the cholera raged on.

Emily lost one patient, an elderly man Mrs. Davenant had referred to as Prince Robert. But Katy's daughter recovered, and Emily had the satisfaction of seeing Katy's face as she brought the little girl into their house in the yard, walking unsteadily, small body wasted from the disease, more bone than flesh, but alive, alive and sensible.

Emily watched them together and thought of her own mother, who had been passed from person to person, hidden and renamed and renamed again.

"Why Lucy?" Laura asked. "Was it a family name?"

"No," said Emily. "My grandfather's mother's name was Sarah."

In the end, she had found herself pouring out the whole story to Laura, Laura, who, despite the inconveniences of her advanced pregnancy, had quietly but firmly taken over the running of the household in Mrs. Davenant's absence.

"My grandfather always said that it was because Lucy meant light, and my mother had been born in a country where the sun always shone." Emily had always thought that very poetic and had been mildly disappointed as a child to learn that she had been named, prosaically, after her father's mother, who kept chickens and occasionally took in boarders. "But now I wonder . . ."

"Yes?" Laura poured her more tea, brewed just the way Emily liked it, in a cup large enough to hold more than just a few genteel sips.

Emily took the cup gratefully, trying to organize her thoughts. "Well, Lottie and Lucy sound rather similar, don't they? And if my mother was quite young . . ."

"She might have been young enough to accept it as her name," Laura finished thoughtfully, setting the tea things back just so. "Yes, I see that."

"Or it might have been how it sounded when she said it," said Emily. "If she was old enough to talk. It would make it less strange than choosing another name entirely."

"And so she went from Lottie to Lucy," said Laura, rubbing the mound of her stomach, where the baby was heaving and kicking as though trying to be part of the conversation. "That poor woman."

"My mother?" There were many things one might say of Emily's mother, but she tended not to inspire pity.

Laura looked up at her, a hand on her stomach. "No, her mother. What did you say her name was? Jenny."

"She died in the fire." Mrs. Davenant had been very clear about that.

"Yes, I know, but what about all the time before? To have a child and not be able to own it—it's beastly. Your mother had your grandparents to love her. But that poor woman . . ." Laura shook her head, blinking back tears. "Goodness, this baby is turning me into a watering pot."

They drank their tea in silence for a moment, each lost in her own thoughts, until Emily said, "But what do I do? Now that I know . . ."

"There isn't really much you can do, is there?" Laura contemplated a lump of sugar, wrinkled her nose at it, and set it aside. "Perhaps had you known as a child that you weren't who you were, it might have changed the way you saw yourself, but you didn't. By now your character is formed. I can't imagine anyone who knew you would say otherwise."

"Thank you?" said Emily, not entirely sure that was a compliment.

"Of course you are who you are. That's not what I meant at all. It's only your grandparents who weren't who you thought they were. And even then . . . Your grandparents were your grandparents for all practical purposes. They loved you and helped raise you."

"But my blood isn't theirs." Emily kept looking at mirrors as though she might see a difference, but she remained, stubbornly, herself.

"What's blood when it comes to it?" Laura turned her cup around in her saucer, once, then twice. "I don't believe it's blood that makes a family. My mother never bothered with that. I'm far more your sister than I am my mother's daughter. That was one of the more compelling reasons for marriage, to be your cousin in truth."

"We would have been sisters even if you hadn't married Adam," said

Emily, and then looked up with a grimace. "Which is what you meant, isn't it?"

Laura nodded. "Your grandfather loved your mother and your mother loved you. It's your mother's real parents I keep thinking about, how they must have suffered, particularly her mother. To carry someone inside you, so close to you, and then have her taken away . . . A great wrong was done, but it wasn't to you."

And all because of the woman gasping for life in the great bed upstairs.

Emily knew her grandfather—the man who had acted as her grandfather—had some part in the tragedy too. But Jonathan Fenty had done what he had done out of love, to save her mother growing up a slave. If there had been some selfishness in that love, there had been sacrifice too. Emily wasn't at all sure what the penalties were for stealing a slave, but she suspected they weren't light. If nothing else, her grandfather's reputation would have been ruined. He, ambitious as he was, would never have been able to do business in Barbados again.

She came again and again to the painting of Jenny, standing behind Mrs. Davenant, Jenny, who had died trying to save the child she had never been allowed to acknowledge.

"I understand now why my grandfather wanted me to have Peverills. It was his way of making things right, giving me what he thought was my birthright."

"Isn't it?" said Laura practically.

"Not legally," said Emily. She thought about George Davenant, about the other Davenants in Bridgetown he had called not really Davenants at all. "Morally, perhaps? Charles Davenant wanted his daughter to have Peverills, that much is clear. Or he would never have gone to such lengths to make her—well, not legitimate, but as close as he could."

Laura tested her tea. "Do you think your mother knew?"

"I doubt it." Emily thought of her mother, her anti-slavery groups, her pamphlets, her meetings, her triumph when emancipation had finally been secured. "I rather think she would have shouted it from the rooftops had she known and gone on lecture tours on the strength of it. But it does still seem odd that she should have taken up the cause she did."

"The Lord works in His own ways," said Laura. "Will you? Tell people, I mean."

"I don't mean to go on lecture tours"—unless someone asked her, of course—"but I shouldn't want to keep it a secret. That wouldn't be right." Emily looked at Laura, trying to put her tangled thoughts into words. She didn't want to minimize the efforts of the grandparents who had raised first her mother and then her. She was beginning to realize, more and more, just how much they had done for her, how much they had cared. But it felt grievously wrong not to acknowledge the grandparents who had never had a chance to see their child grow or hold their only grandchild. She knew so little of them. Would they have liked her? It seemed a silly thing to think about, but she did, all the same. "I don't want to repudiate either set of my grandparents."

Laura nodded. "Some people might snub you, of course, if they knew, but I can't see that bothering you."

"No," said Emily. "They're the same sort who used to snub me for being poor and wearing the wrong sorts of clothes."

"And you had no patience for them then," said Laura. "So I don't see why you would mind them now."

"No." It seemed strange that it was Laura, Laura, whom she had always believed so conventional, so timid, who would cut through all her concerns and put it so simply. But then, maybe there was something to be said for novel reading. "I do worry a bit about Aunt Millicent and Uncle Archibald, that they might think I don't belong to them anymore—but I don't imagine they'd truly disown me. We're too much in the habit of each other. And I'm not sure I mean to go back to Bristol, not to stay."

"Do you mean to stay in Barbados, then?" Laura busied herself with the tea things. "I know there was talk of your marrying Mr. Davenant. . . ."

"Not you too!" Emily grimaced to show Laura she didn't mean it. "That's Mrs. Davenant's scheme. Mr. Davenant and I would be as ill-suited as—" She broke off as she realized the colossal indelicacy of what she had been about to say.

"As Adam and I? It's all right. I don't mind. Oh, how clumsy of me." Laura waved away Emily's help and retrieved the spoon she had dropped, the effort making her cheeks rather pink. "I never did think you and Mr. Davenant would suit. Is it Peverills, then?"

"No." Peverills wasn't what was keeping her here. "It's Dr. Braithwaite."

"Mr. Turner's nephew?" For a moment, Laura looked nonplussed. Then she regarded Emily thoughtfully. "I ought to have known when you wouldn't speak of your time in Bridgetown."

"It was a cholera epidemic. I was hardly going to write to you about boils and bedpans," said Emily defensively. "Dr. Braithwaite is the nephew of Grandfather's oldest business partner—and a doctor. In any other circumstances, he would be accounted a very good match for a vicar's daughter."

But for the color of his skin. But then, what was skin but a covering for bone? It would be nice if the rest of the world felt that way.

Laura took Emily's hands in hers, the gold of her wedding ring very bright against her fair skin. "You are not any vicar's daughter. You're Emily Dawson. You have always gone your own way, and you would be wrong to go any other. Besides," Laura added, her lips loosening into a smile, "I always did think you would fall in love with a physician."

"Not the curate?" said Emily, sniffing a bit and trying to hide it.

"Never the curate," said Laura firmly. Releasing Emily's hands, she said lightly, "Did I tell you I've decided on a name for the baby?"

"Have you?" Emily rubbed at a speck of something in her eye. It was dreadful the way sugar dust got everywhere.

"If it's a boy," said Laura, "I shall call him Emil, and you shall stand godmother."

"Emil?" Emily thought the name dreadful, but, for once, she couldn't find it in her to interfere. If Laura wanted to name her child Esmerelda

Hepzibah Tiddly-Wink or Praise-God Barebones, she would stand there at the font and see it done.

Emily was deeply chagrined at how she had misjudged her oldest friend, how she had misjudged everyone, really. She had dismissed Adam as the carefree scapegrace he had always seemed, when, in truth, he had been riven with the anxious need to make something of himself.

She had prided herself on knowing Laura better than anyone, and yet. She had taken Laura's quietness for weakness, just as she had accepted Mrs. Davenant's assertiveness for strength.

But was it strength, really? It struck her now it wasn't so much strength as selfishness, a blind clinging to what she believed to be hers, and Emily had the uncomfortable feeling that she had been guilty of the same.

She had resented Adam taking Laura from her and Laura taking Adam, not because she had loved Adam, not in that way, but because they had both been hers and she had wanted to come first. She had blamed her father for abandoning the memory of her mother, had looked down on him for marrying again, and dismissed it as the need of a weak character for a stronger. But maybe it wasn't her father who had been weak at all. Maybe it was she. It was easier to blame others than look hard at oneself and see all the spongy bits in one's soul.

She had prided herself so on her common sense, when it wasn't common sense at all, but complacency, a willful refusal to look at anything she didn't want to see.

She was looking now, and the horrible truth was that she didn't much like what she saw.

She went over every excruciating exchange she had ever had with Nathaniel, every thoughtless, prideful, insensitive thing she had said. She cringed at the memory of it. The Bristol and Clifton Ladies' Anti-Slavery Society, indeed. Somehow, knowing that her own grandmother had been a slave, that, but for a bit of sleight of hand, her mother would have been a slave, made sitting at a few meetings and listening to Mr. Frederick Douglass speak seem very thin, indeed.

As the cholera in Bridgetown waned and then disappeared entirely, Nathaniel had resumed his weekly clinic at Peverills. Or so Emily was told. Half a dozen times she reached for her riding habit, and half a dozen times she thought better of it.

She had been smug, prideful, obtuse. She had blamed him for not blazoning his feelings on his sleeve, when she had scarcely been willing to face her own. She was the worst sort of hypocrite and it was no wonder he hadn't written or called.

"You could write to him," suggested Laura.

"But what if he doesn't want to receive a letter from me?"

"Then he can return it unread." When Emily only looked at her, Laura sighed and went back to counting linen.

Slowly, slowly, against all expectations, Mrs. Davenant had begun to mend. On a sunny day in October, six weeks after Mrs. Davenant had descended into insensibility, Queenie came to tell Emily that Mrs. Davenant was sitting up in bed, demanding tea and Emily.

"She knew me," said Queenie significantly, as she led Emily into the room, which had the indefinable smell of the sickroom. "It's the first time she woke up and knew me."

"Of course I knew you. Why wouldn't I know you? Leave us," Mrs. Davenant told Queenie, who raised her brows but went. Mrs. Davenant beckoned Emily peremptorily to her bedside, saying without preamble, "I said a great many things when I was sick, didn't I?"

"Yes." Emily stood by the bed, not wanting to sit down.

"I told you about the child."

The child, as though her mother had been a pawn rather than a person. It was an absurd thought. Her mother had been very much a person, one of the strongest people Emily knew. "My mother, you mean? Yes."

Mrs. Davenant smiled grimly. "You think I was wrong, don't you? Do you think you'd be sitting here in silk and lace if I hadn't done what I'd done?"

Emily wasn't wearing silk and lace; she was wearing poplin and cotton. And that certainly wasn't the way Mrs. Davenant had told the story when she was half-mad with fever.

"It's hard to tell what might have been," said Emily. "But it seems very cruel to let a father think his child burned to death."

"Crueler to tell him otherwise." Mrs. Davenant tried to raise herself on her elbows. "You weren't there. You don't know. At the time, I thought it was for the best."

"For the best to let him think she was dead?"

"I set Charles free! He could marry, have children." Mrs. Davenant subsided against the pillows. "He didn't, though. Instead, he left. He gave each of his slaves a gift of money, and then he went to London and he freed them all. It was something that was done then, to save the manumission fees, selling a slave to a friend in England and having the slave freed there. Just seldom on so grand a scale." She looked sideways at Emily. "Natty Cooper—oh, if you must, Dr. Braithwaite, as he's calling himself now—ridiculous cheek!—his uncle had him freed that way. Your grandfather did the honors in England, I believe."

"It seems hard that he died never knowing his daughter had lived," said Emily.

Mrs. Davenant grimaced at her. "Charles? Charles isn't dead. He's alive and living in Paris. He's married now. A Frenchwoman. They have a whole passel of brats, with impossible French names. I know because Edward wrote me. It was Charles my Edward ran to." She was quiet a moment, the only sound her fingers pleating the fabric of the sheets. "It seemed a bit like justice. I took his child and he took mine. An eye for an eye and a child for a child."

It didn't sound at all like justice to Emily; it sounded more like a justification. Edward had chosen his own path; Emily's mother had had no choice. Not to mention the small matter of Charles Davenant never knowing what had happened to his daughter.

"You still have George," Emily pointed out.

"Yes, I still have George." Lifting her head, she fixed Emily with a red-rimmed gray eye. "There's nothing to stop you marrying George."

There were, Emily thought, many things to stop her marrying George.

Through the window, Emily could see Laura and George, her black head bent near his golden one, consulting on some matter of household management. Or possibly on Sir Walter Scott. It might be either.

They were, Emily thought wistfully, very well matched. They would have to wait out the mandated period of mourning of course, but once that was done . . . Disloyal though it might be, she rather hoped Laura and George didn't let Adam get in the way.

Was it disloyal? Or was it just sense to let the living get on with living? The dead were gone, there was no helping them.

Besides, Emily rather suspected that if there was any justice, it would be watching Laura neatly thwart Mrs. Davenant. Mrs. Davenant had no idea.

Mrs. Davenant was waiting for an answer. Emily turned away from the window. "I'm not sure George and I would suit. In fact, I'm quite sure we wouldn't."

"You needn't worry about George. He'll do as he's told." Mrs. Davenant lowered her voice. "He doesn't ever need to know."

It took Emily a moment to realize what Mrs. Davenant was talking about. "About my grandmother being a slave?" she said, and Mrs. Davenant made a hideous face. "Well, she was. I wouldn't lie to the man I meant to marry, about that or anything. That's no way to start a marriage."

Mrs. Davenant gave a choking laugh. "Oh, my dear. That's little you know about marriage. There's none of that meeting-of-minds nonsense. It's a contract for property, and a license for the creation of heirs. Lawful ones. Everything else is better left aside."

"Not for me," said Emily, feeling her jaw set. "I would rather be honest and take the consequences. I couldn't countenance a marriage based on untruths."

"You're a fool," said Mrs. Davenant bluntly. "There were only the four of us left who knew. Charles is gone, Fenty is dead, London Turner won't tell. He didn't tell you, did he? I didn't think so."

"Why did you tell me, then?" Emily demanded.

"I was out of my mind with lung fever. I would hardly have mentioned it had I been in my right mind." Mrs. Davenant sat in silence for a moment. "When you started asking questions about your grandmother—I was just as happy for you to think your mother might be Boland's get, even if he was an Irishman."

"You never meant to tell me, then?"

"Didn't I just say that? It seemed a way of making amends, to have Jenny's granddaughter mistress of Beckles. It was the only thing left I could do for her." Pulling herself together, Mrs. Davenant said in a very different tone, "And, of course, I'd like to see Beckles and Peverills united. Had Lottie lived, I would have seen her married to Edward."

"She did live. She was my mother." Maybe it was the dismissive way Mrs. Davenant waved her hand, but Emily felt her temper rising. "That girl you call 'the child' grew into a force to be reckoned with. She ignored everyone who told her she ought to sit by the fire and work net bags and went out into the world and did everything she could to remedy what she believed to be the world's greatest ill: slavery."

Emily looked pointedly at Mrs. Davenant, who turned her head away on the pillow, making a show of not listening. Well, she would listen, whether she liked it or not. Emily wasn't going to let her shape the world to her making, not anymore, not even here at Beckles, where she was used to reigning supreme.

"My mother," said Emily, her voice ringing through the high-ceilinged room, "corresponded with ministers of Parliament and American presidents. She never, ever let anyone stand in the way of what she believed. She fought to marry my father when my grandfather refused her, even though he was a lowly minister from a poor family and hadn't a penny to his name."

Emily broke off, her whole body shaking, feeling hot and cold by turns.

"You say all of this as though it were a virtue," said Mrs. Davenant acidly.

"It is." The anger had gone, leaving behind it a strange certainty. Emily felt like a convalescent, as though she had been sickening for months and only now was herself again. "It's a virtue to know one's own heart and mind. It saves a lot of bother and a great deal of unhappiness."

For a moment, it was as though she could see her mother there, in the room, behind Mrs. Davenant's dress, her dark hair dressed in the simple knot she had favored, an expensive Kashmir shawl tossed carelessly around her shoulders, her only ornament the simple gold band on her left hand. Her mother had never let herself be distracted by inconsequentials. When she loved, she loved without reservation, without a care for what the world might say.

As her mother's true parents had done before her, regardless of the costs.

"What day is it? It's Thursday, isn't it?" Emily didn't wait for Mrs. Davenant to answer; she was already hurrying to the door.

"How would I know? One day is much the same as another when you're confined to bed." Pillows and sheets shifted as Mrs. Davenant lifted herself on her elbows. "I didn't tell you that you could go! Where do you think you're going?"

Emily paused in the doorway, looking back over her shoulder at the other woman's outraged face. "To Peverills, of course."

CHAPTER THIRTY-ONE

Christ Church, Barbados
October 1854

THERE WAS THE usual huddle of people outside the bookkeeper's house at Peverills, from which Emily concluded that the doctor must be in.

She had ridden out without a groom, without her habit, without a hat. The habit she didn't regret, not really. The hat she did. There were rainbows at the corners of her eyes and her hair felt as though it had been baked into bronze.

Well, Emily thought giddily, tethering her horse to the old lime hedge, that would give her some excuse for her appearance. She could see the doctor for sunstroke.

But that would be a coward's trick, and she had been coward enough already.

Despite her protests that she could wait her turn, it seemed everyone suddenly discovered that their ailments could wait. Twisted wrists weren't that bad after all and the cut wasn't bleeding so very much. Emily dispensed a bit of commonsense advice, said she wouldn't be a moment and not to go away, steeled herself, and marched inside.

Nathaniel was in his consulting room, which looked much as it had when she had visited with George. The kettle still whistled on the fire; needles and knives, shining with cleanliness, had been set out on a cloth. Nathaniel was setting a dislocated shoulder. Emily watched with professional appreciation as he heaved the arm back and snapped it into place, then bound the arm close to the chest. She had seen the operation performed far less gracefully, and she found herself very aware of the movement of the muscles beneath the fine cloth of his coat.

Goodness, that sun had been hot out there. She could feel her cheeks burning. Or maybe that was the fire in the little room, burning and burning away, boiling away disease, making everything clean and new.

The man on the table saw Emily and started to try to clamber down, earning a strong rebuke from the doctor. "Keep it bound like this for the next week. I don't want you lifting anything heavy for the next month. Yes, I know the head driver won't like it. Ask him if he would prefer to lose your services permanently. You won't be much use with no right arm, would you?"

It gradually dawned on Nathaniel that the patient was staring. Slowly, he turned, and the expression of annoyance on his face froze into . . . nothing.

She wasn't quite sure what she had expected, but it wasn't nothing.

"Miss Dawson," he said, and Emily felt her chest twist, painfully. She had been Emily six weeks ago. She had done this. She had demanded he call her Miss Dawson, had wrenched the right to her name from him in a rage.

"Dr. Braithwaite." He had slept since she had last seen him and had a change of linen. Several, she assumed, given that it had been over a month. His cheeks were smoothly shaved, his mustache recently trimmed, and his cravat was bleached and starched to a nicety. He looked impossibly handsome and very urbane. Urbane and entirely remote. They were, Emily realized, doing a very good job of pretending to be statues, only her statue was wearing an elderly morning gown that hadn't benefited from its contact with a horse, and she had, she was quite sure, the beginnings of an impressive sunburn on the end of her nose.

She really ought to have stopped for her hat.

"You can go out now," Dr. Braithwaite told his patient, without looking away from Emily. Recalling himself, he added briskly, "Mind you. No heavy lifting, or don't blame me if you lose the use of that arm. Tell the next patient . . . Tell the next patient I won't be a moment."

Only a moment.

Now that she was here, Emily found herself at a loss for words. The eloquence that had possessed her at Mrs. Davenant's bedside had deserted her in the face of the reality of Nathaniel, the force of the emotions she felt.

"Dr. Braithwaite." He stood there, elegant and remote, waiting for her to say something else, to state her purpose. She probably ought to have prepared a speech on the way over, but she had been too busy hanging on, so Emily blurted out the first thing that came to mind. "How did you come by the name of Braithwaite? Everyone here calls you Cooper."

"Cooper was my slave name. Braithwaite was the name of the family who fostered me in England." His voice was clipped, inflectionless, but a muscle worked in his cheek. "I was a freeman and an Englishman. I wanted a name that reflected that. I had thought it would make me . . . more free. I thought I could change my nature with my name. But the past is never really past, is it? No matter how hard you try to hide from it. I ran all the way to England, I changed the way I spoke, I changed the way I dressed, I changed my name—and yet, here I am."

"You might have gone anywhere, but you didn't." Emily's voice was strangely husky. She cleared her throat and tried again. "I think it's rather splendid of you."

"*Anywhere* is a relative term," said Nathaniel drily. He busied himself with cleaning the table, scrubbing it with more effort than necessary. "To what do I owe the pleasure of this visit? Do you have a medical question?"

Love wasn't a disease, he had told her once. "Here, let me," Emily said, taking the cloth from him. Her hand brushed his. She felt the shock of the contact straight down to her boots. "You—you're stripping the polish off."

Nathaniel took a step back. He was, she noticed, holding one hand in the other, absently rubbing the spot where their hands had touched. "You didn't come to oversee my domestic efforts," he said gruffly.

Emily paused in her scrubbing, forcing herself to look directly at him. "I've decided to sell Peverills," she began.

Nathaniel didn't give her time to go on. He moved jerkily toward the fire, his boot heels sharp against the wood floor. "I suppose you mean to go back to Bristol? I've been thinking of West Africa. There's a mission going to the Rio Pongo. They need a surgeon to make one of the party."

Emily's hands clenched around the cloth, sending dirty water dripping down the front of her dress. She hastily set it down. "Do you truly mean to go?"

"I'm considering it."

No, no, no. This was all wrong. This wasn't at all how this was meant to go. Emily scrubbed her wet hands down the sides of her dress, which really couldn't get much worse at this point. "I hope you won't. I mean to sell Peverills and use the money to found a clinic, a clinic for the treatment of infectious diseases."

Nathaniel had been leaning over the kettle. He paused, his back toward her, saying slowly, "My uncle would tell you that a clinic is hardly a sound investment."

Emily took a half step forward, her heart in her throat. "I don't want to be mistress of a plantation or learn how to turn sugarcane to gold. I have no interest in investing in ships or railroads." It was amazing how eloquent a back could be. From the way he straightened, she could tell he was listening. "You said it yourself, the rules of the hospital don't allow anyone with an infectious disease. But those people need to be treated too. If there were a special infirmary, one designed for the purpose, one could treat those patients properly and save so many others."

Nathaniel turned to look at her, as though trying to decide what to make of her. But all he said was "It's a noble goal."

"I can't do it alone. I'm not a physician—or a surgeon. I had hoped you might be willing." Emily's voice faltered; she felt, suddenly, very unsure. It had all seemed a grand idea back at Beckles. Some people offered flowers as love tokens; she would give her love a clinic. But Nathaniel wasn't rushing to take her hands and press her to his heart. Hesitantly, she said, "Just think of it. You could study the course and cause of the diseases, really study them. That is what you wanted to do. Isn't it?"

Nathaniel made no move toward her. "Is it a salaried position?" he asked.

"I—I had thought of it more as a spousal one." In a rush, Emily added, "Although it doesn't have to be. I intend to found the clinic either way. If you don't want to take the position, I'm sure I can find someone to run it."

"And the spousal position?"

She couldn't be quite sure if he was mocking her. He was much better than she at controlling his emotions. Emily knew everything she felt showed on her face, particularly now. She twisted her hands together. "That isn't open to anyone else. There's only one candidate I would consider for that role."

Nathaniel tilted his head and looked down at her. "Are you proposing to me, Miss Dawson?"

"Not if you would rather I wouldn't. I wouldn't want to do anything that would put you in an uncomfortable position." Emily could feel her cheeks flushing, her tongue tangling, her words falling over each other. It was now or never; her mother, she knew, wouldn't have faltered. She took a deep breath and tried again. "But you should know, if it makes any difference, that I—I love you."

"Do you?"

The room suddenly felt much smaller, shrunk to the two of them. Emily smiled painfully up at him. "It's either that or measles. Although I have it on the best authority that love isn't a medically verified form of death."

"That wasn't my diagnosis; it was Shakespeare's. And he wasn't, so far as I know, a doctor," said Nathaniel slowly, as though working out what to say next. "Emily—"

"I don't think I should die from loving you." Emily knew she had to say it all now, or she never would. "But I should miss you terribly. I have missed you terribly. I admired you before I loved you. I admired your skill as a surgeon. I admired the way you defied anyone who would make you less than you were. But I ought to have known truly what it was—what I felt—when we were in Bridgetown and I ought to have been mourning Adam and instead all I could think of was you. I could tell myself I was happy because I was doing good and useful work—and I was!—but I've been doing the same work here, and without you, I've felt . . ."

"Empty?" suggested Nathaniel. "Flat?"

"Both of those," said Emily. "I would have written you, but I didn't want to—oh, I don't know. Presume, I suppose." It sounded very silly when put that way.

Nathaniel's lips twisted up on one side. "Half the paper in Bridgetown lies crumpled in the wastebasket next to my desk. I almost wrote you, a dozen times. But I wasn't sure you would welcome a letter from me."

Emily bit her lip, hating herself. "I said awful things."

"No. You didn't." Nathaniel's eyes burned brighter than the coals on the fire. Emily found she couldn't look away. "You asked me to have the courage of my convictions. Here it is. I love you. There's no hypothetical in it. I love you. There has never been anyone like you and there will never be again."

"Some would say that's a good thing," said Emily unevenly.

"Then they're fools," said Nathaniel shortly. "I've never believed in this whole falling-in-love business. Fondness, certainly. Affection. But to be swept away by one's emotions and lose one's reason—it seemed like an absurdity. And then you came to Bridgetown."

"Did you lose your reason?" Emily asked, scarcely daring to breathe.

"I must have done," said Nathaniel ruefully. "There I was, in the midst of the cholera, with everyone dying around us, up to my elbows in excrescence, and I've never been happier, because you were there at the end of it."

"Those evenings together—I didn't want them to end."

"Neither did I. When you left for Beckles—the color left the world. Everything was grim and dark, and smelled horrible."

"That was probably because I wasn't there dousing everything with lime," said Emily practically.

"No," said Nathaniel. "It was because you weren't there. As absurd and impractical as it may be, I love you. And because I love you . . ."

"Yes?" Wasn't this the bit where they were meant to be rushing into each other's arms? But Nathaniel stayed, stubbornly, where he was.

Quietly, he said, "I love you well enough not to marry you."

It took Emily a moment for the words to have meaning. "If you love me—" She caught herself up short. He had already told her there was no *if* about it. "If you love me, why wouldn't you marry me? There's no bar to our union. Unless you have a wife left in Edinburgh you neglected to mention."

"No, only a skeleton named Harold. But he's beside the point." Nathaniel rubbed his temples and the simple gesture tore at Emily's heart. "There might be no legal bar. But have you thought of the consequences? I would be asking you to put yourself beyond the pale, to abandon your friends and relations."

"Is that all? I'm rather good at putting myself beyond the pale. I don't need your help with that." When he failed to smile at that, Emily said passionately, "I mean it. I've never cared for society. My parents always took the view that character was what mattered most, and anyone who would shun one out of snobbery wasn't worth knowing."

Reluctantly, Nathaniel shook his head. "You might say that now . . ."

"If you don't want to marry me, if you cannot imagine a life with me, refuse me then. But not for the horridness of others. I don't care for them if you don't." The memory of her parents and grandparents pressed down upon her. Trying to will Nathaniel to understand, Emily said hurriedly, "When Mrs. Davenant was sick, she told me a story about a family broken apart because the law wouldn't allow them to be together. Well, really, because of her. But the point is, they fought to be together, even when it meant lying and deceiving people and risking prison or worse. And we—we're so very lucky. We don't have to hide or pretend to be anybody other than what we are."

"And what are we?" Nathaniel asked, his voice rough.

Emily took a step toward him, her hands twisted in her skirts. "You're Nathaniel Braithwaite, a doctor. And I'm Emily Dawson. My mother was a reformer and my father is a minister and I might be neither of those things, but I'm rather good at tending to sick people."

Nathaniel grasped her hands in his, so hard that she could feel the bones crunch. "I might be tempted to suspect you only want to marry me to have access to a steady stream of patients."

"It is a benefit," admitted Emily, looking up at him, devouring his familiar, beloved face with her eyes. She loved all of him, even that ridiculous mustache. "I want to marry you because I believe you're the only man I could ever bear to live with. And because I love you."

"High praise, indeed." Nathaniel choked on a laugh. "When you put it that way, it all sounds so simple."

"Isn't it? If it's not, it ought to be." He hadn't let go her hands, which Emily took as rather a good sign. "The people who matter to me won't shun me. Laura's door will always be open to me; my uncle and aunt would never turn me away—they haven't yet, despite considerable provocation. As for the rest, aren't I better off without them? I like your family. I don't think they would close their doors on us, would they?"

"One might wish Cousin Bella would."

"Your cousin Bella was an absolute brick," said Emily stoutly.

"A very noisy brick," muttered Nathaniel.

Emily fixed him with a stern look. "I would choose her over the entirety of Miss Blackwell's Academy for Young Ladies. As for the rest, if we're not invited to the governor's next Viennese breakfast, so be it. I wouldn't want to be received by the sort of people who would stop receiving me for marrying you." Emily glanced up at him sideways. "You don't really want to go to West Africa, do you? If you do, I would go with you, but I would far rather stay here. I'm not really the missionary sort."

Nathaniel gave a shout of amusement. "Aren't you? You would have half the village rebuilding their huts and the other half organizing a benevolent society within a week."

"I've given up ordering people about," said Emily.

"No, you haven't," said Nathaniel, looking at her so tenderly that Emily wondered if it was medically possible to melt into a puddle on the spot. "I wouldn't have you any other way. And no. I have no particular interest in going to West Africa. It was purely a means of getting away and leaving you be. I thought that distance might do what time hadn't. Or if worst came to worst, I could contract a strange and interesting disease and make medical history for the manner of my dying. Braithwaite's Disease, they would call it, and you would read about it in the illustrated papers and think of me with a pang of loss."

"Now you're mocking."

Nathaniel squeezed her hands. "Myself, not you. There's your love token, if you like. I was prepared to offer my corpse to you."

"I would prefer you not die of a strange disease, no matter how interesting," said Emily. "In fact, I would prefer you not die of anything at all."

"We all do, eventually," said her practical lover.

"Yes, but not for some time," warned Emily. "I intend to torment you and our children for many years to come."

"Children," said Nathaniel, looking down at her with an expression composed of equal parts wonder and alarm. "Heaven help us. They'll be strong-willed, that's for certain."

There was a tentative knock on the door.

"Oh dear," said Emily, trying to wiggle her hands free. "We left all your patients waiting."

Without letting go, Nathaniel turned his head and said loudly, "We're engaged. Come back tomorrow."

"But what if someone needs you?"

"They can wait," said Nathaniel, and looked at her in a way that made her bodice feel too tight and her clothes altogether too enveloping.

"Unless it's scarlet fever," said Emily, resting her hands against the wool of his waistcoat. She could feel the way his breath rasped in his chest, the way his muscles tightened at her touch. It was rather wonderful. "Or cholera."

"You say the most romantic things," said Nathaniel huskily.

Cupping her face in his hands, he lowered his mouth to hers, kissing her thoroughly and ruthlessly, kissing her in a way that made her bones turn to liquid and her head spin, and the room feel even hotter than it was.

Emily kissed him back, relying on enthusiasm to make up for lack of experience, her hands sliding beneath his waistcoat, reveling in the warmth of his skin through the thin linen of his shirt, kissing his chin, his neck, the cravat that got in her way until he ruthlessly tore it away, buttons loosening, hairpins tumbling to the floor, lips following hands, hands following lips, bodies and hearts in harmony.

When they could speak again, Emily said breathlessly, "*Are* we engaged?"

"After that," said Nathaniel, running his hands up and down her arms as though he couldn't quite bear to let her go, "I should hope so. I'll get a ring and do it properly if you like. Unless you'd rather propose to me?"

"The queen did," said Emily. "Propose to Prince Albert, I mean."

"If it's good enough for the queen . . ." said Nathaniel, laughter in his eyes, looking so amused that there was nothing for Emily to do but kiss him again, to kiss him and kiss him until neither of them was laughing in the slightest.

"I hope you don't want a long engagement," said Nathaniel seriously, resting his forehead against hers. Somehow, they had come to rest on the examining table, all of his carefully cleaned implements fallen willy-nilly on the floor near a smattering of Emily's hairpins, Nathaniel's impossibly wrinkled cravat, and a jacket that was currently missing at least two buttons. "I don't think I could countenance compromising a vicar's daughter."

Her father wasn't really that sort of vicar, but Emily decided it wasn't the time to go into that. "I should think I've compromised you," she said, nodding toward the window, where the very silence told its own story. She couldn't blame anyone for listening at the shutters; she would have done the same. "It's a very good thing you've told them we're engaged or your reputation would be in tatters."

"My reputation?" said Nathaniel, raising a brow. Looking ruefully down at their scattered belongings, he said, "I'm afraid you'll be the talk of the parish. The news will have spread clear to St. Philip by morning."

"You'd best write your uncle, then, before he hears it from someone else." Emily wiggled down from the table, over Nathaniel's protests. "We'll have to tell Laura properly, even if everyone in the parish already knows. And George. And Mrs. Davenant."

Nathaniel grimaced at her. His hair was mussed, his lips swollen, giving him a delightfully rakish air. "Must we?"

"Oh yes." It would, Emily thought, be rather a useful shock to Mrs. Davenant to have her plans thwarted so thoroughly for once. "I don't mean for there to be anything the least bit hole-and-corner about our marriage. We'll have an announcement in the papers and all that's proper."

Nathaniel reached for her, drawing her back to the table. "And then," he said, his breath tickling her ear, "we can get on with being improper."

"Yes," said Emily breathlessly. "That."

A short engagement, she decided, was really a very good idea. She had never understood, back in her days of delivering baskets and good advice, why so many of her father's parish went to their weddings with swollen bellies. She rather thought she understood it better now. Much, much better. St. Paul, Emily decided, had known what he was talking about when he had said it was better to wed than to burn.

"Do you think your uncle would mind if we were wed from his house?" she asked, after some time.

"If he let us set up a hospice for cholera patients . . ." said Nathaniel, and Emily swatted his arm. Undaunted, Nathaniel smoothed back a lock of her hair that had unaccountably freed itself from its pins. "Where should you like to go on our wedding journey?"

A very long time ago, before her grandfather had died, Adam and Laura had meant to go to France on their wedding journey. Thinking of Paris made Emily remember something else.

Wiggling to a sitting position, propping herself up in the lee of Nathaniel's arm, Emily said, "If you don't mind it, I should like to go to Paris."

"I don't mind at all. Aside from the presence of the French, it's quite a nice place."

Emily looked at him with interest. "Have you been?"

"A time or two." Nathaniel stretched his arms above his head, leaning back lazily against the wall. "I consulted with colleagues there. I'm sure my aunt would be delighted to send us an introduction to her milliner and modiste."

Emily made a face at him. "Can you imagine me in French fashions? No, there's someone I need to see, but it's not your aunt's modiste."

"Or her milliner, I take it?" Seeing she was serious, Nathaniel gave her his full attention. "What is it?"

"There's an old wrong I need to set right." It seemed selfish to be quite so happy when, far away in France, Charles Davenant still didn't know that his child had lived, had grown into a woman of character and conviction, loved and beloved. "Do you remember that story I was telling you about, that Mrs. Davenant told me?"

"Something about love despite the odds?" said Nathaniel, taking her left hand in his.

"Yes, that." Taking strength from his touch, Emily took a deep breath and began, "A long time ago, there was a child who was born to a slave woman and hidden away. . . ."

EPILOGUE

Paris, France
November 1832

EDWARD DAVENANT STOOD in the Place des Vosges, the rain dripping off the edges of his hat onto the already soaked shoulders of his greatcoat.

His hands were frozen through. He blew on them to warm them. He really hadn't expected it to be quite so cold. He'd known it wouldn't be hot here, but the sheer bitterness of the weather had taken him by surprise. The raindrops were needles of ice, cutting through his clothes, chilling him to the bone.

Behind him, a beggar was giving him strange looks. Edward was tempted to slink away, but his empty wallet and the rain decided him.

"I'd like to see Mr. Charles Davenant, please," he asked the concierge, speaking very slowly and clearly in what he had once thought was French, but it seemed wasn't, or at least not if the reactions of the Frenchmen he'd met so far were anything to go by.

He had the uncomfortable feeling his grammar wasn't quite right, but Charles Davenant was Charles Davenant was Charles Davenant in any language. Unless he'd changed his name? Edward began to have an uncomfortable feeling in the pit of his stomach, and not just because he hadn't eaten anything since that highly suspicious stew last night.

This had been the address he'd found in his mother's papers, he was sure of it.

"Charles Davenant?" he repeated, calculating the number of coins left in his pocket and the distance between a bed and the gutter.

It was looking more and more like the gutter. He wanted to tell the man that he was the son of one of the wealthiest planters in Barbados, but, in his bedraggled state, he doubted anyone would believe him. Besides, his teeth were chattering too hard to manage English, much less French.

Edward twisted his blue lips into a hopeful smile. "Monsieur Davenant. *Mon oncle?*"

The concierge shrugged and said something in a French that wasn't at all like the French Edward had learned in the schoolroom at Beckles. It was faster and more guttural and entirely incomprehensible, but the man had opened the door, so Edward took his frozen body through the arch and up a flight of stairs paneled in rich, dark wood.

A bas-relief, depicting something out of classical myth, adorned the turn of the stair. The rain pattered against high-set windows. Edward's feet squelched in his inadequate shoes, leaving damp marks behind him.

He was deposited at a paneled door, where a rapid discussion took place with a maidservant, who disappeared and then reappeared again, gesturing Edward to follow. She took him through a richly papered antechamber into a high-ceilinged room with, thank heavens, a coal fire burning away in the grate.

Edward scooted closer, rubbing his hands over the blaze, and then turned to flip up the damp tails of his coat to dry them.

It was in this very undignified pose that he was caught by his host.

"They tell me that you're my nephew, Ned?" said the man. He had blond hair, graying at the temples, and a lined, dignified face. At the moment, the lines had folded into creases of amusement. He gestured toward the fire. "I would have known it anyway, from your eagerness to get warm."

Edward hastily dropped his coattails. "Yes, sir. I mean, I am. I beg your pardon for not writing in advance."

"You always have a welcome here," said his uncle Charles, quite handsomely, Edward thought, given that he didn't know him from Adam. "Allow me to make you known to my wife, your aunt Jeanne."

He'd been so busy being embarrassed at being caught with his nether end up that he hadn't even noticed the woman behind his uncle.

"I say—that is—I'm, er, delighted." Edward tripped over his tongue and his boots.

His mother had never mentioned that his uncle was married. Or that his uncle's wife was a mulatto. Which might, now that he thought of it, be why his mother had never mentioned it. If they were married.

Could one marry colored people in Paris? He supposed one could do anything in Paris. It was, after all, Paris.

Edward stepped forward, prepared to do the pretty. "Thank you for your hospitality, Mrs.—er—Aunt—er—"

His new aunt took his hands, holding them out, looking at him with bemused gray eyes. "Neddy. Little Neddy."

"I'm afraid I don't—that is, you have the advantage of me." Edward felt stupid and gauche, his wet suit of clothes—his only suit of clothes—clinging to him. His uncle's wife was dressed in a claret-colored gown, richly trimmed with whatever those things were with which women trimmed gowns. She was quite beautiful in an old sort of way.

His uncle's wife dropped his hands, taking a step back. "Forgive me. I've heard so much of you from your uncle that I feel as though I know you already."

"Oh," said Edward, at a loss. He had been not quite three when his uncle had left. He had never imagined that he'd left such an impression. "I'd no idea. . . ."

"It's a pleasure to see you grown," said his uncle gravely. "Even if somewhat unexpectedly."

"And rather damp," added his wife.

"I apologize for appearing like this," said Edward stiffly, trying to reclaim the situation. "If you'll point me to a reasonable inn . . ."

"Don't be absurd," said his uncle. "You'll want a hot drink, I expect."

"And a bath," put in his uncle's wife.

Edward felt his cheeks flush. "I, well, I seem to have underestimated how much it would cost to travel," he admitted. "I lost my baggage in Calais."

Lost, he thought, sounded better than stolen. The man had claimed to be a porter, so Edward had given him a coin and his bags and had never seen either again, or the man neither. He couldn't believe he'd been such a flat, but he had, and here he was, wet and miserable with only the clothes on his back and not quite penniless, but close to it. He could just imagine what his mother would say.

"You haven't come as your mother's emissary, have you?" his uncle asked. Edward saw his uncle exchange a look with his wife. "If you're here about Peverills . . ."

"No!" Edward flushed with embarrassment at his own vehemence. "That is, no. I'm not. I've come away on my own account. My mother— she doesn't know I've come."

Whatever happened, he wasn't going back to his mother. Or to Beckles. His wife had cuckolded him with a half-pay officer at St. Ann's Garrison, had dragged his name through the mud and left him shamed, and then had the nerve to tell him she'd never wanted to marry him anyway, a callow youth barely out of the schoolroom. She'd done it because it was the only way out of her parents' house, but if she'd known what life at Beckles would be like, she would have stayed home with her parents and spared herself his fumbling attentions. The very memory of it made Edward hot with shame and resentment.

Did Julia think he'd wanted to marry her? He'd been bullied and badgered into it. She was nearly a decade his senior, the eldest of six daughters. But she came with a piece of land his mother had wanted, and so there they were, yoked together, although they hadn't a word to say to each other and nothing at all in common. He hated them, he hated them both, his mother and Julia, his mother for using him as a pawn and Julia—Julia for not wanting to use him for anything at all.

Edward felt a moment of guilt at the thought of the baby, but that was succeeded by a flush of resentment. His mother had wanted an heir to Beckles so badly, his mother could raise the child. He wasn't falling in with her plans, not ever again, even if he had to run halfway around the world to get away.

"You won't tell my mother, will you?"

"I won't tell her if you don't want me to," said his uncle. He grimaced. "After she hears I've sold Peverills, I expect she won't want to have anything to do with me at all, so I expect you'll be safe."

"You've sold Peverills?" Even in the midst of his own difficulties, Edward couldn't help but take notice. He'd spent his whole life hearing of Peverills, the legendary Peverills, and how grand it would be once the estates were joined.

"To an old acquaintance. He was rather keen to have it, and I . . . It seemed time to let it go." Uncle Charles exchanged a glance with his wife. "Everything I love is here now. It's best to let the past lie."

"Yes," said Edward fervently. He was all for leaving the past behind. "You won't hear the contrary from me. Let it all sink into the sea, that's what I say."

"Hardly that. There'd be no sugar for your coffee," said his uncle mildly. "Shall we have some coffee? You look like a young man with a story to tell."

Edward nodded. He found he was suddenly bursting to tell all. "Yes, you see—"

"Ah." His uncle lifted a hand, listening to something. "There are your cousins. I expect you'll want to meet them. Philippe! Sybille!"

"Coming!" called a voice from the antechamber. There was the sound of umbrellas being shaken out, and scolding in French from the maid.

"Hercule and Amelie have gone to the Tuileries Garden with their nursemaid, but they'll be back presently," said his aunt Jeanne.

"I have cousins?" said Edward. He hadn't expected cousins. From the way his mother talked, he'd always imagined his uncle leading a hedonistic bachelor existence in the gambling dens and brothels of Paris, not this richly decorated family apartment with aunts and nursemaids and cousins, and, most likely, barley water and hot milk.

His uncle looked at the mantelpiece, at a pencil sketch of a very young girl. "You had another, but she died."

His wife's hand unobtrusively found its way into his. Edward noticed that they seemed to be able to communicate without talking, as though they had their own private language. "It was a very long time ago."

"That was drawn from memory," said his uncle, nodding at the framed sketch on the mantel. "Our poor little girl."

"She's in heaven now, I expect," said Edward uncomfortably, since that was the sort of thing one said.

He was saved by the appearance of two of his cousins, a boy of about thirteen, beautifully turned out in a suit that made Edward all the more aware of his rumpled and very obviously provincial costume, and a girl some years younger, with her mother's beautiful bones and her father's blue eyes.

"This," said his aunt, "is your cousin Edward, come all the way from Barbados."

"Bonjour," said Edward awkwardly.

"You're rather too old for the nursery," said Uncle Charles. "Philippe, if you might find your cousin a place in your room?"

"Come with me," said his cousin Philippe, in accented but beautifully fluent English. "I'll see you settled."

His cousin Sybille trotted along with them.

"Good," said Sybille. "Now come along and I'll take you to my favorite place in the square."

"In the rain?" said Edward, slinking down into his collar. Philippe, he noticed, was quietly laughing, but doing his best to hide it.

"Cousin," said Sybille, "you have so very much to learn."

"Sybille," called his new aunt, taking her daughter firmly in hand. "You can torment your cousin later. Let him have a cup of coffee first."

Edward followed his uncle's wife into the warm drawing room, where he was bustled into a comfortable chair with a cup of coffee out of a flowered china pot and a cake made of almonds, while his cousins teased each other and laughed and the coal crackled merrily, and his uncle held hands with his aunt under the table. His younger cousins appeared and were introduced, and then hustled off to the nursery to have their hands cleaned and their frocks changed, with much commentary and rapid French and some sticky fingerprints left on Edward's pant leg, which he found he didn't mind at all, especially since Philippe had promised to take him to his tailor.

"Cousin!" demanded Sybille, waking him out of a half doze of contented warmth as the conversation ebbed and flowed around him. "Cousin Edouard! How long do you mean to stay?"

Edward looked around the red-papered room, at his smiling cousins and his aunt and uncle, and thought of the echoing rooms of Beckles, sharp with secrets. He hadn't known that people could live like this. How had he thought it cold? He was warm through, a warmth that had nothing to do with the weather.

"As long as you'll have me," he said.

HISTORICAL NOTE

THE HISTORY OF Barbados in the nineteenth century is so rich and complex that to do it justice this note would need to be longer than the book itself. Since the production staff do not seem to like that idea, I have tried to confine myself to those points most important to the story—and, of course, to answering the question that always plagues me upon reading historical fiction: What happened and what didn't?

The Davenants, Beckleses, Fentys, and Turners are my own invention, but all are based on real people. Charles Davenant and his father were inspired by an actual planter and reformer named Joshua Steele. Like Charles's father, Steele came from London to Barbados in the 1780s and set about trying to enact reforms. He believed, essentially, that Barbados's slaves were equivalent to the serfs of medieval England, who had been oppressed and tied to the land, but, once given the proper institutions, became sturdy yeomen and model Englishmen. As David Lambert, author of *White Creole Culture, Politics and Identity during the Age of Abolition*, points out, this won Steele plaudits from abolitionist circles in London, but did not go down well with the majority of the plantocracy. Undaunted, Steele set about implementing his ideas on his own lands, offering wages for work, reorganizing his lands along a copyhold system, setting up courts of law by and for the enslaved. He was also deeply concerned about the plight of the Redlegs, the poor white Barbadians, and made an effort to find them employment upon his estates and to promote the creation of industries that might provide employment.

Sadly, what one remembers about Steele, however, aren't his ambitions during life, but his disappointment in death. Steele maintained an intimate relationship with his housekeeper, an enslaved woman named Ann or Anna Slatia, whom he leased from a neighboring landowner. They appear to have lived together as man and wife, although it is, of course, impossible to ascertain what Ann Slatia's sentiments may have been about the arrangement. Upon his death, he left the bulk of his fortune to his two children by Slatia, Edward and Catherine Ann. There was nothing unusual about a planter leaving a bequest to his natural child: wills of the period are filled with them. Very often, planters would manumit their natural children upon their death, along with some legacy in cash or property. What was unusual in this case was that Steele's children were another man's slaves, and the courts had no idea how to handle this novel and distressing situation. In the end, they ruled that property could not own property. Steele's executor, Francis Bell, belatedly spirited the children to Britain, where he had them manumitted—but he couldn't change the determination of the courts. The children were disinherited. This situation ended as happily as it could under the circumstances: Bell took charge and sent Edward to his own son's school in Norwich and Catherine Ann to a young ladies' academy in Camberwell, fulfilling the spirit of his friend's wishes, if not the letter. But Steele's predicament, unable to free his own children, thwarted in his attempt to make them his heirs, informed Charles and Jenny's story.

We don't know how Ann Slatia felt, whether she cared for Steele or merely submitted to him. As Professor Hilary Beckles points out, in his *Natural Rebels: A Social History of Enslaved Black Women in Barbados*, it's very hard to know the reality of such relationships. Relationships between planters and enslaved women were common: so common that in 1801, the Barbados assembly voted to hike the manumission fees for female slaves from £50 to a whopping £300, a mind-boggling sum (the price of manumitting a male was, in contrast, raised only to £200). The not so subtle purpose of this tax was to prevent men from manumitting their mistresses and children, and, in the process, creating a free colored community that would challenge the distinction between races. People found ways around this, such as "selling" slaves to friends in England, who would manumit them in London, eliminating the fee. But the very fact that the assembly felt it necessary to impose such draconian financial penalties tells us something about the prevalence of planter/slave relationships and the threat that the offspring of these relationships posed to the prevailing paradigm.

One of the hardest challenges in writing *The Summer Country* was trying to reconstruct the life of an enslaved woman. Not the daily toil in the fields or the duties of a body servant—there are plenty of materials there—but the internal life of an enslaved woman. As Andrea Stuart points out in her remarkable family history, *Sugar in the Blood*, in the case of her own many times great-grandmother, who bore a child to the plantation owner, not only can one not know how she felt, it's impossible even to determine her name. For the most part, when we look for the lives of enslaved women, we hear the voices of others: visitors from England, writing back home about the barbarities perpetrated upon women's bodies; planters complaining of their laziness or slyness. It is very hard digging through the propaganda on either side to recover the emotions of the women who lived within this system. As Marisa J. Fuentes comments in *Dispossessed Lives: Enslaved Women, Violence, and the Archive*, "the very nature of slavery in the eighteenth century Caribbean made enslaved life fleeting and rendered access to literacy nearly impossible."

However, that "nearly" is important. One historian places the percentage of literacy among the enslaved at 2 percent—but posits that the majority of that 2 percent were female, particularly housekeepers. We know, for example, that Nanny Grigg, one of the participants in the 1816 rising, was literate. Letters do survive from enslaved women. Dolly and Jenny Lane, daughters of the housekeeper at Newton Plantation, Old Doll, each wrote to their master to request her manumission (Dolly's letter is dated 1807, Jenny's 1804). After making clear that she has her mistress's approval for the request, Jenny explains, "I have a friend who has been generous enough to promise me if I can obtain your consent will pay for my freedom but first I must implore you to take another good slave in my stead, or sell me, which ever you please to do, and you shall be most honestly paid if it should please you to sell me." Jenny acquired her freedom in 1807, and, in 1813, wrote again, this time on behalf of her grown sons, one a tailor on the plantation, the other a joiner, explaining that she has a little put by, as the plantation attorney will attest, and since the boys have such poor constitutions and aren't much good to the estate, she would take the liberty to buy them. After all these years, her voice and character come strongly through the text.

Two important facts stand out about the enslaved population in Barbados in the early nineteenth century: there were more women than men (54.4 percent female) and, in marked contrast to the other sugar islands, the vast majority of enslaved people were Barbados-born. In the year 1817, only 7.1 percent of enslaved people on the island were African-born; 92.9 percent were born in Barbados. In Jamaica and St. Vincent, that same year, 37 percent and 38.8 percent, respectively, of the enslaved population had been brought from Africa; on Demerara, that number was 54.7 percent. There were all sorts of reasons for this, which we don't have space to go into here, but the result was that there was a strong Creole consciousness among the enslaved population, an identification as Barbadian, and, beyond that, to a particular parish and a particular plantation. As Professor Beckles points out, "In 1826, most estates in the colony had been owned by the same family for 100 years, so that several generations of slaves were born, raised, and died in the same villages." Jenny, brought over from Jamaica, is considered a "foreigner," outside the local social structures.

In creating my Jenny, I relied heavily on Professor Hilary Beckles's *Natural Rebels: A Social History of Enslaved Black Women in Barbados*, Marisa J. Fuentes's *Dispossessed Lives: Enslaved Women, Violence, and the Archive*, and Katherine Paugh's *The Politics of Reproduction: Race, Medicine, and Fertility in the Age of Abolition*, all of which I strongly recommend to anyone wishing to learn more about the topic. I am also deeply indebted to Andrea Stuart's *Sugar in the Blood*, which goes beyond bare facts to attempt to reconstruct the emotional and physical environment in which her ancestors lived. Her work was invaluable in helping me flesh out not only Jenny, but also Robert and Mary Anne Davenant.

Mary Anne proved nearly as elusive as Jenny. There is a great deal of writing about Creole women, but it comes largely from English visitors, who enjoyed themselves hugely in deploring the laziness, decadence, and ignorance of Creole womanhood. As Cecily Jones comments in *Engendering Whiteness: White Women and Colonialism in Barbados and North Carolina*, "much of our knowledge about white Caribbean women . . . necessarily derives from the comments of male observers, but their representations of womanhood are largely informed by misogynistic, class-bound perspectives, and must be approached with caution." In an archetypal story, a plantation mistress, desiring some tamarind water from a jug at the far end of the room, shouts for her slaves rather than getting it herself, shouting and shouting until she falls into a fit of coughing. The English observer concludes, "These lazy creoles, if they drop a pin, will not stoop to pick it up." One finds variants on this story again and again, as well as complaints that the voice of the mistress of the plantation, her accent, her diction, her mannerisms, are indistinguishable from those of her slaves. As one critical visitor put it, the white women of Barbados spoke "a vulgar, corrupt dialect," caused by mingling more with their slaves than their own kind.

Taking the biases of observers as a given, it does seem highly likely that there was a fair amount of cultural commonality between mistress and slave. Unlike the other sugar islands, Barbados had a very low level of absenteeism. Planters, while they might send their sons to Eton or Harrow for a bit of Latin, Greek, and social polish, returned, for the most part, to the island, where they served in the assembly, oversaw their own acreage, married the sisters of their peers, and raised their children to do the same. Because of this, the island didn't see the same dearth of women that one found on other sugar colonies, where single men served as overseers for absentee owners. In 1816, the year of the rising, the white population was 52.2 percent female. (By contrast, in Jamaica, the ratio of white men to women was 200:1.) That white female majority did not go to England for their education. They might—theoretically—be educated at a young ladies' academy in Bridgetown, like the one run by novelist and prolific letter writer Eliza Fenwick, but, for the most part, they stayed at home, at the parental plantation. So while a Charles Davenant might go off to England as a young boy and return with a grounding in Enlightenment texts and a pronounced Whig drawl, a Mary Anne Beckles would be more likely to be familiar with folk remedies and plantation lore, and would, in conversation, have an accent very similar to that of her maid.

The Barbados plantocracy believed themselves to be enlightened masters, pursuing a policy known as amelioration, in which they posited that more lenient treatment of the enslaved would lead to increased returns and fewer angry letters from British abolitionists. As proof of the success of their program, they liked to boast that Barbados was the only one of the islands to muster a net increase of slaves rather than a net loss. (Because sugar cultivation was so brutal, the death rate on most of the sugar islands tended to be high and there were few live births.) Although the Barbados slave code was among the harshest on the books, planters insisted that most provisions, such as the need for passes to leave the plantation, were generally ignored, and that their slaves enjoyed great freedom of movement. Although there had been rebellions on neighboring islands, there had not been a slave rising in Barbados since 1692, a fact that planters ascribed to the good relations between themselves and their slaves. No one saw a conflagration coming. As one indignant planter put it, "The night of the insurrection I would and did sleep with my chamber door open, and if I had possessed ten thousand pounds in my house I should not have had any more precaution, so well convinced I was of their attachment." Be that as it may, on Easter Sunday, 1816, about half past eight in the evening, the cane began to go up in flames in the parish of St. Philip.

In writing about the 1816 rising, I've tried to stay as close as I can to the historical information available. Unfortunately, the historical record is patchy and sometimes suspect, much of the information available having been drawn out in interrogations after the fact, or played up to make a point. There's a great deal of debate over what was actually known or intended, why the revolt happened when it did, and who, exactly, was involved. Was the catalyst the registry bill of 1815? That's the generally accepted view, but there are some dissenters who argue that to focus on the registry bill is to play into planter propaganda. (While the registry bill was intended only to enforce the provisions of the Slave Trade Act of 1807, making sure that slaveholders weren't violating the law by importing new slaves, planters argued the very idea of registering their slaves was an incursion of their property rights; the rising was taken as a sign that the legislation had, indeed, been incendiary.) Those historians make the case that the revolt was a reaction to more local concerns: to famine caused by drought, to the harshness of particular masters. The testimony of those involved and the slogans and images that survive do seem to point to a larger consciousness: many of the conspirators, when questioned, referred to the successful rising in Haiti (which they called Saint Domingo or "Mingo"), and to the belief that support was forthcoming from both Crown and Parliament. As the battle banner proclaimed, "Britannier are always happy to assist all such sons as endeavour."

The rising is commonly known as Bussa's Rebellion—now. In fact, it was only in the 1870s, sixty years after the rising, that one sees the first references to "the War of General Bussa." We know there was a Bussa; he figures in the reports compiled immediately after the rebellion, although not as the primary actor. Did he play a seminal role in the rising, or was he just one of many participants? I've included Bussa in the narrative—because it would seem wrong to have Bussa's Rebellion without a Bussa, debates notwithstanding—but I chose to focus on other named conspirators, particularly Nanny Grigg. I did so partly because we have testimony from her own mouth, which we don't for

Bussa, who died in battle, and partly because, as a woman, she made a better counterpart for my own fictional Jenny. There is, sadly, very little known about Nanny Grigg. We know that she was literate and that she was valued at the high sum of £130, but that's about it. Harrow Plantation did change ownership and became Simmons during this period, and the Sunday gatherings and the dance at the River Plantation were all taken from the record. Most of the statements made by Nanny Grigg, Jackey, King Wiltshire, and the other participants in this book were taken, frequently verbatim, from their own testimony. Where I took liberties was in including Jenny and in having Harrow leased by my fictional Mr. and Mrs. Boland, giving me a way for Jenny to meet Nanny Grigg.

Emancipation came to Barbados by imperial edict with the passage of the Slavery Abolition Act of 1833, which came fully into effect in 1838 (technically, it came into effect in 1834, but a period of "apprenticeship" followed, with full emancipation only in 1838). There was, however, already a thriving free Afro-Caribbean community on the island, primarily centered in Bridgetown, where merchants like London Bourne, Thomas Cummins, John Montefiore, and Joseph Thorne impressed English visitors with their elegant homes and the numerous charitable committees run by their wives. My own London Turner is a thinly veiled stand-in for these men, particularly London Bourne. Born a slave, Bourne was manumitted (in London, to save the fee), amassed a considerable fortune, and became a respected member of the Afro-Caribbean merchant elite. The Turner drawing room, however, was stolen in pretty much every particular from Joseph Thorne, whose "taste and judgment" in his collection of books and artefacts was noted by guests from England. For information about the Afro-Caribbean middle class, I am deeply indebted to Melanie J. Newton's *The Children of Africa in the Colonies: Free People of Color in Barbados in the Age of Emancipation*, which provided me with everything from the charitable committees upon which Mrs. Turner would have sat to the furniture in Mr. Turner's parlor. For a picture of London Bourne's life and times, I relied upon Cecilia Karch's "A Man for All Seasons: London Bourne" in the *Journal of the Barbados Museum and Historical Society.*

The real London Bourne did not, to my knowledge, have a nephew who trained as a doctor. There were, however, plenty of real Nathaniels out there. In the early nineteenth century, English and Scottish universities opened their doors to African, African American, and Afro-Caribbean medical students. By the 1820s, there was an Afro-Caribbean doctor in Trinidad who had trained at the University of Edinburgh. James McCune Smith, the first African American to hold a medical degree, graduated from the University of Glasgow in 1837. Nathaniel's near contemporary, the West African Africanus Horton (also known as James Beale) studied at King's College London and the University of Edinburgh, graduating from the latter in 1859.

Where I did take liberties was in adding Nathaniel to the staff of the Barbados General Hospital in 1854. The hospital opened its doors in 1844 with a staff consisting of six doctors: a senior resident surgeon, plus junior house surgeons (resident), and non-resident visiting surgeons. As in England, these doctors worked for free, in the understanding that they would have the opportunity to hone their skills, observe, experiment, and expand their private practice. Hospital positions did not become salaried until 1875. As Olivia Cetinoglu notes in her *A History of the Barbados General Hospital, 1844–1910,* "All of the doctors recruited at the Barbados General Hospital were white and most were recruited from England." Adding Nathaniel to the staff was something of a leap, but one does imagine that, given the hospital's cash flow issues, a hefty donation from London Turner might have helped to cross the color bar. By 1854, the hospital was already experiencing issues with overcrowding, with one exception: during the cholera epidemic, the number of patients admitted dropped dramatically, due to the hospital policy of barring those with infectious diseases. If anyone would like to know more about the hospital, or medical care in Barbados, I recommend

Olivia Cetinoglu's *A History of the Barbados General Hospital, 1844–1910*, as well as Eleane I. Hunte's *The Unsung Nightingales: the Development of Nursing in Barbados from 1844 to the Year 2000.*

I have tried to be as faithful to the actual circumstances of the 1854 cholera epidemic as I could. Fortunately for the historical novelist, Barbados had a thriving newspaper industry, including the *Barbadian*, the *West Indian*, and the *Barbados Globe*, all of which reported on the crisis as it occurred. There are also accounts from those who survived it, including the Reverend Thomas Butcher's grimly named *Mordichim: Recollections of Cholera in Barbados, During the Middle of the Year 1854*, which relates the entirety of the epidemic with impressive thoroughness. Most of the physical details—the phaeton carrying a coffin, the woman who takes on a baby she found alone, the Reverend Bannister's death after kissing his dead child, and so on—are taken directly from *Mordichim* or from the reports in the local papers. The first cases were reported on May 14; notices warning residents that the Asiatic cholera was in the town went up on May 21. One of the first to die was a local merchant, John Castello Montefiore (the same Montefiore with whom Adam visits in this book). One can still see the fountain erected to his memory in Bridgetown by his son. The governor, Sir William Colebrooke, divided the city into seven districts, with two medical officers to each, although there was little they could do. Soup kitchens were opened, with packets of food prepared for the needy, and supplies of lime and drinking water were distributed. Barbados had a population of roughly 126,000. By September of 1854, the death toll had risen to over 20,000. There were no sure remedies, although many were attempted, some more bizarre than others, such as Mrs. Davenant's turpentine wraps. For those wishing to know more, I can only recommend reading through *Mordichim*, which is both chilling and fascinating and contains so much more than I was able to fit in the novel.

For anyone who would like to delve deeper into the fascinating history of Barbados, there is no better general survey than Professor Hilary Beckles's *A History of Barbados*. For a more intimate portrait of the country's history, Andrea Stuart's *Sugar in the Blood* paints a compelling picture of slavery and its legacy through the prism of one family's experience over the generations. For more specific information on various subtopics, you can find a much (much) longer bibliography on my website, www.laurenwillig.com.

ACKNOWLEDGMENTS

THIS BOOK HAS been nearly a decade in the making. It all started on a June day in 2010 when three historians on vacation decided to skip the beach and go on a plantation tour instead—and I first heard the story of the Portuguese ward.

So many thanks to my agent, Alexandra Machinist, for telling me to stop talking about it and just write it already. Huge hugs to my editor, Rachel Kahan, for taking on the project and for completely getting it when I say things like: "This is my M. M. Kaye meets *The Thorn Birds* book!"—and for not only understanding, but knowing exactly which M. M. Kaye book I mean. I cannot imagine having written this book with anyone but you.

Thank you to the many talented people at William Morrow who have helped to turn this book from words in my head to the book in your hands, with special thanks to Mumtaz Mustafa for the gorgeous cover. Thanks go to Liate Stehlik for her support, and to Tavia Kowalchuk and Danielle Bartlett for their infinite resourcefulness and unfailing sense of humor. I am so in awe of all you do.

It took two years of research before I felt competent to tackle the writing of this book. I am so very privileged to have been colleagues with brilliant women who, years later, are willing to put up with random historical questions at odd times of day. So many thanks to Harvard history department buddies Becky Goetz, Elly Truitt, and Maya Jasanoff for fielding questions about slavery, sugar islands, medical practice, and nineteenth-century race relations, for pointing me to appropriate books and bibliographies, and for referring me to relevant colleagues. I am so grateful. The next round of drinks is on me. And, of course, I can't leave out Jenny Davis and Liz Mellyn, who came up with the brilliant idea of a girls' trip to the Caribbean all those years ago. A medievalist, a Renaissance expert, and an Early Modernist walk into a tour . . . and come out with a book.

While I'm dispensing drinks, a bottle of port is owed to Dr. Jonathan Romanyshyn, who not only answered frantic questions like "How DOES cholera work, anyway?" but went through lists of Victorian remedies and explained to me what made medical sense and what didn't (i.e., most of it) and why. Dr. Braithwaite and I both thank you. Thanks go, too, to Georgina Schaeffer for her advice on matters equestrian, and for reminding me (fortunately for me, but unfortunately for Emily!) of that sidesaddle scene in *Auntie Mame*.

There aren't enough thanks in the world for my secret research weapon, librarian extraordinaire Vicki Parsons, who took on this project as though it were her own and spent countless hours hunting down everything from abstruse articles in defunct journals to obscure Victorian travel narratives and journals. The better part of the detail in this book comes from those thousands of files she sent my way, from subaltern's butter to the ornaments in London Turner's drawing room.

If there was ever a reason to use the hashtag "blessed" unironically, it would be in reference to my amazing writer friends. Thank you to Tasha Alexander and Deanna Raybourn for guidance on matters Victorian, to Andrea DaRif for Yale Club cookies and a sympathetic ear, to Alyson Richman and Lynda Cohen Loigman for general jollity, and to my writing sisters, Karen White and Beatriz Williams, for endless text chains, *Daily Telegraph* distraction, and letting me borrow the Unibrain when I need it.

It is a truth universally acknowledged that the writer of a book must be in want of a reader. I am deeply indebted, as both a reader and a writer, to the booksellers and librarians who dedicate their careers to putting the right book into the right hands. If I named all my favorite bookstores, it would take forever, but I want to make special mention of the Corner Bookstore in New York, Diane's Books of Greenwich, FoxTale in Atlanta, the Poisoned Pen in Scottsdale, Murder by the Book in Houston, and the Ripped Bodice in Culver City. Whenever I walk through those doors, I feel like I've come home. (Hand me a latte, and I may never leave.) Thank you, so very much, to all the booksellers and librarians reading this page—and to all the booksellers and librarians who aren't. What you do is pure magic.

Moving from magic to technology, I have many feelings about the electronic age in which we live, some of them more printable than others. On the plus side, the internet has enabled a flourishing of communities dedicated to readers and writers. Thank you to Andrea Peskind Katz, Sharlene Martin Moore, Bobbi Dumas, Robin Kall Homonoff, Jennifer Tropea O'Regan, and to the many, many wonderful readers, bloggers, and reviewers who have nourished and participated in these virtual literary salons. Thank you so much for your support of books and authors. It means the world to all of us—and has increased my TBR pile tenfold.

No acknowledgments section would be complete without a shout-out to my sister, Brooke Willig, and my college roommate, Claudia Brittenham, who both endured endless hours of discussion about character and plot, read multiple drafts of the first three chapters, and kept me from scrapping the whole thing at least a dozen times. For the nineteenth time. They've gone through this with every single book since the first one, way back in 2003. And yet they still pick up the phone when I call. I'm not sure why you put up with me, but I'm so glad you do.

Many thanks go to the staff of my favorite writing Starbucks, particularly Andrea and Jose, for always asking about the book, knowing my drink order better than I do, and never minding when I sit in the same place for six hours straight. You are the best, and I'm so lucky to have you as officemates.

Last but not least, thank you to my family: to my parents, for putting in a ludicrous amount of babysitting time; to my husband, for taking care of pretty much everything I prefer to ignore (which encompasses a wide variety of things, including, but not limited to, garbage disposal and the mysterious art of making the Wi-Fi work); to my brother, for sending gifts of cheese at stressful times; to my sister, for—well, you know about my sister; and to my children, Madeleine and Oliver, for doing their best, in their own unique ways, to delay the writing of this book.

Thank you all!

About the Author

Lauren Willig is the *New York Times* and *USA Today* bestselling author of *The Ashford Affair* and *The English Wife*, the RITA Award–winning Pink Carnation series, and two novels cowritten with Beatriz Williams and Karen White—*The Forgotten Room* and *The Glass Ocean*. An alumna of Yale University, she has a graduate degree in history from Harvard and a JD from Harvard Law School. She lives in New York City with her husband, preschooler, baby, and vast quantities of coffee.